Alan St. Aubyn

Orchard Damerel

A Novel

Alan St. Aubyn

Orchard Damerel
A Novel

ISBN/EAN: 9783337044374

Printed in Europe, USA, Canada, Australia, Japan

Cover: Foto ©Andreas Hilbeck / pixelio.de

More available books at **www.hansebooks.com**

URCHARD
DAMEREL
BY
ALAN ST. AUBYN
Chatto & Windus,
Piccadilly

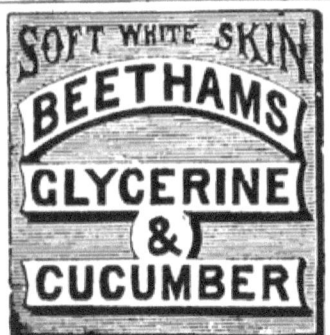

POPULAR TWO-SHILLING NOVELS.

**** This is a SELECTION only.—FULL LISTS of over 600 NOVELS free.*

By GRANT ALLEN.

Strange Stories. | In all Shades. | For Maimie's Sake. | Philistia. | Babylon. | The Great Taboo. | The Beckoning Hand. | The Devil's Die. | This Mortal Coil. | The Tents of Shem. | Dumaresq's Daughter. | Duchess of Powysland. | Blood Royal. | Ivan Greet's Masterpiece. | The Scallywag.

E. LESTER ARNOLD.—Phra the Phœnician

ARTEMUS WARD'S Complete Works.

By Rev. S. BARING GOULD.

Red Spider. | Eve.

By FRANK BARRETT.

Found Guilty. | Fettered for Life. | Between Life & Death. | The Sin of Olga Zassoulich. | A Prodigal's Progress. | A Recoiling Vengeance | For Love and Honour. | John Ford; and His Helpmate. | Honest Davie. | Folly Morrison. | Lieutenant Barnabas. | Little Lady Linton.

By BESANT AND RICE.

Ready-Money Mortiboy | With Harp and Crown. | This Son of Vulcan. | My Little Girl. | The Case of Mr. Lucraft | The Golden Butterfly. | By Celia's Arbour. | The Monks of Thelema | 'Twas in Trafalgar's Bay | The Seamy Side. | Ten Years' Tenant. | Chaplain of the Fleet.

By WALTER BESANT.

All Sorts & Conditions. | The Captains' Room. | All in a Garden Fair. | Dorothy Forster. | Uncle Jack. | Children of Gibeon. | Armorel of Lyonesse. | The Ivory Gate. | World went well then. | Herr Paulus. | For Faith & Freedom. | To Call her Mine. | The Bell of St. Paul's. | The Holy Rose. | S. Katherine's by Tower | The Rebel Queen. | Verbena Camellia Stephanotis.

By BRET HARTE.

An Heiress of Red Dog. | Luck of Roaring Camp | Californian Stories. | Gabriel Conroy. | Maruja. | Flip. | A Phyllis of the Sierras | A Waif of the Plains. | A Ward of the Golden Gate.

By ROBERT BUCHANAN.

Shadow of the Sword. | A Child of Nature. | God and the Man. | Annan Water. | Matt. | The New Abelard. | Martyrdom of Madeline | Love Me for Ever. | Foxglove Manor. | Master of the Mine. | The Heir of Linne.

By HALL CAINE.

Shadow of a Crime. | Son of Hagar. | Deemster.

By MACLAREN COBBAN.

The Cure of Souls. | The Red Sultan.

By MORTIMER & FRANCES COLLINS.

Sweet Anne Page. | Midnight to Midnight. | Sweet and Twenty. | Frances. | Transmigration. | A Fight with Fortune. | The Village Comedy. | You Play me False. | Blacksmith and Scholar.

By WILKIE COLLINS.

Armadale. | AfterDark. | Antonina. | No Name. | Hide and Seek | Basil. | The Dead Secret. | Queen of Hearts. | My Miscellanies. | The Woman in White. | Moonstone | Legacy of Cain. | Man and Wife. | Poor Miss Finch. | Miss or Mrs.? | The New Magdalen. | The Frozen Deep. | The Law and the Lady. | The Two Destinies. | The Haunted Hotel. | The Fallen Leaves. | Jezebel's Daughter. | The Black Robe. | Heart and Science | "I say No." | Blind Love | The Evil Genius. | Little Novels. | A Rogue's Life.

By C. EGBERT CRADDOCK.

The Prophet of the Great Smoky Mountains.

By B. M. CROKER.

Pretty Miss Neville. | Proper Pride. | A Bird of Passage. | Diana Barrington. | "To Let." | A Family Likeness.

By DICK DONOVAN.

The Man-Hunter. | Caught at Last! | Tracked and Taken. | Man from Manchester. | Hetty Duncan. | Detective's Triumphs. | In the Grip of the Law. | Wanted! | Information Received. | Tracked to Doom. | Link by Link. | Suspicion Aroused. | Dark Deeds. | Long Arm of the Law

By G. MANVILLE FENN.

The New Mistress. | Witness to the Deed.

By PERCY FITZGERALD.

Bella Donna. | Polly. | Fatal Zero. | Second Mrs. Tillotson. | 75 Brooke Street. | Never Forgotten. | The Lady of Brantome.

By R. E. FRANCILLON.

Olympia. | One by One. | Queen Cophetua. | A Real Queen. | King or Knave? | Romances of the Law. | Ropes of Sand. | A Dog and his Shadow.

By CHARLES GIBBON.

Robin Gray. | For Lack of Gold. | What will World Say? | In Honour Bound. | In Love and War. | For the King. | In Pastures Green. | Queen of the Meadow. | Flower of the Forest. | Fancy Free. | A Heart's Problem. | The Braes of Yarrow. | The Golden Shaft. | Of High Degree. | Loving a Dream. | By Mead and Stream. | A Hard Knot. | Heart's Delight. | The Dead Heart. | Blood-Money.

By ERNEST GLANVILLE.

The Lost Heiress. | The Fossicker. | A Fair Colonist.

By SYDNEY GRUNDY.

The Days of his Vanity.

By THOMAS HARDY.

Under the Greenwood Tree.

By JULIAN HAWTHORNE.

Garth. | Dust. | Ellice Quentin. | Sebastian Strome. | Spectre of Camera. | Fortune's Fool. | Beatrix Randolph. | Miss Cadogna. | Love—or a Name! | David Poindexter's Disappearance.

HEADON HILL —Zambra the Detective.

Mrs. CASHEL HOEY.—The Lover's Creed.

By Mrs. HUNGERFORD.

A Modern Circe. | In Durance Vile. | A Maiden all Forlorn. | Marvel. | A Mental Struggle. | Lady Verner's Flight.

By Mrs. ALFRED HUNT.

Thornicroft's Model. | Self-Condemned. | The Leaden Casket | That Other Person.

By JEAN INGELOW.—Fated to be Free.

By WILLIAM JAMESON.—My Dead Self.

By HARRIETT JAY.

The Dark Colleen. | Queen of Connaught.

By R. ASHE KING.

A Drawn Game. | Passion's Slave. | 'The Wearing of the Green.' | Bell Barry.

By E. LYNN LINTON.

Patricia Kemball. | Atonement of Leam Dundas. | The World Well Lost. | Under which Lord? | With a Silken Thread. | Rebel of the Family. | "My Love!" | Ione. | Paston Carew. | Sowing the Wind.

By JUSTIN McCARTHY.

Dear Lady Disdain. | Waterdale Neighbours. | My Enemy's Daughter. | A Fair Saxon. | Miss Misanthrope. | Linley Rochford. | Donna Quixote. | The Comet of a Season | Maid of Athens. | Camiola. | The Dictator. | Red Diamonds.

London: CHATTO & WINDUS, 214, Piccadilly, W.

POPULAR TWO-SHILLING NOVELS.

⁂ This is a SELECTION only.—FULL LISTS of over 600 NOVELS free.

By KATHARINE S. MACQUOID.
The Evil Eye. | Lost Rose.

By W. H. MALLOCK.
New Republic. | Romance of 19th Century.

By FLORENCE MARRYAT.
Open! Sesame! | Written in Fire.
Fighting the Air. | A Harvest of Wild Oats.

By Mrs. MOLESWORTH.
Hathercourt Rectory.

J. E. MUDDOCK.—The Dead Man's Secret.

By CHRISTIE MURRAY.
A Life's Atonement. | The Way of the World.
A Model Father. | Bit of Human Nature.
Joseph's Coat. | Cynic Fortune.
Coals of Fire. | Old Blazer's Hero.
First Person Singular. | Bob Martin's Little Girl
By the Gate of the Sea | Time's Revenges.
Val Strange. | Hearts. | A Wasted Crime.

CHRISTIE MURRAY and H. HERMAN.
One Traveller Returns. | Paul Jones's Alias.
The Bishops' Bible.

By HENRY MURRAY.
A Game of Bluff. | A Song of Sixpence.

By HUME NISBET.
"Bail Up!" | Dr. Bernard St. Vincent.

By GEORGES OHNET.
Doctor Rameau. | A Last Love. | A Weird Gift.

By Mrs. OLIPHANT.
Whiteladies | Primrose Path | Greatest Heiress

By OUIDA.
Held in Bondage. | Ariadne. | Moths.
Strathmore. | Friendship | Pipistrello.
Chandos. | Idalia. | A Village Commune.
Under Two Flags. | Bimbi. | In Maremma.
Cecil Castlemaine. | Wanda. | Frescoes.
Tricotrin. | Puck. | Princess Napraxine.
Folle Farine. | Othmar. | Guilderoy.
A Dog of Flanders. | Ruffino. | Syrlin.
Two Wooden Shoes. | Santa Barbara.
Pascarel. | Signa. | Wisdom, Wit, & Pathos.
In a Winter City.

By JAMES PAYN.
Lost Sir Massingberd. | Mirk Abbey.
A Perfect Treasure. | Not Wooed, but Won.
Bentinck's Tutor. | £200 Reward.
Murphy's Master. | Less Black than We're
A County Family. | By Proxy. [Painted.
At Her Mercy. | Under One Roof.
A Woman's Vengeance. | High Spirits.
Cecil's Tryst. | Carlyon's Year.
The Clyffards of Clyffe. | A Confidential Agent.
The Family Scapegrace. | Some Private Views.
The Foster Brothers. | From Exile.
Found Dead. | Halves. | A Grape from a Thorn.
The Best of Husbands. | For Cash Only.
Walter's Word. | Kit.
Fallen Fortunes. | The Canon's Ward.
What He Cost Her. | Holiday Tasks.
Humorous Stories. | Glow-worm Tales.
Gwendoline's Harvest. | Mystery of Mirbridge.
The Talk of the Town. | The Burnt Million.
Like Father, Like Son. | The Word & the Will.
A Marine Residence. | A Prince of the Blood.
Married Beneath Him | Sunny Stories.
A Trying Patient.

By Mrs. CAMPBELL PRAED.
Romance of Station. | Soul of Countess Adrian.
Outlaw and Lawmaker.

By E. C. PRICE.
Valentina. | The Foreigners.
Mrs. Lancaster's Rival. | Gerald.

RICH. PRICE.—Miss Maxwell's Affections.

By Mrs. J. H. RIDDELL.
Her Mother's Darling | Fairy Water.
Uninhabited House. | The Prince of Wales's
The Mystery in Palace | Garden Party.
Gardens. | The Nun's Curse.
Weird Stories. | Idle Tales.

AMÉLIE RIVES—Barbara Dering.

By F. W. ROBINSON.
Women are Strange. | The Hands of Justice.

By CHARLES READE.
Never too Late to Mend | Course of True Love.
Hard Cash. | Autobiog. of a Thief.
Peg Woffington. | A Terrible Temptation.
Christie Johnstone. | The Wandering Heir.
Griffith Gaunt. | A Woman-Hater
Put Y'rself in His Place | A Simpleton. [face.
The Double Marriage | Singleheart & Double-
Love Little, Love Long. | Good Stories.
Foul Play. | The Jilt | Readiana.
Cloister and the Hearth | A Perilous Secret.

By JAMES RUNCIMAN.
Skippers and Shellbacks. | Schools and Scholars.
Grace Balmaign's Sweetheart.

By W. CLARK RUSSELL.
Round the Galley Fire. | On the Fo'k'sle Head.
In the Middle Watch. | A Voyage to the Cape.
Book for the Hammock. | Jenny Harlowe.
Mystery of 'Ocean Star.' | An Ocean Tragedy.
My Shipmate Louise | Alone on a Wide Wide Sea.

By ALAN ST. AUBYN.
A Fellow of Trinity. | The Junior Dean.
Master St. Benedict's. | To his Own Master.

By G. A. SALA.—Gaslight and Daylight.

By JOHN SAUNDERS.
Bound to the Wheel. | The Lion in the Path.
One Against the World. | The Two Dreamers.
Guy Waterman.

By KATHARINE SAUNDERS.
Joan Merryweather. | Sebastian.
The High Mills. | Heart Salvage.
Margaret and Elizabeth.

By GEORGE R. SIMS.
Rogues and Vagabonds. | Dramas of Life.
Mary Jane's Memoirs. | Tinkletop's Crime.
The Ring o' Bells. | Zeph. | My Two Wives
Mary Jane Married. | Memoirs of a Landlady.
Tales of To-day. | Scenes from the Show.

By HAWLEY SMART.—Love or Licence.

By T. W. SPEIGHT.
Mysteries of Heron Dyke. | Hoodwinked.
Golden Hoop | Back to Life | Londwater Tragedy
By Devious Ways. | Burgo's Romance.
Quittance in Full.

R. L. STEVENSON.—New Arabian Nights.

By BERTHA THOMAS.
Cressida. | Proud Maisie. | The Violin-player.

By WALTER THORNBURY.
Tales for the Marines. | Old Stories Re-told.

By ANTHONY TROLLOPE.
The Way We Live Now. | The Land-Leaguers.
American Senator. | Mr. Scarborough's
Frau Frohmann. | Family.
Marion Fay. | John Caldigate.
Kept in the Dark. | The Golden Lion.

By FRANCES ELEANOR TROLLOPE.
Anne Furness. | Mabel's Progress.
Like Ships upon the Sea.

By MARK TWAIN.
Tom Sawyer. | Huckleberry Finn.
A Tramp Abroad | Prince and the Pauper.
Stolen White Elephant. | Mark Twain's Sketches.
Life on the Mississippi. | The Gilded Age.
A Pleasure Trip on the Continent of Europe. | A Yankee at the Court of King Arthur.
The £1,000,000 Bank-note.

By SARAH TYTLER.
What She Came Through | St. Mungo's City.
Beauty and the Beast. | Lady Bell.
Noblesse Oblige. | Disappeared.
Citoyenne Jacqueline. | Buried Diamonds.
The Bride's Pass. | The Blackhall Ghosts.

ALLEN UPWARD.—The Queen against Owen

By WILLIAM WESTALL.—Trust-Money.

By J. S. WINTER.
Cavalry Life. | Regimental Legends.

By H. F. WOOD.
The Passenger from Scotland Yard.
The Englishman of the Rue Cain.

By EDMUND YATES.
Forlorn Hope. | Land at Last. | Castaway.

 London: CHATTO & WINDUS, 214, Piccadilly, W.

ORCHARD DAMEREL

Opinions of the Press

ON

ORCHARD DAMEREL.

'There is a good deal more in Mr. St. Aubyn's delightful novel than can be indicated within the scope of a short notice. The characters are like living persons. . The book is healthy throughout. Its general tone inclines to be sad; and the richest effects are those of tenderness and pathos. But there is also plenty of humour in the course of the story. . Taken altogether, the work is the strongest that has come from its author's pen, and does not gain its strength by any abandonment of the peculiar refinement which characterizes this writer's books. It is a thoroughly enjoyable story.'—*Scotsman.*

'"Orchard Damerel" is a warm-coloured and somewhat gushing story, told with girlish simplicity. The most poignant sorrows and the most ecstatic joys recorded in this volume spring from the loss or the acquisition of little sums of money; but such is Alan St. Aubyn's artless skill that the reader inclines to accept everything on her own showing—to grieve with her women's grief and to rejoice with her women's joy. "Orchard Damerel" will certainly be voted a nice and a pretty story.'—*Athenæum.*

'The story is told in a straightforward and interesting fashion, and Phyllis is a very attractive girl. Mr. St. Aubyn writes pleasant and easy English, and his pretty story is likely to be in considerable demand.'—*Glasgow Herald.*

'There is a good deal of charm and prettiness about this story.'—*Queen.*

'"Orchard Damerel" is a thoroughly pleasant and readable book.'—*Dundee Advertiser.*

'The story is fairly good and quite wholesome—a quality that is not so common as it might be nowadays. On the whole, the book leaves a good taste in the mouth.'—*Spectator.*

'The idea of the book is fresh and the writing is natural.'—*Standard.*

'"Orchard Damerel" is a very good novel, with plenty of character. . . The story is very well told.'—*Guardian.*

'Always a pleasing novelist, Mr. St. Aubyn in "Orchard Damerel" is strong as well as pathetic, realistic in no ordinary degree, but with a refined realism of which few authors possess the secret. He has the mind and eye of a poet, a faculty of painting everyday life with a delicacy of touch rare, but strikingly truthful. . Few unsophisticated readers will come to the end of this novel without genuine regret.'—*Morning Post.*

'There is a fine natural simplicity and unaffected spontaneity about "Orchard Damerel." . For the ingenious and romantic contrivances by which the characters are extricated from their formidable difficulties we must refer our readers to Mr. St. Aubyn's delightful story, the interest of which is brightly and steadily sustained. Greatly to its author's credit, he is neither oppressively interpretative nor sedulously analytical, but always straightforward, fluent, graceful, and pleasantly humorous.'—*Daily Telegraph.*

ORCHARD DAMEREL

A NOVEL

BY

ALAN ST AUBYN

AUTHOR OF

'A FELLOW OF TRINITY,' 'THE MASTER OF ST. BENEDICT'S'
'AN OLD MAID'S SWEETHEART,' ETC.

A NEW EDITION

LONDON
CHATTO & WINDUS, PICCADILLY
1896

CONTENTS

ORCHARD DAMEREL

CHAPTER I.

THE CURATE OF STOKE LUCY.

It is hard upon a man to make a choice between sisters, three sisters exactly alike. It would be less difficult if one of the three were lame, or afflicted with a squint, and another had a mole on her cheek—an unpleasant mole—or bore the traces of small-pox; but when all three sisters are equally fair and sweet and gracious, it is hard upon a man to have to choose between them.

He has an excuse, at any rate, for not making up his mind in a hurry—a quite sufficient excuse for any reasonable delay.

The curate of Stoke Lucy had this excuse, but it was not his only reason for delay.

There were three Miss Penroses for him to choose from, and he fell in love with them all, one after the other. He fell in love with the eldest first. He fell in love with Bertha Penrose the moment he saw her. He saw her for the first time at a mothers'-meeting, and he told himself during that blissful half-hour he sat watching her cutting out pinafores and little shirts, that she was the woman he had been looking for all his life. Perhaps she was.

Bertha Penrose was very good at cutting out shirts. She was very good at cutting out everything; nothing came amiss to her that came within reach of her scissors.

She would have been invaluable in the Sandwich Islands, or in Central Africa, or anywhere where wardrobes are scarce and scanty. She would soon have clothed the whole population.

She was not only good with her scissors at mothers'-meetings, but she was skilful with her pasteboard and with her frying-pan at cookery lectures. She taught the mothers of Stoke Lucy to mend and make their children's clothes and cook their husbands' dinners; and she did a good deal of district-visiting besides.

She was exactly cut out for a curate's wife.

It was no wonder that Robert Lyon watched her snipping away at the calico for those little shirts. Bertha Penrose was worth watching. She had a kind, good face, which is better than beauty any day. Beauty is vain and deceitful, and soon wears off, like the bloom on a peach, but kindness and goodness are homely qualities and endure. They are among the few things that do not pass away in the using.

But Bertha Penrose had beauty besides: she was one of the beauties of Stoke Lucy. A sound, healthy, active girl, with a dainty profile and lovely brown hair with red tints in it, and gray-blue eyes that looked straight at you beneath the most beautiful dark eyelashes in the world. Nature had been in a kindly mood when she mixed the colour on her palette for the Penrose girls.

She had given them all this beautiful brown hair with the red tints in it, that set off so well their fresh, healthy complexions; she had pencilled with a cunning hand their brown, level brows, and she had bestowed on them this delightful gift of lovely dark eyelashes.

If her mood had not been kindly, and she had given them sandy hair, and drab eyebrows, and pale lashes, they would have been the most commonplace girls in Stoke Lucy, and the curate would not have looked at Bertha twice, however deftly she snipped away at those little shirts.

It was not the goodness, it was not the kindness in her sweet face, as she bent over that homely work, which touched the foolish, emotional curate, and set his heart thumping in that ridiculous way; it was the rich, warm colouring that Dame Nature—who is always setting traps for men—had laid on with such a generous hand.

Beauty, like fortune, is merely the result of a happy accident. It is a distinction—a delightful distinction—but it is not a merit. One is so apt to forget this. Robert Lyon forgot it; he overlooked it, at any rate, as he sat watching Bertha Penrose plying her scissors, and fixing and planning those little garments. He looked at her sweet face and her lovely gray eyes, and he endowed her with all the virtues in the world. There was a freckled, red-haired girl, who wore glasses, and who was reading a goody-goody book to the mothers of Stoke Lucy while they worked, who really possessed most of the virtues with which he had credited Bertha, but he did not look at her once during the afternoon. He only remarked that she had a most unpleasant voice, and that the book she was reading was a great deal above the heads of the women who were yawning over their sewing.

His allegiance to Bertha Penrose lasted until the following Sunday, when he saw her sister Phyllis—the second Miss Penrose—in the Sunday-school. He thought it was Bertha for a moment, but the gray-blue eyes were softer; there was a droop in the eyelids, and about the corners of the mouth, that he had not remarked in Bertha, and the lips had a quiver, a tremulous motion in them at times that he had not seen in the firm, decided mouth of the young woman who handled the shears.

Her voice was softer, like her eyes, and there was the least little bit of an Irish accent in it. He had not remarked it in Bertha; there was nothing timid, or shy, or nervous about her; it was with that tremulous quiver of the lips, and the shyness, that the Irish accent came in.

The curate of Stoke Lucy was desperately in love for a whole week with the second Miss Penrose. His cheeks used to get quite hot when he recalled that delightful Irish voice, and his heart repeated that ridiculous thumping performance, and he told himself over again that he had found the woman he had been looking for all his life.

No doubt he had. If he had been wise he would have

accepted his fate thankfully. He could not have done better if he had searched the world over. He would have had the tenderest and most loving wife in—well, in Stoke Lucy. But he was not wise. If he had been, if he had known what was good for him, this story would not have been written. He would have lived a blameless life, and not have made the many mistakes, the sad blunders, that this veracious history has to recount for a warning and an example to all weak-minded, emotional curates.

The Reverend Robert Lyon was faithful in his allegiance to Phyllis Penrose until the next mothers'-meeting. It was not long to be faithful: it was exactly a week and three days.

He went to the meeting half an hour late: he had to pay some visits, and he could not get there before. He was quite ashamed of himself for going in so late; he ought to have opened the meeting. He made up for it by climbing the stairs two at a time, and arriving on the scene hot and breathless.

He knew exactly what he should see: a row of colourless-looking women, with plain tired faces, seamed with sordid cares, sewing away at coarse homely garments; and there would be a few babies squalling, perhaps, and a young woman with red hair reading at a table—reading in an unpleasant voice an impossible story—and there would be a girl with gray eyes snipping away at little shirts.

The curate of Stoke Lucy was wrong for once.

The women were there, and the babies were there, and Bertha Penrose and her scissors were there, but the girl at the table—to be more accurate, the girl sitting *on* the table and swinging her legs—had not red hair. Her voice was not the least unpleasant, there was just a suspicion, a *soupçon*, of delightful Irish brogue in it, and the book she was reading was not a bit above the heads of the audience she was addressing.

The faces of the women were no longer dull and vacuous, and nobody was yawning.

A ripple of laughter had gone round the room and greeted the curate when he opened the door. He was so astonished that he left the door open, and when he had got half-way across the room, the girl sitting on the table called out to him, before all the mothers, 'Oh, would you shut the door, please!' And he went back humbly and shut it.

She did not thank him for shutting it, and she did not look up from her book; she went on reading and swinging her legs.

It was the youngest Miss Penrose, and when the reading and the working were over, and he had closed the meeting with a short prayer, Bertha took him over to the table, and introduced the girl to him as her sister Joan.

Joan was exactly like her sisters; that is, she had the same brown hair, and the same bright complexion, and the same dainty profile, and the same gray-blue eyes. The same, but not the same.

No superficial observer could have told where the difference in the Penrose girls lay—whether in eyes or lips, or in the droop of the dark-fringed eyelids. There was a difference; nobody in the world would have mistaken Joan Penrose for either of her sisters, but she was exactly like both.

It was the unlikeness rather than the likeness that finished the poor curate of Stoke Lucy. He had never been in love that he could remember before in his life, and now he had fallen in love three times in as many weeks. It was rapid work; he could not keep on falling in love at that rate. It was clearly time to stop—he stopped with the youngest Miss Penrose.

He was a superficial, unbalanced young man, not unlike most young fellows of the nineteenth century; he had no ballast whatever to speak of, but he had a genuine passion of admiration and reverence in his heart, which once awakened could never go to sleep again.

The sight of Joan Penrose sitting on the table in that bare, whitewashed parish-room set the tremble in his heart a-going. He had no need to tell himself for the third time that he had found the woman he had been looking for all his life. He was only conscious that the woman had found him.

He made up his mind at once, directly he saw her, that no other woman on earth should be the partner of his fate, and of that magnificent stipend of one hundred and fifty pounds a year. He did not lay himself and his stipend at her feet all at once, but he made up his mind, as he watched her swinging her legs on that deal table, that the very first moment he had a home to offer her, he would lay himself, and the dear little snug nest that was waiting for him somewhere, at her feet, and that he would fly away with her into some sweet sequestered spot, where they would live as happy as two doves for ever after.

It was not the difficulty of choosing between the three Miss Penroses that kept him from declaring his passion for six whole months, after that day when Joan had sent him back to shut the door; he had no hesitation about his choice; he was only waiting until the dear little nest should be ready.

It was ready sooner than he expected. Most men who enter the Church as a profession have to wait years and years, if they have no private means, before they are in a position to keep a wife.

Of course there are exceptions; some men are born lucky, and fall naturally into good things. Doors fly open to them wherever they go; they have only to open their hands wide—very wide—and they are filled to overflowing. Fortune, good fortune, never does things by halves. It is all or nothing.

Robert Lyon was born lucky; he was certainly not born rich. His father, a poor country parson, had left little behind him except a lot of musty old books and a cupboard full of yellow, discoloured old sermons. Robert came across these old sermons on the day of the sale at the Rectory after his father's death, when the house was full of Jew brokers, pulling about all the old familiar things, and making coarse jokes at the shabbiness and poverty of the dear old home that was sacred to him by oh! so many tender associations—the most sacred place on earth.

The brokers were kicking about those yellow, discoloured old manuscripts that had just been unearthed from a locked cupboard, when he came across them. They had been written years and years ago; the ink was faded, and they were covered with dust and cobwebs. They were fit for nothing but to light fires. They were scarcely fit for that; they were damp and mildewed, and had an earthy smell, as papers have that have been locked up in a damp cupboard for half a century. They were only waste-paper; they would not even sell for a song, the auctioneer's clerk said, as he kicked them over, and put them into a lot with a fire-guard, a foot-rest, and a waste-paper basket.

Robert Lyon took up one of the old faded manuscripts, and the sight of the dear familiar handwriting brought a rush of tears to his eyes. It would be a very sad song, he thought, and who so fit to sing it as he? He bought the lot—waste-paper basket, and foot-rest, and fire-guard.

The auctioneer's clerk was right: he bought the sermons that had cost the old Rector hours and hours of toil—weary laborious hours, the best part of the best years of his life—for a song. He stuffed them into a carpet-bag, but he left the waste-paper basket and the fire-guard behind.

And this was his fortune.

Years after, when called upon suddenly to preach an Advent sermon for a college friend in a distant town, he had thrust his hand into the bag that was bulging out with those old manuscripts—he had never thought of them till that moment—and had drawn forth a yellow musty sermon that his father had written and preached twenty years before he was born.

By a lucky accident—call it fate or fortune—he drew forth an Advent sermon. He never stopped to read it; he only read the superscription, '*Preached the second Sunday in Advent*, 1836, *in my own church*.' He stuffed the yellow, musty manuscript into his pocket, and he went his way. He preached the musty old sermon the next day. It was dry and wordy and flavourless, and was full of old-fashioned doctrines about the Second Advent. It had been written when men saw things differently, before the age of scepticism and doubt. There was no uncertainty about it, no vagueness. It was an old-fashioned discourse on the great truths of the Gospel, the promises of God, the immortality of the soul.

The man who had penned those faded characters on the yellow page had lived and died in an obscure country parish. Nobody outside its narrow limits had ever heard of him, but he had done his little part faithfully. He had buoyed up men in his time by his own definite and unconquerable faith in the immortality of the soul, and in God.

That old musty sermon of his, that his son took hap-hazard out of the bag fifty years after, was like the blood of righteous Abel: being dead, it yet spoke. It spoke so well, it went so directly home to the heart of one member of the congregation to whom Robert Lyon preached it on that second Sunday in Advent, that six months after it brought him the offer of a living. It was the luckiest sermon he ever preached in his life.

CHAPTER II.

JOAN PENROSE'S GOOD FORTUNE.

The living came just in time. It came at a most opportune moment. A dreadful thing had happened to the Penrose girls. They had lost all their money; they were plunged in the deepest despair, when, at the darkest moment, there came the timely offer of the living to Joan's lover, and lifted them out of their trouble, and gave them something to think about.

Mrs. Penrose was the widow of an army surgeon, and she had the magnificent pension of seventy pounds a year. She had, besides this fortune, several thousand pounds invested in a colonial bank, and she had in addition a large landed property of her own in Ireland.

The property in Ireland had not brought her in anything for years, and the house that she had inherited from her forefathers was untenanted and falling into decay. Nobody who would pay any rent could be found to live in it, so it remained empty year after year, and fell to pieces bit by bit. If she had had any spirit she would have gone back to Ireland and lived in the house herself, and looked after her agent, who managed, or rather mismanaged, her estate. She had not the spirit of a mouse; she had her children to educate—two boys and three girls—and there were no grammar-schools or high-schools handy to Ballycoran.

The boys would go back to Ireland by-and-by, when they were able to fight their own battles; but the girls grew quite pale at the thought, and vowed they would never set foot in 'the horrid place.' So Mrs. Penrose lived on her pension and the interest of her small capital at Stoke Lucy, where there was a good grammar-school for her boys, and her girls had the advantage of select (provincial) society.

The blow had fallen on the Penrose household on the very day that Robert Lyon received that unexpected offer of a living. It had been a modest household, and the handsome pension and the small dividends had covered all its wants, quite covered them, but there had never been a penny to spare. Now the little dividends were gone, and there would be nothing but the pension left. The bank in which all Mrs. Penrose's money was invested had failed. It is no new thing for a bank to fail. Banks and companies are failing every day, and causing widespread ruin and desolation to hundreds of families. A bank failure is so common a thing that people soon cease to talk about it. It is only when the failure touches one's own immediate circle, and brings unexpected and quite unmerited suffering to helpless, innocent women and children, that one recognises what an awful thing it is. Wrong and robbery and injustice are so common in the world. Somebody makes a blunder, or a whole community go wrong and get into a muddle, and confidence is shaken, and there is a run upon the banks, and a general scramble, each for his own, and the weak go to the wall.

There had been a run upon the bank in which Mrs. Penrose's money was invested, and she had gone to the wall.

The blow had fallen with dreadful suddenness. She was not in the least prepared for it.

A moment before she had been rich, comparatively rich, prosperous, and happy—the girls had just been planning some new summer gowns; and now—in a moment after the receipt of that wretched letter—the whole baseless fabric of prosperity, like Alnaschar's vision, had melted quite away.

Mrs. Penrose's trustee had written to inform her of the failure of the bank. It was the time when he was in the habit of sending her half-yearly dividends; instead of the usual cheque for her dividends, he sent her a formal announcement of the collapse of the concern in which the money was invested.

The poor woman sat like one stunned after reading that miserable letter. The girls came in half an hour after the postman had brought it, and saw it still open in her hand.

Something in her face struck them as they came towards her in the June sunset.

It was a sweet, balmy evening; it had been a perfect golden June day, and it was a perfect golden June evening. It was still only evening, a long, soft, rosy sunset slowly gilding the lilac bushes and the tops of the tall rose-trees in the border, and the white jasmine on the wall. The sunlight had already slipped off the grass, but it lingered on the tall climbing red rose over the window, and on the laburnum-tree that stood near, dropping its pale gold on the path. The two elder girls, Bertha and Phyllis, had been sitting out in the garden until now planning those summer frocks.

They had heard the postman come half an hour ago, but his knock did not quicken their pulses, or bring their hearts to their lips, as it is said to do to some young people of their age. They had no lovers to write to them like other girls. No *billets-doux* ever fluttered in at the windows, or dropped prosaically into the letter-box of the Poplars.

The dear little house that the widow Penrose occupied had three tall poplars quivering at the front-gate; there had once been a knot of poplars standing there, tall and bare in winter, gray and quivering in summer, and from these grim sentinels, or what remained of them, the house had taken its name.

They were quivering in the still June air, and casting long shadows across the grass, when the girls ran up the steps of the silent house.

Mrs. Penrose was sitting with that letter in her hands, beside the open window, when the girls entered the room. They had burst in, as girls do when they are hot and eager. They were very eager just now. They had settled a burning question. They had been considering it all day, not to say disputing it, and they had settled it at last. The beauty of the warm June sunset, the sweet, soft haze that was creeping up from the valley, the golden light that was lingering upon the hills, the fragrance of that jasmine flower, the breath of the tall white lilies in the border, did not touch them as they discussed that burning question.

They did not heed the swallows circling overhead, or the twittering of the finches in the apple-trees, or the rooks cawing on their way to bed; they were so full of that question they had to settle before the London post went out that they did not notice any of these familiar sights and sounds.

One gets so used to Nature: the Penrose girls had lived in the midst of these sweet scents and sounds half their life; they had grown accustomed to the quivering of the poplars and the sunlight slipping off the grass. They had watched it hundreds of times before; there was no reason why they should look at it with different eyes to-night; besides, they had the colour of those new Liberty-silk dresses to settle before the post went out.

'We have quite made up our minds, mamma!' they exclaimed, in a breath, as they burst into the room where the poor woman was sitting with that wretched letter. 'It is to be old rose——'

They stopped, with the door still open, and the words on their lips, and looked at the stricken face at the window.

Mrs. Penrose was sitting bolt upright, with her knitting in her lap, as she had dropped it when she opened that letter, and she was looking straight before her, not at anything in particular, but something a long way off.

Whatever it was she was looking at, it had taken all the colour out of her cheeks, and drawn down the corners of her mouth, and her jaw had fallen, and a hard, upright line had come out on her forehead. She looked ten—twenty years older.

'Oh, mamma, mamma! what is the matter?'

They were both by her side in a moment; and Bertha had her arms around her, and Phyllis had sunk down at her feet, and was holding her cold hands within her own. They had forgotten all about those 'old rose' summer frocks.

It ought to have been a relief to the stricken mother, having those tender arms around her; but she was not thinking about the girls. She was thinking only about her boys, about Clement and Chris, who were doing their 'home-work' in an adjoining room. She was thinking of the future she had planned for them: the prosperous careers that she had mapped out for them—school scholarships, University successes, college fellowships—the Church, the Bar, opening their doors wide to receive them—a long, long vista of success and distinction that only a mother's fancy could create.

Alnaschar's vision was all over now; the stately edifice had toppled over. The poor woman was sitting in the midst of the ruins when the girls came upon her with that open letter in her hand; she was not thinking of them, she had not a thought for anyone but the dear boys scratching away with their pens in the next room.

'Is it all gone, mother—all?' Bertha asked, when she had read the letter, and folded it up, and put it back into the envelope. She always did things methodically.

Phyllis did not say a word; she only knelt on the ground, chafing the poor woman's cold hands; she hardly dared to look up into her face.

'All, everything, except the pension.'

'Is there nothing else left, mother—nothing?'

'Nothing!'

The hopelessness of that one word made the girl kneeling at her feet shiver.

There was silence in the shaded room looking out into the green garden.

The sun was slowly, very slowly, sliding off the jasmine-bush and the laburnum; it had reached already the top-most boughs of the cherry-tree in the kitchen-garden below; it would soon be climbing up the wall of the cottages in the lane—up the wall, and over the red roofs. Bertha, standing by her mother's side at the open window, saw the sunlight slipping off all these familiar things with a strange sense that it was slipping out of her life, and that the shadows were creeping in.

The silence was broken by the sound of voices in the next room, fresh young voices and laughter. Work was over, and the boys were putting away their books. They would be here in a moment—and they would know all.

'Oh, my boys! my poor boys!' the stricken mother moaned. Her stony calmness was shaken, and she broke down in a sudden passion of tears.

The girls had never seen their mother so moved before—not in this way. It was no summer tempest; it was a fierce, wild storm of weeping, it was a passion of despair.

Bertha let her weep her tears out on her bosom, but she could not shed a single tear herself. She could not understand her mother being so moved at the loss of money, mere money. If one of them had died suddenly, or had been injured, she could have understood it—but for mere money!

The boys were already in the passage outside, and one of them was turning the handle of the door, but Phyllis was beforehand with them. She had jumped up at the sound of their footsteps outside, and set her back against the door.

'Go away!' she cried sharply, not in her usual voice, 'go away—you can't come in!'

'Oh, can't we? We'll see about that,' came a cheerful response from outside, and another young back was set against the other side of the door.

It was a tussle between two strong young backs. Phyllis set her shoulders firmly, and her heels firmly, and the door creaked ominously with the weight of the heavy body on the other side; but Phyllis did not give way, she did not budge an inch.

'Go away!' she said, between her teeth, 'go away! I'm ashamed of you. Mother's got a headache.'

'You should have said that before,' the boy said sulkily, as he stamped down the passage.

He did not seem to make much account of the maternal headache as he went whistling and stamping down the passage. He was strong and healthy and sixteen; what should he know about headaches—or heartaches?

Phyllis locked the door when he was gone—at least, she slipped the latch; there was no key in the lock—and then she came over and shut the window. The evening was growing chilly, she remarked, and the boys would hear outside the sound of her mother weeping.

'I don't think everything has gone, mother,' she said, speaking very slowly, and in a voice she made an effort to keep steady. 'It might have been worse. We are not gone—not any of us. We are all left—and we are all strong; you don't know how strong we are.'

She was thinking of that tussle at the door, and how hard Clem had pushed, and what a difficulty she had to keep her feet—but she *had* kept them. It seemed to her like the struggle she would have to go through. It quite braced her up for it.

'I don't see why the boys shouldn't have come in; they will have to know some time. You can't keep it from them,' Bertha said drearily.

'They needn't know yet, not till we've had time to think it over. Perhaps it won't look so bad, mother, when we've thought it over.'

Mrs. Penrose could only moan and wring her hands. She refused to be comforted.

'It couldn't be worse!' she sobbed.

'Oh yes, it could, mother! It could be a great deal worse. The pension might have gone too. We are all big and grown up, all but the boys, and we are all strong and able to work, and if we all cling together and help each other, it will not be so very bad.'

No one, looking at Phyllis Penrose, with her soft eyes and her shy, timid manner, would have believed it of her. No one would have given her credit for having the courage of a mouse, and here she was the champion of the family, preaching hope, and faith, and courage!

Bertha kissed her mother, and soothed her with her soft, clinging arms around her neck, but her lips faltered, and she could not find a word of comfort to say to her.

She was thinking of the butcher's book and the baker's book, which she had added up that afternoon, and the boys' school-bills, and the quarter's rent that was just due—she never gave a single thought to those 'old rose' Liberty frocks.

She thought of the tradespeople, and the tax-collectors, and the midsummer bills that would all be coming in in a week or two—and that there would be nothing but that miserable pension to meet them with.

Phyllis was not so practical as her elder sister; she could not have cut out a little shirt without a pattern if her life had depended upon it—she thought of nothing but comforting and sustaining her mother under the blow that had fallen upon her.

'If we all do our best, mother,' she said, almost cheerfully, choking down that foolish tremor in her voice, 'it will not be so bad as it seems. Perhaps it may be all for the best; we don't know. Things, when you come to look at them and get used to them, are never so bad as they seem.'

Mrs. Penrose could only moan. She was not a philosopher like Phyllis.

While they were still talking—or, to be more accurate, while Phyllis was talking and her mother was moaning—somebody was coming up the path; somebody with a quick, eager, eager step: no one could mistake that footstep.

Joy! joy! joy! rang in every beat of it on the gravelled path, on the stones, on the passage outside. A quick, imperative step with a message going before it.

Joy, joy, joy!

The two girls looked at each other. They knew the footstep quite well; they had heard it every day since it first pattered over the floor eighteen years ago, but they did not know the message.

'Mamma! mamma!' someone was calling outside.

The voice was eager and imperative like the footstep.

Phyllis unlocked the door of the room, and the youngest Miss Penrose burst in. She did not come in —she burst in.

'Oh, mamma! girls! I am—going—to be married!'

The youngest Miss Penrose was so breathless that she had to make a pause between each word. Her heart was beating so high that she could scarcely get the words out. Her eyes were shining, her cheeks were crimson, and she was quivering all over with this strange, delicious happiness.

'Going to be married!' Mrs. Penrose murmured faintly.

'Going to be *married!*' echoed Bertha and Phyllis in a breath.

'Yes, it is settled. I am going—to—to marry—Robert Lyon, and he has got a living—a lovely living!'

Mrs. Penrose wiped her tears away, and embraced her youngest daughter.

'Mother has got a headache,' the girls explained, when she feebly brandished that damp pocket-handkerchief.

How could they mar the joy of that supreme moment with their miserable news?

CHAPTER III.

A TIME OF ROSES.

'It was the time of roses;
We plucked them as we passed.'

It was quite true. Joan Penrose was going to be married immediately. There was nothing to wait for. Robert Lyon had got a living, a good living, and a lovely Rectory-house, and a fine glebe in the sweet, fruitful West Country.

A wealthy old lady, who had the living in her gift, had been impressed on the one occasion that she had heard him preach with his beautiful sermon—with his doctrine, rather. 'It was not often,' she remarked to her friends when they questioned her choice, 'that one heard such doctrine nowadays.'

This was quite true.

The new Rector remembered with a pang, when Lady Aylmerton's words were repeated to him, that the sermon was fifty years old if it was a day.

He had no qualms of conscience about accepting this great gift in those early days when the living of Coombe Damerel was offered to him. He had not the remotest idea why it had been offered to him. He could not think how the old lady had heard of him: he had forgotten all about that Advent sermon he had preached months ago at a place a hundred miles away from Coombe.

He only remembered at that happy time that he could offer the woman he loved a home. He would not have spoken to Joan of love for the world before that living fell into his lap. He would not have asked her for any consideration to share the lot of a poor curate. He shrank from the thought of bringing the woman he loved and reverenced, above every other woman in the world, down to that low level. He could not have borne to have dragged her down into poverty, to have seen her grow prematurely anxious, and careworn, and troubled, to have watched her beauty fade, and seen her strength and her heart failing as the sad burdened years wore on.

He would rather have been silent for ever. It was this that had kept him silent so long, not the difficulty of choosing. He had made his choice the first moment he saw her at that mothers'-meeting. He had been led up to it by degrees, step by step; first Bertha, then Phyllis, and last of all Joan.

He came up to the Poplars the next day, and saw Mrs. Penrose and the girls. He saw the mother first, and then he saw the girls, and received their congratulations.

He told them all he knew, or as much as he knew, about his living. He was as happy and pleased as a schoolboy.

'There is a tennis-lawn,' he said, 'and you must, both of you, come down and play tennis; and there is a big orchard—I believe there are three big orchards—the boys must come down and pick the apples; and there are a lot of old trees on the lawn, and no end of birds' nests; and the place is overrun with rabbits and hares. Chris must bring his gun when he comes down in the Christmas holidays; I dare say we shall be able to borrow some ferrets.'

'You will never be able to take them all in,' Mrs. Penrose said, pleased and smiling. She had forgotten for the moment all about that wretched bank.

'Oh, you don't know how big the house is! It is a great, old-fashioned country house, with I'm afraid to say how many rooms. We shall not be able to occupy a quarter of it. There is stabling for a dozen horses, and a great coach-house, and barns.'

Mrs. Penrose smiled and smoothed her silk gown. She had a habit of smoothing her gown when she was pleased.

'What will you do with so much stabling?'

'Oh, we shall want a good deal of it. I shall keep a quiet mare for Joan to ride, and a hack that we can use in the carriage, and I should like Joan to have a pair of ponies to drive.'

All this sounded delightful. A big country house that they could not fill; orchards, and tennis-lawn, and ferreting for the boys, and a pair of ponies for Joan to drive. No wonder Mrs. Penrose smoothed her gown.

They did not tell Joan anything about that bank failure. What was the use? She would soon be married and away, and it would be time enough then to begin to pare, and scrape, and live upon nothing. Why should they cloud the brightness of that glad, glad time with their sad tale of poverty and misfortune? Joan would never have to bear it; it was their own special trouble, not hers. She would be away in her own home, the big Rectory with the orchards, and tennis-lawn, and flower-gardens; she would be driving that pair of ponies through the green lanes and over the lovely hills of the sweet West Country, while they were pinching and scraping in a mean little house in a stifling street.

Joan was to be married at once, as soon as her few

frocks, her little humble trousseau, could be got ready. It would have been a thousand pities to have marred that glad, happy time with the story of the failure of that wretched bank.

The glad, sunshiny June days passed as no other June days had passed since the world began—at least, Robert Lyon thought there never had been such a June—there never could be such a June again! And Joan—well, Joan trod on air. She was not alone in that delicious experience. Every engaged girl who is going to marry the man she loves goes through exactly the same amazing performance during the first weeks of her engagement. Joan's life had never been anything but a happy one; everything and everybody had always given way to her, but now—now—the happy, tranquil days that were past looked gray and colourless against the bright colours, the golden light of joy, the rosy lines of love and hope that had suddenly come into her life.

There was a flutter at her heart, and her cheeks were alive with blushes, and she could not keep the smiles and the dimples from breaking out on her face at all times and seasons.

She could not keep the joy out of it. She was so brimming over with happiness that it *would* bubble to the surface.

There was a great deal to be done before putting up the banns and ordering the bride-cake. There was that great country Rectory to be furnished, and servants to be engaged, and the ponies to be bought—the ponies and the low basket-carriage. It would take a long time to get a perfectly matching pair; they could not be bought in a hurry. A week after the engagement Robert Lyon took his betrothed down to Coombe Damerel. He had never seen this wonderful great fortune that Providence had bestowed upon him: the big roomy house, the wide lawns and orchards, the fields and gardens that were his for life—his freehold as much as if he had inherited them through a long line of descent.

No one could ever take them away from him: they were his, his own freehold, as if they had been handed down from father to son since the Conquest.

It was right that they should see this House Beautiful, this great estate, together. They started for Carlingford in the early June morning, and came back in the dewy June night, and had six hours to wander over their new domain.

They did a good deal in that six hours, or, rather, four whole hours. The train put them down at Carlingford Station, and they had one hour's drive through a lovely country in the blue June weather before they reached Coombe.

They could have done the distance in half the time, but they would not let the driver hurry. They delayed their happiness; they were not at all eager when it came to those last few miles; they liked to dally with it, and put it off like children. They wanted to see all that lay between them and their future home; they could not afford to miss anything. There was something at every turn to stop and wonder at: green, glowing valleys, and hills with a purple mantle of mist still about them. There never were such hills, Joan declared, they were like mountains! There never were such rich orchards—apples and pears, plums and cherries—nothing came amiss in this fruitful land. And the flowers—it was a world of colour and fragrance; and over all was an intense blue heaven, all melting into light.

The hedgerows rose up tall on either side the road, banks of rosy-fingered honeysuckle, and trailing branches of wild roses, and flowering elder-bushes, and foxgloves tall and dappled.

It was June, the blossoming time of the year. The summer air was full of sweet scents and sweet sounds as they drove through the leafy green lanes to Coombe. A lark, a hundred larks, were singing overhead, and there was a blackbird, or a chaffinch, or some other delightful creature, singing in every bush, and a thrush was calling after them all the way—of course he was addressing Joan:

'Pretty dear! pretty dear!'

First the chimneys, then the gables, then the house itself, came in view. A lovely mellow old house in the midst of wide lawns and stately trees.

It was an old Rectory-house, built years and years ago in those good old days when tithes had suffered no depreciation, and the living had been worth twice, three times as much as it was worth now. The tithes had dwindled year by year, but the old house had stood unchanged. It had only grown mellower and statelier with the years. The ivy had grown around its walls, and moss and lichen had crept among the stones. It quite took Joan's breath away to see the rows and rows of tall, staring windows, and the stacks of chimneys, and the flower-gardens, and the greenhouses, and the stabling and outbuildings.

She did not see them all at once; she saw enough to bring her heart into her mouth; she could not find a single word to say as she drove up beneath the chestnuts to the great gravelled sweep in front of the house. She had expected to see a big, rambling, roomy old house, but she had not expected this. The wide greenness of the lawns, the giant trees that had seen so many rectors come and go, the shady drive beneath the chestnuts, the orchards spreading downward to the river, the gardens ablaze with flowers, had a great effect upon Joan. It was like being set down in an enchanted land.

All hers—all, everything: lawns, gardens, orchards, conservatories—actually conservatories—big house, giant trees, shady avenues, great wide stretches of tranquil greenness—it was all hers, every bit of it. It quite took her breath away.

There was no one living in the house, no caretaker. It was not to let like an ordinary house; there was no one to show people over it, and expatiate on its advantages. There were no men working in the gardens, no grooms in the stables; everything was deserted and standing still like the Sleeping Palace. It might have been standing still for a hundred years. Everything was in its place as it had been ordered ages since. Thought and time might have stood still, too. Perhaps they had, and care and pleasure, hope and pain, had brought the fated fairy prince—and princess—to awake them.

It was no use hammering away at that closed door and sending dreadful echoes on ghostly errands through all the silent house; there was nothing to be done but to send the man who had driven them over into the village to find out who had the key of the house, and to bring it back with him.

While he was away on this errand the lovers walked round the deserted house and saw all they could of it from the outside. They were not content with the outside, though there was a good deal of it to see, and it took them a long time to go round it. They looked in at all the windows they could reach; they flattened their noses against the panes in their eagerness to see what the rooms were like. They would have looked ridiculous objects inside, with their faces pressed tight against the glass, if there had been anybody there to see them.

'This must be your study, Robin,' Joan said, with her lips against the pane. She called him 'Robin' already. It had been 'Mr. Lyon' a week ago, then, shyly, 'Robert.' Now it was 'Robin.'

'See, there are the bookcases for your books; I am so glad they have left the bookcases; it would have pulled the walls about so to have taken them down. And there is a big cupboard by the fireplace for your sermons. Do you see, the door is open? it has got one, two, three shelves. Oh, it will hold such a lot of sermons!'

The new Rector of Coombe Damerel dutifully flattened his nose against the pane to get a view of that cupboard and its gaping shelves. He owned, with a sigh, it would take a lot of sermons.

Joan did not waste much time over the study; she was burning to see the drawing-room. There was a wide bay-window to the drawing-room that was as big as any ordinary room, and there was a door that opened into the conservatory.

The bay-window was rather high up above the steep bank of velvet lawn that sloped away on the western side of the house to the flower-gardens that spread out beneath. Joan ran up the bank and peeped in at the window.

'Oh, Robin!' she said.

She had not heart left in her for another word.

It was a long lofty room like a church, and it had a grand marble mantelpiece, and it was painted white and gold; a big old-fashioned wainscoted room, with great white panels, with gilding round, and a beautiful ceiling with white moulded panels. It would take waggon-loads of furniture to fill it. It ought to be lovely old furniture to match the lovely old room.

The dining-room was nearly as large—a stately, spacious room that would accommodate twenty or thirty people and leave room to spare. They would be quite lost in it, Joan thought, as she stood at the window flattening her nose against the pane.

It had been built in the old hospitable days when money was plentiful, and the owners of the house were not dependent on their tithes and glebe. The house had been built for, and occupied for generations by the descendants of, the great family at Orchard Damerel. It had been the younger brother's portion. It had been occupied by men who had large private incomes, rich squire-parsons, who enjoyed the best society in the county, and spent their days in hunting, shooting, fishing, giving dinner-parties, and playing whist till midnight, and on Sundays donned a surplice and went into the pulpit.

There were no younger sons now at Orchard Damerel; the old family had languished out; there was no one left but that old woman who had listened to Robert Lyon's Advent sermon.

When the happy, quite bewildered young people had seen all they could through the windows of the house, they wandered off into the flower-garden. It was the time of roses—the time of red geraniums, of scarlet poppies, of limp, drooping laburnum, of heliotrope, mignonette, double stocks, of lilies tall and white—of every sweet blossoming thing.

It was an old-fashioned garden, like the house, and it was full of old-fashioned flowers, the dear old favourites that everybody loves.

The borders were full of perennials that had been there years and years, and their ancestors before them. They had gone down into the earth every winter, and come up every spring, and blossomed every summer as they were blossoming now. The varying year had clothed and reclothed the thorns and ivies and woodbines in the hedge, and the tall lilac-tree that nodded over the wall, and sent its new blood up into the old gnarled apple-trees that stood all aslant in the orchard below. There had been little change here for generations—the same old trees, the same flowers springing up in the borders; only the hedge had grown into a little wood, close matted with thorn and woodbine and briar. The briar roses were in bloom in the hedge now, and they covered it with their pink, starry blossoms.

The lovers passed through the sweet-smelling flower-garden, where the colour and the light almost dazzled Joan. It seemed more than she could bear, this brimming over of the cup, these bubbles of delight breaking in the sunshine. They opened a gate in the rose-covered hedge and passed into the enclosure beyond, an enclosure sacred to vegetables.

There was a great deal that was practical in Joan.

The sight of those homely vegetables—the rows of peas and beans, the dear little potatoes, the asparagus, the little green lettuces, and the slender young carrots all desiring to be pulled, or dug, or gathered, and to be boiled and eaten, or chopped up and consumed with a due proportion of oil and vinegar—touched her deeply, more than the flowers had done, with all their sweetness.

Everything was ready for them—ready and waiting. The lovely crinkly green cabbages were literally breaking their hearts in their desire to be promptly cut, and boiled, and eaten. They had burst their tight outside leaves with the vehemence of their desire, and their beautiful white hearts were breaking to pieces.

Joan felt quite sorry for them. She walked up and down the garden paths, making fresh discoveries every minute. There was a lovely bed of strawberries, and there was nobody to pick them. If only the boys had been there! The kitchen-garden was as full of fruit as the flower-garden was full of flowers. The wants of great families had been amply supplied from that old garden. Currants and raspberries, plums and peaches, pears and apricots, all ripened in their season. It made one's mouth water on that hot summer day to see the provision that the old dead and gone rectors had made for those that came after.

Joan devoured the ripe, red strawberries that her lover gathered for her—his first-fruits—but he could not swallow any himself. There was an unaccountable lump in his throat which he had not remarked before. There was a lump in his throat, and a mist before his eyes. He could not understand these things being his.

'What have I done? What have I done?' he asked himself a dozen times as he walked up and down between those homely bean-stalks and currant-bushes.

Joan was much more practical. She was thinking what a quantity of jam she would make with that fruit, and that she would feed the household, the maids, and the grooms upon vegetables.

She was feeling the white hearts of the cabbages, and remarking how hard and solid they were, when the driver came back with the key.

CHAPTER IV.

COOMBE DAMEREL.

It was more and more like a dream, a blissful unreality, unlocking that great hall-door, and going together into the empty house.

They went in hand-in-hand. There was something that even in the midst of their happiness struck them with a feeling of awe as they went over the empty house.

They began at the big rooms on the basement, and went slowly through the place, floor after floor. Every room was sacred to some silent memories; men and women had lived in them, and suffered in them, and, let us hope, rejoiced in them, years before they were born.

They passed through the empty, silent birth chambers and death chambers with hushed footsteps, and speaking involuntarily in whispers. They went up into the garrets last of all—the dusty old garrets with the lean-to roof, where there was not room enough between floor and ceiling for a decent-sized ghost to stand upright.

When they had been in every room, they came downstairs again into the hall. It was quite a relief to come down into the hall, where the door was open, and the beautiful green world could be seen outside, and the balmy June air was blowing in.

They sat down on the stairs—there was no other place for them to sit down—and they talked over this great good fortune that had come to them.

'It will take a lot of furniture to fill all those rooms,' the new Rector said presently. His face was a little long, not to say grave; he did not look nearly so bright and eager as when he was pacing up and down between the bean-stalks in the kitchen-garden, and he had left off murmuring to himself that ridiculous, unanswerable question: 'What have I done?' Perhaps he was tired, or it was the close air of the shut-up house.

'We needn't furnish them all at once,' Joan said sharply. 'We can furnish a few at a time, as we want them. We must furnish all the downstair rooms—the drawing-room and the dining-room; and you can't do without a library. We needn't furnish more rooms upstairs than we need. We can lock the doors, and nobody will know but what they are furnished.'

'I am afraid it will take a great deal to furnish those big rooms downstairs; we shall have very little left for the—horses—and carriage, and we shall want a lot of servants, living in this great house.'

He could not keep back a sigh, though he tried to cover it up. He did not see his way clear about those ponies for Joan on which he had set his heart.

'How much will it take, Robin? How much can we afford?'

'I have not got very much, dear—not quite two thousand pounds. I am afraid it will not go a very long way in furnishing this great house, and in buying carriages and horses.'

'Two thousand pounds! Why, that is quite a fortune, Robin! We shall be able to do a great deal with two thousand pounds. We will write to Maple's, and the Stores, and get catalogues, and pick out the things very carefully. We shall be able to furnish the house beautifully on a thousand pounds, and then you will have nearly another thousand left for the carriage and horses.'

Robert Lyon looked into the clear eyes, so full of hope and courage, and took heart. Of course she knew best. Women have so much better heads for business than men. He was quite angry with himself for being disheartened.

When they had quite finished the house, they went over the stables. They were lovely stables, with accommodation for fifteen horses, and several loose-boxes. They were exactly what the stables of a great country house should be; there was every convenience, and they were in capital order. To a man with a couple of thousands a year and a taste for hunting, they would have been delightful. One ought to have been able to keep at least half a dozen grooms washing carriages and rubbing down horses from morning till night in that capacious stable-yard.

The new Rector stifled another sigh as he left the stables, and went across the paddock, and through one of the wide apple-orchards to the church. There was a path in the grass all the way that the grooms had worn in passing. He had forgotten all about the church until he had quite finished with the stables. He felt himself so exactly like a country gentleman who had succeeded to the paternal estate that he had quite overlooked the church.

The driver had brought over the key of the church with the key of the house; they were tied together on the same string—it was the Rector's key to the little door in the chancel, and it went with the house. When Robert locked the hall-door he saw the other key, and then he suddenly remembered that he had got to see the church.

Side by side they walked together through the apple-orchard. They had gone through so many experiences together since the morning that they felt like old married people. They were grave, almost silent, as they walked beneath the apple-trees in the orchard; the weight of all this wealth and happiness seemed more than they could bear. The world was full of love and happiness—full, brimming over. The sunlight was dropping down on their path between the apple-boughs overhead—Joan could not help remarking how laden they were as she looked up, how full of promise—and the buttercups, tall and golden, were crowding up at their feet. The fields were quite ablaze, like a dappled cloth of gold, with yellow buttercups, and the meadow grasses were in bloom. The grass was quite ready for cutting; there would be a heavy shear this year. There would be quite a respectable rick of hay with all these fields and orchards.

The new Rector was thinking of the hay when they reached the church-gate. They could not see the church till they came upon it.

A little low-roofed country church, with an old gray tower, with a sharp-pointed shingled spire rising from it. The tower was centuries older than the spire, but they were both gray and covered with lichens. The churchyard was full of graves and moss-covered tombstones.

'What a dear little church!' Joan said, as they walked up through the yard; but the new Rector said nothing. His conscience rather pricked him for having thought so much about the hay, and the stables, and the furnishing, and leaving such a small corner in his mind for the church.

A dear old country churchyard full of green mounds, and tombstones all aslant. It must have been a very old yard to be so full of old tombs and lichen-covered slabs. The grass grew tall and rank between the graves, and the falling tombstones were green with moss, and yellow lichens had crept over the slabs and obliterated the inscriptions.

Robert paused as he walked up the path to read, or try to read, the records on the old worn stones. He could not but think, as he walked slowly up the path, over which four centuries of men and women had passed, of his predecessors, who had come, as he had come, full of hope, and youth maybe, and strength and courage, up that same path, and had grown gray and feeble as the years went on, and by-and-by were laid beneath the chancel-stones, one after the other living and dying amid his flock, yielding up his charge to another, and going to his solemn account.

He trod softly between the graves, and paused at the chancel-door, and took off his hat. He did not know why he took off his hat in the yard before he unlocked the door; the air was heavy with—he did not know what the air was heavy with.

He turned the old key in the old door, and went in with a strange feeling in his heart that he could not understand, and he stood bare-headed in the church that was his—his always, so long as God gave him life and strength to deliver His sacred message.

A solemn charge!

It was rather a dark little church, with big round pillars supporting the arches of the roof, and there was an old painted screen across the chancel and the aisle, which, though horribly mutilated, was still beautiful.

There were triple lancets in the east end, and some single lancets in the south wall, and a lovely Decorated west window. It was difficult to determine the date of the various parts, as scarcely one window remained in its original state, and plaster had at various times been liberally applied to the walls and roof. Divided by a carved screen from the chancel was a north chapel, belonging to the noble family at the Court.

It was more like a vault than a chapel; it was so full of old tombs and brasses of dead and gone Damerels that there was scarcely room for the living. Two seats with high carven backs were crowded into one corner of the chapel for the use of the living representatives of the race, and the rest of the space was reserved for the dead.

Joan shivered when she peeped into the chapel through the carved screen—she could not go in, as the door was locked; she could only peep in between the rails. She would not have sat alone in that chill, ghostly place for the world, with all those effigies of dead and gone Damerels around her.

It was a lovely church, and it was in lovely order. There was nothing wanting—nothing—not even a cushion for the pulpit or a book-marker for the lectern.

The only way in which the new Rector could show his gratitude for this great gift, this wonderful providence that had fallen into his lap unasked, was to do his duty, his simple duty—nothing more—in that sacred place unto which God had certainly called him.

Before Joan went away, she gathered some flowers in the Rectory garden to take back with her.

She was so full of her good fortune that she wanted to take back some of the fruits and flowers of this rich, fruitful land—this Canaan flowing with milk and honey in which her lot had fallen—to show her mother and the girls. They would not believe half of it if she did not take away with her, like the spies of old, an earnest of the exceeding richness of the land.

She gathered a great armful of roses, a rich lovely bunch of foam and freshness, to take back with her; she snipped off the sweet fragrant rosebuds with reckless wantonness. It would have gone to the heart of a rose-grower to have seen the havoc she made in that Rectory garden.

In the sweet summer dusk they drove back through the leafy lanes. Soft, blue mists were creeping up from the valleys, and purple tints were lingering on the hills; the sun was setting in a ball of fire behind the church and the village, gilding the tall shingled spire and the red roofs; the blue smoke was curling up from the farm-house chimneys, and the dappled cows were grazing in the rich grass, and everything was golden, and peaceful, and prosperous.

CHAPTER V.

A WONDERFUL PROVIDENCE.

ROBERT LYON never forgot as long as he lived—perhaps he will not forget it when life is finished—this life—he will go on remembering it—the sweet-smelling gloaming of that June night, when he drove through the dusky lanes, with his heart full to bursting of the smell of the new-mown hay, and the honeysuckle in the hedge, and of the strange wonderful thing that had happened to him.

It did not occur to him then, it did not occur to him till long after, that this great gift which had fallen into his lap could be anything but an unmixed good.

What man in his senses would question the wisdom and the goodness of the kind Providence that showered upon him such rich gifts?—a lovely old country house and grounds, a wide estate in the midst of the loveliest country in the world, and an income of nearly three hundred a year.

To be more accurate, the Rector of Coombe Damerel had a net income of exactly two hundred and seventy-eight pounds a year to keep up an establishment that might—well, that had indeed cost his predecessor one to two thousand a year to keep up. The house was exactly fitted for a tenant with at least three times his income. There was extensive stabling, accommodation for numerous servants, large reception-rooms, expensive flower-gardens and hot-houses—what more could a man with large private means desire?

It showed exactly the extreme wisdom of the adage we all quote impatiently, and with a sense of injustice, 'Unto him that hath much shall much be given.' The rich man was precisely the right person to receive this rich gift. It was out of the question for a poor man; it was like that unpleasant comparison people sometimes make when they see riches and beauty—female beauty—grossly misplaced.

It did not occur to Joan for a single moment that this rich jewel which had fallen to her lot was misplaced. She looked upon it as a wonderful dispensation of Providence—a proof, if one were wanting, of the wisdom and far-sightedness of the Great Dispenser, who had recognised Robert's great merits, and had rewarded them as was meet. She accepted her jewel of gold, and wore it, not in her ear, but in her heart of hearts. It was nothing more than Robert deserved.

If the two people most concerned did not question the wisdom of the gift and the prudence of accepting it, there was no one else to question it. Mrs. Penrose feebly remonstrated when Joan put down big sums in her store-list for the sideboards and couches she had set her heart upon to furnish those great rooms.

'My dear,' her mother would say, with a weak smile, remembering what these big sums would represent in that bare household—boys' education, rent, wages, food, coals—'my dear,' she said, smothering a sigh, 'I don't think the sum you have set aside for furnishing will cover all those expensive items. You must recollect that there are other things besides furniture, chairs, and tables, and hangings. There is the linen. The linen, as you will have to buy all new, will be quite an expensive item. And then there will be the plate——'

'Oh, we shall get a lot given us for wedding-presents, mamma. You must tell everybody to give us silver. We shan't buy any until we see what is given us. You might drop a hint to people, you know, of what things we want: spoons, and forks, and entrée-dishes, and tea-sets—silver tea-sets—and things for the table. I hope no one will work us anything. I do hate needlework presents. I like something solid.'

With all her frivolity Joan was practical.

'Mamma doesn't think the two thousand pounds will last out, Robin,' she said to her betrothed in her blunt way, as they were looking over the lists together. 'She thinks we ought to begin in a smaller way, and buy things as we can afford them.'

Robert Lyon laughed a low, happy laugh.

'If we cannot afford them now, we shall never be able to afford them,' he said gaily; 'my income is not likely to increase.'

'We don't want it to increase, Robin. It will be quite enough. We shall never be able to spend so much money. Think! nearly three hundred pounds a year on only two people; and no rent to pay, and that great garden, that will supply us with vegetables and fruit—more than we can eat if we had nothing else—all the year round!'

Robin had thought it over dozens of times. He thought, considering the garden and no rent to pay, that it would be enough, quite enough—but there would not be anything to spare.

They were as happy as Cock Robin and Jenny Wren in the old nursery rhyme. They were going to live on love and red-currant wine. This source of income was never likely to fail, whatever else happened.

The furnishing was a more serious undertaking than Joan had anticipated. It is astonishing what a lot of things a house of the most modest dimensions requires. Not chairs and tables only—one can count these off on one's fingers—but odds and ends. There seemed to be no end to that long, long list that Joan made of odds and ends, and they seemed to swallow up most of the money.

Mrs. Penrose went up to town with the lovers to select the furniture and to buy the linen, and while she was there she bought the wedding-gown. No one had told Joan about that bank failure, but she understood, somehow, that great economy was needful, and that she would have to be content with very few frocks.

She was so happy, so ridiculously happy, that she would have been content with one. She would have been content to have gone on wearing that wedding-gown till it dropped from her back.

The wedding-frocks were made up at home. A pale young woman used to come early every morning, and stay till late at night, sewing all day at those gowns; and Joan was called away from her accounts and her store-lists a dozen times a day to try them on a bit at a time—a sleeve, or a collar, or the lining of a bodice that was stuck so full of pins that it was a marvel how she ever got into it, or out of it, without being torn to pieces.

Sometimes she used to come into the busy workroom, where the girls were stitching for their lives, to help a bit—to run a seam or hem a frill; but she did not hem it very long, and she used generally to stop in the middle of the seam. Her hands would fall down softly into her lap, and a dreamy, far-off smile would come over her face as she looked beyond that tiresome work out into the little green garden.

Phyllis, stitching away for her life at those wedding-garments, would watch her with her soft eyes and wonder at the strangeness of that smile. There was nothing to make Joan blush and look up surprised with such a depth of happiness in her absent eyes when some-one called across the table, 'I'll trouble you for the white cotton,' or, 'Pass the scissors, please.'

Phyllis had never seen that blissful look on her sister's face before, or on any other girl's face; but, then, she had not seen much. She used to look in the glass sometimes when she was doing her hair, to see if her own eyes had any blissful depths in them. They were very like Joan's eyes, only softer and sweeter; calm, tranquil eyes, whose depths—if they had any—had never been disturbed.

She could see nothing in the glass but her soft sad face, and her pretty brown hair, and the long lashes that cast such a dark shadow on her cheek. She had a little nervous trick of blinking those tremulous lids, and the corners of her mouth quivered when she was moved. They quivered now as she looked in the glass and recalled Joan's strange look of happiness. It might have been hers, this wonderful happiness that had come to her younger sister; it would have been hers but for Joan.

The wedding-gowns were made at last; there were not many new ones to make besides the wedding-gown, but there were a lot of old ones to freshen up, and, with the addition of some frills and furbelows, to make as good as new.

There were three new ones—hightum, tightum, and scrub, as Joan called them. Scrub was an everyday sort of gown for home wear; tightum was a gown to return calls in, and to wear at church and garden-parties and hightum was an evening gown—a rosy Liberty silk one of those gowns the girls had given up so bravely it is not a small thing to give up a Liberty frock when one's evening frocks are few and shabby.

It meant a lot of pinching and scraping for another year, those few gowns, and the necessary additions to that little humble trousseau that the girls worked so hard at from morning till night, that Joan might not go to her new home naked and ashamed. It was the first wedding in the family, and they did their best. Never mind how poor it was, it was their best—their loving, generous best. Joan never knew what it cost them, or what pinching and paring it entailed. If she thought anything at all about it, she thought it was mean and stingy.

The girls had never told her anything about the bank failure, and the loss of income, and that, as soon as she was married and away, they would all go to live in a stuffy little house in a mean, shabby street.

It would be time enough for her to know it when she was married and settled in her beautiful home, and then she need not know the worst. Love is like a sheltering tree. It would fain bear itself the sweeping storm of adversity, and shelter those it loves from the rude blast.

The furnishing of the Rectory went on apace. It is quite astonishing how quickly one can turn a dreary, empty, barrack-like place into a delightful cosy dwelling, if one has a thousand pounds at hand to do it with. When Joan had completed her lists, the upholsterers went down to Coombe Damerel and took the place in hand, and filled up the details that she had forgotten. She had forgotten a good many.

She had reckoned a good deal on the wedding-presents. She knew so many people in Stoke Lucy, and this was the first wedding in the family; they had never been asked to give any presents before, and they might never be asked again. Only one of the girls left could marry in any case; the other would have to stay at home with her mother.

Robert Lyon, until his engagement, had been the most popular curate that could be remembered in Stoke Lucy for years, judging by the number of slippers that were worked for him, and the lovely sermon-cases and book-markers, and the knitted vests and mufflers for his tender throat. They did not come in so freely after his engagement was made known, nor were the wedding-presents exactly what Joan had expected. They made up, however, for their other shortcomings in their number and variety. There was not much table-silver among them, nothing like what Joan had counted upon.

There was a lovely pair of old apostle-spoons fit only

for a cabinet, and a sweet little antique Queen Anne cream-jug with an unreliable handle, and a butter-knife. To be more accurate, there were half a dozen butter-knives, but five of them were plated. The same defect applied to the butter-dishes and muffineers and pepper-pots and sugar-basins. But there was a lovely variety of other useful things. There were four smelling-bottles, a crocodile brush-case, two walking-sticks, six china *menu*-holders, three pin-cushions, a silver cigarette-case, a pair of tall glass vases, a Prayer-Book, a *point-de-gaze* pocket-handkerchief, a glove-box, a sandal-wood card-case, a pair of brass scissors, a set of toilet-mats, a paper-cutter, a melodeon gong, a silver hand-mirror, six photograph frames, a pickle-fork, a tea-cosy, a shaving-glass, and a pair of fire-screens hand-painted.

Nobody could have desired a greater variety, and, as Joan remarked, they were all useful—very useful.

The wedding was a very quiet one. It was not one of those old-fashioned showy affairs with a dozen carriages, and big white satin favours for the coachmen, and guests in hundreds, and a ridiculous wedding-breakfast where the champagne flowed like water. It was a modest little wedding, with not more than a dozen people present besides the congregation, which overflowed the aisles, and allowed the little bridal party scarcely room enough to pass to the altar. There was no breakfast after. The present delightful two p.m. arrangement does not allow of formal sitting-down wedding-breakfasts.

People who desired to offer their congratulations called in the afternoon and sipped a cup of tea and swallowed a few crumbs of cake or a lump of sugar-icing, as the case might be.

The little tearful bride—Joan was not at all a tearful bride—had stripped off her finery, and packed up her small trousseau, and started on her wedding-journey before these dear friends began to arrive. The world was before her, and, like adventurous Eve, she had stepped out of the calm Eden of her youth and ignorance, and an angel with a flaming sword barred the way of return.

Perhaps she would never desire to return. Why

should she? She had Adam by her side, or his lineal descendant. The old tangled way was before them; the thorns and the briars, and the print of the old footsteps. Who can blame them if, in their youth and their ignorance, they repeated the old mistakes; if they suffered the same failures and losses; if they stumbled by the way, and got up again bruised, and torn, and wound-d? The world teaches now, as it taught then, by experience. Schools change with the times, but there is only one schoolmaster.

CHAPTER VI.

WEDDING-BELLS.

It is all very well for happy people to get married and go away, and leave the poor, dear, tearful people at home to cut up the wedding-cake, and pack it into nice little boxes—in clean-cut, wedge-shaped pieces, with a due proportion of icing—and tie it up with satin ribbon in dear little true-lovers' knots. They should try what it is themselves to cut through the icing of a wedding-cake, before they devolve upon those poor, dear, tearful things they have left behind the unthankful task.

Phyllis and Bertha Penrose spent the whole of the day after the wedding cutting up that wretched cake. It was not for its size—it was quite a modest little cake—but no amount of persuasion would induce the sharpest of knives to penetrate that awful sugary crust. They tried a hammer when everything else failed, and then the icing all broke to pieces, and the cake crumbled, and there was nothing left but a heap of powdered sugar and crumbs.

It was the first time they had ever attempted to cut a wedding-cake, and Phyllis remarked, almost in tears, when she saw what a mess they had made of it, she hoped it would be the last!

When the cake was cut up and sent off, they had to begin about the moving. They had to move into a stuffy little house in a back street, and they had to send away the servants and get rid of a lot of the furniture.

Perhaps this was the hardest part of all, getting rid of the old familiar things they had known and loved all their lives—the old furniture, and the old china, and the old pictures. The pictures were so large that they were out of proportion to the little house they were moving into; they would have quite covered the walls, and made the rooms look smaller than they were.

Mrs. Penrose thankfully accepted the offer of the man who moved the furniture for a dozen of them; they were only in the way, and she was glad of the small sum of money he offered. It was a very small sum for such a lot of big pictures, but it covered the cost of the moving, and left a little balance.

She stopped one of the pictures as she saw it carried out of the house. It was a portrait of a woman, a girl, rather, in an old-fashioned gown, who had been a beauty in her time.

'You must bring that back,' she said; 'it is a family picture. I cannot sell that. It is the portrait of my great-aunt.'

The man grumbled, and brought the picture back, and then the small amount had to be reduced still further.

'It is the portrait of my Aunt Joan,' she explained to the girls; 'I don't think it ought to go out of the family. Joan was named after her. If no one else cares for it, I should like to give it to Joan. It is the only wedding-present I can give her.'

'Let Joan have it by all means,' said the girls. 'It is a hideous old thing; no one else would give it a place!'

The despised portrait of her ancestress completed the list of Joan's wedding-presents.

It was a terrible affair going into that little house. It was not only a little house, but the street was wretchedly mean and narrow, and there were mean houses on either side and poor neighbours. It was not the poverty of the neighbourhood that tried the girls and their mother in the early days of their change of fortune; it was its unutterable shabbiness and dreariness that weighed upon them.

'I'm sure nobody will ever find us out here,' Bertha said, with tears in her eyes, as she looked round the dull rooms, and glanced hopelessly down the dull street. 'We can't expect people to call in this horrid place!'

'I don't see why they shouldn't call,' Phyllis said stoutly. 'I'm sure everybody we care about will call. We have done nothing. It is not our fault that that horrid bank has failed!'

'Ah, you don't know,' Bertha moaned, shaking her head with an air of superior wisdom; 'how should you know? People don't value you for what you are, but for what you possess. If you are rich and prosperous, you will have plenty of friends—everybody is glad to know you—but if you happen to be unfortunate, and have come down in the world, it doesn't matter by whose fault, it is astonishing how soon people forgot you.'

Phyllis gave a sniff of disapproval.

'I don't believe it,' she said stoutly. 'We shall see if people forget us—people we've known and been brought up among all our lives. I wouldn't take such a mean view of human nature for all the world!'

Phyllis *saw* that very afternoon. A frequent visitor at the Poplars in the days of their prosperity—the donor of one of those plated butter-knives—met Phyllis in the High Street, and looked the other way. She did not cut her—nobody cuts people in these days—but she did not see her. She had grown suddenly short-sighted.

Phyllis came home furious. It filled her with indignation that the world—her little world—should be so base and mean as to turn its back upon her because she was no longer rich and prosperous. It required all her courage to face the situation and bear up under the change of fortune. Bertha did not attempt to bear up; she broke down after the first day or two when the excitement of moving was over. She did not pretend to be cheerful or contented; she went about in a sort of sullen despair, chafing under the injustice of her lot, and planning futile schemes for retrieving their ruined fortunes.

'What have we done?' she was always asking Phyllis when they were alone and out of reach of their mother's anxious ears and eyes. 'What have we done that this should happen to us?'

'I don't think it's for anything we've done, dear,' Phyllis would say, with her eyelids blinking in their nervous way; 'but I'm not sure it isn't a kind of discipline, or something of the sort——'

'Discipline! What do you mean?' Bertha interrupted, in quite a shocked voice. 'What have we done that we should need discipline—this sort of discipline?'

She might well ask.

'I don't know, dear,' Phyllis said humbly; 'I only thought——'

'Oh, you are always thinking foolish things! I dare-say you think that it has happened for our good—that poverty and misfortune were just the discipline we needed; that prosperity and ease were spoiling us, and that we shall be ever so much better by-and-by for enduring these wretched shifts and humiliations. Oh, I have no patience with such notions!'

Phyllis sighed.

'I don't know,' she said, hanging her head, and her eyelids quivering; 'nobody knows why such things happen, why they are permitted to happen, why the world is so full of sorrow, and loss, and pain. There must be a reason for it. It can't be a matter of chance. I don't think I could go on living if I didn't believe that there is a Providence over all, shaping our lives, and sending us exactly the things that are best for us.'

It was Bertha's turn to sniff now.

'How about Joan, then? Is prosperity—happiness—ease—love, the best kind of discipline for Joan?'

'It may be,' Phyllis said softly; 'who can say?'

'I don't believe any such nonsense. Why should there be such distinctions? What have we done that our lot should be different from hers?'

It was the old question. It was a difficult question to answer.

While Bertha brooded over her wrongs, Phyllis tucked up her sleeves, and set to work to get the little house in order, and put the best face on things. It did not look nearly so shabby after a week's rubbing and scrubbing and polishing up. It is astonishing what a transformation willing hands can make in the dreariest dwelling.

Love and labour, a box of mignonette on the window-ledge, a bowl of roses on the table, and white curtains fluttering in the breeze that came in at the open window, looking out into the shabby street, quite transformed that little bare room that was bare and mean no longer.

Things did not look nearly so bad at the end of the week, when the chairs and tables and the dainty knick-knacks were all put in their places, and the white curtains were up, and the dull windows were bright and shining.

With great economy that seventy pounds a year would cover the bare cost of living, and there was enough left from the sale of the furniture to pay for the boys' schooling for a year or two, and the rent of the shabby little house, and at the end of that time who could say what might not have happened? A fairy prince might have come and carried away another of the girls, or the bank might have recovered itself, and there might be a small dividend, after all.

'We can't wait for that,' Bertha said impatiently, when Phyllis suggested those possibilities. 'What fairy prince would come to us now? The very sight of the house would frighten him away. No one but a workman with a bag of tools over his back would ever seek for a wife in this wretched street. We shall have to go out in the world and look for the fairy prince, Phil; he will never come here to look for us.'

Phyllis' face flushed, and her lips quivered, and her long eyelashes drooped over her cheek.

'Do you think mother would let us go out?' she said, with bated breath. 'Oh, do you think she would let me go out?'

She was anxious to begin that search for the fairy prince at once.

'She must. She can't expect to keep two girls at home—on seventy pounds a year.'

'Then, I think we ought—one of us ought to go out at once. Oh, I wish she would let *me* go!'

'You! What can you do?'

It was rather a cruel question, but Bertha was not considerate of the feelings of other people. She was sharp—like her scissors.

'I? Oh! I could do something.'

'Something, yes; but you could do nothing well, not well enough to earn a living at it.'

'I could teach—a little.'

This very humbly.

'Yes, you could teach a Sunday class, or you might teach the Catechism in a school, the Commandments, and the "duties"—which the children never remember—and teach them a few hymns. I don't think you can teach anything else. You don't know a single rule of English grammar, Phil; you never could recollect dates; and I don't believe you could repeat the counties of England. If you don't know things, you can't teach them.'

'No,' Phyllis said despondently. 'I'm not clever like you, Bertha; I couldn't teach French and German. I always hated French; I wish I had liked it better now. You remember what dreadful trouble I had with those French verbs?'

'I remember you were always a goose at school, Phil—a goose at everything. I never knew you do anything well. You were always at the bottom of the class, and your reports were shocking—and you talk about going out as a teacher!'

Phyllis hung her head. The tears were gathering under her dark lashes, but she kept them back; she was not going to give in yet.

'There is something else I could do besides teaching. All girls do not go out as governesses. I could be a companion—a companion to a lady.'

Bertha burst out into an unfeeling laugh.

'Nobody thought you could be a companion to a gentleman!' she said; and then Phyllis began to blush in the most ridiculous way. 'No, no, Phil, your duty is quite clear. You must stay at home and take care of mother, and let me go out. Perhaps I shall find the fairy prince; who knows? I shall never find him if I stay here; never—never.'

CHAPTER VII.

A QUESTION OF CONSCIENCE.

THE village of Coombe Damerel was an out-of-the-way nook, hidden among the green hills of Devon.

The nearest railway-station was five miles off by the highroad, though there was a nearer way of reaching it if you cut across the fields and did not mind a few stiles and gates by the way.

The village consisted of a single twisting street—a delightful, irregular old street, with whitewashed cottages on either side, with red roofs and quaint gable-ends, and lattice-panes glittering in the sun.

The village led up to the great house, but it did not approach too near to it; it kept a respectful distance from the gates. If it had approached the gates, over which a hideous griffin that frightened the village children into fits kept watch and ward, it would still have been a mile and a half from the house.

The carriage-drive that led up to the house wound round the shrubberies and the home fields before it reached the park proper. Then, instead of the conventional wide stretch of tranquil greenness, with giant trees casting their great shadows on the grass, and looking as if they had pushed the world aside to clear a wide breathing-space for their fortunate possessors, a lovely coombe ran through the grounds, and the thickly wooded deer-park rose up on either side. The road wound round the coombe and the gently sloping hills, and through a dense shrubbery that even at that late time in the year was ablaze with rhododendrons.

At the end of the shrubbery one came upon the house—a beautiful old house amid shady glades, and with a wide stretch of tranquil greenness before it, and the hills rising up behind. It was like a house in a picture.

Orchard Damerel, as the place was called—it was one of the country-seats of the Earl of Aylmerton—was an unpretending house for such a great estate. It was a pleasant place enough—it had been a favourite residence of the late Earl during the later years of his life—but it had no pretension to dignity.

A long, irregular, picturesque old house, with sunny windows opening out upon velvet lawns, and looking as little like the residence of a belted earl as a rambling old red-brick country mansion could look.

The Countess of Aylmerton had lived here ever since the late Earl's death, some seven years before our story opens. She lived here to economize. Her income would not allow her to live at Aylmerton Court, the old family place of the Damerels. The Earl had died in debt—up to his ears in debt—and the place was mortgaged to the chimneys.

He was the last of his race, and he had run through all the money. There was no one of his name to come after, no one to save up for, and the Earl had spent his money in his lifetime like a lord—like an earl, rather. The only legacy he left behind him was a legacy of debt, some hundred thousand pounds. He had no heir to leave it to: the title died with him.

He took some trouble during his last illness to find out a distant—far distant—kinsman, who bore the name of Damerel; and having found one, in the most handsome manner he bequeathed him this weighty legacy. Besides the legacy, he left him, at the decease of the Countess, the family place of the Damerels in Norfolk and the beautiful old house of Orchard Damerel, with all their priceless heirlooms. There was only one condition attached to the bequest—that the late Earl's debts should be paid in full, every shilling of them, before the next owner entered into possession of the estates.

Considering that there was the heavy interest of all those mortgages to be paid, and the place to be kept up, and the little that remained had to accumulate year by year until it could pay off that hundred thousand pounds, the fortunate legatee was not likely to come into possession very soon.

It would have been different—at any rate, it would have altered the aspect of things—if any portion of the property, the outlying lands, the acres and acres of shooting, could have been sold, or the plate, or the pictures, or the china that were locked up in the great empty house in Norfolk. There was a special clause to provide against this: the great estate and the heirlooms were to descend intact to the legatee, or his heirs, when the debt was paid—and not before. It was not likely to be paid, with those slow accumulations year by year, for a generation or two. It was not at all likely to be paid in the lifetime of Hugh Damerel, the fortunate legatee.

The property was vested in the hands of trustees, and a small income was paid to Lady Aylmerton, which her marriage settlement had fortunately secured to her.

It was a small settlement for a countess, but her ladyship was a second wife; the Earl had already run through his money when he married her. The bankrupt Earl was a very good match for the daughter of a small country attorney—her ladyship's father had been the Earl's legal adviser, and had assisted at those mortgages. Maria Burrough had really done very well for herself when she married the Earl: she had lived in some splendour during his lifetime, and she had been received at Court. After his death she had nothing to complain of. She had the beautiful old house of Orchard Damerel for her life, and she had an income that, considering her humble bringing-up, was not only ample, but liberal enough for her to put by a small sum yearly for those who came after.

The Countess lived at Orchard Damerel all the year, except when at rare intervals she paid a visit to her married nephews and nieces. She was paying a visit to a married niece when she heard that Advent sermon of Robert Lyon's.

She was looking out for a successor for the living of Coombe Damerel, the next presentation being in her gift. She had no nephews of her own to give it to, and there were no Damerels left, no second sons, or cousins, or nephews. There had not been a Damerel at the Rectory within the memory of the present generation.

Lady Aylmerton had decided views on religious matters—not very broad views—and she held rather unusual opinions on the Second Advent.

She had never heard anyone in the pulpit express those opinions of hers—she was a disciple of Dr. Cumming; she was more than a disciple, she was a worshipper of that great mistaken man—she had never heard anyone, except the great man himself, express opinions on that all-absorbing subject that so exactly agreed with her own as Robert Lyon in that Advent sermon.

She desired nothing better than to sit beneath such teaching for the rest of her life. It was exactly the teaching she had been thirsting for for years; nothing could have happened more providentially She believed in Providence. It is an old-fashioned belief; it is going out fast, like those old foolish notions about earthly millenniums.

The Countess of Aylmerton was an old fashioned person: she had not had much education, and she believed in both. She found out all about Robert Lyon after he had preached that sermon, and when the living of Coombe Damerel became vacant she desired the Earl's trustees, who acted for her in the matter, to offer it to him.

He never knew until he was instituted in the living to what happy circumstances he owed that unlooked-for presentation.

When the new Rector of Coombe Damerel came back from his wedding-tour, and settled down in the near neighbourhood of his unknown patron, or rather patroness, it was his duty to call upon her without delay and express his gratitude.

He called the day after he came back. He did not take Joan with him; it was not a proper call, he explained to her; it was not even a parochial visit, it was a call of duty; and, if the truth must be told, he would much rather that his bride was not present while he expressed his gratitude to the great lady who had honoured him by her choice.

He knew nothing about the settlement of the property, or the late Earl's debts, or the antecedents of Lady Aylmerton. He only knew that the village and the land for miles around belonged to the Damerels, and that they had come in with the Conqueror or thereabouts, and that so far as he was concerned they were, or, rather, the last representative of the noble line was, the greatest potentate on earth. All things are relative, and the little hill a mile off is bigger, much bigger, than the mountains on the horizon.

Orchard Damerel was scarcely a mile away from the Rector, if he took the short path through the shrubbery, the path that had been worn in those old days when a Damerel held the family living; and the Countess of Aylmerton was a much greater person in Robert Lyon's eyes than her Most Gracious Majesty herself in her distant castle of Windsor.

With his heart beating dreadfully, Robert walked through the blossoming rhododendrons, and came out upon the head of the coombe and the wide tranquil greenness of the park.

He had never seen an Earl's house before, and he had expected to see a great gloomy castle frowning down upon him, or a big Tudor mansion at the least. The sight of the unpretentious red-brick house reassured him, and gave him courage to ring the front-door bell.

The door was opened by an ancient butler of very solemn aspect, who led him through the wide roomy hall, into which the door opened, into the great drawing-room beyond.

He had time while he sat there waiting for the Countess to look round the great stately room. It really was a stately room, and it was furnished in the stiff, conventional taste of the early years of the century. Everything was massive and gilt, and stiff and formal. The heavy old hangings were of rich brocade with great conventional flowers, and trophies, and true-lovers'-knots in the funny old taste of those unæsthetic days.

The chairs and couches were covered with old faded embroideries of the same outrageous pattern, and there were immense roses and carnations and fuchsias sprawling over the carpet in the same old faded colours. The mantelpiece was a wonderful erection of pure white marble that the late Earl had brought from Italy some years ago, and that must have cost a fortune; and there were two big statuary marble figures, one at each end, in hideous gilt alcoves, lined with red velvet, and a great marble clock in the middle.

It would have been quite an appalling room, with all that gilding and upholstery, and those marble busts and figures, if it had not been for the beautiful old pictures and the china.

The pictures on the walls were family portraits, and had all been painted by great masters in their day. Whatever other gifts the Damerels had lacked, they had never lacked beauty.

A lovely portrait of Henrietta, fifth Countess of Aylmerton, painted by Van Dyck, hung over the mantelpiece, between the hideous gilt alcoves and the classical statuary marble figures. A lovely Gainsborough, representing the beautiful Countess, wife of the eighth Earl, hung opposite the big bay window; the blue satin dress that Gainsborough was so fond of painting had faded in that strong light, and the roses in her bosom, and the paler roses in her cheeks, had faded too, but the soft, dark eyes were as bright as ever, and the vermilion of the thin red lips was untouched, and time had only mellowed to a diviner tint the rich abundant auburn hair beneath the great hat and its drooping feathers.

There were some delightful portraits by Reynolds, and Lawrence, and Hoppner on the walls, but Robert Lyon could look at nothing but the Gainsborough. The gilding, and the colouring of those wonderful floral devices on the carpets, and the curtains, and the presence of all those marble figures, had dazzled and bewildered him. He had not any eyes for the priceless old china on the tables and in the cabinets; he could do nothing but sit with his mouth open staring at that figure of a woman in a blue gown.

He was still staring at her when the Countess came into the room. He had expected—well, he did not exactly know what he had expected a countess to be like. He had never seen a countess before, only those painted ones on the walls. He could not have expected an old woman over seventy to be like those sweet creatures that were looking down at him with their painted eyes and their best company smiles. He could not have expected her to have come in, at that time of the day, in a pale-blue satin gown, with her poor old withered shoulders very much *en évidence*, with a gauzy scarf about her, and a great hat with sweeping plumes nodding above her scanty locks.

Whatever he expected a real live countess to look like, the old lady who came into the room was not the least like anything that he had expected—a large, stout, commonplace-looking woman, with a florid face, and wearing a decidedly dowdy cap.

Robert got up awkwardly and set the Countess a chair, and then he found himself thanking her for having chosen him above all the world for this great gift—he called it a great gift—and saying some idiotic things about her confidence not being misplaced.

'Oh, I knew all about you before I wrote to Mr. Greatorex to offer you the living, Mr. Lyon,' her ladyship said. (Mr. Greatorex was one of the trustees of the Damerel estate.) 'I heard you preach a sermon on the millennium last Advent, when I was staying with my niece at Clifton, and your views exactly agreed with mine. I could wish nothing better than to sit under such teaching for the rest of my days.'

This ought to have been very gratifying to the new Rector; it ought to have made him blush with modest pride and satisfaction. He did blush to his fingers' ends, but, alas! not by any means with pride or satisfaction.

He had not written a word of that sermon, and, so far as he could recall it, he did not agree with a single opinion that it expressed. He had never even read it over until he smoothed it out on the pulpit cushion, and then he had to go on with it, whether he agreed with it or not.

His first thought as he sat there, amid the old faded roses and the gilding, crimson and ashamed, was to confess his fault—if fault it could be called—and own that the sermon was not his own; that he had, in fact, without knowing it, obtained a living by false pretences.

First thoughts are always best.

The Countess had made the mistake, not he; it was

too late for her to take back the gift she had bestowed on such slight provocation.

He looked up at the picture of the lady in blue, and saw the soft, dark eyes fixed upon him, and then he remembered Joan, and her innocent joy in her new house and her beautiful grounds. He had a ridiculous notion that all this would slip out of his hands, and that he should have to give up the living and go away if he explained to the Countess the mistake she had made.

For Joan's sake—only for Joan's sake—he was silent.

He was quite relieved when Lady Aylmerton changed the hateful subject and asked after his wife.

'I must call and see Mrs. Lyon,' she said. 'I will bring my niece; I should like them to be friends. Cecilia is very dull living alone with me in this gloomy house, and seeing so few people. She will be very glad to know your wife.'

As the Rector walked back through the rhododendrons he was troubled with a great many qualms of conscience. He was sorry and sad and ashamed. He would have to go on living a lie; he would never be able to preach any different doctrine. For the rest of his life he would be hampered by these old-fashioned, exploded views which he did not hold, which he could never bring himself to hold; he would have to lay aside the beautiful broad modern theology he had learnt in the schools, and on which he prided himself, to pander to the narrow prejudices of a bigoted old woman.

Oh, it was humiliating!

'Should he tell Joan?' he asked himself.

And then he found himself getting quite hot at the thought of confessing to his bride of a month that he had done this contemptible thing.

'It was for Joan's sake he had done it.' If it had not been for Joan, he would certainly have told the truth about that sermon, and Lady Aylmerton would have seen her mistake. If he had been a single man, with no one dependent upon him, he would not have hesitated for a moment.

Whatever happened, it was for Joan's sake that he had kept silence.

It was perhaps quite as well that he had paid that first visit to Orchard Damerel alone, that he had not taken his bride with him.

CHAPTER VIII.

A BLUE-BEARD CUPBOARD.

LADY AYLMERTON called on the Rector's wife the next day.

It was very early to call; Joan had only arrived in her new home two days before, and the place was, if not exactly in confusion, not in that perfect order in which Mrs. Robert Lyon would have desired it to be when she received so august a visitor.

The carpets were down, of course, and there were some curtains before the windows, but the furniture was in that transition state common to new households and youthful housekeepers, who cannot make up their minds, without a great deal of moving about, where the things ought to stand.

The things had been moving about Mrs. Robert Lyon's drawing-room ever since she came back. She could not make up her mind where the chairs and the tables and the cabinets ought to go. The piano, after a great deal of wandering, had settled down in a corner, with its face to the wall, and its ugly bare back exposed to view. It would be draped by-and-by, but it was ugly and bare now, and the chairs were heaped up in the middle of the room when the Countess called.

She did not call alone. She brought her niece with her, a pale, spiritless young woman with light ringlets, who followed the great lady like a shadow.

They were shown into the drawing-room at once, where they found the Rector in his shirt-sleeves, with his coat off, helping Joan to move a big cabinet across the floor. They had been so occupied coaxing that unwieldy piece of furniture back to the exact spot from which it had been three times ignobly removed, that they did not hear the sound of wheels on the gravel outside, or the front-door bell ring.

Joan stopped the cabinet half-way and shook hands with the Countess, not exactly in that deferential way in which a rector's wife should greet the patroness of her husband's living.

She could hardly believe that that fat, dowdy old woman was a countess. She was not a bit afraid of her: she hardly thought it worth while to apologize for the confusion they were in. She had no patience with Robert blushing in that absurd way because an old woman had caught him in his shirt-sleeves. As for the Countess's niece, Cecilia Burrough, Joan put her down as of very small account from the first.

She had a rapid way of making up her mind about people the first time she saw them, and she seldom found reason to change it.

'I ought not to have called so soon,' the Countess said, flopping down into a chair in the midst of the barricade, 'but I wanted to know your wife, Mr. Lyon. I could not wait till after Sunday.'

This ought to have propitiated Joan, but it did not. She had no patience with people calling at all sorts of hours, before lunch of all times in the day, as if she were a churchwarden, or a pew-opener, or a sexton, anything but the wife of the Rector of the parish. She did not think even an earl's coronet on the panels of the great yellow chariot on the gravel outside an excuse for such rudeness.

Cecilia Burrough, her ladyship's niece, was not very young nor very beautiful; perhaps this was why Joan took to her. She was soft-spoken and commonplace, like her noble relative; but she had a kind face, which is better than beauty: perhaps it *is* beauty—the substance, not the shadow.

'It is my fault that my aunt came over so early,' she explained shyly to Joan. 'I wanted to speak to you about the church; there has been no one to play the harmonium, or to take the Sunday-school, since Mr. Finch left'—Mr. Finch was the late Rector—'and I have helped a little. I have done what I could——'

'Cecilia has taken the Sunday-school ever since the Finches went away,' Lady Aylmerton said, interrupting her niece with some asperity, 'and she has played the harmonium; now you're here, Mrs. Lyon, she will not be wanted any more. It is very troublesome to have to give Cecilia up so much on Sundays.'

'I hope Miss Burrough will still help in the parish,' the Rector said; he could not think of anything else to say.

'I shall be very glad to help,' Lady Aylmerton's niece said eagerly; 'that is, if my aunt can spare me——' And then she stopped in her shy, frightened way and looked timidly at the Countess.

'The Finches did not require any help when they were here,' her ladyship said rather stiffly; 'they were quite able to manage the parish without help. Mr. Finch was everything that a parish clergyman should be, and the schools were in excellent order. He managed the schools entirely. He gave religious instruction in them every day. He was very particular about the religious education of the children.'

The new Rector winced; the prospect that opened before him was not quite agreeable. He had not come down to Coombe Damerel as a schoolmaster, and he did not quite like being dictated to by an old woman.

He felt it was dictation, that her ladyship was trying it on, and that she would for ever be flinging the Finches in his face if he did not make a stand at first and let her understand that he was quite able to manage the parish without her assistance.

'Of course,' he said gravely, 'the religious training of the young is a very important feature of parish work. With such an energetic man as Mr. Finch, the Sunday-schools will be in excellent order.'

'I don't think you must expect too much, Mr. Lyon,' Cecilia said, blushing. 'I have taken the Sunday-school since Mrs. Finch went away, and I'm afraid you will find the children very backward. They are rather stupid children, and they don't seem to understand anything, but I dare say you will get on better with them than I did. The infant-school teacher, who helps in the school, and plays the harmonium in church, has been away ill for a month, so I had to do it all myself. I'm afraid I did it very badly.'

'And is she away still?' Joan asked.

'Yes; she was no better when my aunt last heard. I'm afraid she will not be back yet.'

'And what is to be done till she comes back?' Joan asked, quite breathlessly. She had never played the harmonium in her life.

'I'm afraid you will have to do the work yourself, unless my aunt will let me help you till Mary Bailey comes back. The Sunday-school is not very large, and there are no big girls; and the schoolmaster takes the boys. There is no one else in the village to help.'

'But about the music in the church—and training the choir—I never played a harmonium in my life!'

Joan was quite pale. She had never reckoned upon this. There was always a proper organist at Stoke Lucy, and choir practices in the church. There were a dozen dear little boys in white surplices at St. Matthias's; the girls had nothing to do with the singing.

There was some more talk about parish matters, and then the Countess rose to go; but she did not offer to let Cecilia play the harmonium the next day before she went away.

'You must come over to Orchard Damerel, Mrs. Lyon,' she said very graciously, before she went; 'we shall expect to see a good deal of you.'

When she had gone, Joan sat down in the midst of the furniture piled up in the middle of the room and made her moan. She did not exactly burst into tears, but the tears were not very far off.

'Oh, Robin!' she said, in her little exaggerated way, 'oh, Robin! what are we to do? I can't play that horrid harmonium! I can't train the choir—and—and I never took a Sunday-school class in my life!'

Clearly she had mistaken her vocation: she should not have married a clergyman if she could not do these things.

Robert Lyon comforted his tearful bride. He thought she had been rather hardly dealt with; and he thought his patroness was dictating to his wife, as she had dictated to him. He was very grateful to her for what she had done for him, but he was not so grateful as he would have been if the recollection of that Advent sermon had not been rankling in his mind.

'Darling,' he said, sitting down beside her, and getting his arm round her waist—he was no longer in his shirt-sleeves; he had put his coat on—'there is nothing to be unhappy about. If we can't have any music in the church to-morrow, we must do without. I will find a person who can play the harmonium and take the choir before next Sunday; we must do what we can to-morrow. It will be our first Sunday. People can't expect everything to go right at first.'

'And about the Sunday-school, Rob? Oh, I'm sure you ought to have married Phyllis; she would have been able to take the school beautifully. There is nothing she loves so much as a Sunday-school. You have made a mistake, Rob; you have married the wrong Miss Penrose. Is it quite too late to change?'

Robert Lyon assured his bride that it was quite too late to change, that he had no desire to change, and that—this really was a 'stretcher'—if she had been anybody else but the useless, ignorant creature that she was—if she had been able to play the harmonium—if she had known anything about Sunday-schools—he would not for any consideration have married her!

Thus comforted, Joan plucked up heart afresh and set about putting the furniture in order.

Considering that the next day was Sunday—Robert Lyon's first Sunday in his new parish—he ought not to have been moving that furniture about. He ought by rights to have been preparing the sermon, or sermons, rather, he had to preach the following day. He had thought a good deal about these sermons during the last few weeks; he had gone so far as to decide upon the text for each, and he had made some notes of the headings of various parts of his discourse. He was very anxious to begin well. It is everything to begin well in a new position; it gives people confidence. The new Rector was very anxious to win the confidence of his parishioners, and he desired above all things to do his duty by them.

It was not because the place was small and the duty

was light he was going to sit down and do nothing; on the contrary, he had quite made up his mind that the little he had to do he would do well: he would do better than his predecessor—than Mr. Finch had done. He had settled all this in his mind before he came to Coombe Damerel, and then came the matter of that unhappy Advent sermon and upset it all.

Robert Lyon did not go into his study until quite late in the day—until after dinner, in fact. He put off that humiliating ordeal until he could put it off no longer. When he pulled himself together, and braced up his nerves for that miserable task, he went into his study alone and locked the door after him.

He locked the door, he explained to Joan, while he was preparing his sermons, in order that he might have no interruption. It broke the thread of his reasoning, it interrupted the flow of his eloquence, if anyone disturbed him.

When he had locked the door behind him, he went at once to the big cupboard in the wall—that Joan had said would hold such a lot of sermons—and drew forth a bag. It was a shabby old carpet-bag, and the sides were bulging out as only the sides of a carpet-bat can bulge. It was the bag that he had stuffed full of those old sermons that were put up at his father's sale with a waste-paper basket and a fire-guard.

His face grew pink as he drew forth the bag from its hiding-place, and it grew pinker and pinker as he thrust his hand into it, as he had thrust it in on the memorable day when he went to Clifton to take the duty for his friend.

It was a wonderful bag; whatever he wanted seemed to come uppermost. The first sermons he took out were exactly the sermons that he wanted. If he had searched the bag through he could not have found any better suited for his purpose.

They were dry and wordy and old-fashioned—and narrow; he could not have believed that his own father, that any reasoning man, could have held such narrow views. It made him quite sick to copy them. He copied them religiously, word for word, and when he had finished them he put the originals back in the bag, and restored the bag to the cupboard. He would not have had Joan come in and catch him copying them for the world. He would not have believed two days ago that he could have a Bluebeard cupboard in that delightful house, a cupboard of which he could never trust his wife with the key—never, never.

CHAPTER IX.

A RED-LETTER DAY.

The first Sunday in his new parish ought to have been the happiest day in the world to Robert Lyon. If it were not exactly the happiest day in his life, it ought to have been a red-letter day, at the least.

The preaching of that first sermon, carefully thought out and prepared, as a sermon befitting such a solemn occasion should have been, ought to have afforded him both pride and satisfaction.

Modest pride, that he should have been called upon to fill that responsible position, that he should have been thought worthy to have the souls of all these rustic people committed to his care; and satisfaction, not unmixed with gratitude, that the work was so easy—so pleasant—so exactly the work that he could do well, that he could do best.

That first Sunday at Coombe Damerel was anything but a red-letter day to the new Rector, and the preaching of those wretched sermons did not give him unalloyed satisfaction.

In the sweet summer weather, with all the brightness and warmth of the August sunshine about him, he walked up through the churchyard path, between the green graves and the slanting old tombstones, to the vestry door. His bride of a month was by his side in the sweetest of summer costumes ('tightum'), and the little tinkling church-bell—his own church-bell—was summoning his widespread flock with its insistent invitation: 'Come-to-church! Come-to-church!'

His heart ought to have burned within him at this supreme moment of his life, as he walked up the churchyard path on this first sweet Sabbath day; but it was as cold and unresponsive as the hearts of his dead and gone predecessors, whose graves he passed as he walked over on his way to the vestry door.

The church struck unaccountably chill, too, on this warm August day, and he remarked for the first time that it was not at all a good church to be heard in, and that in some places the plaster was peeling off the walls.

Several people came in late and forgot to close the door after them, and insisted upon walking up the church to the most distant seats in their great hob-nailed boots, and disturbing the kneeling congregation.

The music, too, went very badly. Lady Aylmerton had ungraciously consented at the last moment to let her niece play the harmonium for this Sunday, but there had been no choir practice, and the hymns had not been selected till just before the service. The children were shy, and would not open their mouths, and there was no one to lead them. He could hear Joan's little flat voice singing almost alone all through the hymns.

He ought not to have let these things irritate him; they were such very small worries, and they could all be altered, but they jarred through every nerve.

He went home disappointed and sad. He had thought so much about this day ever since the living had been given to him; and now that it had come, all that he had pictured—the dear little country church, the rustic congregation, the dearest voice in the world leading the choir, and, in addition to all these things, a real Countess sitting in solemn state in an adjoining chapel, drinking in every word of his eloquent discourse—it was all—everything—even the rapt attention of the Countess—Dead Sea fruit; it was dust and ashes to his taste.

Lady Aylmerton met the new Rector coming out of church; she had stayed behind to speak to him, and he walked down the path beside her, and put her in her carriage, which was waiting for her at the gate.

'I was much impressed by your sermon this morning, Mr. Lyon,' her ladyship said. 'I hope you will continue the subject this afternoon; the arguments were exactly the ones I have always wanted to hear brought forward. I hope you will follow up the subject next Sunday.'

Robert gave a gloomy assent, and then he put her ladyship in her carriage, and waited, with the handle of the door in his hand, while Cecilia Burrough, who had lingered behind with Joan, came up.

'I am much obliged to you for allowing your niece to play for us to-day,' he said; 'but we must not trespass upon her kindness too much. I will see about getting a person to play in church, and train the choir, before next Sunday—that is, if you do not think the infant school teacher is likely to come back.'

'She is not at all likely to come back at present,' Lady Aylmerton said; and then the carriage drove away.

'How gloomy you look, Rob!' his wife said to him as they walked back to the Rectory. 'Has her ladyship been scolding you?'

'She has been praising my sermon.'

Joan made a little *moue.* She had not listened very much, but what she had heard she could not make anything of; she could not understand, in fact. It was not a bit like Robert's delightful little sermons at Stoke Lucy.

He saw the cloud on his wife's bright face, and that made him more angry. Should he make a clean breast of it, and tell her now that he had got the living by false pretences, and that, for the present, at least, he must continue the deception? Surely there could be no better time.

He put it off weakly, as he had put it off when he came back from Orchard Damerel. He could not bring himself to tell the woman he loved that he had done this meanness. He put away the thought of those wretched sermons for another week; he locked it up with them in that Bluebeard cupboard, and he tried to forget all about it till the following Sunday.

He had a good deal to occupy his attention meanwhile. Everybody within twenty miles around called upon his wife during the next week, and he had to make the acquaintance of his brother clergy. Most of the people who called were much better off than he was, he remarked rather bitterly. He had come to the end of the thousand pounds he had set aside for furnishing that big Rectory-house and for preliminary expenses. The preliminary expenses had been much heavier than he had reckoned upon.

The upholsterer's bill amounted to more than twice as much as Joan had calculated from those wonderful lists upon which she had spent so much time. The house was not completely furnished now; there were only two spare bedrooms furnished, and the walls were quite bare. There were miles and miles of walls, as Joan expressed it, to cover with plates and mirrors and pictures and prints. They had bought nothing but useful things so far—furniture and linen and plate—they were obliged to buy some silver forks and spoons; they could not eat with their fingers, as Joan put it in her exaggerated way. There were all these things still to buy, and the horses and carriage. They could not return any calls until they had a carriage.

The people who came from a distance usually drove a pair. The roads were very hilly about Coombe Damerel, up and down every few hundred yards. A single horse would have no chance in a carriage, unless it were a dog-cart, over those hills.

Robert Lyon told himself that he could not possibly take his wife to return calls in a dog-cart, and that his first duty was to buy her a low carriage and a pair of nicely matching ponies that she could drive herself, and in which she could return the visits of her new friends.

He bought the carriage and the ponies, and the silver-plated harness, and a handsome opossum rug within the week—and a pretty penny he paid for them.

It is astonishing what one can get for money.

The old troublesome conjuring business of rubbing up old lamps has quite gone out. There is a greater conjurer now than the frightful Genii of the Lamp. The conjurer did his work so well, he matched that pair of ponies for Joan so exactly, that Robert Lyon could do nothing less than commission him to provide another equipage: a gig this time—he called it a gig—a brand-new dog-cart with a high-stepping mare. This was not a luxury, he assured himself; it was a necessary. He could not always be driven about by his wife in a low pony-carriage. He would have all his neighbours laughing at him. Besides, there were always things to be fetched from the station, or from Carlingford, which was fifteen miles off—groceries and all sorts of household things—and they could not be packed away in a pony-carriage.

Having quite satisfied himself that the second carriage was a positive necessity, he lost no time in setting up the gig and the high-stepping mare.

When the bill for these necessaries came in, he winced just a little; he had no idea things cost so much money. There were so many details that he had never counted upon in setting up these vehicles, and the horse-flesh to draw them. The stable equipment was something tremendous; it embraced so many things he had never counted upon.

In the old boyish days, at the old country Rectory, there had been a rough, shaggy Exmoor pony, and a gig—and the stable equipment had been, to say the least of it, primitive. Robert had had these things in his mind when he commissioned his smart groom to get such things as were necessary. And then there was the livery. One cannot do these things by halves.

When the carriages had come home, and the horses were in the stable, and the harness-room was duly furnished, and the stable equipment was complete, quite complete, and the fodder had been brought in, and the cornbins were overflowing—then, and not till then, Robert Lyon added up his money.

It was a lovely August day—a fine drying day—and the extra woman who had come over to help in the laundry was hanging out the clothes in the orchard behind the house, and Joan was eating, not exactly bread and honey—honey is apt to be sticky for afternoon tea—she was in the drawing-room with her guests, at any rate, and a pair of prancing steeds were tearing up the gravel at the front-door, and the Rector was in his study adding up his bank-book. He was not quite literally counting out his money; he was doing the more prosaic thing, he was adding the figures up in his bank-book.

If there is one kind of literature that is of more absorbing interest than any other to a large class of readers, it is the perusal of a bank-book. The emotions that it excites are pleasingly varied. Satisfaction—surprise—disgust. Generally the two latter.

It was with both surprise and disgust that Robert Lyon compared the figures on the two opposite pages of that wretched book. No one could have been more surprised than he was at the way those horrible figures mounted up, nor more disgusted at the result.

He went over them two or three times to make sure. He was quite certain that there was a mistake, that the figures were wrong.

He was still adding them up when Joan came into the study. She had finished her bread and honey, and she had got rid of her visitors, and she came to see what had become of Robert.

'Oh, why didn't you come in, Robert? It was Lady Alicia Mainwaring, and she stayed nearly half an hour on purpose to see you. Her husband wants to know you so much. He would have called with her, but he was away on some election business. There's going to be a contest, and people want him to stand for the county—for the Eastern Division——'

Joan stopped abruptly in the midst of her gay, eager talk. Something in her husband's face stopped her, and she came over to his side and saw that wretched book open before him.

He covered it up guiltily; why should it worry her as it had worried him?

'Good gracious! is anything the matter, Robin?' she asked anxiously. 'Are you ill? Have you been catching something in the parish—measles, or whooping-cough, or——'

'No, I've not caught either the measles or the whooping-cough,' he said, interrupting her with a weak attempt at a smile. 'I have been going through my accounts, and the result is not quite so satisfactory as I had expected.'

'You have not got through all that two thousand pounds yet, Robin?'

'No, dear, I haven't got through it all, thank God! There is still a little left—enough to keep us going till—till the tithes come in.'

'Then, what are you worrying about? They will be coming in soon, and then we shall be quite rich; we shall have such a lot of money; we shall not know what to do with it.'

Robert smiled. He did not tell her that tithes do not come in the very moment they fall due, that there is an interval—often a long interval—between the date when they are due and the time they are paid.

He got up from his seat and put his arm round her waist.

'I was not worrying,' he said; 'I was only thinking that, just at present, we shall not be able to afford another horse. Will you be much disappointed, dear, if you have to forego a horse to ride at present?'

Joan's bright face clouded, and she made a little *moue*. She was very fond of pursing up her lips and making provoking little mouths.

'It will be rather horrid,' she said. 'I—I have promised Lady Alicia to go to the meet. It would be so awfully jolly if I could ride with you. You would ride, of course; you need not follow the hounds, but you could ride to the meet. I have never been to a meet in my life, and I should enjoy it awfully.'

'Would you?' he said. He rather winced as he said it; he had never denied her anything yet; it was rather hard to begin now.

'I should, dearest; indeed, I don't know how to get out of it. I've promised the Mainwarings I'll be there. I told Lady Alicia you were going to see about getting me a horse at once, and—I have ordered a habit.'

'I didn't know you had ordered the habit,' Robert said, with a little catch in his voice. 'Wasn't it rather premature to order the habit before you got the horse? Something like that cookery-book mistake about cooking the hare before you caught it?'

Joan laughed a gay little laugh.

'You silly old man!' she said, 'you have got hold of the wrong end of the story; but we shall catch the hare after all—you will be able to manage it, won't you, Robin?'

The new riding-habit came home the next day, and Joan tried it on. It fitted her to perfection. It fitted her so well, it was so perfectly irresistible, that if Robert had been wavering in the matter of that extra horse which he had decided he could not afford—or thought he had decided—the sight of Joan in that riding-habit left him in doubt no longer. Whatever else he did without, Joan must have the horse. What is the use of having a smart riding-habit if one has not got a horse?

CHAPTER X.

LORDS AND LADIES.

JOAN did not order that riding-habit in vain. Robert Lyon had not the heart to tell his bride to fold up that beautifully-fitting garment and put it away, with plenty of camphor between the folds, for use on some future day.

The horse for Joan to ride to the first meet of the Wynnstay hounds was forthcoming when the day arrived. It was rather a costly affair, but then, as Robert reflected, he had his place to keep up in the county; and the world —represented by the county families of the Eastern Division—already regarded him as a rich man; he could not afford to let his wife ride a screw. She must have a good mount or none, so a good mount, at a fancy price, was forthcoming for Joan when the day arrived.

Before the opening meet of the hunt, which was a memorable day in the Eastern Division of the county, Robert made the acquaintance of the Mainwarings.

He drove over to Wytchanger, in his wife's pony-carriage, to return Lady Alicia Mainwaring's call.

The Mainwarings were the great people of the Eastern Division of the county—greater people and richer people than the Aylmertons. Wytchanger was a house of much greater pretensions than Orchard Damerel. It was a great big modern house; it had cost thousands to build; it was complete with every convenience and improvement that money could command. The grounds were not so extensive as the grounds of the Damerels, but they were not encumbered. There was not a mortgage on a single acre of the property. There was a wide park, not so wide as Orchard Damerel, but much more park-like in its way. It had been laid out a dozen years ago by an eminent landscape-gardener, with an eye to effect, and now that the little beeches had grown up, and the shrubberies had put on their beautiful summer green, the place was perfect—quite perfect. It was the gem of the county.

The ancestors of the Mainwarings had made their money in trade, made it not so long ago. It was quite within memory when the place had another owner, when the father of the present Squire bought the land, and pulled down the old house, which was nearly tumbling to pieces, and built up the present handsome modern mansion.

His son had married the daughter of an earl, the Lady Alicia Fane Tempest, and brought her home to his spick-and-span new mansion a dozen years ago. It was the Lady Alicia who had employed the landscape-gardener to lay out the shrubberies at Wytchanger, and plant those little beeches and the avenues of chestnuts that were now the glories of the park. It was she who had raised those orchid-houses, the graperies, and pineries, and acres of glass, that were the wonder and admiration of the county.

She had done a great deal for her husband besides spending his money. She had given him a position in the county, and now she had set her heart upon giving him a seat in Parliament. There were not many things that Lady Alicia set her heart upon that she failed to get; she was not troubled with scruples, and if she could not get what she wanted by 'hook,' she generally got it by 'crook.'

If she succeeded in getting the vacant seat for the Eastern Division for her husband, she would certainly have to get it by 'crook.'

It was a Conservative seat, and Lady Alicia had been a Conservative all her life. She had been born and brought up in the hot-bed of Conservatism, and she had married a Whig. The distinctions of parties were more marked in the days to which our story belongs. There were not so many political 'blends.' A Tory and a Whig meant certain distinct things, they could not possibly amalgamate; they could never become Unionists. The Aylmerton interest in the late Earl's days had always been sufficient to return one, sometimes two, members for the Eastern Division of the county. The Earl was dead now, and there was no one to take his place. Two out of the four executors in whom the control of the Damerel property was vested were moderate Whigs. They would not be likely to use any coercion to induce the tenants to vote for a Conservative candidate.

There could not have been a better time for Lady Alicia's husband to have come forward to contest the county in the Liberal interest. He was the richest commoner in the neighbourhood, and his wife was one of the most popular women in that division of the county.

Lady Aylmerton had little or nothing to do with the administration of the late Earl's estate, and she took no interest in politics, and there was no other great landowner who could influence the election to any great extent. There was no reason why Mr. Thomas Mainwaring should not ride over the course easily.

When Robert Lyon and his wife returned Lady Alicia's call, the conversation naturally turned upon politics; there was nothing else talked of just then.

'I hope you are on our side, Mr. Lyon,' her ladyship had said, and Robert had answered that he had been so little time in the county that he did not know which was Lady Alicia's side.

It was a safe thing to say, seeing she had come of an old Tory family, and had married a Liberal lord.

Then Lady Alicia laughed her rather loud, harsh laugh —it would have been pronounced loud, distinctly loud, if it had proceeded from a less aristocratic throat.

'Oh, we are all in the same boat here,' she said; her voice was loud like her laugh, but it was not an unpleasant voice. 'I am a feminine edition of the Vicar of Bray. I am a Tory at home—and a Liberal here. I hope your politics are equally elastic, and that you will help us in this election. I would not have Tom beaten for the world.'

Robert Lyon blushed, and assured her ladyship that he was a stanch Liberal, and that he would give her husband all the support that lay in his power.

He would have returned exactly the same answer if she had asked him to support a Conservative candidate. His politics—if he had any—were rather more elastic than her ladyship's. He was so ridiculously elated at being made much of by an Earl's daughter that he was ready to promise anything. He had not yet got accustomed to countesses and their descendants. And he could not receive overtures of friendship from these great people without feelings of considerable elation.

An invitation to dinner followed that call at Wytchanger, and Joan found herself among the great people of the county. Lady Aylmerton did not give dinner-parties. She had asked the Rector's wife over to tea several times, and once she had pressed her to stay to lunch. This was the only hospitality she had ever received at Orchard Damerel.

This dinner-party at the Mainwarings' was really Joan's first introduction to the county. She had never met anybody at Lady Aylmerton's but Cecilia Burrough and a few of her ladyship's pet old women; nobody she would give a fig to know, or could talk to for five minutes without yawning. Here at Wytchanger everything was different; there were no old women, and there were no bores. All the best people of the neighbourhood were here, and there were some great titled people staying in the house. Lord George Fane Tempest, Lady Alicia's brother, was there, and two or three members of the Upper House.

Joan had never been among such great people in her life. It had cost a good deal to get there. A close carriage and pair had to be sent over from the post-town, fifteen miles away, the day before, and it could not return until the following day, after that long drive to Wytchanger. Of course Joan could not go out to dinner in a pony-carriage or a gig. If she accepted the invitation, she must have a fly from Carlingford; there was no alternative. To see her drive up through the great gateway, with the horses steaming, and the servants in their brand-new liveries, with shining gilt buttons, and a frightful griffin sprawling over every one of them, anyone would have taken her for the wife of one of the leading magnates of the county, instead of the wife of a country rector with the ridiculous income of two hundred and seventy pounds a year.

She was wearing for the first time that pretty pink evening gown, and there were flowers in her hair and roses on her cheeks, and she was by far the prettiest woman in the room. Nobody who saw her there for the first time could understand why she had married that beggarly country parson. With her sweet eyes, and her damask cheeks, and that lovely brown hair with the red lights in it, she might have married anybody.

Lady Alicia took her up at once—she always took up attractive people—and introduced her to her own set.

They made so much of her that Joan's pretty head was turned. Her husband received a deal of attention, too, but in another way. There was nothing talked but politics among the men. It was the eve of an election, and the subject was uppermost in everybody's mind.

Mr. Mainwaring entertained his guests as befitted a man who was about to stand for the county. If he did not talk politics himself, his friends did for him. It was quite understood that all those who gathered round that hospitable board would support the Liberal candidate. They were not exactly pledged to it, but they would not have been there, eating his venison and drinking his champagne, if they were not prepared to give him their support.

'How many votes have you got in your place?' Lord George asked Robert Lyon, as they sat over their wine after dinner.

'Votes? I—I'm sure I don't know,' the Rector said, with a little hesitation; he had an idea that he was getting on dangerous ground. 'I am new to the place.

I have only just settled down. I don't suppose that I have got a vote.'

'No, of course you haven't—you've got to be on the rates twelve months before you get a vote--but there are all the farmers and labourers on the estate. All the parish, I believe, belongs to the Damerels?'

Robert said that so he had heard—all but a spinney and a few fields the other side of the coombe that belonged to his host.

'Ah, I remember there was a dispute over that spinney,' said Lord George, with rather a knowing look; 'perhaps you have not heard about it. The Earl raised a stiffish sum on some land about there, and a portion of the property was sold to his neighbour, the old Tom Mainwaring. He was buying up every acre he could get hold of just then, and the spinney went with the rest. There was a dispute about it, and a lawsuit which was decided against the Earl. There has been bad blood between the families ever since.'

Robert was very sorry to hear this. He was not at all sure that his patroness would approve of his getting himself mixed up with this Liberal set, with the late Earl's enemies. He had a conviction that she could take things to heart—mundane things—though she was daily expecting some kind of millennium.

'The old lady doesn't take any interest in politics, I hear,' Lord George said, in his off-hand way. 'She let everybody vote as they liked at the last election.'

This was quite true, but his lordship did not say that there had been no opposition, that the Conservative candidate had been returned unopposed. It was always understood that the Damerels could return whom they liked, and now there were no Damerels left, only that poor beggar of an heir, who had not a penny to spend on an election if he could get returned to-morrow.

Lord George told Robert something of this while they lingered over their wine. There was no one, he assured him, that the Countess could have any interest in. All the old stock was gone—all, every one. They had to search the country over to find out a sixteenth cousin to take the property. It could not matter tuppence to Lady

Aylmerton—his lordship said 'tuppence'—who was returned for the county.

A great deal of this was true—a great deal—but not quite all.

Before Robert left Wytchanger that night he had promised to do what he could among the tenants and the labourers in Coombe Damerel, and he had consented to let his name appear among the members of Mr. Mainwaring's committee.

Joan was so elated as they drove back in the silence of the summer night that she did not know whether she were on her head or her heels.

'Lady Alicia is a duck!' she said; 'she has invited me to spend a week at Wytchanger for the hunting. They are going to have a lot of grand people down—lords and ladies—and the Earl and Countess will be there, and they have asked poor little me!'

CHAPTER XI.

ROBERT LYON WORKS HIMSELF UP.

It must not be supposed, while Joan was in the midst of such grand doings, driving about in her carriage and pair, and feasting with lords and ladies, that she had forgotten all about the dear people at home.

'The poor dear things,' as she called them, wrote to her every week—sometimes they wrote twice a week—and she in her turn wrote pages and pages back. She was never tired of telling them of her gay doings, of the great people that she knew. Her letters quite bristled with titles. It is very wrong, no doubt, to like titles, and those who bear them. Joan did not like them; she *loved* them. She positively revelled in them. Her letters for months after that dinner-party were full of Lady Alicia and Lord George, and the Earl and Countess.

She was so full of her new friends and her gay doings that she had not time or thought to spare for 'the poor things' living their dull lives in the mean little house in the shabby street. She remembered the street well. It quite shocked her at first to hear that her mother and sisters had gone to live there. Something dreadful must have happened, she knew, to have brought about such a change; but the extent of the calamity she did not know. She certainly did not realize that her mother and sisters and the two boys had to live upon, year by year, the exact sum that Robert had spent upon the horse she rode to the meet.

Not that the expense of that luxury, like the expenses of that bare household, stopped at the seventy pounds. There was a new lady's-saddle, and a silver-mounted riding-whip, and that becoming riding-habit and hat, and many other things. The actual cost of that whim of Joan's did not stop within a long way of seventy pounds.

To be more accurate, it was only her mother and Phyllis and the two boys who had to live on that munificent sum. Bertha had gone out—that is to say, she had accepted a situation as governess to teach little boys, and she had gone away from home. There was only Phyllis at home now, and she was rubbing and scrubbing, and cooking and mending, from morning till night.

There was only a small servant kept in that poor establishment, and Phyllis, with her soft eyes and her busy hands, was working like a horse.

While Phyllis was scrubbing, and Bertha teaching the Latin accidence to her unwilling scholars, Joan was driving her ponies through the sweet green country, and basking in the society of lords.

There was one day in the week when she did not bask, when she felt the weight of her new position. On Sundays her hands were full; she had to sit in a stuffy room for an hour before the afternoon service, hearing the infant population of Coombe Damerel stumbling through the Church Catechism. Joan had never taken a Sunday-school before in her life; she had not the gift of teaching that Phyllis had. The only thing in the way of parish work that she had ever done was to read to the women at the mothers'-meeting. It was here that Robert had first met her; he never forgot that memorable day when he had seen her sitting on the table in the midst of the women, swinging her legs.

Besides taking the Sunday-school, the Rector's wife had to assist in the choir. It was not so easy a thing as Robert had thought to get a person to come over from Carlingford, fifteen miles every Sunday, to play the harmonium in church and train the choir. Her ladyship's niece still presided at the harmonium, and Joan's flat little voice led the choir.

She hated sitting there in her husband's church singing with the village children, when she ought to be sitting in state in the Rector's pew in the chancel, behind the screen. Any stranger coming into the church might take her for the village schoolmistress.

A stranger sitting in the Aylmerton chapel, and looking out between the bars of the screen, did take her for the schoolmistress on that Sunday after the dinner-party at Wytchanger. He thought, as he heard her flat voice leading the singing, and when his eyes wandered over to where she was sitting yawning during Robert's long, dreary discourse, that he had never seen so sweet a woman's face in his life.

The Rector caught him looking across the pews two or three times during that long sermon. He was wondering all through the service who this gaunt, red-bearded man could be in the Aylmerton pew. He did not belong to the neighbourhood; he was not the least like the country squires of the West Country. A big, broad-shouldered, gloomy-looking man, with a shaggy red beard, and gaunt, hollow eyes.

The Countess was not at church that day; it was the first Sunday she had been absent, and the gloomy stranger sat alone in the great family pew among the old stony monuments of the Damerels.

The Rector, looking over the top of his sermon-case, saw him staring about as strangers stare about in a church that is not familiar to them. He had eyes for other things besides the schoolmistress singing in the village choir—sad, hopeless, hollow eyes that took in every detail of the building, the painted hatchment on the walls, the old tombs of the Damerels in the chapel, the arms and escutcheons of the noble families who had intermarried with the Aylmertons in the windows. The stranger, sitting alone in that high seat, took in all these things—all, everything, except the sermon.

He was still lingering in the churchyard, looking at the graves and reading the inscriptions on the old stones, when Robert and his wife left the church, and then Cecilia Burrough, who had come out with Joan, introduced him as Mr. Hugh Damerel.

It was the Earl of Aylmerton's heir.

Robert walked back with him through the village as far as the entrance to the park. He had only arrived the night before, he said; the Countess had sent for him in haste. If he had known why she had sent for him he certainly would not have come, he told Robert.

He laughed—a hollow, mirthless laugh—as he spoke of her ladyship's hasty summons, but he did not say why she had sent for him.

Robert learned why from the Countess's own lips the next day.

A messenger from Orchard Damerel came over the following morning while he was at breakfast, requesting him to call upon the Countess without delay. He was going to ride with Joan after breakfast, but he had to put off his ride and walk over to the great house instead.

'I hope you won't let Lady Aylmerton bully you, Rob,' the Rector's wife said, while he was putting on his hat and brushing himself down in the hall; he always gave himself an extra brush when he went over to Orchard Damerel.

'Why should she bully me, darling?' the Rector asked.

'Oh, she'll have heard of your going over to Wytchanger. She hates the Mainwarings; they had an old quarrel years ago, and she has never forgiven them.'

'How did you hear about the quarrel?'

'Cecilia told me. They brought a lawsuit, I believe, against the Earl, and offended him dreadfully. When he lost the lawsuit, they brought a man down from London to oppose his candidate at the election. A Radical, Cecilia said—a shocking Radical, who would have turned the country upside down. The Earl was furious; it was his own seat, it had never been out of the family. He spent so much money over the election that it ruined him; it was the last straw.'

'Cecilia seems to have told you a good deal. What made her tell you all this?'

Joan's face flushed, and just a little cloud passed over it.

'She knew we were going to Wytchanger—I told her about the dinner-party—and—and I dare say she said it to warn us.'

'To warn us? Why should we want warning?' Robert said impatiently. 'We can choose our own friends. Lady Aylmerton has no right to dictate to us. Her quarrels have nothing to do with us—her quarrels, or her prejudices, or her whims. I have given way enough already.'

In this frame of mind the Rector went across the lawn and through the shrubbery, by way of the short-cut, to see his patroness. He was anxious to get the interview over, and he went the short way. He had an idea that it would not be a pleasant interview. There had been differences between them of late, differences of opinion, and Robert would not give way if he thought he was right. He had given way in the matter of those wretched sermons, and it had rankled in his mind ever since; it had become a burden on his conscience, and he would not give way again, if he felt he was right. If he allowed this old woman to dictate to him what he should do in his own parish, and what friends he should choose, he might as well be a toad under a pair of harrows.

He told himself this as he walked through the shrubbery. It was disgraceful that a clergyman should be hampered in his work by the whims and fancies of an old woman. He knew what was best for the parish better than her ladyship did, who never came among the people except in her carriage.

There had been a difference lately about the management of the school, and he had been obliged to tell her ladyship this truth, and it had made a breach between them.

The infant school could not go on possibly any longer without a teacher. The schoolmaster, a weak-minded, incapable young man, a *protégé* of her ladyship's, had been taking it, or pretending to take it, during the absence of the female teacher, who had gone away ill. His hands were quite full already, without the infants, and his own school had suffered. No village school could be in worse condition. There was no order, no discipline, and there was really nothing properly taught. When the inspector came round, the report would be shocking, and there would be no grant to augment the funds of the school.

Under these circumstances, the Rector had taken the matter in hand. He had expressed his determination to wait no longer for the schoolmistress, who was still away ill, but to appoint another teacher. He had also expressed himself strongly about the schoolmaster's inefficiency.

Lady Aylmerton had chosen to take umbrage at his remarks. The schoolmaster, and the young woman who had gone away ill, were her especial pets. It was rumoured that they were engaged to be married, and that her ladyship had favoured the match. When she made up her mind to anything, she was accustomed to have it. Nothing was allowed to stand in the way of her caprice. She had made up her mind that Albert Beckett, the schoolmaster, should marry poor Mary Bailey, who was in an advanced stage of consumption, and she would not hear of her place being filled up.

The Rector had already advertised for an infant-school teacher, and that morning's post had brought him a host of applications. He was quite prepared to fight the matter out with her ladyship.

He was working himself up for the battle all the way through the shrubbery. He never noticed the sunlight dropping down on the path before him, or the birds singing in the branches overhead; the sweetness, the delightful dewy freshness of the morning did not move him the least. He was so engrossed with these petty parish squabbles that he had no eyes or ears for the loveliest sights or sounds in Nature.

It was necessary to remind himself that Lady Aylmerton was in the wrong, and to work himself up, as he walked rapidly through the shrubbery in the morning sunshine.

There was just a little lingering suspicion in his mind that he had been hasty, a little too hasty, in promising his support to Mr. Tom Mainwaring, and in allowing his name to appear among the members of his committee. He had a suspicion that his patroness would not be too well pleased when she heard of it, and so, to cover up his hesitation, weakness, doubt, and fear, he worked himself up before he presented himself at Orchard Damerel.

CHAPTER XII.

THE EARL OF AYLMERTON'S HEIR.

Robert Lyon was not shown into the great drawing-room where the family portraits were; he was taken upstairs to the Countess's own private sanctum.

Wilkins, her ladyship's maid, was crossing the hall when he came in, and she took him up at once to her mistress's apartments.

'Dear my lady,' she explained by the way—she always spoke of the Countess as 'dear my lady'—had not been well for several days; she had caught a chill out driving, and was confined to her room.

Robert had never been farther than the inner hall in his previous visits to the house, and he looked round with a certain feeling of awe as he followed Wilkins up the wide staircase. Portraits of generations of Damerels looked down upon him with their dull painted eyes as he climbed the stairs. There was a marble bust of the late Earl, done in Italy, at the head of the stairs, and marble figures and busts on pedestals in the corridor, and trophies of armour on the walls, and big Oriental jars and vases on the high Chippendale cabinets between the windows, which were filled, he observed, with quite priceless old china.

The sight of the old Worcester gleaming through the glazed doors of the cabinets, as Robert slowly followed her ladyship's maid down the long gallery, made his mouth water. Lovely blue-scale vases with long-tailed birds, sets of Oriental fan-pattern, and crisp, delightful turquoise cups and saucers—oh, it was enough to make anyone's mouth water! He knew something about china. He had picked up a few bits already in the village—an old delft plate or two, and some cracked teacups, and the possession of these treasures had whetted his appetite.

Lady Aylmerton received him in her boudoir, a delightful little oriel chamber in the eastern wing of the building. No two rooms could be more unlike than the drawing-room and the Countess's boudoir at Orchard Damerel. There was nothing crude or harsh or glaring here. The colouring of the walls was subdued, and the beautiful old furniture, which had all the dainty grace of a bygone time, was covered with delicate, faded embroideries. There was nothing new. The pictures on the walls were lovely creations by Greuze, and Lancret, and Watteau. The curtains of the big oriel window, that looked out over the green park and the coombe, were embroidered in old faded crewels, with flowers and quaint long-tailed birds, worked by some noble ancestress in bygone pains-taking days. There was china on the walls, in the cabinets, on the high, beautiful Adams' mantelpiece.

It quite took Robert's breath away to see that mantelpiece, with its graceful moulded urns and garlands, and the wealth of priceless china that it bore. He could not keep his eyes from wandering, during that interview, from the old woman at the table to the dainty shepberdesses in their rich bosquets on that Adams' mantelpiece.

The Countess was wrapped up in a shawl, and she was looking decidedly glum.

Robert thought he had never seen her look so coarse and vulgar before as she looked in that beautiful old room amid all these treasures.

Evidently she had not lived up to her surroundings. It takes generations of culture to fit an ignoble soul to noble surroundings.

'I sent for you, Mr. Lyon,' her ladyship explained, 'to consult you about the election. You saw Mr. Damerel at church yesterday?'

Robert murmured that he had had that pleasure. He was rather afraid of her ladyship, if the truth must be told, in spite of the efforts he had made to work himself up. The sight of all that grandeur, the painted Damerels on the staircase, the marble busts in the gallery, the armour on the walls, the beautiful china in the cabinets, the soft harmonious colouring of that delightful old room, with its associations of rank and wealth and culture, had affected him like the splendour of the great King had affected that poor-spirited Queen of Sheba.

'I brought him down here,' the Countess continued, 'to induce him to stand for the county. The Eastern Division has been in the family for years. It is the Damerels' seat. There is no one but Hugh Damerel left; he is the heir to the property, though he is never likely to succeed to it. He is the right person to stand; he would be returned unopposed; nobody in their senses would think of opposing a Damerel.'

'And is Mr. Hugh Damerel willing to stand?' Robert asked. He felt he must say something.

'No; that is the difficulty—that is why I sent for you. Of course, the poor young man has not the money; no one expected him to have the money. The expenses would not be much—not to a Damerel; there would be no canvassing needed. He would ride over the course, as the rest have done, and what money was wanted would be forthcoming. The election would not cost him a penny.' Her ladyship was more eager than Robert had ever seen her.

'And knowing this, he refuses to stand?'

'He refuses decidedly. He is angry at being sent for: he is an unreasonable young man. I didn't know whether you would have any influence with him. Perhaps if you talked to him, Mr. Lyon, and showed him it was his duty to his Church and to his country, and to the name he bears, to come forward, he might be persuaded.'

What could Robert say?

He should have to tell her that he had promised to support her enemy; that his name was already down among his committee. He ought to have told her at once; it would have been better to have got it over. He had not the spirit of a mouse, or he would have told the truth.

'I will speak to him if you wish, Lady Aylmerton,'

he said awkwardly, 'though nothing I can say will, I'm sure, have any weight with Mr. Damerel. We were strangers to each other until yesterday—and—and——' He was just going to tell her his promise to Tom Mainwaring, but she interrupted him.

'It is your duty to speak to him,' she said, impatiently striking her shaky old stick on the floor. She could not understand his being so lukewarm. 'Show Mr. Damerel what will happen if the seat is sacrificed; it will be a gain of two seats to the other side, and a Radical Government will get in. You cannot put it too strongly, Mr. Lyon. For the sake of the Church you must make an effort.'

She ordered Robert about in her under-bred, domineering way. It made him quite hot to be treated like—well, not like a parish priest who had a right to have opinions of his own.

Mr. Hugh Damerel was in the library, and Robert went down unwillingly to speak to him there.

He felt dreadfully ashamed of himself as he went down the stairs on this errand, with the eyes of all the Damerels watching him. He was ashamed of himself for being mean and cowardly, and afraid of telling the truth to an old woman.

Hugh Damerel was turning over some prints when the Rector went in.

The library was one of the largest rooms in the house; it occupied the ground-floor of the west wing, and looked out upon the rising ground and the heather-covered heights that rose up in gloomy grandeur behind the house.

A library should look out upon a noble scene—it should not look out upon anything mean, or base, or trivial—the mind dwelling apart on noble themes is insensibly affected by external scenes.

The student reading in the library of Orchard Damerel had nothing but noble things before his eyes when he raised them from the printed page—a wide uprising landscape lit up here and there with sunny gleams. The heather was purple now on the distant height, the gorse was golden, and the sunlight was shining upon the summit, and there were deep cool shadows at its base. It was a perpetual Mentor—a moral lesson of hope and aspiration.

The great room was lined with book-shelves from floor to ceiling, and it had that delightful suggestive smell which a great library always has. The late Earl must have been a solitary man, for there were few tables or chairs in the room, and the books were all confined behind wire screens. There were hundreds, thousands, of volumes on those well-filled shelves, but not one of them could be removed without the master-key.

Hugh Damerel was not reading when Robert Lyon came in; he was turning over some prints at a table. An open portfolio was before him, and he was examining the contents with critical eyes and a lowering brow.

He looked older standing there in the cool shade of that gloomy room, and with those hard lines on his forehead, and his bushy eyebrows drawn together, as he critically examined the pictures in the light.

They were worth examining. It was a portfolio of engravings by Bartolozzi he was turning over, early impressions, proofs before letters, etchings fresh from the master's hand.

He looked up when Robert came in, but his brow did not unbend, and those two upright lines on his forehead were as plain as ever.

He could not think what that parson wanted disturbing him. Had Lady Aylmerton sent him to pry upon him, to see that he was not carrying off those prints—his own prints?

'Lady Aylmerton tells me you have refused to stand for the county,' Robert began awkwardly; 'that the seat will go begging.'

'Hang the seat!' Mr. Damerel said fiercely; and Robert heard him muttering a naughty oath or two as he turned over the prints before him.

'Her ladyship has asked me to beg you to reconsider it,' Robert said, but he could not put any heartiness into his voice. 'She thinks it a pity the seat should go out of the family.'

He did not say anything about his duty to the Church

or the State, that the Countess had laid so much stress on.

Hugh Damerel laughed a harsh, discordant laugh.

'What is the family to me?' he demanded fiercely. 'I care as much for the family as I care for the seat. They are both a sham and a pretence. The seat will no doubt go to the best man—the man who has most money to spend—and the family may go to the devil!' the heir of the Damerels said, as he stood glaring angrily across the portfolio of prints at the Countess's ambassador.

'I don't think money need be a consideration,' Robert said, feeling more and more ashamed of his errand. 'Lady Aylmerton assures me the money will be forthcoming. The election will not cost you a penny. You have only to consent to stand. I don't know anything about it myself; I only give you her ladyship's message.'

'I have already told Lady Aylmerton I will not stand; I will not make myself the laughing-stock of the county. Everyone knows I am a beggar—a beggar—and the heir to thirty thousand a year! No; I have been made fool enough of already without being held up to the derision of the county!'

Hugh Damerel was very much in earnest, and he began to walk up and down the room. Like Robert when he came through the shrubbery, he was working himself up.

'Look here, Lyon,' he said, stopping before Robert, 'did you ever hear of a man being fooled as I have been? I tell you this cursed property has ruined my life! I was a young man, with the world before me, when that miserable old dotard found me out; I had no claim upon him but the claim to be let alone. He would not let me alone. He sent for me, when I had just settled down into a profession, and informed me he had made me his heir, that he had put my name down in his cursed will for the whole thing—this place is nothing to what the Damerels own in the North—that he had left it all—all to me, for the mere accident that I bore his name, Hugh Damerel. What man after having been told this, with the prospect of such a fortune before him, could settle down to work? I did what every other man in my case would do—I threw up my profession—and ran into debt.'

He walked twice the length of the room while he was talking to Robert, leaving him standing dumb and confounded by the table, looking down at the Bartolozzi prints.

'I had a right to run into debt,' he said, turning savagely on Robert, as if he had disputed this privilege. 'I, with my expectations, had a perfect right to run into debt. It was only anticipating my fortune—my great fortune. I availed myself of my right. I plunged into debt as if I had already the rent-roll of the Damerels at my back. The Earl himself couldn't have spent money more freely than I did. I ran through every farthing I had; I had nothing to save for; and when everything was gone, I raised money upon my expectations. Can you blame me? Some people are ready enough to blame me, and say things hard to bear. I swear to you, Lyon, that I did not know how this cursed property was tied down when I raised money upon it!'

His wrath and resentment against the man who had made him his heir was terrible. Robert had never seen a man so moved.

'No; I cannot blame you,' he said, 'no one can blame you.'

'I tell you,' he went on, speaking hurriedly, and the perspiration standing out in great beads on his forehead, 'that man has robbed me. He has robbed me of everything in life worth having—of my youth, my hope, my ambition. I had aspirations and aims like other men. I had a future before me once, before he found me out, and blasted my life with his cursed gift. Look at me now, a ruined man, soured by poverty and hardship and disappointment! Everything has gone from me: my independence, my place in the world, my ambition, my hopes, aims—everything has gone—and left me a pauper—a puppet of a rich man's caprice!'

He threw himself into a chair beside the table where the portfolio of prints was lying open, and covered his face with his hands.

It was terrible to see a man so shaken with passion. Robert laid his hand on his shoulder.

'*De mortuis nil nisi bonum*,' he said gravely.

He could not be silent in that house and hear the husband of his patroness spoken of in those terms.

'Ah!' Hugh Damerel said fiercely, 'it is all very well for you to preach, who have not suffered. I have been a fool, and worse than a fool, I know; but I have been duped, cruelly duped as never man was. I knew, of course I knew, everyone knew, that the Earl was over head and ears in debt. But think of the estate—the acres and acres of land, the great mansion that no one has lived in for years, the treasures that are locked up in this place, and at Aylmerton. Why, the things that are locked up here, that no eye has ever seen, are worth a fortune. I tell you, Lyon, if these things were sold—things that would never be missed—the debt could be paid off at once.'

Robert looked round the room as he spoke, but he did not see anything that looked like fetching a hundred thousand pounds. He saw shelves upon shelves of books in their fragrant russia-leather bindings, and a case, the door of which was open, where there were portfolios of prints instead of books—rows of bulky portfolios, one on top of the other, reaching up to the ceiling. There were no pictures on the walls, there was no room for pictures, but on the top of the bookcases were big Oriental jars. He did not know anything about books, rare books, but he knew something about prints and china, and those old jars had caught his eye when he came into the room. He found himself wondering what that big yellow jar would fetch with the hideous green dragon sprawling over it, and the ruby jar—he never remembered having seen a ruby jar of that size before—and the set of big turquoise-blue enamelled vases with fierce-looking vampires on the lids. They would fetch something at Christie's, he was sure, but they would not fetch a hundred thousand pounds.

'Have you seen the pictures in this house?' Hugh Damerel asked, speaking in his rapid way—'the Gainsboroughs, and the Reynoldses, and the Vandykes? Why, the portraits of the women alone would nearly pay off that debt. The house is full, brimming over, with works of art, every one of them a gem in itself. The Earl knew what he was about: he bought nothing but gems, and the treasures here have been accumulating generation after generation. There has never been anything sold, everything has accumulated. The money has not been spent, it has been invested; it could not have been invested better. Everything in this house is worth a hundred times its original cost. It has been heaping up and heaping up. It has been kept quite intact, and now it is all mine—and I cannot touch a penny of it.'

Robert remarked that he had noticed the beautiful old china—he could not help seeing the china—he had never seen anything like it in his life.

Hugh Damerel laughed his hollow, mirthless laugh.

'The china is all very well,' he said. 'It is good of its kind; but it is nothing to the other things there are in this house: the pictures, the books, the silver. There is a service of silver here that was used at the Restoration—great tankards and winecups in which the King's health was drunk—and gold and silver bowls and dishes and fruit-baskets. There are dozens of old apostle-spoons, and rat-tailed spoons, and that sort of thing. I wonder the old woman isn't afraid to sleep in the house with all this valuable old plate. It was brought over here from Aylmerton for safety. If it were known to be here, all the thieves in London would be down after it, and she would be murdered in her bed.'

'Then, I am sure that you ought to use great caution in speaking about it,' the Rector said gravely. 'It would never do for it to be known.'

'It isn't likely to be known. The people here are all blind and deaf; they don't see anything that is under their very nose. Nobody here dreams of the value of those old portraits on the walls, the miniatures, the enamels in the cases, the ivories that are lying about these rooms, the engravings locked up in these cases. I tell you, sir, some of the things in this house are priceless. Look at these engravings.'

He turned over the beautiful red prints and etchings on the table as he spoke with his eager, nervous hand.

'See these portraits fresh from the artist's hand, proofs before all letters, some with Bartolozzi's own touches upon them! There are portfolios of his engravings in that case, all as fine as these. Every portfolio contains different subjects—see!' And he ran his finger down the gilt titles on the backs of the crimson leather cases. '"Mythological Subjects," "Dramatic and Poetical Subjects," "Portraits," "Vignettes," "Allegorical Compositions," "Historical Subjects," "Marlborough Gems," "Cameos," "Illustrations," "Religious Subjects." There is not such another collection of Bartolozzi prints in the world! A man could carry away a fortune under his arm. I wonder the old woman trusted me with the key. All these things are mine, sir—mine—and I can't lay a finger on a single one! No, thank you; I will not accept the Countess's munificent offer. Let who will have the seat. Let it go with the rest.'

CHAPTER XIII.

JOAN'S GREAT-AUNT.

Robert Lyon told his wife all about that interview with Hugh Damerel, and the failure of his errand.

'I think she is a very unreasonable old woman,' Joan said, referring to the Countess. 'How can she expect the poor young man to stand? Everyone would know that he was only a puppet. Cecilia tells me that he hasn't a penny in the world; that he ran through all his money—what little he had—before the Earl's death. He thought he was coming into a great fortune at once; he never understood that there was to be this unreasonable delay.'

'He is very bitter about it; I never saw a man so moved before. I am afraid he will do something rash—something he will be sorry for. He is so indignant at the injustice of the whole thing, particularly at the treatment of the trustees; he thinks they are exceeding their authority. If he should do anything rash in his resentment, I don't think he would be quite answerable for it.

'You don't mean, Rob, that the poor fellow is going out of his mind—that this disappointment has turned his head? I thought I saw a wild look in his eyes yesterday. I never saw such an unhappy-looking man.'

'No, I don't think he is going out of his mind; but I think he is reckless. He believes that he has been ill-used; that he is kept out of his property illegally. I shouldn't be surprised to hear that he had taken some hasty, ill-advised step to get possession of it.'

'I think he has been shamefully used! He has been duped and deceived; the Earl's ridiculous will was a mockery, nothing short of a mockery Fancy a man, the heir to all that place, the owner of all those lovely things, not having a penny in the world, being obliged to earn his living by painting pictures! He painted a picture of his own place when he was down here last, and the Countess actually bought it of him!'

'Perhaps he wouldn't take the money from her else; it might be her only way of helping him. He wouldn't accept the expenses of the election at her hands.'

Hugh Damerel left the neighbourhood the next day. Before he went, he came over to the Rectory to see Robert. He was looking as gloomy and discontented as ever, but the excitement of that election proposal which had stirred his indignation was over, and he had cooled down.

'The Countess has not given it up,' he explained, speaking of the election; 'she has sent for one of the trustees, Greatorex, a London lawyer; he is coming down to-day, and I have waited to see him.'

'I thought she had given up all idea of keeping the seat,' Robert said, with a sudden sinking of heart. He had hoped that there would be no opposition, and that that hasty promise of his to the enemy would never be known.

'No; she is an obstinate old woman; she never gives up anything until she is obliged. She would stand for the seat herself if they would return her. I don't care a hang who gets the seat! I'd as soon see Mainwaring in as anyone. I saw your name on his committee, Lyon.

You can tell him from me that I wish him luck. I hope he will get the seat, with all my heart!'

Then Robert had to explain that he had promised his support to his neighbour, Mr. Mainwaring, before he knew that there was a probability of a candidate representing the Damerel interest coming forward.

'The Damerels have no interest here now,' the heir said, turning upon him savagely. He was a dreadfully touchy young man; he would go off in a rage at a moment's notice. 'There are no Damerels left, only trustees. You don't call that old woman a Damerel! She was Maria Burrough, a pettifogging country attorney's daughter, the other day. Her father was the man who helped the Earl on to his ruin, who made it easy for him to raise money on the place—money that I've got to pay. What was it to him? Whenever the Earl was more than usually hard up, he went to old Burrough instead of going to his own lawyers, to honest men who would not have seen him robbed, and he got the money. It didn't matter to him how the estate suffered; he raised the money. Oh, there is no greed like the greed of these low country attorneys who lend money on mortgage. He got his rascally fees, and he burdened the place with a debt that will take a lifetime—two or three lifetimes—to pay off.'

'I didn't know that Lady Aylmerton's friends, relations, were such large creditors of the estate,' Robert said, in a tone of surprise; he had always understood that her ladyship's relatives were quite humble people; that her brother, Cecilia's father, was a small attorney, with a very second-rate, shady sort of *clientèle*, practising in the adjoining town.

'Oh, the old rascal overreached himself; he got mixed up with a bank that failed, and he came to grief, and the mortgages fell into other hands.'

'And Cecilia Burrough?' Joan asked anxiously; she was rather fond of Cecilia Burrough.

'Oh, Cecilia is very well. It is no fault of hers. We are not answerable for the sins of our grandfathers. I am always sorry for Cecilia; she has a hard life with that old woman, and she will get nothing when she dies.

It is too bad to bring a girl up in luxury, as she is brought up in that house, and then to turn her penniless upon the world. Cecilia is the only redeeming feature in Orchard Damerel.'

'The Countess will leave her something; she will not be quite unprovided for,' Joan said warmly. She was always ready to do battle for her friends.

'The Countess has very little to leave,' Hugh Damerel said, with a laugh. 'She has to keep up her small state, and when she dies she will leave every penny she has got in the world for Masses to be said for her soul, or whatever newer form that kind of spiritual legacy may take. She is not likely to leave anything to poor Cecilia.'

'It will be very horrid of her if she doesn't,' Joan said warmly. 'To see what a slave she makes of that poor girl! She never allows her to leave her side; she keeps her shut up for hours and hours all through the bright summer days, shut up in a stuffy room, reading those dreary prophetic sermons. She was so tired and hysterical from being shut up so long that she broke down the other night when I met her walking by the coombe; she said she wished Dr. Cumming had never been born!'

'A good thing the Countess didn't hear her!' Mr. Damerel said, with his mirthless laugh. 'I got the poor girl into trouble the other day—God knows unwittingly. We had been walking in the grounds, and Cecilia had gone in to read the everlasting sermons to my lady, and I asked her to leave the door, the front-door, unlocked—they always keep that cursed door locked when I am in the house—and I came in, unannounced, and without ringing, an hour or two later, and there was the devil to pay.'

'Why?' asked Robert. 'What was the difficulty?'

'Oh, I am not allowed to go into my own house without knocking. I am only a guest under my own roof. I am not allowed to open the hall-door and walk in, lest I should treat the house as my own, and take forced possession of it—and they might not be able to dislodge me if they tried. I don't know that I shall not some day—some day—when the right time comes.'

'I should take possession of it to-morrow if it were mine!' Joan said hotly. 'If they wouldn't let me in at the door, I should get in at the window. All the old women and all the trustees in the world shouldn't keep me out of my own!'

She looked so delightful, standing there with that bright colour in her cheeks, and her eyes shining, puckering up her pretty white forehead and her red lips—she looked so exactly a painter's ideal of warm, generous, impulsive womanhood, that the artist-heir sighed as he looked at her.

'If I had so warm and true a champion as your wife, Lyon,' he said to Robert, 'I would not be kept out of it another hour!'

They had been talking in the library—to be more accurate, the study, the Rector's study—and Mr. Damerel, as was his wont, had been pacing up and down the room rehearsing his wrongs very much like a caged bear. He was very fond of rehearsing his wrongs—they were of paramount interest to him, the most interesting theme in the world—and he thought they were of equal interest to others, and he generally behaved like a bear while he was reciting them.

He was behaving like a bear now. He was not exactly tearing up and down the room like a caged wild creature, but he was striding with his great steps up and down the study with his moody, dejected air, and running his long lean fingers through his great tawny beard.

'I tell you, sir,' he was saying to the Rector, who had tried to get him into a chair, and to look at the situation calmly—'I tell you there is not a tenant on the estate that is treated as I am. I am not allowed to walk in the grounds without permission of the trustees. I cannot throw a line into the river, or carry a gun in the plantation, without being liable to be prosecuted as a trespasser, or thrown into prison as a poacher and a felon. The trustees have absolutely forbidden me to fish or shoot on my own place!'

He was reciting his wrongs with great vehemence as he walked up and down that nondescript room that the Rector called his study, and that the Rector's wife dignified by the name of the library.

'Show the person into the library, Mary,' she used to say to the maid, with great dignity, when anyone came to see the Rector on parish matters.

It was not the least like the library at Orchard Damerel. There were Robert's few theological books partly occupying two or three of the long shelves of that big bookcase. They did not nearly fill them up; and there were some old schoolbooks of Joan's, and some yellow-backs, and a litter of newspapers and magazines on the lower shelves. It was a most unclerical collection for a rector's study; it was a very poor stock-in-trade for a professional career. Perhaps the Rector's real stock-in-trade was out of sight, behind the door of that locked cupboard.

There was only that half-filled book-shelf to cover the library walls, so that there was plenty of room for other things. Robert had hunted out some old photographs of his college clubs, and had them hung up to take off the bareness of the walls: the crew of the May boat of St. Benedict's when he rowed in it; the cricket eleven and the football team, in each of which his pleasing countenance was portrayed at various stages of his University career.

Hugh Damerel stopped before each of these interesting groups in turn, examining them with his unseeing eyes.

Joan was hoping that he would remark how nice Robert looked in 'shorts,' and how much more becoming the scanty dress of that May boat crew was than his clerical habiliments; but Mr. Damerel made no such remark.

He did remark one picture that hung on the wall—a picture of a woman in an old-fashioned dress, that hung in a dark corner. It was the picture of Joan's great-great-aunt, that had been sent to her with her wedding-presents. She never could understand why her mother had sent her the poor faded old thing in its shabby frame. She would not give it a place in any other room in the house—she would not have had it in her pretty, gay drawing-room for the world. She had tried it in the dining-room, being a family portrait, but it would not do, and she had banished it the next day. The only place in the house that could be found for it was a dark corner in Robert's study, behind the door.

Hugh Damerel stopped in the midst of reciting his wrongs, and looked at the picture. Perhaps he was thinking of those old family portraits on the walls of Orchard Damerel that were his.

'It is my wife's great-aunt,' Robert said, seeing he paused before it.

'My great-great-aunt, Rob,' Joan interrupted gaily; 'the dear old thing has been dead over a century.'

'Ah! I see—a family portrait. I could not think how it got here.'

He continued his walk, and said no more about the picture.

After he was gone, Joan suggested that it should be banished to one of the empty rooms upstairs.

'I don't wonder Mr. Damerel was surprised at seeing such a shabby old thing here,' she said; 'it's only fit for a lumber-room.'

Robert would not have the picture displaced. It was a family portrait, and it had been a wedding-present. There was something, too, in the beautiful wilful face that reminded him of Joan, a likeness in the bright eyes and the red lips. He could not bear to think of the beautiful face looking out upon bare walls and an empty room. He had got used to the picture now, and the face looked down kindly upon him out of its shabby frame.

CHAPTER XIV.

CONFIDENCES.

JOAN met Cecilia walking in the grounds the day after Mr. Hugh Damerel returned to London.

The Countess kept her niece a close prisoner all day, but in the cool of the evening, just before dinner, she was allowed to walk in the grounds for half an hour. After dinner she had to read or play to the Countess for the rest of the evening. She always walked in the direction of the Rectory, and Joan, whenever she had nothing else to do, would meet her half-way.

She was very anxious to meet her to-night; she wanted

to hear the result of Mr. Greatorex's visit, and if the poor young man—she always called the Earl of Aylmerton's heir 'the poor young man'—had been able to come to any arrangement with him before he went away.

Cecilia had a good deal to tell her. There had been a row royal between the heir and the trustee, and Mr. Damerel had gone away in a rage. He had asked for permission to shoot in the Aylmerton covers; the covers were full of game, and the place was strictly preserved. The trustees and their friends came down shooting in the season, and had capital sport; but they would not give the heir permission for a single day.

'I think the trustees are behaving shamefully!' Joan said, blazing up. 'I wonder Mr. Damerel stands it. I wouldn't if I were a man. What are they afraid of that they will not let him shoot on his own place?'

'They are afraid of his claiming the right, I suppose,' Cecilia said, with the least possible flush creeping up under her white skin. 'I got into dreadful disgrace the other day for leaving the hall-door unfastened for him to come in. They are so afraid of his making it a precedent, and claiming it as a right. I don't see how they are to dislodge him if he once gets possession.'

Joan saw that flush on Cecilia's white face, and she drew her own conclusions. Poor girl! of course she was in love with him; how could she help being in love with this ill-used hero? No hero of romance was ever more cruelly ill-used, and had a greater claim upon a woman's tender compassion; and pity, we know, is akin to love. Joan was quite sure that if she had been in Cecilia's place she would have been desperately in love with the gloomy heir; she would have been his champion, and stood up between him and those dreadful trustees. *She* would have left the hall-door open; she would have left every door in the house open all hours of the day and night for him.

'I think you were quite right to leave that door open,' she said warmly. 'Mr. Damerel says that you are the only friend that he has in the house.'

Cecilia's face drooped rosily.

'There is the Countess,' she said, with a little quiver

in her voice. 'I am sure my aunt is his friend. She would help him if she could, but she has no authority here; everything is in the hands of the trustees.'

'Will he ever come into the property?' Joan asked impatiently.

She could not understand Cecilia taking it so quietly. She would not have taken things so quietly if it had been her lover.

Cecilia shook her head.

'No,' she said, with the tell-tale blood in her face, and head drooping, 'I don't think—I'm afraid he will never come into it. The late Earl's debts are so large, it will take years and years to pay them. It will take several lifetimes. There is such heavy interest to be paid—quite shocking interest to be paid on some of the mortgages.' Cecilia's head drooped lower as she spoke. She must have known that it was her own relative who had laid this heavy tribute on the estate. 'It takes all the income to pay the interest only. When the Countess dies her small jointure will fall in, and that will accumulate, and —and perhaps they will let the house.'

'And what will you do?' Joan asked. 'Will you go on living here if the house is not let? There must be someone left here to take charge of all those valuable things.'

'Oh no; I should have to go away at once. I should not be allowed to stay here a single day.'

'What would you do? The Countess would have made some provision for you, surely?'

Joan was thinking of what Hugh Damerel said the day before about Cecilia being left unprovided for.

The girl shook her head, and there was a little throaty quaver in her voice.

'No, Lady Aylmerton has left her money elsewhere—to the Jews, I believe. She has not much to leave, but she is very fond of the Jews. She is always asking me to read the prophecies about them. She thinks they are going back to their own land shortly, and everything she has got to leave she will leave to the Jews' Society.'

'To take them back?'

'I suppose so. It will take a lot of money to rebuild

their cities and carry them all back,' Cecilia said with a sigh.

Joan gave a little impatient sniff.

'I thought queens were going to be their nursing mothers, and carry them back,' she said shortly. 'I'm sure they could do very well without Lady Aylmerton's help. Robert ought to speak to her, and tell her that charity begins at home. If she is so selfish and narrow-minded that she chooses to overlook the claims of her own people, and leave her money for that ridiculous object'—Joan called it 'ridiculous'; she did not believe in that kind of millennium—'she ought to be reminded of her duty.'

'I wouldn't have Mr. Lyon speak to her about it for the world!' Cecilia said, turning quite pale.

'Why not? She ought to be told her duty, if she doesn't know it. What's the use of a clergyman in a parish if he doesn't tell people their duty?'

'Oh, pray, pray, don't ask him to speak to my aunt,' said her ladyship's niece, trembling, 'she would be sure to know that I had been complaining.'

'And why shouldn't you complain? You have a right to complain.'

'No, I have no right. Lady Aylmerton has been very good to me. She took me away from a wretched home, and she brought me to this beautiful place, and she has surrounded me with every luxury. I have no right to expect any more.'

'Oh, you poor thing!' the Rector's wife said, with a scorn she could not keep out of her voice. 'What do you intend to do when her ladyship dies? You can't expect her to live for ever.'

Cecilia Burrough was a poor-spirited little trembling thing; she shook all over when the Countess was in her tantrums—she used to have her tantrums like other people less distinguished—and she wept when she bullied her, but she had a little bit of spirit left.

'Do?' she said, with a little throaty quaver in her voice that Joan had remarked before—'do? Why, I must get my own living. Thank heaven! I need not be dependent upon anyone; I can always get my own living. I shall go out as a governess.'

'A governess!' Joan repeated in her mocking voice.

'Oh, you poor dear! you don't know what you are talking about. Do you know what a governess's life is?'

Cecilia admitted humbly that she did not, but that other girls went out as governesses. She was not less brave or more thin-skinned than other girls. What other girls had done, and were doing, she could do.

'Do you know what other girls are doing?' Joan said eagerly, her cheeks flushing with excitement, and her eyes shining. 'Would you like to hear what a girl brought up as you have been, and who was compelled by circumstances to go out in the world and get her living as a governess, is now doing—now, at this very moment? I have had a letter from one this morning; I have it with me now. It's from my own sister. She is as brave as a lion; she would suffer anything before she would complain, and this is what she writes.'

Joan took a letter from her pocket, and spread it open, and laid it on Cecilia Burrough's knee. They were sitting on one of the rustic benches in the park, and the twilight was falling.

Cecilia read it as well as the failing light would allow.

'DARLING' (it began),—'I promised to write and tell you exactly what my life is here, and about my work.

'How shall I begin?

'Remember, this is under the seal of confidence, and the dear things at home are *never* to hear a word about it.

'In the first place, I made a mistake in coming here. I ought never, never, never to have gone into a private family; I ought to have stuck to a school.

'This is the programme of my day:

'5.30: Awoke by children talking; two of them—boys—sleep in my room; make them keep quiet if possible, and doze till 7. Get up, and dress two boys. 8: Breakfast. 9 to 12.30: Lessons. 12.30: Walk. 1.30: Dinner. 2.30 to 4: Lessons. At 4 children go out for walk with maid, and I stay at home and mend their clothes. 5.30: Tea. 6.30: Start putting them to bed. 7.30 to 10: My own time.

'I have all my meals in the nursery with the children. I never go downstairs by any chance. I am in the nursery all day. Mrs. Brown does not shake hands, if she happens to say good morning; and Mr. Brown actually tipped me a nod the first time I saw him out of the house! He has realized at last that he ought to take his hat off to the governess! The boys—my boys that I counted so much upon (four, seven, and eight)—are the naughtiest, rudest, most dreadfully spoilt children I ever met with.

'The loneliness of this wretched life is simply dreadful! I never speak to anyone all day long but the children, and a German servant who cannot speak one word of English. At first it nearly drove me mad; but I am getting used to it now.

'It is hard work, too, being on the "go" all day long; the lesson-hours are much too long for such small children. When I suggested less, Mrs. Brown politely said I was shirking the work! If the children were the least lovable or nice, it wouldn't be so bad, but they are truly dreadful!

'I have said more than I ought to have said, but it is such a relief to pour it out. Remember, not a word of this is to reach Stoke Lucy.

'I shall certainly leave here as soon as I can hear of anything else. If I were a housemaid or a cook, I could get a situation at once. I could get a hundred situations—and I could get any salary I liked to ask. Mrs. Brown does not pay me a quarter the wages that she gives to her cook, who is quite a magnificent person, which perhaps accounts for the fact that she has altogether ceased to remember that I am a lady.

'Burn this horrid letter; don't let anyone see it; I would not send it if I had time to write another. Darling, I am so thankful to hear of your happiness. I am a wretch to try to cloud it. Don't let this trouble you; forget my complainings, and remember only, with deep, deep thankfulness, how good God has been to you in giving you such a beautiful home, and a loving husband, and everything to make your life happy! Write me a long gossiping letter; it will do me so much good. Getting letters is my *only* pleasure.

'Always, darling,

'Your loving BERTHA.'

It was almost too dark to read the last lines, but dark as it was, Joan saw tears in Cecilia's eyes as she handed the letter back.

'It is too horrid,' she said huskily; 'it is much too horrid!'

And then she had to hurry back to the house to be in time for dinner.

CHAPTER XV.

THE EARL OF AYLMERTON'S TRUSTEE.

CECILIA was late for dinner after all. She had to dress when she got back, and she had stayed out longer than usual, and she had barely five minutes left to dress in. The Countess always expected her niece to dress for dinner; she kept up very little state, but she still clung to the old form of putting on an evening gown and a French blonde cap with a flower in it, as she had been used to do when the Earl was living, when she came down to dinner.

She had had no new evening gowns since the Earl's death; she was wearing out the faded gray and lavender satins and brocades that used to make such a brave show in the old days of her magnificence.

They made a brave show still when seen by candle-light and veiled with French blondes and laces. Her ladyship had a weakness for blonde; the glistening surface and the large patterns suited her large person and her florid face. She was covered with blonde to-night, a little faded and yellow, and looking as if it had been lying by for years, and some ghosts of artificial flowers were in her cap.

She sat in great state at the head of the table, and Mr. Greatorex, the trustee of the Damerel estate, ought to have sat at the other end, where a cover was laid for him, but he chose to sit opposite Cecilia, where he could see her pretty meek face the other side of the table.

It really was pretty to-night. The excitement of being late—she had never been late before in her life—had brought a colour into her white cheeks, and her eyes were shining. She was wearing one of the Countess's old gowns. Her ladyship's gowns were so ample that they required considerable reduction for her niece's slender figure—reduction and restoration. There was quite enough in one of Lady Aylmerton's gowns to make two frocks for Cecilia. There was no French blonde on the low neck of Cecilia's simple satin frock to hide her white bosom and her pretty bare arms. She wore no ornament but a coral necklace round her slender throat, but the Earl of Aylmerton's trustee, sitting opposite to her through that dreary dinner, thought he had never seen such a becoming ornament for a woman's throat before in all his life.

Mr. Greatorex ought to have known better at his age than to have stared at Cecilia's pretty face, and her white shoulders, and her lilac satin gown, and that red coral necklace, all the time he was eating his dinner.

He was an elderly lawyer of grave aspect, with keen gray eyes that looked across the table at her ladyship's niece from beneath immense bushy eyebrows.

There was very little conversation at the dinner-table; the Countess, in spite of her satins and her blondes, was not in the best of tempers. She found fault with all the dishes; she snapped up Cecilia when she ventured to make a remark; she had been quarrelling with the late Earl's trustee all day, and she had not quite forgiven him yet. It took Lady Aylmerton a long time to forgive people.

The old family lawyer had been persuading her to put all this election nonsense out of her head. It would have been the height of folly, he explained to her, for Mr. Hugh Damerel, who, everybody knew, had not a penny in the world, to stand for this or any other seat. The Earl's trustees would not have supported him; they would not spend a penny in supporting any candidate The seat must go, as the title and everything else had gone; there was nothing to be gained by keeping it in the family.

'And that man at Wytchanger will go in unopposed!' her ladyship had said, bridling up.

'I hope so,' the lawyer had answered; 'the county couldn't return a better man.'

'Do you know that his father was the Earl's enemy, that he brought an action—a lawsuit—against the Earl, and robbed him of all the land on the other side of the coombe, the spinney that you can see from this window?'

'I know that Mr. Tom Mainwaring holds the largest mortgage on the Damerel property. The estate is virtually his. It would be madness to oppose him,' the Earl's trustee had answered; and then her ladyship had gone off in a huff.

When the solemn stately dinner was over, and the ladies had taken themselves to the drawing-room, Cecilia sat down to the grand piano at the end of the big dusky room to play to her aunt. She could not read Dr. Cumming's sermons to-night, as a visitor was staying in the house, so she sat down at the piano and played some gloomy old melodies instead.

The Earl of Aylmerton's trustee came in while she was playing, but he did not go over to the piano; he sat down at the farther end of the room, beside the chair where her ladyship was nodding after her dinner. The far end of the long drawing-room was in the shadow; but he could see Cecilia's white arms gleaming at the piano, and the curve of her white throat against the great stiff brocaded curtains that swept from their ancient cornices behind her.

While they talked in low whispers, Cecilia played. She did not put much heart into her playing; she was thinking all the time of that letter that she had read in the shrubbery. Should she go away from this place some day, away from the old-fashioned state and the dreary splendour, the lumbering old family chariot with an earl's coronet on the panels? should she ever go away from these things that had come to be part of her life, and go out into the world, as that other girl had gone, and pass her days in a bare schoolroom, teaching rude, dreadful, troublesome little boys?

The gray black shadows of the stately room loomed around her as she asked herself these questions; she could see the Countess's blonde cap nodding in her chair by the fireplace—they had already begun fires these chill autumn evenings—and the eagle-like profile of the great London lawyer, with his immense eyebrows and his close-cut gray hair, as he leaned over her ladyship's chair. She did not know that they were talking about her; she would not have taken any interest in their conversation if she had known.

She was thinking about the letter that the Rector's wife had shown her, and wondered if her fate would be like Bertha's. Silent and dull and monotonous as this life was, she was used to it; it seemed impossible that it should ever cease, and that one day, perhaps at no distant day, she would have to go away.

While Cecilia was playing a low, melancholy accompaniment to her gloomy thoughts, the Earl of Aylmerton's trustee was asking the Countess some questions about her niece's future.

'I hope your ladyship has made some provision for Miss Cecilia,' he was saying, as he watched the girl's white fingers straying over the keys. 'During all these years you have been able to lay aside a sufficient sum, I trust, to provide for her future.'

'I have done a great deal for Cecilia already,' her ladyship said. 'I don't know what more she can expect.'

'I don't suppose she expects anything,' the lawyer answered, still watching the white fingers straying over the keys; 'still, there is her future to consider. She cannot always go on living here. She has been accustomed to a certain style of living—to ease, comfort, and luxury,' he added, as he paused and looked round the stately room.

It was all the more stately for the shadows, the rich brocades, the beautiful old china, the white marble statuary, the old family portraits on the walls looking down out of their gilded frames in their faded beauty, the white figure playing in the dusky corner, and the great curtains sweeping behind her. It was a lovely room in that dim lamplight, and the old lawyer, sitting by the Countess's chair, pictured to himself what the change would be to the girl playing in the shadows, when she should go back from this place to her father's house.

'Cecilia has had every comfort while she has been here,' the Countess said sharply. She objected to being called to account. 'If she had been my own child, I could not have done more for her.'

'Exactly; the fact of her having been brought up in all this luxury, amid these surroundings, will make the change greater when it comes. It will be cruel to send her back to her father's house; there are seven others, I believe, all of them at home. And his practice cannot bring in very much. I know something of what a country attorney's practice is worth; and he has had losses, I hear, lately—considerable losses. I don't think it would be fair to send Cecilia back.'

The Countess sniffed in a peculiarly disagreeable way. She was only a parvenu Countess; she was not to the manner born, and she had a plebeian way of showing her displeasure; her manners had none of the repose that marks the caste of Vere de Vere.

'I have done a great deal for my family,' she said, 'from first to last. I have let James have a great deal of money'—James was her ladyship's brother, Cecilia's father—'and I shall never see any of it back; I have paid for the education of the boys; and I have given Cecilia a home here for I don't know how many years. I have done more than my duty, and I have a right to do what I like with the little money I have been able to put aside.'

'Your ladyship has a perfect right,' said the old lawyer stiffly.

Before breakfast the next morning, the Earl of Aylmerton's trustee took an early walk through the beautiful grounds of Orchard Damerel.

It was a strange sight to him, after his dreary Temple chambers, to look out upon the purple hills and valleys of this sweet West Country. It was yet early autumn. The leaves had only just begun to change from green to gold, and from gold to russet. The hills were melting into delightful hues of morning mist and sunshire and shadow, and a thin purple haze, like a veil, hung about them. The dew was heavy on the grass, and hung like sparkling gems on the branches of the trees as he passed beneath them, a shimmer of gold and green and amber light and russet leaves dropping down on to the path before him. It was quite worth while to get up an hour or two earlier to see the lovely blaze and glitter of the woods and hedges on this glowing autumn morning.

Mr. Greatorex walked slowly along the winding path that led beside the coombe. He was an elderly gentleman, and he knew better than to take the short cut across the grass with the dew still heavy upon it. He would not have gained much if he had; he would only have met Cecilia earlier. He met her coming across the fields, with her cheeks glowing, and a trail of rosy honeysuckle in her hand.

The grave London lawyer watched her with a strange interest, perhaps with some admiration in his keen blue eyes. She was ever so much better worth looking at than those statuary marble figures upon which the Earl had expended such fabulous sums. He had been looking at those figures the night before, as he sat listening to Cecilia playing her sad tunes, and wondering what they would fetch. He was thinking about them when he met her walking towards him with that branch of woodbine in her hand.

'You are out early,' he remarked, when he came up to her. 'Do you always take such an early walk?'

Cecilia blushed; she was not accustomed to go out before breakfast. She had passed a sleepless night, tossing about, dreaming that she was immured in a bare schoolroom with a dozen rude, dreadful boys, and that she could not teach them anything. They all knew a great deal more than she did, and they were laughing at her ignorance. She got up feeling miserable, and haunted by that dreadful dream, and she had come out into the fresh morning air to shake it off.

She did not tell the Earl of Aylmerton's trustee all this, but she told him something of it. She had known him for years and years, coming and going to and from Orchard Damerel, and sometimes staying weeks together in the house. She had long ceased to regard him as a stranger; she looked upon him as a friend—an old friend. She did not hesitate to tell him what troubled her, and she told him something of the letter Joan had given her to read in the shrubbery.

'And in the face of this,' he asked, when she had poured out her artless tale, 'do you still intend to go out as a governess—in a family?'

'What else can I do?' she asked him, with her lips quivering, and the tears rushing to her eyes. 'There is nothing else a girl, brought up as I have been, can do. I can only teach children.'

The lawyer smiled.

'I thought the market was already overstocked,' he said.

'So it is; but perhaps room can be found for me. I don't expect so much as most people. I shall be content with very little. I am not clever; I have no accomplishments. There is so little that I can teach, but I would make myself useful. I shouldn't mind doing things.'

She was thinking of Bertha's letter while she was speaking, of the little boys—the dreadful, naughty, rude, spoilt little boys—that Bertha Penrose had to dress and undress every night and morning, and how she was taking only a lady's wage, and doing a servant's work.

The London lawyer looked at her with a strange pity in his eyes, as she spoke in her brave, hopeful way of the hard life and the hard, uncongenial tasks that were awaiting her in the future.

He said no more about the future as he walked back beside Cecilia to breakfast. He talked about the mists on the hills, and the violet shadows in the valleys, and the songs of the birds, and the shimmer of the dewy leaves. When he came near the house, he spoke about himself, and then Cecilia learnt for the first time that he was a lonely old man spending most of the day in chambers, and living in a big desolate London house; that his wife had been dead years and years, and that he was living quite by himself, a lonely, cheerless bachelor life.

He went away after breakfast, and Cecilia found herself thinking about him several times during that day, and picturing him going back at night to his dreary, desolate house.

CHAPTER XVI.

BLACK BEAUTY.

ROBERT LYON was immensely relieved when he heard the result of Mr. Greatorex's visit. There was to be no contest after all, and Lady Alicia's husband would be returned unopposed.

There was no necessity now, he told himself, to say anything to Lady Aylmerton about the hasty promise he had given Tom Mainwaring to support him in the event of a contest, or that he had allowed his name to be put down on the list of his committee. Hugh Damerel had seen the list somewhere, but it did not follow that her ladyship had seen it. Besides, as he was always reminding himself, he was not Lady Aylmerton's dependent. He had a right to be a judge of his own actions. He was not answerable to her for his opinions, and as a parish priest it was his duty to consider the welfare of his flock.

It was for the welfare of the flock—the tender lambs of the flock, who had been running wild during the schoolmistress's long illness—that he had advertised for a new teacher. He had received a great many answers to his advertisement. The world is full of teachers; soon there will be as many teachers as learners.

Among the many applications for the vacant post, he had selected a teacher with a great number of certificates —'parchments,' she called them—who could play the harmonium in church and train the choir.

He engaged the young woman, who undertook all these duties, without consulting his patroness, and when he had engaged her he went down into the village to make arrangements for her reception. The school-house adjoined the school—it was a part of the school-building, and it was divided into two unequal portions; the lower portion—with the domestic offices, the kitchen and back-yard, and the small well-stocked kitchen-garden, where great pears were already ripening against the wall—was set aside for the schoolmistress, and a couple of rooms in the adjoining building were occupied by the schoolmaster.

The young woman who had gone away ill had been engaged to the schoolmaster, and Lady Aylmerton, to whom the school-buildings belonged, had promised to turn the two houses into one when they were married, and enlarge the boundaries of the kitchen-garden.

The schoolmaster already looked upon the place as his own. He had worked in the garden all the summer. He had planted and hoed the potatoes, and trained the scarlet-runners, and pruned the apple-trees, and nailed up the big brown pears against the wall. He had found time to plant a little border of flowers round the grass-plot that led up to the front-door. It was brilliant now with geraniums, and double stocks, and fuchsias, and fragrant with mignonette and lad's-love. A tall yellow sunflower stared solemnly at the Rector over the garden wall as he went up to the gate. There was a bush of gray lavender under the window, and, late as it was, the sweet-scented white jasmine was in bloom over the porch.

The schoolmaster was at work in the garden, nailing up a rose-tree beside the window. He had taken his coat off, and was working in his shirt-sleeves. He was whistling at his work—Robert heard him whistling a long way down the lane.

He was rather a stoutly-built young man, with stooping shoulders and a pale flabby face, and he was cultivating an incipient black moustache. He stopped whistling when he saw the Rector enter the gate, and a dull red colour came into his cheeks.

'I am putting the place a bit in order,' he explained. 'Mary—Miss Bailey is better. She will be well enough to come back in another week.'

Then the Rector had to tell him that he had engaged another schoolmistress; that he could wait no longer for Miss Bailey to come back.

The young man's face fell while Robert was speaking, and the colour went out of his flabby cheeks; he turned quite the unpleasant colour of chalk, Robert remarked, and his lips turned pale like his cheeks.

'But she is coming back,' he gasped. He was so agitated that he could not keep his voice steady. 'Mary—Miss Bailey—is—coming back.'

'She could have come back a week ago,' the Rector said, 'but her place is filled up; she cannot come back now. If she is better, if she is so far recovered that she can take another situation, perhaps something can be found for her.'

'She is much better, she is quite able to return to her work,' the young man said eagerly. 'With a little care and looking after, in this nice air, she will soon be quite strong. As soon as she is sufficiently recovered, and we have got the place in order—her ladyship is going to throw the two houses into one—we are to be married. The Countess has given her consent; everything is settled.'

If Robert had been at all sorry for the young man's disappointment before, the mention of his patroness—their mutual patroness—hardened his heart. He did not acknowledge Lady Aylmerton's right to interfere in this matter. It was his business, not hers. She had nothing whatever to do with the schools. The late Earl's trustees paid what sums were necessary, what they were compelled by law to pay, for their maintenance, and her ladyship had no authority in the matter. He had waited months for this young woman to get well, and the school had been shockingly neglected meanwhile, and now, when he had found another person to fill her place, he was told that the Countess had arranged for her to come back—this girl in her weak health—that the school-buildings were to be altered to accommodate her; and when once settled here she would be a burden to the parish, and it would be next to impossible to get rid of her.

'The appointment of a schoolmistress has nothing to do with Lady Aylmerton,' the Rector said, with just a perceptible note of irritation in his voice; 'I have waited long enough for Mary Bailey'—he did not say Miss Bailey—'and the school is nearly ruined. It will take months—a year, at least—to make up for the time that has been lost.'

'I have done what I could,' the young man said, reddening: he did not turn a healthy red, he grew a sickening brickdust colour under his chalky skin. 'I have taken the children every day. The school has not suffered for her absence. I will go on taking it now; I would help her with the elder girls; I could spare the time very well without neglecting my own work.'

He was flushed and eager, and his voice was painfully anxious.

'You have quite enough to do, Mr. Beckett, to attend to your own school,' the Rector said almost impatiently. He was vexed and angry at the man's persistence. 'The examinations will be coming on soon, and the children, both boys and girls, are very backward. I never met with children so backward for their age. You have not a child to present in the sixth standard. The report will be the worst that the school has ever had, and there will be no grant.'

'I have done what I could,' the schoolmaster said, with that dusky brickdust red glow suffusing his face and his heavy under-lip quivering. 'I have worked day and night to bring the boys on. It is not my fault if they are dull and stupid.'

'No, perhaps not; but the fact remains that they are quite unprepared for the examination. I do not think you will find their dulness a sufficient excuse for the—I'm sorry to say it—the unsatisfactory condition of the school when the examiner comes round.'

'I have done my best,' the schoolmaster pleaded. He did not attempt any other plea.

'You have attempted too much in taking the schoolmistress's work as well as your own, and the school has suffered for it. I am afraid the examiner will say, with very good reason, that there has been neglect somewhere.'

'Nothing has been neglected that I know of. I have done my best,' the young man weakly pleaded.

'I do not say that you have not, but this state of things has been allowed to go on too long. I ought to have interfered before. However, now things will be altered. The new teacher is coming on Saturday; the place must be got ready for her. She will begin her work in the school on Monday morning.'

Having said all that he had come to say, the Rector was going away, but the young man followed him to the gate.

His face was working strangely, and his hand trembled as he took hold of the garden gate to steady himself.

'Is it quite settled, sir?' he said, with a catch in his voice that made the words difficult to get out. 'Ma—Miss Bailey—is quite ready—is expecting to come back. I don't know how she will bear it.'

'It is quite settled,' the Rector said decidedly. 'I am sorry for Miss Bailey, but she has recovered too late. Her place is filled up.'

The schoolmaster looked after him as he went down the road, carelessly flicking the ferns and nettles by the wayside with his cane, and when he turned to go back to the house to pick up his coat, he reeled as if he had received a blow, and his face grew suddenly pale, all the brickdust colour dropping out of it.

He picked up his coat and put it on mechanically, but he did not finish nailing up that rose by the window.

He groped his way blindly, like one stunned, to his own quarters at the other side of the school-house, feebly repeating in a dazed, foolish way, like a child repeating a lesson—he could not grasp the meaning of the Rector's words—'She has recovered too late—too late!'

Robert dismissed the man and his disappointment from his thoughts before he got to the corner of the lane. He was a coarse, common soul—a dull, inefficient, commonplace young man, not at all fit for his position—and he had no sympathy with him. He was only sorry that he was not going too, as well as poor Miss Bailey.

It would be very humiliating for the school to have the worst report of any school in the neighbourhood now that he had come there. Everyone would say that he had been neglecting his duties.

Robert was dreadfully thin-skinned about what his neighbours said or thought of him. He had shaken off some of his awe—or reverence, call it what you will—for that old woman at Orchard Damerel; he had found out that she was only a parvenu Countess after all, and that the neighbourhood did not think much of her. He was anxious above everything to stand well with the county.

So many great people had called upon him, people who did not call on the neighbouring clergy, and Lady Alicia had made a great fuss with him. He had got into quite the best set. His head was turned, quite turned. He looked down, as he drove through the country roads, behind his swift-stepping roan, or Joan's perfectly-matching ponies, upon the poor country clergy and their wives he met jogging along the road in their homely vehicles. He acknowledged their greeting in quite a condescending way.

He was already of importance in the diocese; he had dined with Joan at the Palace more than once, and the Bishop's wife had driven over from Carlingford, fifteen miles, to make a formal call.

He had really got a position in the county. He had the finest Rectory-house, and the finest grounds, and by far the finest horses and carriages, of any parson in the neighbourhood, and he ought to have had the finest income. People gave him credit for having it whether he had it or not. Nobody was surprised when they saw Joan riding beside him on a beautiful chestnut; it was only another sign of his wealth.

Robert did not exactly hunt, but when there was a meet in the neighbourhood he rode over with Joan, and loitered about among the distinguished company, while the hounds drew the neighbouring coverts. He did not race across the country after the hounds in a pink coat and shout himself hoarse like the independent squire-parsons of the county; he was content to wait about among the carriages and renew his acquaintance with his titled friends.

Joan accepted that kind invitation of Lady Alicia's, and spent a delightful week at Wytchanger while all the fun of the election was going on. It was really fun—nothing serious; only making speeches out of hotel windows amid immense cheering, and driving about with bows of blue ribbon on the horses' ears. Mr. Tom Mainwaring was returned unopposed. It was the first time that a Liberal had been returned for the Eastern Division of the county, and there were big demonstrations to celebrate the event.

There had been equally big rejoicings when the late Earl of Aylmerton's candidate had been returned at the last election. They were both dead, the Earl and his nominee, and the old cry had gone up with the old enthusiasm unabated, 'The King is dead! Long live the King!'

Lady Alicia's husband was the most popular man in the district quite an affectionate relationship existed between him and his constituency. If Hugh Damerel had been induced to stand, he would not have polled a dozen votes. There were great doings at Wytchanger after the election, and Robert and his wife were staying as guests in the house.

It was at a meet on one of these red-letter days that Lord George persuaded Joan to change horses with him.

'That horse is too hard in the mouth for your wife,' he remarked to Robert, as they rode together. 'See how the brute pulls; it's as much as she can do to hold it in. There'll be a nasty accident some day, when it gets its head, after the hounds; she won't be able to hold it in.'

There seemed some truth in what he said. The brute did pull. Joan was quite flushed and breathless with the exertion of trying to hold it in; but, then, she was not a very experienced horsewoman. The horse went beautifully in an ordinary way—a handsome chestnut, with splendid legs and mild eyes. It did not look the least like running away. It woke up when following the hounds, as men and beasts do wake up when their blood is stirred with the excitement of the chase, and then it certainly pulled rather hard. What creature would not, with any spirit in it, at such a moment?

Joan acknowledged, when she came up panting, that it was as much as she could do to hold it in. So the saddles were changed, and Joan rode Lord George's horse, Black Beauty, which did not pull at all hard, and carried her beautifully. It was a lovely creature, with a coal-black shining coat, taller and more shapely than the chestnut, and with slender legs. It was exactly what a lady's hunter should be—at least, that is what Joan said, and she ought to be able to express an opinion, as she rode it for the rest of the day, and it carried her splendidly.

Robert rode beside her. He had not intended to hunt with the rest that day when he started; he had only intended to ride over to the meet, and wait about while the hounds drew the coverts, and then go back with the carriages and the guests to the house. He could not go away and leave his wife tearing across the fields on another man's horse; he had to go with her whether he wanted to or not. It was absurd to take her away just as she was enjoying herself immensely, and everybody was saying how well she looked on the back of that splendid hunter.

A pretty woman looks pretty anywhere, but a handsome woman never looks so handsome as on horseback, and it was quite settled before the day was over that Joan was the handsomest woman on the field. She was in the best possible spirits; the admiration she excited, or the run, or the exhilarating air of those breezy moors, had quite turned her head. She left Robert a long way behind her several times during that day, and galloped away beside Lord George, leaving him to follow. Perhaps she could not help it; Black Beauty would go, whether she wanted to or not. What is the use of riding a hunter if it holds back when the houuds are in full cry, and streaming across the field?

'Oh, Rob!' she exclaimed, riding up to her husband, who was coming towards her on his slow, steady old roan. 'Oh, Rob, it was too lovely!'

She was too breathless to say what was too lovely, whether it was the run or the horse; but she was patting and fondling the handsome creature, and bending over it as women do over their four-footed favourites when they have accomplished some great thing.

'He took me over a hedge, Rob, like a bird. It was like flying; he didn't stop at anything. He's worth a hundred of that humdrum old chestnut!'

'The chestnut was never fit for your wife, Lyon,' Lord

George said, coming up on the despised beast; 'it is too big and heavy for a lady's horse, and its mouth is too hard. It would pull her arms off. As Mrs. Lyon says, Black Beauty is worth a dozen of her.'

Robert hung his head. He was not any judge of horseflesh, but it was not pleasant to hear that a horse he had just given seventy guineas for, for his wife to ride, was but a poor creature.

He rode home in silence. He had not spent a delightful day. He had not been by his wife's side an hour, though that had been the excuse, the reason, rather, for his presence in the hunting-field. He had a suspicion that he was out of place there—a poor country parson with two hundred and seventy pounds a year. He would have been better at home in his study, writing his Sunday's sermon.

He went home the next day, but before he went Lord George took him aside and spoke to him about the horse.

'Look here, Lyon,' he said, in his affable way—Lady Alicia's brother had a great deal of her ladyship's affability, and her loud, free-and-easy ways; there was not a bit of pride about him, people used to say—that is, people who did not know him very well, who had never had any dealings with him, and very few people have dealings with lords—'Look here, Lyon, that beast isn't fit for your wife to ride. It's too big and heavy a thing for her, and too hard in the mouth. There'll be a nasty accident some day, when she lets him get his head. I don't see how she's to prevent it. The brute might break her neck at any moment.'

The picture was so appalling that Robert turned quite pale at the thought.

'If that's the case, I had better get rid of him at once,' the Rector said.

'I tell you what I'll do, Lyon,' Lord George said, in a sudden access of generosity—he was so concerned about the safety of the Rector's beautiful wife—'I'll make a swop with you for him—you know, our West-Country phrase for an exchange—I'll swop that hunter of mine, that carried your wife so well, for him. It'll suit me as well as any other; it can pull as hard as it likes with me. Black Beauty is worth a couple of hundred as a hunter, and cheap at the money.'

Then Robert had to explain modestly that he could not afford to give such a sum for a horse for his wife to ride.

Lord George laughed his great good-humoured laugh.

'Nobody expected you to, my dear fellow,' he said, in the most friendly way in the world. 'How much did you give for that brute?'

He always spoke of Robert's last purchase as a 'brute.'

'I gave seventy guineas for him,' the Rector said ruefully.

'Five-and-twenty more than he's worth, with a mouth like leather.'

Robert feebly protested that he had taken a veterinary's opinion on the horse before he bought it, and it had been warranted not only sound, but faultless—he had been assured, in fact, that he had got it a bargain.

Lord George laughed again. He had a big, good-tempered, genial laugh that always set people at their ease and inspired confidence.

'You don't know so much about horses as I do, Lyon,' he said, which was quite true. 'You should have had an independent opinion before you gave that money for a brute that pulls like the very devil. He isn't fit for any lady to ride. If I took him of you, it would be only to prevent an accident. I shouldn't like to see your wife on his back again. I'll tell you what I'll do: I don't mind dropping some money to oblige a friend; if you like to swop him with me, and give me another fifty, I'll take him off your hands!'

This generous offer quite took Robert's breath away. He did not close with it until he had talked the matter over with his wife.

'You don't mean that Lord George is willing to give Black Beauty up for fifty pounds!' Joan said, as if fifty pounds could be picked any day off blackberry-bushes.

'Fifty pounds and the chestnut I bought for you,' the Rector said, in not quite so enthusiastic a voice.

'Oh, that brute! I could never ride him again, Robin.

It is very good of Lord George to take him at any price. I thought that hunter of his was worth hundreds of pounds. You should have seen the way he cleared the hedges!'

'It is more than I had intended to give for a horse,' Robert said thoughtfully; 'more, I think, than we can afford, and I don't know just now how we can spare another fifty pounds. It will be a long time before the tithes come in.'

'We shall be ever so rich when they come in, Rob. We shan't know how to get through so much money. There will be no expenses after this first settling in, and buying the things that are necessary. There are only two of us to live on all that money.'

Joan really thought what she said. She never could understand how they could get through nearly three hundred a year in eating and drinking. They would not want any more clothes for years, and they had bought and paid for all their furniture, and the horses and carriages; there would be no more expenses now.

She reasoned this over with Robert, as he stood pale and unwilling beside her writing-table, where she was answering poor Bertha's letter.

'The saddle fits him beautifully, Rob,' she said, by way of argument—'it might have been made for him; and it will cost just the same keeping a good horse as keeping that brute; he won't eat a bit more.'

There were other arguments equally convincing that Joan brought forward for the 'swop,' as Lord George had good-naturedly termed it, and for the payment of that fifty pounds in addition that he was so generous as to offer to accept for the splendid hunter that had carried her so well.

She was quite sure that Lord George had only offered it out of charity. He was dreadfully afraid she would break her neck if she ever went out on that brute again.

The Rector and his wife returned to Coombe Damerel the next day; 'the brute,' that he had given seventy guineas for, was left behind in the stables at Wytchanger, and a groom rode Black Beauty over to the Rectory early in the next week.

CHAPTER XVII.

THE SCHOOLMASTER'S APPEAL.

THE summer had quite gone. It had gone slowly, lingeringly, as if unwilling to depart.

It had been a long lovely summer, full of sunshiny days, and the songs of birds, and the fragrance of flowers. There never had been such a summer for flowers; there had never been such long unclouded sunshiny days.

The autumn had been as rich and as golden as the summer. The yellow harvest fields had yielded their rich store of golden grain, and the stack-yards were full, and the barns brimming over. The orchards had yielded their ruddy store: no one could remember such a season for apples! The wild things too, the wayfarer's harvest, had not failed. The nut-bushes and the wild sloe, the green bullace and the luscious blackberry, had each yielded fruit after its kind.

The sunshiny days and the gracious glamour of harvest were over now, and everything had changed. The gold of the woods had turned to russet, and the russet to brown. The colours of the landscape had shifted, and the song of the birds was over, and the swallows had flown away.

The chill dreary days of late autumn, almost winter, had set in, and the rainy season had begun. When they have not frost in the West Country, they have rain, and a great deal of it.

There had been so much this year that Joan had not been able to go a-hunting so often as she had fondly anticipated. Black Beauty was eating his head off in the stable, while his mistress was kept a prisoner indoors.

She had only ridden him a few times before the rains set in. She had only once met Lady Alicia since that visit to Wytchanger. The new member for the Eastern Division and his wife had gone up to town, and Lord George had returned to his own place, and taken 'the brute' with him.

It was hardly worth while to give so much money for a horse and keep it in the stable all the winter. Even if the weather had been fine, and Joan could have got out, it was hardly the kind of horse to ride about country lanes, and through village streets, and over the steep hills of that hilly country. A sure-footed Exmoor pony would have been much better. There would have been more 'fun' to be got out of it, and less danger.

It was too big a mount, if the truth must be told, for the Rector's wife. Joan saw it after a time, but she did not see it at first. It was such a lovely sensation flying over the country like a bird, that it swallowed up every other feeling; she could think of nothing else. Robert had never experienced that exhilarating sensation. He did not care for the paces of that high-flying Black Beauty. He preferred the steady jog-trot of his roan.

The horse had been bought for Joan, and when Joan could not ride it, it stayed in the Rectory stables eating its head off. Joan was not likely to ride it for some time to come; she had been ailing lately, and a doctor had been consulted—he ought to have been consulted months before—and he had forbidden horse-exercise for the present.

Robert never could understand what had made him buy that hunter. He had never liked it; and now he had no further use for it, and was not likely to have for some months to come. It was like a white elephant—he had encumbered himself with it, and he did not know how to get rid of it.

The winter wore on with its occupations and cares. Joan did not go out very much; she sat in the room he called his study all day, employed with some fine needlework, which, considering the hours she devoted to it, seemed of absorbing interest. The room did not look at all like a study if anyone happened to call to see the Rector on parish business. Joan's things were always lying about it, and her work-table had taken up a permanent place by the fire. There were always scraps of lace, and bits of cambric, and tags of tape, and shreds of cotton, lying about that untidy room if anyone happened to come in.

There were not many people to come in now. Cecilia

sometimes found an opportunity to run over from the great house for a few minutes' chat. The walks in the shrubbery in the gloaming were over now. The days were short and dark, and the paths in the shrubbery were too damp to loiter about in exchanging confidences and reading letters. She could never get away long from her noble relative; the rainy weather kept the Countess a prisoner indoors a great deal, and she could seldom spare Cecilia for more than half an hour at a time.

The Countess never called at the Rectory herself now. She used to send kind messages to Joan by her niece, but a coldness had sprung up between her and the Rector. She had found out all about that promise of his to support her enemy. He had not behaved with the candour and openness she had a right to expect in that election business. He had been reticent, to say the least. Her ladyship did not call it reticence; she gave it a broader name. She called him 'double-faced.' She was not very particular what she called people when she was angry. She had still greater cause for wrath in the matter of the appointment of the new infant-school teacher. Robert had not consulted her in this matter; he had appointed a successor to poor Mary Bailey without consulting her.

The schoolmaster had come over to the house and poured out his grievances to the Countess. Cecilia, who had been present at the interview, declared that he had wept. All his little schemes of happiness and domestic bliss were shattered at a blow, and the little humble castle of love in a cottage—a dear little cottage, fragrant with lavender and lad's-love, with jasmine over the porch, and roses looking in at the window; he was training that rose-tree when the blow came—had toppled over, and had nearly buried him and poor Miss Bailey in the ruins. The sick girl had had a relapse when the news of her lover's disappointment reached her; it was her disappointment too, and she was less able to bear it than he was—she had been weak and ailing ever since. The doctors did not think she would ever get over it; she was a poor weak thing, without any backbone; she had no stamina in her to stand a sudden shock.

The Countess was angry and indignant; she was very fond of Mary Bailey; she had made up the match, people said—at any rate, she had encouraged it—and she had set her heart on having Mary Bailey near her for the rest of her time.

Now all these things were at an end; the matter had been taken out of her hands, and she had not been consulted. She had a right to be angry.

The schoolmaster had not given up his hope of happiness without another effort. He wanted his happiness so much; he had waited for it so long; he could not give it up without an effort.

He made a last appeal to Joan. It was like a drowning man clutching at a straw. The Rector's wife took very little interest in parish matters. She did not concern herself about the place or the people; why should she? She could not be always running about the village on little fussy errands concerning the children in the Sunday-school, the Bands of Hope, the clothing club, and the mothers'-meetings. She could not always be prying into poor people's houses and catching things; she could not be expected to sit by the hour in stuffy rooms listening to the complainings of bed-ridden old men and women, who would insist on telling her all about their unpleasant complaints.

She gave up sick-visiting when she found how trying it was and what a lot of time it took up; and as to the Sunday-school, and the Bands of Hope, and the mothers'-meetings—well, 'if the people, or the children, came, they came, and if they did not, they stayed away.'

This was Joan's way of putting it when her husband remonstrated because the Sunday-school was falling off, and the mothers seldom came to the meetings. If the truth must be told, she was just as well pleased when they stayed away as when they came.

It was very little use the schoolmaster coming to her with his grievance; like the children, he might as well have stayed away.

She was busy when he called putting up some fresh hangings in the drawing-room. He could not have chosen a more unpropitious time. She was fond of altering the hangings in the drawing-room—the hangings, and the arrangement of the plates and pictures. Whenever she had nothing else to do she took these all down and put them up afresh. She had only just returned from Wytchanger, and the 'set' of Lady Alicia's hangings had touched her deeply. She was very susceptible to these influences. The lovely embroideries and silken tissues, the delicate, soft-falling draperies of rich Eastern stuffs, that made so dainty and luxurious the beautiful rooms at Wytchanger, had moved the country-bred wife of the Rector to envy. The paradise of subdued colour, harmonious tints, and artistic drapery had stirred the deeper depths of Joan's nature. She could no longer live, she told herself, amid these crude surroundings; everything must be changed.

So all the curtains in the drawing-room had been taken down, and the walls had been cleared of their little humble attempts at decoration, and Joan was seated on a high pair of steps planning a wonderful scheme of artistic drapery, when the schoolmaster was ushered in.

The maid who ushered him in did not know that her mistress was pulling the room to pieces, and that she was not exactly prepared to receive visitors. Joan received him at the top of the steps.

She did not take the trouble to come down. She looked down from her high seat upon the poor commonplace fellow, with his clumsy manners and his chalky face, with a feeling of impatience and disgust.

'I have come to speak to you about the school—the infant-school,' the young man began awkwardly.

It is rather hard to talk to a person up a ladder.

'Oh, you have made a mistake; it's Mr. Lyon you want to see. I know nothing about the school,' Joan said, in her unsympathetic voice.

'There is no mistake. It is not about the school—it is about the new schoolmistress I wanted to speak to you,' he went on nervously. 'Mary—Miss Bailey is better——'

Joan interrupted him hastily; she did not want to hear that story over again.

'Oh, I'm very glad to hear she is better; it was a pity

she didn't get better before. I hope she will get a nice school somewhere else.'

'It is about that I came to speak to you.'

He was a very awkward young man; he did not know what to do with his hat, which he kept changing from one hand to the other, and he did not know what to do with his feet; and he had not wiped his boots, Joan remarked, and he was making a dreadful mess on her new carpet. Why had not Mary told the young man to wipe his feet?

'It's no use coming to me,' she said, with some asperity. She had no patience with people coming into her rooms without wiping their feet. 'I don't know anything about it. I believe the matter is quite settled. If you have anything to say, you must say it to Mr. Lyon.'

'I have already spoken to Mr. Lyon,' he went on desperately, with a clammy sweat breaking out on his forehead, and his lips working nervously. 'He does not seem to realize what a serious matter this is to me, and to Ma—Miss Bailey.'

He always checked himself when he got to Mary, and gave his betrothed the full dignity of the prefix.

'We were to be married——'

He said this with a gasp and waited, as if he were sure of Joan's sympathy.

'So I have heard,' she said, calling down to him from the top of the ladder. 'You must put it off, I suppose. A lot of people put off their weddings.'

The man was silent, and Joan revolved in her mind the set of the curtain she held doubtfully in her hand.

She had been trying to remember all the morning how those window-curtains at Wytchanger were draped, and it had just flashed across her mind while she was speaking, like a revelation.

'It would kill Ma—Miss Bailey, in her weak health, to put it off!' he said desperately.

Joan laughed.

'People are not killed so easily,' she called down from her high perch. 'Miss Bailey will soon get used to it. It will give her time to get strong——'

'Oh, you don't know!' the young man burst in. He

could not control his feelings any longer. He was a poor sort of a young man, without any self-restraint. 'Mary has counted upon it so long; she has been looking forward to it all the summer. We have been getting the house ready, and I have planted the garden. It is all ready for her—quite ready—she was coming next week. We were going to have the banns read on Sunday—and now—it will break her heart!'

He had dropped his hat on the floor, and he buried his face in his hands. He could not keep the tears back. He had no control whatever over his feelings.

Joan looked down at him sobbing there, from her giddy height, with disgust and impatience. She could not understand a man being so weak and so easily moved. She had no sympathy whatever with his disappointment. If Mary Bailey wanted to get married, she ought to have got better earlier. It was clearly her fault, not theirs, that the place had been filled up. It was unreasonable to think that it could be kept vacant any longer.

'It was a great pity she didn't get better before,' she said in her hard voice, which no trouble of her own had ever softened, 'and then there would have been no fuss.'

'It is not too late now for her to come back,' the foolish fellow said eagerly. Joan had never seen anyone so eager in her life; he was trembling all over, and the perspiration was standing in great beads on his forehead, and his face was working strangely. 'Oh, don't say that it is too late! Think of your own wedding—how you looked forward to it, and got your things ready for it. Mary—Miss Bailey—has been getting her things ready all the summer. Think, if anything had happened to prevent your own wedding; if it had been put off—perhaps for ever—if you had been in weak health, and could not bear things very well—think what it would have been to you!'

He had come over to the foot of the ladder where Joan was standing, or sitting, rather, and he was looking up to her with his agitated face, and his trembling hands clasped and upraised. It was as if she had taken the place of Providence, and he was a wretched suppliant, imploring her to alter her decrees.

He implored in vain. Providence, in the shape of Joan, turned her back upon him. She had just recollected the set of that window drapery at Wytchanger, and she went up to the top of the steps and began to arrange it. She was arranging it beautifully, and the poor wretch at the foot of the steps looked up at her through his tears and waited.

'I should have had to put it off, I suppose, like other people,' she said impatiently. She did not even turn round to speak to him. He looked so absurd standing there that she turned her back to him, and called down to him from the top round of the ladder. 'I am quite sure it is too late now to alter anything. I heard Mr. Lyon say it was all settled, and the young woman is coming to-day—this afternoon.'

'And you will not interfere?' he said hoarsely, 'for Mary—Miss Bailey's sake, you will not interfere? She is your own age; she is not unlike you—she is tall and slight, and has a fresh colour, and she is the dearest girl in the world. If you knew her, you would intercede for her.'

'It is too late for anyone to interfere,' Joan said sharply; 'and I am so busy this morning, it is really no use your talking to me.'

She was very anxious to get rid of him; she had no patience with the foolish young man standing there.

The young man turned away from the foot of the steps, and picked up his hat from the carpet, as he had picked up his coat from the doorstep of the house. A change came over his face as he stooped to pick it up—a white, awful change, as of one that had abandoned hope, and rigid, upright lines came out on his damp forehead.

'You may be in trouble yourself some day,' he said, speaking thickly—so thickly that Joan on the top of the ladder could scarcely catch what he said; perhaps she did not try to. 'You may have to ask a favour, a kindness, like me, some day; maybe you will ask in vain. Remember how you have refused Mary Bailey'—he did not say *Miss* Bailey now—'with what measure you mete, it shall surely be measured to you again!'

He walked out of the room looking older than when he

came in a few minutes before, and with the awful rigid lines on his gray, stricken face.

He let himself out, and walked across the lawn between the Rector's flower-beds with a strange sense of change and loss. The flowers looked different to him now as he passed by them, the flowers and the trees, and the ruddy colour of the autumn leaves lying on the grass. Perhaps he could not see clearly, but a change had come over the face of the sky and the earth; all the bright colour had gone out of his life, and the songs of the birds had ceased.

Joan had caught the schoolmaster's last words, and she came down from the high steps flushed and angry.

'That impudent young man at the school-house has been up here threatening me,' she told her husband, when he came in. 'He has been crying like a baby, because you will not have Mary Bailey back; he behaved disgracefully, and quite spoilt the carpet with his dirty boots. I wish you would send him away, Rob, as well as his sweetheart.'

The Rector's wife did well to be angry, for that troublesome young man's visit had quite put the lovely arrangement of those curtains at Wytchanger out of her head. She spent the rest of the morning trying to arrange them to her satisfaction, but they would not 'drape' artistically, do what she would. The interview with Mary Bailey's *fiancée* had taken all the grace out of these draperies, or the deftness from her touch. They would only hang in rigid, upright lines, like the lines she had seen on a white face that had hurried past the window as she came down the steps.

CHAPTER XVIII.

PHYLLIS'S CHRISTMAS VISIT.

WHEN Christmas came round, Lady Aylmerton did an unexpected thing. She sent for Hugh Damerel to spend Christmas with her.

It was not a strange thing that the heir of the Earl of

Aylmerton should come down among his own people and spend Christmas in his own place.

The wonder was that her ladyship should have asked him. They had parted in anger, or, if not exactly in anger, in ill-will. Lady Aylmerton would not forgive him for giving up the family seat so easily, and he, on his part, could not forgive her for asking him to contest it with her money.

Under the circumstances, and as Christmas is the best time in the world for making up quarrels and reconciling old grievances, for kissing and making friends—else what is the use of hanging up mistletoe?—it was quite in the course of things that the heir should come down to Orchard Damerel, and eat his Christmas dinner with her ladyship.

It was not a very cheerful Christmas gathering; and it was rather ominous, if anyone happened to be superstitious, to sit down a party of three to a Christmas dinner. If there is anything in old wives' tales, the seat of one of the party would surely be vacant when another Christmas came round.

The solemn, not to say glum, party which gathered round that stately board on that festive occasion, had attended service at the village church on the Christmas morning, and listened to a long windy discourse suitable for the season.

At least, the Countess and her niece had listened, and Hugh Damerel, sitting with them in the Aylmerton chapel, had looked about him as was his custom, while the Rector turned over the yellow pages of his sermon. He did not take the trouble to copy them now. He slipped the old faded manuscript into his sermon-case, and carried it up into the pulpit.

The new infant-school teacher had taken Cecilia's place at the harmonium now—she played it uncommonly well—and she kept a sharp eye on the children while she played. But Mr. Damerel was not looking at that admirable young person, nor was he admiring her playing, though she was playing her best, her very best. He was looking at the sweet downcast face of the girl beside her, who was leading the singing.

The voice of the Rector's wife, he remarked, had grown sweeter while he had been away. If she had been singing about 'Peace on earth, good-will to men all the time, how could it help being sweeter?

There is a great deal of truth in the dear old fairy-tales of our youth. It is the pearls and precious stones dropping from the lips that sweeten the most commonplace voices.

But the change that Hugh Damerel noted, looking across the hymns and the prayers and the long windy sermon, to the seat among the village children where the Rector's wife usually sat, was not in the voice only, but in the downcast face that bent over the book. It never looked over to the Aylmerton chapel once through the service; it was never conscious of being an object of scrutiny. It was a pleasure to look at it, and feel that it would not suddenly look up and meet one's eyes with a swift embarrassing glance, and make one feel dreadfully conscious and ashamed.

Mr. Damerel stared at the girl singing in the village choir all through the service, as he stared at the Christmas decorations, which Cecilia had been busy about all the week. There were bits of holly stuck about the church in a primitive, tasteless fashion; there was not much to show for a week's work. Cecilia had done it alone, as Joan had been ailing, and the doctor had forbidden her to go out.

After the service, Lady Aylmerton waited to speak to the Rector, and inquired for his wife—she was fond of Joan—and then he introduced Phyllis to her, who had only come down from Stoke Lucy the night before.

Her ladyship charged Phyllis with some kind messages to her sister, and asked her to come over to tea at the house the next day, and to bring Joan with her, if it were safe for her to go out.

Hugh Damerel let the ladies return alone, and when he had put them into the big yellow chariot, and watched it drive away, he walked back to the Rectory with Robert.

Phyllis thought she had never seen such a gloomy, morose young man in her life, as the Earl of Aylmerton's heir. He did not speak half a dozen words to her as he walked beside her on his way to the Rectory. He did not take the trouble to notice the few shy remarks she ventured to make, as he walked by her side pulling the ends of his moustache, and gnawing his under-lip, and behaving generally like a bear. Perhaps he did not hear her, or he was too much occupied with his gloomy thoughts to take much interest in the weather, or in discussing the decorations of the church. He did not walk exactly by her side all the way back. The path was narrow that led up to the Rectory, and three persons could not walk abreast, so he dropped behind, only far enough to catch a view—an artist's view—of the girl's dainty profile, the charming curve of her cheek, and the pensive—the decidedly pensive—droop of her red lips, and the quiver of her white eyelids.

He had been puzzling himself all through the service, while he had been staring at the girl, as if she were part of the decorations, to find out what was the charm, the piquant charm, of her face.

Beauty is made up of so many things; sometimes it is only made up of one thing. An attractive face, when pulled to pieces, may not have one perfect feature in it; it may have no beauty of form or colour; but the charm is there, the quite unmistakable charm, and the world goes down before it.

Hugh Damerel found out, or thought he had found out, the secret of Phyllis's pensive beauty; he had hit upon the lines and curves—he put them down on paper when he got home—wherein the charm lay. He was used to appraising the beauty of women, and putting it on paper or canvas. It was his trade.

Joan was not very ill. She was only confined to the house. She had been suffering from a cold, and the doctor had forbidden her to go out while the snow was on the ground. She was watching for them to come back from church at the drawing-room window. The fire had been lighted in the drawing-room to-day in honour of Phyllis, perhaps also in honour of the season, but the big bare room felt cold and chilly, and the fire did not seem to give out any heat.

Joan had taken a dislike to the room since that scene with the schoolmaster, when he made that ridiculous appeal to her at the foot of the ladder. She had arranged the hangings quite beautifully, after all; and she had hung up the plates in fresh places, and draped the mirrors, and moved the old cabinet about again, and put the piano in another corner; but she could not get any satisfaction out of it when she had done it. The fire crackling on the hearth, the Christmas holly on the walls, the beautiful hot-house flowers on the tables, did not seem to relieve the gloom of the place. She could not shake off the remembrance of that importunate young man. There was a soil that his dirty boots had made on the pretty new carpet still; her eyes would always go over to that spot when she entered the room.

She was thinking of him now, as she stood at the window, watching her husband and Phyllis and Hugh Damerel coming back from the Christmas service, and his words were in her ears, 'With what measure you mete, it shall surely be measured to you again.'

She was looking paler and thinner, Mr. Damerel thought when he shook hands with her, and she was not nearly so lovely as her sister. Seeing the two women standing together, he could not understand how he could have taken one for the other.

'What has brought you down?' Joan inquired eagerly. 'Has anything happened?'

Mr. Damerel shook his head.

'Nothing is likely to happen,' he said bitterly. 'The Countess has sent for me to eat my Christmas dinner under my own roof, as if I were a pauper dependent on her bounty.'

Phyllis opened her shy eyes to the widest. She had never heard of the Earl of Aylmerton's ridiculous will, and she thought the ill-mannered young man was mad.

'I'm very glad you've come,' Joan said, with a laugh, 'for Cecilia's sake. Poor Cecilia! Think of spending Christmas alone with that dear, solemn old thing in that dreary house! It was quite worth while to come down for Cecilia's sake.'

Hugh Damerel ought to have blushed up to the roots

of his tawny red hair, and looked dreadfully confused; but the mention of Cecilia's name did not move him the least.

'I'm very sorry for Miss Burrough,' he said, 'but I fear I can lay claim to no such disinterested motives in coming down. Hang it!' he exclaimed, with a sudden vehemence, and beginning to walk up and down Mrs. Lyon's drawing-room as if it were a bear-garden; 'can you blame a fellow for coming down to his own? It may never be mine—it never can or will be mine—but I cannot resist the temptation—no, not the temptation; there is a word stronger than that—I cannot resist the attraction that draws me down to this place, whether I will or not. If I were wise, I should throw the whole thing up. It is nothing to me—it has wrecked my life. If I had any sense or judgment left, I should go away to Australia, New Zealand, anywhere, and begin life afresh. I have thought a hundred times of taking a cattle-ranche, and forgetting all about the cursed thing.'

He was very much in earnest; he had quite forgotten that he was in a lady's drawing-room, and that he was behaving like a bear.

Something in Phyllis's face made him pause in his walk as he was striding with his great steps away down the room.

'I beg your pardon,' he said humbly; 'I had forgotten where I was. I forget everything when I am once on that cur—— I beg your pardon, that miserable subject. I am the victim of a ghastly joke, Miss Penrose—a cruel mockery which has spoilt my life.'

He went away and left Phyllis standing there looking after him with a strange pity in her kind eyes. She thought the poor man was mad, quite mad, and she was dreadfully sorry for him.

She thought of nothing but that raving madman all through that first day in her sister's beautiful new home, when there were so many other things of more absorbing interest that ought to have occupied her attention.

She had come down late the previous night—Christmas Eve—she could not come earlier. She could not come away and leave her mother alone. She had to wait until Bertha came home. Bertha had got permission to spend a short Christmas holiday at home, but she was not suffered to leave her delightful pupils until the day before Christmas. When she arrived Phyllis came away. She had only a few days to spend at the Rectory; she would have to go back at the end of the week to set Bertha free.

There were so many things to talk over when the sisters met after such a long absence. They had never been parted so long before in their lives. Joan had to tell Phyllis all about her new friends, the lords and ladies, and the county people who had made so much of her, and that delightful week she had spent at Wytch-auger; the dinner-parties, and the election ball, and the fun in the hunting-field, and the delightful run she had had on Black Beauty, who had carried her over everything.

Black Beauty was in the stable now, a trifle stiff in the legs this cold weather. Phyllis went out into the stable-yard with Robert to see it, and Joan's ponies, and the roan, and the dear little pony-carriage, and the high dogcart.

The sight of all these grand things took her breath away. She had no heart to tell Joan about the pinching and scraping at home after that; the contrast was too great. There could be nothing gained by telling Joan, who was much too full of her own delightful surroundings to trouble herself about other people's trials and difficulties.

Phyllis got rather weary, when the novelty had worn off, of hearing about the lords and ladies and the splendid runs in the hunting-field. Perhaps she was envious. She was not made on the same lines as Joan, though they were so much alike that Hugh Damerel had mistaken one for the other.

In the midst of these glowing descriptions, just as Black Beauty was taking that fence so splendidly, or Lord George was taking Joan in to dinner, a picture would arise before her listener's eyes of poor Bertha shut up in the nursery with her troubles and pupils, and her mother patching the boys' well-worn garments. Phyllis did not think of herself at these times; she was so used to rubbing and scrubbing, and washing and ironing, and pinching and paring, from morning till night, that she was personally quite out of the question.

She hoped that none of these great people would come to the Rectory while she was there during her short week. She was quite sure she should sink into the earth if a lord, a real lord, were to offer to take her in to dinner; she would not be able to swallow one morsel.

She did not hear anything about the parish, Robert's new parish. She remembered that he used to talk a great deal about it before he came here. He had been a model creature—a simple, earnest, hard-working curate—who had been a favourite with the bed-ridden old people of Stoke Lucy.

She had expected to hear a great deal about the schools, and the parish work, and the poor of Coombe Damerel, but they were never mentioned during that first day. There were so many more engrossing topics.

Phyllis was fond of schools, and parish work, and visiting poor people; these things were more in her way than lords and ladies and riding across country on a magnificent coal-black steed. Robert Lyon had made a mistake; men often do make mistakes of this kind when there are two or three girls to choose from. He had married the wrong sister.

He had not found out his mistake yet; he had not repented of his bargain. He was quite as full of those delightful topics as Joan, and, if the truth must be told, there was nothing he liked better than driving through the country roads in that high dogcart with his sleek, well-fed, spirited roan, frightening all the people out of his way. It was much more delightful seeing the little children scuttling out of his path, and the old people standing at their doors making their curtsies as he passed, than plodding through the country lanes on foot and paying formal parochial visits.

He gave his parishioners 'good-day' in the most affable manner, and he nodded in a patronizing, superior way to the children and the old women when they scuttled out of his path. If Joan happened to be driving with him, or whipping her ponies through the village street, she would smile and nod to the people, and say, 'How d'ye do?' in the cheerfullest way in the world. The people could see them, the Rector and his wife, every day of their lives, living—or driving, at least—in their midst, and distributing smiles and 'How d'ye do's?' and if they wanted them they knew where to find them.

What more could they expect?

CHAPTER XIX.

A SWANSEA TEACUP.

The next day being cold, with fitful gusts of sleet and rain, it was not safe for Joan to go out, so Phyllis and the Rector went up to tea with the Countess at Orchard Damerel without her.

Phyllis would much rather have stayed at home; there were so many things she wanted to talk to Joan about, and they would have had a cosy tea together in the study—Robert's study—and spent a lovely evening over that fine needlework.

There were other reasons why she went reluctantly to drink tea with the Countess at the great house.

She was a miserable little coward; she was dreadfully afraid of countesses. She had been picturing all night the unpretending little great house that had once been the home of an earl, a stately castle with a moat, and warders at the gate, and a flag flying from the topmost turret.

The moat was there in the shape of the coombe, which wound round Orchard Damerel and gave the village its name. It was not a dry moat now: a broad, swollen stream flowed through it, winding like a black ribbon through the white, wintry landscape.

'I don't wonder at the poor young man being nearly out of his mind,' Phyllis said, as she walked beside Robert through the beautiful grounds of Orchard Damerel, with the wooded sides of the coombe sloping steeply down beneath them, and the snow-covered hills rising above. 'It was a cruel, unjust thing to mock a man with such a will.'

Joan had told her all about the late Earl's will and its hard conditions, and how the victim of this cruel joke had squandered his small patrimony, and was now a beggar at his own gates, dependent for a night's lodging in his own house on the Countess's hospitality.

Phyllis did not know anything about law, nor the duties of executors. Her soft, tender heart was touched by the hard fate of the penniless heir. She thought the trustees of the late Earl must be very hard-hearted to keep the poor fellow out of his own. She had not any patience with them, or the Countess either. What was the use of being a countess if she could not see justice done? She had heard that story about the services of old silver, and the priceless china that Lady Aylmerton used every day, and the pictures that hung upon the walls, and the treasures locked up in the cabinets, that would sell, if brought to the hammer, for more—far more—than the debts that encumbered the estate; and she fretted and fumed all the way up to the house at the selfishness and injustice of the old woman and the lawyers who were keeping the young man out of his own.

She looked round the great drawing-room with a feeling akin to awe as she sat drinking the Countess's tea. There, around her, were the things that could—that would—pay off that load of debt, and bring the heir back to his own. She found herself mentally appraising the furniture and the bric-à-brac around her, while Cecilia poured out the tea, and Lady Aylmerton talked to Robert. If the truth must be told, she did not think much of them; she could not imagine where the value lay.

All the brightness had gone out of the carpet and the hangings and the embroideries on the chairs. The gilded scrolls of the furniture and the picture-frames were tarnished, and the pictures themselves were old and faded—they were no better than that old likeness of her great-aunt, Joan's namesake, that hung behind the door in Robert's study. She could not understand how such dingy, faded, old-fashioned things could be worth so much money.

Mr. Damerel came in while they were drinking tea, and began talking to Robert; he did not take much notice of Phyllis. He had to be reminded by Cecilia to take her cup and saucer, and to bring her some cake. He took the cup and saucer so awkwardly that he let it fall on the way, and smashed the delicate china cup to atoms. He had a right to smash it; it was his own china; but the Countess made a fuss about it, and Cecilia went on her knees on the floor and picked up the pieces.

It was a Swansea cup, the Countess explained; it belonged to a set that had been made expressly for the Earl sixty years ago. It was unique of its kind, and had been painted by a great flower-painter, celebrated for his roses, every piece with a different rose, and now there would be a rose missing.

Hugh Damerel listened with a half-cynical smile on his face while the Countess told the tale of the Swansea tea-set.

'This is the first time I have exercised my rights in this house,' he said, sitting down beside Phyllis. 'I have to thank you for giving me the opportunity.'

Phyllis did not think he had much to be thankful for; he had broken one of the priceless family heirlooms.

'Oh, a cup more or less doesn't matter,' he said; 'there are services of every kind of china under the sun in this house. They dine off a different one every day, I believe; I have heard that they used to in the Earl's time. If people go on collecting things for generations, there must be a pretty big accumulation some day. I should like to show you the inventory of this place.'

He was always talking about his place and his property, that were no more his than they were Phyllis's.

She was very sorry for him. She was dreadfully afraid that he would get up and begin to tear about the room, as he had the day before at the Rectory, and then there was no saying what valuable things he would be knocking over. He would be exercising his rights with a vengeance.

'Who is that woman over there in the picture?' she asked, to distract his attention. 'Is it an ancestress of yours?'

She was sitting on the couch where Robert had sat on the occasion of his first visit, and the portrait was that of the beautiful Countess, wife of the eighth Earl, painted by Gainsborough, that he had stared at with open mouth and wondering eyes. Phyllis knew no more than her brother-in-law about pictures, and the beauty of women did not touch her as it touched him. The picture had attracted her, she could not say why. The woman, so long dead, had seemed to greet her when she came into the room, and the soft eyes and the sweet lips were smiling upon her, as she sat talking to the Earl of Aylmerton's penniless heir.

'That woman?' he said, nodding gloomily over in the direction of the picture, 'she is no ancestress of mine. I am a stranger here—a stranger and a pauper—I have no right in this house. I am only here on sufferance.'

Why would he be always harping upon his wrongs? He tired himself out, and he tired everybody else out.

'I thought she might be a relation,' Phyllis said hastily; 'I thought I saw a likeness. Her hair is exactly like yours, and there is a likeness in the eyes——'

She stopped and blushed divinely. What right had she to be taking notes of young men's eyes and hair? She had not the excuse that Hugh Damerel had when he was studying the curve of her cheek, and the pensive droop of her eyelids on the way from church. An artist must take note of these things—it is his trade.

'She is no relation of mine,' he said, with a smile. He was taking a mental note of the rosy red that was suffusing Phyllis's downcast face, and wondering what colours on his palette would reproduce it.

Coming out of the great house in the winter dusk, Phyllis drew her cloak closely around her; it was not a very warm cloak, and it was rather shabby for a countess's guest. She shivered in spite of herself as she came out into the cold, damp air; the blank gloom of the place seemed to have fallen upon her, and she did not brighten up until they were outside the park gates.

The dusk had closed in while they had been sitting there, and they walked back in the twilight through the gray park, with the mists rising up from the dark waters of the coombe below, and the sombre shadows of the hills closing in around them.

'How angry the Countess was when Mr. Damerel broke the Swansea teacup,' Phyllis said to her brother-in-law when they had got outside. 'It was his own china; he had a perfect right to break it.'

'By Jove!' said the Rector, with unusual warmth, 'I wish he had smashed the lot!'

'Oh, Robert! and it's worth no end of money! The girl who picked up the bits told me that it was worth five guineas a cup and saucer. Think of that! The cup he broke was worth as much as a whole set of other china.'

'Still, I wish he had broken the lot.'

'Why do you wish it? It would be wanton destruction.'

'I think a little wanton destruction would be the best thing that could happen in that house. It might bring things to a crisis. Mr. Damerel would have a chance of asserting his rights, and the trustees would have to defend their position.'

'You think they take too much upon themselves, Robert?'

'I am not a lawyer, my dear, and I know nothing about the Earl of Aylmerton's extraordinary will but what I have heard from Damerel. Still, I think the trustees are afraid of him. I fancy that if he once got possession of the place they couldn't turn him out——'

'And that if he smashed the tea-things he would only be exercising his rights?' Phyllis said eagerly. She was thinking of what Hugh Damerel had said when he sat down beside her.

'Exactly.'

'Did you notice that picture, Robert?' she asked presently, breaking in upon the Rector's meditation. He had been wondering what the Earl's trustees would do if the heir should break all the beautiful old china in the place, and destroy the pictures, and tear up all those valuable Bartolozzi engravings, what action they could take in the matter. A man has a right to do what he will with his own.

'What picture?' he asked absently; 'there are so many pictures in the room and on the staircase—the house is full of pictures.' He was still thinking, if Mr. Damerel were such a Vandal as to take a brush and paint all these pictures out, what action the trustees could bring against him. They were all his—his very own—he was only waiting the fulfilment of a certain condition to be put in formal possession of them. It was a ridiculous idea.

'The portrait of the lady in the blue dress, between the windows, opposite to where I was sitting.'

Robert remembered the picture well.

'Yes,' he said, 'I know the picture.' It gave him quite a pang to think of the lovely face being 'painted out.' 'What did you see in it remarkable?'

'I thought it so like Mr. Damerel; the hair and eyes are exactly like his. I thought it must be the portrait of one of his ancestors; but he tells me that he does not belong to the family, that the beautiful Countess was no relation of his.'

'He belongs to a very distant branch of the Damerels; he was not related in any way to the late Earl, so I don't see how he could be a descendant of the beautiful Countess. It was quite an accident the Earl leaving the property to him, the mere accident of his bearing an old family name—Hugh. There was a Sir Hugh Damerel once, whose portrait hangs in the hall; probably he is one of his descendants.'

Phyllis's cheeks were glowing, and her eyes were shining, when she came into the warm lighted 'study' where Joan was sitting busy over that fine cambric work.

The cold, keen air had brought the colour into her cheeks, and the remembrance of that little scene in the Countess's drawing-room had brightened her eyes.

'Oh, Joan!' she exclaimed, 'Mr. Damerel has begun to exercise his rights. He has begun to break up the family china!'

CHAPTER XX.

LADY AYLMERTON'S OFFER.

The Countess of Aylmerton had not sent for Hugh Damerel only to eat his Christmas dinner off his own silver dishes and beneath his own roof; she had another reason for sending for him.

Mr. Greatorex, the Earl's trustee, had written her several letters since his return to London. The letters were not connected with the business of the estate. They were of a private nature; they related to the Countess's niece. Mr. Greatorex had remonstrated with her ladyship on the disposition of her money, and he had pointed out to her the duty of providing in some measure for poor Cecilia's future.

The Countess had listened to his remonstrance, and she had gone so far as to promise she would do what she could for Cecilia's welfare.

With this promise in her mind her ladyship had sent for Hugh Damerel.

She did not speak to him on the subject that was weighing upon her heart until the third day of his visit. She sent for him on the morning of the third day, and Wilkins, her ladyship's maid, ushered him into the little upstair room that was known as 'my lady's boudoir.'

It was the same room that the Rector had been shown into on the occasion of that interview on the subject of the coming election.

Hugh Damerel had only been in that room once or twice during all the years that he had gone backwards and forwards to Orchard Damerel.

He looked round it with a strange mixed feeling of awe and wonder when Wilkins had shut the door upon him and left him in her ladyship's presence.

His eyes travelled over the beautiful appointments of the lovely old room, the Chippendale furniture, the pictures on the walls, the faded embroideries, the priceless old china, to the Countess herself, sitting in an armchair by the fireplace.

He had never remarked before how coarse and commonplace she looked, what an incongruous figure she seemed amid these surroundings.

Her ladyship was wearing a plaid shawl over her shoulders, as the air of the room was chilly, and a lace cap with bows of ribbon. It was not such a dignified cap as the blonde affair she wore at dinner, and the dingy old plaid shawl was not so becoming as the gray satin. She did not look the least like a countess. Hugh Damerel could not think, as he looked at her sitting there, what had made the Earl marry her. She had never been a handsome woman, and she was undeniably vulgar.

He took the seat Lady Damerel motioned him to on the other side of the fireplace, and his eyes wandered round the room while she was speaking to him. He could not keep his eyes from wandering. All this was his, he told himself with a strange feeling of awe, his—his very own; it had been his for seven years, and he had hardly seen it until now. Some of the things he saw now for the first time; his former visits had been so hasty that he had not been able to take in half the contents of the room. There was a case of miniatures over the mantelpiece that was quite new to him. He knew most of the portraits and miniatures in the house, but these were quite new to him.

There were three miniatures framed in one case, and all of them were the heads of children, two little girls of different ages, and a boy.

While Hugh Damerel looked up at the sweet, fair faces of the children of the house, the children of long ago, whose little footsteps had pattered over the floors, whose merry laughter had awoke the echoes of the silent corridors and the deserted rooms, the Countess told him why she had sent for him.

'Mr. Greatorex has written to me about Cecilia,' she began. She did not know how to begin, and she plunged into the subject in a hurried, nervous way. 'He thinks some provision ought to be made for Cecilia.'

Hugh Damerel had not much interest in her ladyship's niece, but he bowed a polite assent.

'Certainly,' he said absently, 'certainly; it would never do to leave Miss Burrough unprovided for.'

'She has no claim upon me to provide for her. I have done my duty by her for years. She has had a good home here, and every luxury; she has no right to expect any more,' her ladyship said, as if defending herself. 'She has had advantages that few girls have had.'

Mr. Damerel bowed. He did not think it was worth her ladyship's while to send for him to discuss this question.

'I am willing to do what I can for Cecilia; she is my own, she is nearer to me than the rest. She is a pious, good girl; she has read more Christian literature than most girls of her age, and in the event of—of her marrying, I would do what I could for her.'

Again Mr. Damerel bowed. He could not think what the old woman meant. He was wondering who those little people were over the mantelpiece, who were looking down upon him with their arch smiles and their sweet fresh faces.

'I had arranged to leave what little I have to leave for a cause that is very near my heart,' her ladyship went on, growing more and more nervous and confused; 'but if Cecilia married as I would wish to see her married, I would put my own inclination aside, and leave what little I have to leave to her. It would be enough to keep her in comfort, to enable her to live quietly, as I have lived, and to keep up the same style. The carriages and the horses are mine, and—and I dare say—I am sure—an arrangement could be made with the trustees for her to live in this house. It would not cost much to keep up.'

Hugh Damerel opened his eyes. He could not think what she was driving at. He did not quite see, if he could not be suffered to live at Orchard Damerel, why this permission should be accorded to her ladyship's niece.

'She would not be a very good match, perhaps, but it would be in the family; and I could promise the use of the house—and the gardens—the produce is sold now to pay the wages, but that might be arranged; and I would leave Cecilia enough to keep it up, and the carriages and the horses.'

Hugh Damerel could not tell for the life of him what the old woman meant.

'What do you think?' she said, turning to him sharply, seeing that he did not speak.

'I—I am afraid I am no judge. I should think it would be rather dull for Miss Burrough living here alone.'

'Who talked of her living here alone? If she were to live here alone, she would never touch a penny of my money,' her ladyship interrupted sharply. 'I have my duty to my husband to consider. Whatever I have been able to put aside I owe to the Earl's bounty. I would sacrifice my own wishes, and leave it as he would have it left, if—if Cecilia's future could be provided for. It is a sacrifice—I own it is a sacrifice on my part—but I am willing to make it, if you and Cecilia are willing.'

Hugh Damerel's heart began to beat, and he felt himself turning sick.

'I'm afraid I do not catch your ladyship's meaning,' he said stiffly.

'Oh yes, you do,' she said impatiently. 'You know quite well what I mean. When I die, you and Cecilia will both have to turn out. Cecilia will go back to her own people, and you—there will be no home here for you—you will be no more here than a stranger. You could not keep up the place if it were yours to-morrow.'

'No,' he said bitterly; 'I could not keep it up a single day.'

'If you marry my niece—if you marry Cecilia—you will be able to keep it up; and I will arrange with the trustees that you shall have the place for your life.'

Hugh Damerel flushed crimson. He blushed as if with shame to his finger-tips.

'I think there must be some mistake,' he said, interrupting her. 'I—I have no intention of marrying Miss Burrough. Your ladyship does me too much honour.'

'Wait,' she said eagerly, 'wait; hear what I have to say before you speak.'

'I don't think I had better hear what your ladyship has to say,' he said, getting up from his seat by the fire, and feeling dreadfully hot and uncomfortable. 'Nothing that you could say would influence me—in—in this matter. It would be better for your niece's sake and my own that it should be left unsaid.'

The Countess stopped him with an impatient gesture.

'Sit down,' she said, 'sit down; don't decide in a hurry. You will regret it; you will have cause to regret it all your life if you refuse this offer.'

Hugh Damerel sat down rather ungraciously. He would have given anything to be on the other side of that closed door.

'It is not the little that I can give Cecilia,' Lady Aylmerton went on, speaking in an agitated voice, 'there is something else. You must remember that in telling you this, in making this sacrifice, it is not altogether for Cecilia's sake, nor is it for your sake. It is for the sake of the late Earl's memory. The encumbrance on the estate hung like a chain about his neck; it galled him more than it has ever galled you. He was ill advised. He wanted money, and he let others raise it for him, and he didn't trouble himself at what cost. Those who advised him are dead and gone. The ill-gotten gains never benefited them; it brought loss and dishonour with it, and they have gone to their reward.'

Hugh Damerel could not but be sorry for the old woman's agitation; he had never seen her so moved before, not even at the reading of the late Earl's will. He remembered, as he saw her mopping the damp off her red, coarse face, that it was her father who had been the Earl's adviser.

'It may not, even now, be too late to remedy the wrong that was done—to make some atonement. There is a way—I cannot tell you how—I cannot explain. If you marry Cecilia, the way will be made clear—*the papers are in her father's hands.*'

She had sunk her voice to a mysterious whisper, and all the colour had gone out of her face, and her lips were trembling.

'Good heavens!' Hugh Damerel exclaimed, jumping up and flushing darkly, 'do you mean to say, Lady Aylmerton, that there has been fraud as well as usury?'

'I do not mean to say anything of the kind. I only

mean that if you married Cecilia, you would be likely to come into possession of the place earlier than if you married anyone else. God forbid that I should say there had been fraud—there has been mistaken counsel, but not fraud—oh no, not fraud!'

Her lips were white and trembling, and great beads of perspiration were on her forehead, and she could not meet the scorn and disdain that were blazing in Hugh Damerel's eyes as he stood before her.

'There has been fraud somewhere, Lady Aylmerton,' he said bitterly, 'fraud and usury, and—and you have done me the honour to send for me to propose that I shall condone it by marrying your niece——'

'You mistake my meaning; I said nothing about fraud,' she interrupted eagerly.

'You have said quite enough to convince me of what I have suspected all along, that the Earl was not only ill advised, but that he was entrapped by usurers—and that those who advised him and entrapped him were members of your ladyship's own family.'

'You are mistaken; you are altogether mistaken!' she moaned, wringing her hands. 'Oh, why will you mistake my words?'

'I beg your pardon if I have mistaken them, Lady Aylmerton,' he said coldly, with the scorn and fury in his eyes blazing down upon her. 'I understood you to say that if I availed myself of the privilege of forming an alliance with a member of your ladyship's honourable family, a way would be opened to me for entering into possession of my own estates. It is plain that the way could only be opened by fraud, or that it is kept closed by fraud.'

The old woman sitting by the fireplace cowered in her chair before the passion in his voice and eyes.

'You are mistaken, Hugh—Mr. Damerel,' she moaned; 'you have twisted and distorted my words. I only meant to help you—you and Cecilia—for—for my husband the Earl's sake I would have helped you—and I thought, being in the family, it might be arranged—and now you turn upon me, and charge my family with fraud!'

The Countess had broken down, and she was weeping

now like any commonplace person. An old woman weeping is always a very sad picture. The close of life should be calm and placid, untroubled by storms.

It touched Hugh Damerel to see her weeping there. She had done him no wrong. What she had said she had said in kindness, and to help him to his own.

Looking down at the trembling old woman weeping among all her grandeur, he was ashamed of himself for the scorn and passion he had heaped on her poor old bowed head.

'I beg your pardon, Lady Aylmerton,' he said humbly. 'I am sure what you have said, you have said in kindness. I am sorry I cannot accept your help on—on the conditions you name. I am not a marrying man—I shall never marry until I come into my own—I shall never ask a wife to share my poverty and my wandering life. Forgive me if I have spoken harshly.'

He pressed the hand that lay nerveless on her lap; he was astonished to find how damp and tremulous it was. He could not have believed that an old woman could have been so moved.

He went out of the room and left her weeping there, and in the gallery outside he met Cecilia.

'Does the Countess want me—is she ill?' she asked anxiously. Something in his face had struck her.

'No,' he said, speaking with difficulty; 'no, she is not ill, and—and I don't think she wants anyone at present.'

He was dreadfully humiliated and ashamed; the sight of poor Cecilia covered him with confusion.

CHAPTER XXI.

MR. GREATOREX'S LETTER.

Hugh Damerel went back to town the same day. He did not wait to come over to the Rectory to say good-bye before he went. The lumbering old yellow chariot drove him to the railway-station. Phyllis caught sight of it as it passed the Rectory gate, and she stood aside by the hedge to let it pass. She thought the Countess and her niece were inside, and she could not think why they were tearing along at such a rate.

The carriage drew up abruptly, and someone jumped out. It was not the Countess. It was the Earl of Aylmerton's heir who was driving away from his own house as fast as a pair of well-fed horses could carry him, and he was not likely soon to come back again.

Phyllis had been dreaming about the young man all night—she had been helping him to break up the china—and she blushed scarlet like a poppy when he stood in the road beside her.

'I am going away,' he said hurriedly; 'I am going away for a long time—perhaps I shall never come back—and I should like to have said good-bye to your sister and Mr. Lyon.'

'Can't you come in now?' Phyllis said eagerly, 'they are both at home; they will be so sorry if you go away without seeing them.'

'I have no time, or I would. I shall only just catch the train. I could not go away and see you here without thanking you for the good omen of yesterday.'

'Have you been breaking any more china?' Phyllis asked, turning quite pale at the thought.

Hugh Damerel laughed.

'If you had been there to help me, I would have finished the Swansea set. I could not do it without you. The charm would have been gone. I shall always remember that you helped me to assert my rights.'

He shook hands with her and jumped into the carriage, and in a few moments it was out of sight.

Phyllis went back slowly to the house. She had never been so sorry for anyone in her life as she was for this stranger, who was being driven away from his own place in that big lumbering yellow coach, and who might never, never come back.

Lady Aylmerton was angry with Cecilia for a whole week. She made her read Dr. Cumming's excellent sermons aloud to her an extra hour every afternoon, by way of penance, and she never once let her during that time—she had the excuse of the weather being bad—walk over to the Rectory to inquire for Joan.

Cecilia read the familiar sermons without a murmur. She hated the prophetic preacher in her heart, but she read his beautiful discourses hour by hour without murmuring. She used to read her ladyship to sleep of afternoons, and when she had quite gone off she closed the book. Lady Aylmerton did not 'go off' once during the week after Hugh Damerel's visit; when poor Cecilia, dropping her voice lower and lower at every page, ventured at last to stop altogether, her ladyship would wake up with a start and desire her to go on. She had not a minute's rest all that miserable week.

To make matters worse, Mr. Greatorex wrote again before the week was over, to ask what provision her ladyship had decided to make for her niece.

The Countess wrote back by return, not exactly telling the Earl's trustee to mind his own business, but telling him pretty plainly that his interference on Cecilia's behalf had not done Cecilia any good, that the project she had in her mind for advancing her niece's interest had fallen through, and that she was not prepared to do anything further. Cecilia had had a good home for years; she would have a home at Orchard Damerel so long as the Countess lived, and when the time came that it would be her home no longer, she would return to her own people. Her ladyship had done a great deal for her family, her nephews and nieces, and she had done more for Cecilia than for any of them.

She did not tell her niece anything about this correspondence with her trustee, nor did she allow her to read her letters.

It was a part of Cecilia's duties to open and read aloud her ladyship's letters, and to answer them from her dictation. This correspondence with the late Earl's trustee was an exception to the rule; the letters were laid aside by Cecilia unread, and the Countess replied to them in her own shaky handwriting.

Cecilia opened the post-bag and took out her ladyship's letters of mornings. There were not many to take out. Very few people wrote to the Countess now; those who knew her in the Earl's lifetime had forgotten her: it is astonishing how soon one is forgotten. The bag seldom contained anything but printed circulars and begging letters.

It contained something else one fine morning early in the new year. The snow had all melted, and the year had opened with blue skies and sunshine, and the glad singing of birds. They had been silent all through the snow—silent and sad—and many had died. There was quite a fringe of thrushes lying dead and crumpled up beneath the great trees in the avenue in the park, when the snow cleared. It had not all cleared yet, though a south wind was blowing, and the sun was shining.

Deep down in the coombe the snow lay white and deep, and the black oaks stood out stark and straight against the white background. The black line of firs on the ridge of the distant hills was outlined sharp and clear against the blue of the sky, and the rooks were cawing as they flew over the park. They had been silent for weeks—silent and glum and shrivelled up on their bare tree tops; but they were cawing to-day, and going about their business. Whatever their business was, they were making a great deal of fuss about it—fuss and mystery. Perhaps they were already thinking of building.

Cecilia watched them from the breakfast-room window, as she waited on that bright January morning for the Countess to come down. Her ladyship always came down to breakfast; she generally came down in that old plaid woollen shawl, and sometimes she came down late. However late she came, Cecilia waited for her. She was waiting now, as she stood at the window looking over the park, and watching the sunlit clouds sailing by, and listening to the cawing of the rooks.

There was something different in the cawing of the rooks to-day, she remarked, and in the song of the lark—there was one going up just outside the window—and the wood-pigeons were cooing, cooing, cooing, as she had never heard them coo before. Cecilia did not notice many things; she did not care a fig for birds and trees and the clouds sailing by; but she looked at these things to-day, and listened to the tender cooing of the wood-pigeons with a new interest.

She was so busy watching the course of the rooks from

the tree-tops to the distant copse, that she did not hear the Countess come in, until she called to her sharply from the breakfast-table.

Poor Cecilia blushed as if she had been detected in a crime, and she came hurriedly over to the table, and began to pour out the tea.

'You haven't opened the bag,' her ladyship said, rather snappishly. 'What are you thinking of this morning?'

Cecilia left the cup of tea half poured out, and meekly opened the post-bag.

There were quite a dozen circulars addressed to her ladyship, and one letter, only one letter, and that was addressed to her ladyship's niece. Cecilia knew the writing quite well. The sight of it did not stir her pulses the least.

She put the letter beside her plate unopened, and then she filled up the teacup. The tea already in it was cold, but she did not dare to throw it away: her ladyship was very particular about small things.

She drank the lukewarm mixture meekly while the Countess looked through her circulars. She did not read them, she only looked through them indifferently, and then she caught sight of that letter beside Cecilia's plate —at least, she caught sight of the envelope—Cecilia was reading the letter. She had her back to the window, and the big tea-urn was in front of her. Perhaps it was quite as well that the urn was in front of her.

'What letter is that?' the Countess asked across the table.

'A letter—for me—aunt.'

'A letter for you?' Anyone would have thought, from the tone of her ladyship's voice, that her niece had never received a letter before in her life. 'Who is the letter from?' she demanded rather sharply.

'From—from—Mr. Greatorex, aunt.'

'From Mr. Greatorex? What is Mr. Greatorex writing to you about?' her ladyship inquired, with a touch of asperity.

He—he has asked me to marry him, aunt.'

'To marry *him!—him!* Whatever answer shall you give him, child?'

'I shall accept him, aunt.'

The old London lawyer had taken the matter out of her ladyship's hands, and had provided for Cecilia's future himself.

CHAPTER XXII.

A PERFECT TREASURE.

THEY were busy days at the Rectory after Christmas. There were the school-treats, and the tea for the old people, and a supper for the ringers, besides a magic-lantern entertainment in the schoolroom, to which everybody in the village was invited.

Joan's cold kept her indoors through all that busy time, but Phyllis was able to help a good deal. She was in her element among Sunday-school children and old women. Before the end of the week—she had to go away to set Bertha free before the end of the week—everybody in the village said the Rector had made a mistake; he had married the wrong sister. A parson's wife coming in and out among them, and entering into all their homely cares, was more what they wanted than a lady galloping through the village on a coal-black steed, or driving a perfectly matching pair of ponies, and scattering the little children and the old women out of her way.

Though Phyllis had to leave Coombe Damerel before the Christmas festivities were over, the Rector was not left singlehanded. He had an invaluable helper in the new schoolmistress.

Matilda Bray was a pattern schoolmistress—she was a pattern young woman altogether. The Rector was always telling himself how lucky he had been to get her. She had come to him with the best testimonials; she had yards and yards of parchments all testifying to her admirable qualities. The school-inspector had signed them after every inspection of her pupils, and he had expressed on each occasion his satisfaction at the high standard of order and excellence that the school she presided over had attained.

It was fortunate for the parish that the Rector had

made such a happy choice. He had received quite a dozen applications for the post, and he had chosen the best.

At this Christmas season, when there was so much to be done, and Joan was shut up at home, Matilda Bray was invaluable. Robert could not have got on a single day without her. Cecilia was kept a close prisoner at Orchard Damerel, and the schoolmaster had gone away for a holiday. He had gone to spend his Christmas with Miss Bailey. Poor Miss Bailey had had a relapse—the disappointment may have had something to do with it—at any rate, the poor thing was laid up again, and there seemed little chance of her rallying before the spring. It was very lucky, the Rector told himself, she had not been laid up there. He would have had to provide a nurse and a doctor for her, and someone to look after the school.

Phyllis had to go back to Stoke Lucy before the school-treat, and as the doctor would not hear of Joan leaving the house, the new schoolmistress had to manage the whole thing herself. Robert was perfectly useless, except to say grace and pay the bills.

There was a Christmas-tree for the children, the articles for which were provided by the Countess. She still liked to do something for the parish; she had been accustomed to do a good deal in the Earl's lifetime. She could not do a great deal now, but she kept Wilkins her maid and Cecilia employed for months before Christmas, making flannel petticoats for the women, and dressing dolls for the children, and these gifts were distributed on the evening of the school-treat. The flannel petticoats were tied up in bundles, and the dolls were hung on the tree, and the tying up and the hanging on were done by Matilda Bray. Who ever heard of a man trimming a Christmas-tree?

But her work did not stop here. She cut up the cake—she made it go twice as far as Mary Bailey had made the same quantity go the year before; she poured out the tea—she observed the same economy in sugar; and she kept the children in order.

She kept them as still as little mice; they would not

have dared to ask for another slice of cake, with Matilda's eye upon them, for the world, and they drank their unsweetened tea without a murmur.

When the festivities were all over, there were half a dozen dolls still left hanging on the tree, and one old woman had not turned up to claim her flannel petticoat. Matilda made these articles into a neat little bundle, and sent them up with a polite note to Orchard Damerel, and begged her ladyship to put them aside for another year.

If the Rector had searched the kingdom over, he could not have met with a more careful or conscientious young woman. She refused to take a well-earned holiday at Christmas, in order to work up the children for the examination. The inspector had not come down in the autumn as he was expected to have come; he had put off his visit to Coombe Damerel till the spring. It was well that he had put it off; it would give the school a chance.

The school had been shamefully neglected during the late schoolmistress's illness and absence; the children were dreadfully backward; it would have been quite hopeless to present them for examination in the autumn if the inspector had come; but with the winter before them, a winter of hard work, they would be better prepared in the spring.

Matilda Bray spent her brief holiday in working up the elder girls for the inspector's visit. She had them in her own little house in twos and threes, and spent every hour of her holiday upon them. The boys were not so well off—perhaps they were better off—the schoolmaster was away comforting Mary Bailey, and the boys were throwing snowballs in the lanes, and breaking down the farmers' hedges.

Robert Lyon had other things to think of in those opening days of the new year, besides the village treats and the school examinations. His Christmas bills had come in, and he had added them up. It required a great deal of moral courage to add them up. It would have been much easier to have stuck them on the file and hung them up somewhere out of the way, and forgotten all about them—easier and pleasanter.

The totting up of that simple addition sum, if it did not exactly make Robert Lyon's knees quake beneath him, certainly took away his breath. He had no idea that he owed so much money. If he paid all these bills he would have nothing left, and there would be no money coming in for another six months.

He added those wretched bills up over again to make sure that there was no mistake. He could not understand how he could have got through so much money in such a short time. There was the coming in, and the furnishing, and the carriages and horses, and the saddler's bill, and all those stable requisites, the wages of the men and women servants, and the housekeeping. He could not think of anything else. He had not spent anything on the church or schools, and the charities in the village had not amounted to anything to speak of.

There was one item he had forgotten, but he did not forget it long. The groom sent in the stable-book that afternoon, and then Robert found out something of what the stable cost him—was costing him—every day.

He had left that quite out of his calculations when he made those little fanciful tables of expenditure in the early days of his settling here. He and Joan had amused themselves in those happy, careless days with making these fanciful tables; they were not only going to live within their income, but they were going to put by a great deal of it towards a rainy day. They were going to live like Cock Robin and Jenny Wren, and feast off currant wine; and, as Joan had observed on the occasion of her first visit to the Rectory garden, when she felt the hard green hearts of the cabbages, the servants were going to live entirely on vegetables.

The butcher's book had mounted up, nevertheless. It was quite astonishing how those items in the butcher's book had mounted up. When Robert remembered the solitary chop that used to figure so frequently as the *pièce de résistance* of his bachelor board, he looked with wonder, not unmixed with dismay, at the long, long list of legs of mutton that confronted him on the greasy pages of that butcher's book.

How his appetite must have grown! Unfortunately, it was not his appetite only that had increased to such abnormal dimensions.

Those four idle, useless animals out in the stables were positively voracious. The sight of the groom's book with the stable accounts made the silly fellow's hair stand on end. When he had bought those horses, it had never entered into his head what it would cost him to feed them. There was some hay on the place, and the grass in the orchard; but the hay had not lasted a month, and no one could ride grass-fed horses—at least, so his groom had told him.

If he paid the stable bills, and the housekeeping bills, and the other odds and ends that came in so unexpectedly at Christmas, he would not have any money left to carry him on till June. There was nothing to be done but to retrench. He had made a mistake—he had begun too expensively, but it was not too late to retrench. He would sell that Black Beauty of Joan's; she would have no use for it for months and months, and it would do no good shut up in the stable. It ought to fetch a big sum, at least a hundred or a hundred and fifty pounds. It would be dirt cheap, Lord George had said, at two hundred.

He spoke to Joan about it the same day. He did not tell her that he had been adding up the butcher's book, or that if he paid all those bills that had come in he would not have a penny left.

The doctor had given directions that Joan was not to be worried; it was just now most important that she should be kept quiet. Robert would not for the world have given her a cause for uneasiness.

'I have been thinking about that horse in the stable, dear,' he said at dinner, approaching the subject over a leg of mutton he was carving.

Joan was a young housekeeper; she had not the benefit of experience, and she did not introduce much variety in the choice of her joints. She rang the changes between roast leg of mutton and boiled leg of mutton, and when Robert remonstrated, she ordered a leg of beef by way of variety.

It was a boiled leg of mutton to-day, and it was rather under-dressed. Joan's appetite was fanciful, and she sniffed at it with evident distaste, and pushed her plate aside untouched, and Robert had the great steaming joint to himself.

'Well,' Joan said fretfully—she hated being treated as an invalid, and she hated having no appetite for her dinner—'well, what about Beauty? Are you going to ride him?'

'He is not heavy enough for me,' Robert said evasively. 'He is too good for these rough country roads. I wouldn't ride him on any account this frosty weather. I should be afraid every step he would come down, and I should knock fifty or a hundred pounds out of him.'

Joan laughed.

'I wish Paget would let me ride him,' she said, with some animation. 'I'd run the risk of his coming down. He wouldn't be likely to come down. Lord George said he was as firm as a rock.'

'I thought his knees were a little weak,' Robert answered behind the joint. 'He tripped with me once or twice coming downhill the other day, when I rode him out. Perhaps it was for want of exercise; he has been shut up in the stable doing nothing for more than a month.'

'Of course it is for want of exercise. Bennett does not take him out enough. Lord George said we were to be very careful with him. He had been used to a first-rate groom. The poor thing couldn't help going back with only Bennett to look after him. I'm sure, if you want the horses to live through the winter, you ought to keep another groom, a man used to hunters.'

Robert shivered, and laid down his knife and fork. He had no more appetite for that boiled mutton than Joan.

'I think the better way would be to sell him,' he said, with a little cough.

'Sell him! What are you thinking of, Robin?'

Then Robert had to explain to his wife that it was not likely that she would ride Black Beauty for some months to come, and that meanwhile he would not be improving under Bennett's care in the Rectory stables. He said nothing about his eating his head off.

Joan pouted, and declined to swallow another morsel of her favourite sweet pudding.

'I thought Beauty was a present,' she said, with an injured air, 'and that he was my own, my very own; and you talk of selling him!'

'I thought it would be a great pity for him to stay in the stable all the winter with no one to ride him,' Robert said humbly.

'You should have thought of that when you gave him to me. You couldn't expect me to be tearing about the country on his back every day; if you did you should have said so at the time, and I wouldn't have let you buy him.'

Joan was getting quite excited; her cheeks were scarlet, and her lips were quivering, and there were tears in her eyes.

'I only suggested it for his good,' Robert said guiltily. 'I thought it would be a pity to run the risk of ruining such a splendid animal by keeping it in the stable all the winter—and spring.'

'You may as well say summer, too, Robert, and autumn, while you are about it. You may as well say what you think—if—if—you don't think I am ever likely to ride him again, you should say so. It would be better to say so, than to pretend that you think his legs are giving way. I—I sometimes think, myself, I shall—never—never—ride him again——'

Joan was getting hysterical. Her eyes had brimmed over, and she was sobbing behind that plate of sweet pudding at the other end of the table.

Robert jumped up to comfort her.

'My darling! my darling!' he murmured, feeling dreadfully guilty and ashamed.

Joan took a great deal of comforting.

After that there could be no more talk of selling Black Beauty.

CHAPTER XXIII.

THE WIDOW AND THE FATHERLESS.

THERE could be no more talk at present, with Joan in this weak, hysterical state, about selling her favourite horse. It would have gone on eating its head off in the Rectory stable until it sickened of that unappetising meal if something had not happened to make Joan change her mind.

Phyllis had gone back home, after that brief Christmas visit to the Rectory, full of the wonders she had seen there.

She did nothing but talk about Joan's beautiful house and its big rooms—some of them as big as a church—when she got back. Perhaps it was the narrowness and meanness of their own small surroundings that made the Rectory seem bigger by contrast. She sat up all the first night after her return—at least, she lay awake—telling Bertha about the great house, and the lovely new furniture, and the horses and carriages. The stables were full of horses, and there was a hunter, a noble creature, as black and shiny as a coal—Phyllis was very exact in her description—kept entirely for their fortunate sister's use.

There were other things besides the appointments of the house and the stable that kept Phyllis awake. She had looked through the card-basket on the Rectory table, and she had reckoned up Joan's new friends. There were dozens of country clergy among them, and the Bishop of the diocese, and the Bishop's wife and daughters, a viscountess, and several honourables, a lord and a lady, the wife of the member for the county, to say nothing of the real Countess, dear Lady Aylmerton, whose house was always open to them, and who was so friendly and affectionate in her inquiries for Joan.

Bertha lay awake long after Phyllis had fallen asleep thinking over Joan's good-fortune. She could not understand—people never can understand these things—why this good-fortune should have come to Joan, and the hard work, the poverty, the slights, and the drudgery should have fallen to her share.

It did not occur to her, as she lay awake staring blankly out of the uncurtained window at the faint gray streak of the low wintry dawn, that perhaps the discipline was best suited to her—best suited to each—the discipline of happiness and prosperity, the discipline of loss and failure.

Bertha was getting rather impatient of the discipline, however good it might be for her; she was chafing under it. She would go back to-morrow to her uncongenial tasks, to the little troublesome boys, and the upper room, and the loneliness that nearly drove her mad. Her brief holiday was over; she would go away on the morrow and not catch a glimpse of the dear faces, or hear the sound of the dear voices—she never knew how dear they were till now—not for months and months. It was too dreadful to think of; she was grateful that the darkness and the bed-clothes covered her up, and that she could weep out her discontent unnoticed on the sympathetic pillow.

While she was weeping there, comparing Joan's good-fortune with her own hard lot, her costly establishment and luxurious fare with the pinching and paring of this poor household, she made up her mind to write to Joan and tell her something of the poverty and shifts that had been kept so carefully from her.

She talked it over with Phyllis and her mother before she went away the next day; but Mrs. Penrose would not hear of it. The utmost she would consent to do was to write to Robert, she would not write to Joan; she would write direct to Robert, and ask him for the loan of fifty pounds towards the boys' education.

Chris was going up to Cambridge in the spring to try for a scholarship, and he could not go without help; a little help on the threshold meant a great deal for Chris. It means a great deal for most boys. It is just the difference between success and failure. Help is not much good when the success is assured, when the failure is complete.

Mrs. Penrose promised Bertha, when she clung to her

in the anguish of that sad parting, that she would write to Robert. Bertha would not leave her until she had promised to write that very day.

She was as good as her word. She wrote to her son-in-law by the next post and asked him for the loan of fifty pounds.

She explained to him, with a certain amount of dignity, her reasons for asking this loan. She was no common suppliant asking for the needful crust. Chris was going up to Cambridge for a scholarship. He was encouraged by every hope of success to go—he was in the sixth form of his school; he had carried off the form prizes at the last examination. With a little help now, at the opening of his career, he would do well—he would do very well; why should he not do very well, like other boys? He had the ability, why should he not go in and win some of those great prizes that the University dangles every year before the bright eyes of her youthful scholars?

So Chrysostom's mother wrote; she believed in her boy as only a mother can believe in a boy, and she was ready to cringe and humiliate herself in the dust for his sake, when she would have starved rather than ask a favour for her own.

It is the way of mothers. Let us thank God humbly that they are made of that soft, weak, tender stuff, and not made of any sterner material.

Robert came into the room where his wife was working, with the letter from his mother-in-law in his hand, after breakfast. Joan was not always down to breakfast these chill wintry mornings. She used to have her breakfast carried upstairs, and she came down when the rooms were warmed and aired.

She had just come down, and she had got that little work-table over by the fire, and she was holding a little scrap of cambric up to the light. Robert used to compare her to a little nesting-bird in these days—he seldom came across her but she was carrying a scrap of cambric in her hand, and had a work-bag full of tags of tape and cotton on her arm—a happy, anxious bird, collecting the twigs and litter for its little soft, warm nest.

'What have you got there?' Joan asked, when he

came into the room with the letter in his hand. He laid the open letter before her, and stood by her side while she read it. His face was looking grave and troubled, and there was an upright line between his eyebrows. He was wondering how he could spare this money.

'Oh, poor mamma! I didn't know that things were so bad. Of course you will lend her the money, Robin?'

She looked up in his face with her clear eyes; there was no doubt or mistrust in them. He would not have disappointed her for the world.

'Of course,' he said, with an effort to speak cheerfully; but there was a nasty lump in his throat that took all the heartiness out of his words. It was a damp, drizzly morning; perhaps that accounted for it.

'You will send it her at once; you will not lose a post, Robin?'

'I will send it her—to-day,' he answered quite readily, and in as steady a voice as that lump in his throat would allow. 'I—I am sorry for her own sake, and the boys', she has need to ask it. I wish we could do more for the boys, Joan. We must have them down here in the spring, when you are about again.'

'Yes, oh yes; they must come down by-and-by.'

Joan was not thinking about the boys, or, indeed, about her mother and her troubles and cares; she was thinking about that upright line on her husband's face, and that quiver in his voice. She did not often notice such small things, but she noticed them to day. She had been shut up indoors for the last week or two, and perhaps that had made her nervous and fanciful.

When Robert came back with the letter to her mother written, and the cheque drawn for the sum she had asked him to lend her, Joan looked up at him sharply, but his forehead was quite smooth; the upright line was no longer there.

The writing of that letter to the widow in her affliction, the ministering to her need in the shape of that neatly-written cheque, had smoothed the ugly little wrinkle quite out.

'I have been thinking, Rob,' Joan said humbly, while her pretty pink face bent over her work, 'of what you said the other day about Black Beauty. I am sure he will be ruined if he stays in the stable doing nothing for —for another year, perhaps. I wish you could do something with him. I wish you could sell him.'

Robert wrote off to Tattersall's the same night, and asked what their terms would be for selling a capital hunter that he had no further use for, and if they could include it in an early sale.

He received a reply to his letter by return. The same post brought his mother-in-law's acknowledgment of the cheque, and Messrs. Tattersall's courteous and business-like answer to his inquiries. He took it quite as a good omen, the two letters coming together; the one with a widow's blessing and thanks, the other making a way clear out of his difficulties.

He quite believed in the old promise; he had seen it fulfilled in a hundred ways: perhaps he was superstitious, but that touching letter of the poor, thankful widow seemed like a benediction.

It was quite a simple thing to get rid of that useless horse, which had been a thorn in his side all the winter. The cost would not be very great in any case; there would be the carriage of the horse up to town, the charge for a loose-box until the day of the sale, and the commission for selling. It was quite easy. He had only to write to Messrs. Tattersall to send a groom to meet Black Beauty at the London terminus on a certain day, and to fix a reserve price, and the thing was done.

The horse could be included in the next sale; it could be sent off at once. Robert was afraid that his wife would change her mind at the last moment, and refuse to let her favourite go; but Joan was more anxious now than her husband that the horse should be sold; she would not have kept it back for the world.

His mistrust showed how little he knew about his wife.

Perhaps he was not singular. How little, how very, very little, the wisest of men know about women! Uncertain, coy—no, not always coy—and hard to please. If they knew more about them they would not make such mistakes.

Robert sent off Joan's hunter at once, and he fixed a

reserve price—rather a stiff reserve—and instructed Messrs. Tattersall not to sell it for a shilling less than the sum named.

He breathed quite freely when Black Beauty had gone out of the Rectory yard. It was like getting rid of a white elephant. It had been preying upon him all through the winter; it had weighed him down in spite of himself. He had a conviction—he would not have breathed it to Joan for the world—that it was the height of folly, that it was nothing short of madness. for a country parson with an income under three hundred a year—the income of a City clerk—to keep a hunter!

The ponies, he told himself, were a necessary expense; Joan could not do without a carriage and the dogcart. There were always things to be fetched from the distant railway-station, or groceries and housekeeping items from the town, and visits to be paid to the neighbouring clergy, and meetings to be attended. It would be impossible to go on a single day without the dogcart.

When this incubus—Black Beauty was nothing short of an incubus—was off his mind, Robert Lyon could give his attention to other things. He could do a little visiting, to begin with. If the truth must be told, he had rather neglected his parish work lately. Those few sheep that were committed to him were wandering over the hills without a shepherd. Very few of the male population of the village were ever seen in church. Some of them wandered away on Sundays, when they ought to have been in church, to the cross-roads, where there was a wayside public-house, and there they stayed smoking and drinking all the evening; others wandered over the fields to the next village, where there was a humble conventicle and an unlettered preacher, who won their hearts by his homely earnestness.

The congregation was certainly falling off. It was small to begin with, and it grew smaller Sunday by Sunday. The people were growing cold and indifferent, and those who were not indifferent, who had a desire for good things, were drifting into Dissent.

The fault was not his, the Rector told himself bitterly; it was the fault of that bigoted old woman who sat in the

Aylmerton pew. She would not suffer him to preach any other doctrine than the old-fashioned, narrow-minded theology that suited her taste. He had made a bargain with her and he could not go back from it.

He still visited that Bluebeard cupboard. He generally visited it on Saturday nights, when the household had gone to rest. He was ashamed of Joan seeing him go to that bag. He kept it carefully locked up, and week by week, when the house was silent and the inmates were wrapped in sleep, he went stealthily to that hateful cupboard and drew out the faded manuscripts from the shabby old bag he had stuffed them in at the sale. He felt like a culprit as he drew them out, and folded them afresh, and wiped off the dust, and slipped them into that dainty sermon-case Joan had made for him.

It was her ladyship's fault that he preached these musty old sermons. She would not let him give the people anything of his own—any fresh thoughts, any helpful sympathy, hope, or promise. He was obliged to go on in the old, lifeless, formal groove, and—and it saved a lot of trouble.

CHAPTER XXIV.

A FRIEND IN NEED.

A DAY of reckoning came to Robert Lyon. It comes to most men; to some early, to some late. It never fails to come, but it does not always come in the same form.

It came to the Rector of Coombe Damerel in the most prosaic form; it came in the literal vulgar form of pounds, shillings, and pence.

Christmas, if it had brought nothing else, had brought a cartload of bills. The Rectory post-bag had never been so full as it was on the morning after Black Beauty went up to Tattersall's.

It was not delightful correspondence, by any means; there was a singular unanimity in it that would have made him smile at any other time, but that brought out two upright lines on his forehead now—two lines where there used to be only one.

The letters were all from Carlingford tradespeople, and they were all pressing for the payment of their 'little' bills.

Robert had not intended to pay them all just at present; he would pay a few, and the rest, he thought, could wait—could very well afford to wait; but they all with one accord desired to be paid at once. He could not at all understand it. He could not think how it came about that his credit should be so suddenly shaken.

It never occurred to him that everybody in Carlingford had heard of that horse being sent up to London for sale. The groom who rode it to the station and put it into the train had made no secret of it. Servants never make secrets of these things. He had carefully explained to everybody his own view of the case—that his master could not afford to keep the brute any longer, and the tradespeople, acting on the hint—the first sign of the reduction of that splendid establishment that was to be maintained on two hundred and eighty pounds a year; everybody knew that it was only two hundred and eighty pounds a year—sent in their little bills.

Robert paid what he could. He sat down at once and wrote cheques for the most pressing accounts, but he could not pay them all.

He added up his bank-book, and he added up the amounts of the cheques he had drawn, and he made an awful discovery. People are making the same discovery every day, and it is invariably attended with the same results—extreme astonishment and cold shivers in the region of the spine.

He had overdrawn his account.

It was clearly no use sending people cheques for their bills when there was no money in the bank to meet them. That cheque for fifty pounds which he had sent so readily to Mrs. Penrose had put the balance on the wrong side.

He must write and tell the people to wait. When he had sold Black Beauty, and got the money, he would be able to pay them.

Robert pushed the letters and the cheques aside—it made him sick to see them—when he came across a letter unopened that he had overlooked. It had been lying at the bottom of the post-bag, and he took it out from beneath all the others.

His fingers trembled as he opened it; he did not know why.

It was not a bill; it was not a request for the payment of money; it was—it was—an offer of money to any amount.

It was like the old story of Pandora's box of evils. He had gone on taking one unpleasant missive out of that bag after another, until he had come to the bitter end—no, not quite the end; there was Hope at the bottom.

It was a delightful letter, and it had come just at the right moment. A kind, courteous letter, thoughtfully written, from a quite unknown correspondent, offering Robert an immediate loan of any sum of money he desired, on his own personal security. It set forth, in the most considerate way, the advantages of a temporary loan to incumbents who have recently come into a living; and have found the initial expenses far exceeding their expectations, and the emoluments slow in coming in.

It was exactly Robert's case.

His expenses this first six months had been more than double the amount he had reckoned upon, and there would be nothing coming in for months. A temporary loan would be the very thing for him.

He had never had anything to do with money-lenders before, but this was quite an exceptional case; besides, hundreds of other clergymen in his position did the same thing.

Appended to the circular enclosed were a dozen testimonials from beneficed clergymen who had availed themselves of Mr. Wilberforce's generous offer of assistance rather than, as they expressed it, submit to a snub from their bankers.

It would only be a temporary loan Robert would want. When Black Beauty was sold he would be able to repay it at once, and meanwhile he could pay these wretched bills.

He wrote off by the next post, and asked Mr. Wilberforce to oblige him with the loan of one hundred and fifty pounds for three or six months.

The philanthropist replied by return, saying he should be delighted to arrange this trivial loan for any term to suit Mr. Lyon's convenience, say six or nine months, and that a young gentleman—an architect—should wait upon him the following day to take his signature.

The young gentleman arrived during the morning. Fortunately, Joan was not in the library when he was shown in. Robert would not have had her know anything about this transaction for the world.

He was a delightful young gentleman, full of interest in the country, and with a great passion for Decorated churches. He waived the question of the loan when he heard that Robert's church was a Decorated church, and proposed to go over and examine it at once, and return to the little matter of business that had brought him there when they came back.

If there was anything in the world Robert hated, it was Late Perpendicular. He could put up with quite early buildings of that interesting style, with pointed arches and that sort of thing, but what his soul loved was a Decorated church.

He was as proud of that Decorated west window in his little dark church, and the monuments in the Aylmerton chapel, and the round pillars that supported the arches, and the old painted screen, as if the church had belonged to his family since the Conquest—since it was built, at any rate.

Mr. Wilberforce's young gentleman went into raptures over the mouldy, ill-smelling little church. It was a damp, drizzly January morning, and it had been shut up for nearly a week, and the old stones in the aisles were 'giving,' as the sexton used to say in his homely way of describing mildew and damp; and there was a musty, suggestive odour of old Damerels in the Aylmerton chapel.

They stayed so long in the church examining the windows and the monuments, that when they got back to the house it was time for lunch. Robert could not do less than ask the pleasant young gentleman to stay to lunch, and he introduced him to Joan as an architect and surveyor who had come over to see the church.

This was no misrepresentation, though Robert's conscience gave a twinge when he made it. The young man *had* come over to see the church, and he had come over to see a great deal more.

Whatever he saw must have given him confidence. He was quite ready to return to business when he went back with Robert to the library after lunch. He produced a bill from his pocket-book, drawn for one hundred and eighty pounds, thirty pounds in excess of the sum Robert had asked for. This, he explained, was the usual rate of interest—twenty per cent.—not such a great amount of interest, considering the risk and the absence of security—only the incumbent's note of hand.

It really did not seem very much, after all, considering the convenience, and the strictly private nature of the transaction.

'It is made payable in three months,' Robert remarked, as he sat twiddling the bit of stamped paper between his finger and thumb. 'I understood it was not to fall due for six or nine months.'

'Oh, that is a mere matter of form,' the young gentleman said, in his pleasant, reassuring way. 'All our bills are dated three months; at the end of that time you can renew them for another three or six months, until the time Mr. Wilberforce named expires.'

'It need not be paid, then, for six or nine months?' Robert asked, a little nervously. He was not quite so sure of Black Beauty fetching the price he had put upon him, and if it would not sell, it was quite evident that he would not be able to raise the money until his tithes came in.

'Oh no, not at all. You will quite consult your own convenience whether you pay it at the end of three, six, or nine months.'

'I would rather it had been drawn for six months,' Robert said doubtfully. 'I am not sure of being able to meet it at the end of three months—not until my tithes come in. I hope there will be no difficulty.'

'No, certainly not. You are not expected to meet it until the time expires. You will have due notice. There is no reason whatever why you should think about it, meanwhile.'

Robert laid the long strip of paper on the blotting-pad before him, and dipped his pen in the ink and hesitated, while the young gentleman smiled reassuringly and waited.

Why should he doubt him?

If he had not been so keen on early English and Decorated churches, Robert might have doubted him; but a man who hated—who positively loathed Perpendicular——

He did not put the base thought in words, but he dipped his pen in the ink and scrawled his name across the paper.

The young gentleman carefully blotted the trumpery bit of blue paper, and folded it up slowly, and put it into his pocket-book. Something in the action reminded Robert of an absurd picture he had once seen of some one folding up somebody else's shadow, a limp, spiritless, backboneless shadow, and putting it into his pocket. But this was not all the transaction.

The young gentleman, having pocketed the bill, put a sheet of blank paper before Robert, and dictated a rambling rigmarole, of which he did not understand one word, purporting to authorize him to draw this sum of one hundred and eighty pounds from his superior.

Robert drew out the paper and signed it meekly—in faith—it was too late now to question anything.

But even this was not quite all. Before the pleasant youn gman, who took such intelligent interest in Decorated churches, went away, he asked for his fee, the ordinary fee for preliminary inquiries, just the railway fare and the day's work.

The fee was five guineas, which the young man put into his pocket-book with the bill, and buttoned his coat carefully over it.

The next day Robert received a cheque for one hundred and fifty pounds.

The ease and the expedition with which the loan was effected quite charmed him. He had no idea the money could be raised so easily. He was not at all surprised at those other incumbents having written the testimonials that were printed on the philanthropist's circular, with those words of encouragement and sympathetic advice addressed to their younger brethren.

He was ready to sit down—with that hundred and fifty pounds in his pocket—and write a testimonial on the spot.

CHAPTER XXV.

CECILIA.

The first mild day that the doctor allowed Joan to drive out, she went over to Orchard Damerel.

She had not seen Cecilia since her engagement, and there was a great deal to tell. While Robert was talking to the Countess, Cecilia took her apart and told her all about it. She was so brimming over with her unexpected good fortune, that she could not rest till she had told Joan all about it.

There was very little to tell.

Cecilia had accepted Mr. Greatorex's offer gratefully. She had not hesitated a moment. She had had a bad time, she told Joan confidentially, since she had accepted it: the Countess had not ceased bullying her. If it had not been for the hope of speedy release, she would have wept her eyes out, she would have been unable to read any more sermons. They were heavy now and red, but there was a light in them, beneath their heavy lids, that Joan had not seen in them before.

'There is nothing to wait for,' Cecilia whispered, in her hurried, frightened way, as she poured out her eager blushing confidence into Joan's sympathetic ear. 'We are to be married as soon as the Countess can get somebody. Oh, I wish she would get somebody soon!'

Then Joan had congratulated her softly, as a young happy bride alone could congratulate her.

'I hope you will be very happy, dear,' she said; 'I am sure you will be happy. I should have accepted Mr. Greatorex myself, if he had asked me, before I had met Robin. He is not a bit too old. I hate young men; they are always so conceited, and want so much waiting upon. I think he is a duck!'

Joan was quite full of Cecilia's engagement all the way home; she could talk of nothing else. It was all very well for poor Cecilia to say that there was nothing to wait for; the Countess was not very likely to get anyone to fill her place. If she waited until her aunt could give her up, she would have to wait a long time.

While Joan was talking it over with Robert after dinner by that cosy fireside in the study, where a big screen kept off all the draughts, and shut them in with the warmth, and the comfort, and the shaded lamplight, an idea struck her, and she jumped up and almost upset the little table with all the cambric treasures.

'Why shouldn't one of the girls go to Orchard Damerel?' she asked Robert eagerly, when the inspiration struck her.

'One of the girls? You mean Phyllis or Bertha?'

'Yes, of course; who else should I mean, Rob? They are *the* girls to me. There are no other girls in the world like them!'

And then quite suddenly Joan's eyes filled with tears.

'I think Phyllis, if your mother could give her up, would suit the Countess admirably, and it would be nice for you to have her so near.'

'Nice? It would be lovely!'

The Rector smiled.

'I am afraid it would not be lovely for Phyllis,' he said dryly. 'She would get tired of reading those sermons all day, and talking to an ill-tempered, narrow-minded old woman.'

'Oh, Phyllis wouldn't mind; she isn't like some people. She doesn't mind old women, and she loves reading sermons. It will be just the thing for Phyllis.'

Joan wrote to her sister the same night before she went to bed; she covered two whole sheets of paper. She told Phyllis all about the sermons she would have to read, and the hymn-tunes she would have to play night after night, and the long, dreary, uneventful days she would have to spend shut up with a grumpy old woman. Robert made her enumerate all these things. She did not keep anything back; she knew that none of them would come amiss to Phyllis. She was not like other girls. She was created solely for the benefit of Sunday-school children and old women.

It was quite a mistake for Nature to have painted her cheeks such a lovely carnation, and shaded her sweet eyes with such long dark lashes, and made her beautiful brown hair so crisp and curly. It was wasted upon old women, whose eyes were too dim to see if her eyes were blue or green, and upon little children, who are not judges of beauty, who love a brown, wrinkled old crone better than a professional beauty with the loveliest complexion in the world.

The day that Phyllis received Joan's letter was a day of the deepest humiliation at Stoke Lucy. Bertha had come back like a bad penny. It is harder to return to one's work after a holiday than to go away for the first time. There is no novelty in going back to take off the bitterness. It is ever so much harder. The contrast between the warm welcome of home—ever so humble a home—and the chilling reception that awaits the poor dependent, going back fresh from the tender, clinging arms of love to the dull routine of duty, is more than some natures can bear.

Most people—weak people—suffer in silence, weep by night and sulk by day, till time, the reconciler, blunts the dear memory of the happy days, and by-and-by the wheel goes round as if there had never been a break. Others grow restless, and refuse to settle down in the old groove, till by-and-by the discontent culminates into open rebellion, and they pack their boxes and go away.

Bertha packed her box before she had been back a week. The troublesome little boys that she had tried so hard to love, and could not love, the upstair room, the loneliness, and the isolation, were more than she could bear. When the father of the little unmannerly boys 'tipped her a nod' when he met her in the square, and the mother of her charges bullied her for half an hour because she had cut the children's long, dreary lessons short, a few minutes short, a day or two after her arrival, Bertha's spirit broke down, or rather it flared up, and she packed her box and came away.

She was dreadfully ashamed of herself the next morning. She had not been used to slights and being bullied; she had not gone through a preliminary course of bullying and got used to it. She was not fit to go out into the world and get her living, she told herself, if she could not stand being bullied; and then she sat down and wept, and declared herself ready to go back and ask Mrs. Brown to give her another trial.

She was still weeping when Joan's letter came.

It was quite a Providence, Mrs. Penrose said, reading Joan's letter through a mist. She was always seeing the leading of a Kind Hand through all their misfortunes and poverty.

'Depend upon it,' she used to say, when the boys were grumbling, and the girls were murmuring at their hard lot, 'God knows what is best for you, dears. Perhaps you couldn't have borne prosperity; very few people can;' and then she would comfort herself by repeating the lines of her favourite hymn:

> 'Judge not the Lord by fearful sense,
> But *trust* Him for His grace;
> Behind a frowning Providence
> He hides a smiling face.'

What would she have done without that hymn?

Phyllis wrote back by the next post, and said that she would be willing to come, that she would be delighted to come, that she would come at once!

It was exactly the situation that would suit her. It would suit her much better than teaching little boys, dreadful, unlovable little boys, like Bertha's. She liked old women; she would never, never tire of an old woman's whims—why should she? She would be old herself some day—and the literature that she adored was sermons!

It was her turn to go out now; Bertha had gone out, and—and failed. Bertha did not admit that she had failed, but her experience had not been a happy one, and she was quite willing to stay at home with her mother, and pare and scrape, and sew and scrub—no, not scrub, she stopped short at scrubbing—as Phyllis had done.

When Joan received this letter, she had the ponies

brought round at once, and drove over to Orchard Damerel.

It was earlier in the day than she was in the habit of calling, and the Countess was still in her boudoir, and Joan managed to get a few minutes' talk with Cecilia before she went upstairs to see her.

Poor Cecilia was delighted with the proposition; she was sure that Phyllis would fill her place exactly. It was not an easy place to fill, she admitted; and then she broke down and had a little weep. Her eyes were red as if she had been crying all the morning; the Countess had been unusually cross: something had happened to upset her, and when she was upset, she generally vented her ill-humours upon Cecilia.

Mr. Greatorex had written to her ladyship, and had asked her to name an early day when she could dispense with the attendance of her niece; and the Countess had fallen into a passion upon reading the letter, and wept, and raved, and called him an unfeeling brute for seeking to take away from her the prop of her old age.

There had been a scene.

Cecilia was sure, she told Joan, that her aunt would never, never willingly give her up, that she would keep her in that dull house, reading those hateful sermons as long as she lived, unless she ran away, or—or Mr. Greatorex came and carried her off by force.

Joan could not help smiling at the picture she drew of Cecilia's elderly lover carrying her off by force.

The Countess had not smoothed all the signs of her recent agitation from her face when Joan went in. It was redder than ever, quite purple red under her eyes, which were still angry and disturbed, and she was shaking all over like a jelly. She was still wearing that old warm plaid shawl, and a hideous erection of a cap. She had never looked more unlike a countess.

When she saw Joan, she began to whimper and bemoan the ingratitude of her niece.

'After all I have done for her!' the Countess moaned. 'If she had been my own child I could not have done more; and now—to think of her ingratitude! She is ready to leave me at a minute's notice for the sake of an old man, old enough to be her father—to be her grandfather. I'm ashamed of Cecilia!'

Her ladyship's niece stood by, blushing and weeping.

'Mr. Greatorex is only sixty,' she said, with some spirit.

'Hold your tongue, miss! he is sixty-five, if he is a day! If he had been a young man I could understand your infatuation, but with an old man—a man old enough to be your grandfather—it is quite indecent!'

The late Earl had been considerably over sixty when her ladyship had married him.

'A girl like Cecilia, with her expectations—the niece of—of an earl——'

'A countess,' Cecilia murmured inaudibly.

'To throw herself away on a mere London attorney, a man old enough to be her grandfather,' the Countess went on severely, 'is worse than folly; it is madness, nothing short of madness—her friends ought to interfere. If her father will not interfere, I shall take it upon myself. I have always stood in the place of a mother to Cecilia. I shall take it upon myself to write to Mr. Greatorex, and put a stop to this folly. He is one of the Earl's trustees, and he is taking a great liberty in paying his addresses to the Earl's niece. If he has forgotten his place, I should not be doing my duty to my family and my position if I did not remind him of it.'

Cecilia began to weep copiously.

'I have promised to marry him, aunt,' was all she could say.

'Marry him indeed! What does a chit like you know about marrying? How old are you—eighteen or nineteen?'

'I am twenty-six, aunt.'

'Good gracious, how time flies! I thought you were still in your teens, child. Twenty-six! Well, there is plenty of time yet to talk about marrying.'

Cecilia shook her head, and two big tears coursed down her despairing face.

Joan was very angry with the selfish old woman, and she thought Cecilia was a goose, a big goose, to stand crying there because the Countess would not let her get married. She would have liked to shake her.

It was hardly a propitious time to tell the Countess what had brought her there so early, but Joan was not accustomed to let small things stand in her way.

She told her ladyship about Bertha having come home, and Phyllis wanting to go out into a situation—wanting exactly such a place as Cecilia's—and how fond she was of reading sermons, and that she would play hymn-tunes by the hour.

She could not have put the matter more clearly, but the Countess did not jump at Phyllis's offer.

'I don't think I could do with a stranger about me,' she said quite crossly. 'Cecilia knows all my ways. I am not fidgety, but I like people to know what I want without telling. I couldn't begin teaching a stranger at my age; most likely, after I had taken a lot of trouble with your sister, she would be ungrateful enough to go away and get married!'

It was clearly no use reasoning with her. Joan came away and left her ladyship grumbling and vowing she would have no more ungrateful minxes about her.

A week after this unsatisfactory interview Mr. Greatorex came down. He did not stop at Orchard Damerel as he was accustomed to do; he put up at the Aylmerton Arms in the village. He was closeted with the Countess for an hour on the night of his arrival, but he refused her invitation to stay to dinner. He had never required an invitation before, and the Countess did not make it very graciously. She could not bully the Earl's trustee very well, so she bullied Cecilia after he had gone. It was always a consolation to her to remember that she had bullied Cecilia on that memorable night.

Her ladyship's niece was out walking with her lover in the grounds betimes the next morning. It was a dismal January morning; a damp mist was rising from the ground, and the trees in the shrubbery were dripping as they passed beneath them. The shrubbery was the last place in the world for anyone but lovers to walk in on this damp, dreary morning. A wilderness of laurels and evergreens, unpruned and untrained, and meeting in some places across the path—a more forlorn, melancholy walk they could not have chosen.

Cecilia could not think why her elderly lover had chosen this walk, but she did not venture to remonstrate. She was always used to giving in to other people; she had no will of her own.

Mr. Greatorex talked about all sorts of things as they walked through this tangled wilderness—about his beautiful old house in the country that Cecilia had never heard of, and his gloomy old mansion in town that the upholsterers were already busy about, and his sad, lonely bachelor life that would be lonely and sad no longer.

He talked about everything but the Countess; he never mentioned her name once during that morning's walk.

Cecilia was so interested in what he was telling her of the strange, stirring world that lay outside the dreary splendour of Orchard Damerel that she did not notice that they had left the shrubbery behind and were walking across the meadows in the direction of the church.

The mists that had been so thick in the shrubbery were rising when they passed out of the tangled wilderness into the meadows beyond. They melted and opened out before Cecilia in a strange, mysterious way, as if to reveal to her the unknown world that lay beyond. The soft blue mists were rising, and the sun was shining on the distant hills, and there was a rustle and sparkle on the scarlet berries of the hollies by the church gate, and they were walking up the church path before Cecilia knew it.

'I want to go into the church for a few minutes,' Mr. Greatorex explained; and Cecilia followed meekly.

By the strangest coincidence, the Rector was walking towards them through the churchyard from the gate that led into the Rectory garden, and they went into the church together. The door was open, and Fowler, the gardener from the Rectory, who sang in the choir and looked after the church, was putting down some cushions in the chancel.

Cecilia could not imagine why he should be putting down the cushions in the middle of the week.

She followed her elderly lover up the aisle, and waited for him while he went into the vestry with the Rector.

She waited in the chancel, looking down at the

cushions, and at the flowers, the sweet fresh Christmas roses on the altar, wondering what it meant.

She was still wondering when Robert came out of the vestry in his surplice, and passed inside the Communion-rails, and she was standing, with Mr. Greatorex by her side, before them, and someone—Fowler, the gardener, or another—was standing at her elbow.

She could not tell what it all meant. The marriage-service had begun, and the Rector had asked her if she would have this man—who had come down from London with a special license all ready in his pocket—for her wedded husband before she realized what was happening.

It was too late to draw back. She would not have drawn back if she could.

The service went on to the end, and then Cecilia broke down. She did not break down till she got into the vestry, and then, when it was quite too late, her tears poured down like rain. She had suddenly remembered the poor old woman at Orchard Damerel, and what a good friend she had been to her.

It was quite too late to weep now; the old dreary, monotonous days were all over. The mists had risen from the hills when she came out of the church door, and the world was before her.

Joan wrote the same night for Phyllis to come down to Coombe Damerel at once, to come down without delay, not to let anything detain her.

CHAPTER XXVI.

MARY BAILEY.

There was great consternation in Coombe Damerel when it was known that her ladyship's niece had been whisked away.

There was still a halo around the little household at the great house; an atmosphere of greatness still surrounded the Countess. Everybody remembered that she was the Earl's widow. The sight of that lumbering old yellow chariot in the village street, with the red face of the Countess and her dingy lilac plumes nodding inside, still filled the simple minds of the country folk with awe and admiration.

The news of Cecilia's elopement—it really seemed like an elopement, a mid dle-aged, orderly elopement—fell like a thunderbolt in the village.

Everybody in Coombe Damerel knew all about it an hour after the event. It upset the day's work. Women stood about at the corners of the street, or collected together at their doorsteps to gossip about it, and men paused in their work; even the school-children neglected their lessons, and put their heads together behind their slates, and whispered the wonderful news.

Perhaps the schoolmaster was to blame for the children's inattention. He was *distrait* and inattentive himself. He forgot all about the lessons he was giving; he was absent and preoccupied all the morning; and when the school was over, when he had got rid of the children for the day, he brushed himself up very carefully, and walked over to Orchard Damerel.

He walked through the wet shrubbery, where Cecilia had walked in the morning, scrunching the dead leaves under his great awkward feet, and pushing aside the invading boughs that obstructed his path. He was very much in earnest; he was always in earnest: he was not of a frivolous nature, like some young men. He had a long upper lip, and a square jaw, and a heavy, overhanging forehead, and there was not a gleam of fun in his eyes. When he whacked a boy—he could not trust himself to whack a boy very often—he whacked him within an inch of his life. That deadly earnestness of his had got him into trouble, in the matter of discipline, more than once in his scholastic career.

He was very much in earnest now, as he walked with a heavy, rapid step through the tangled wilderness of shrubbery. It was a delightful meeting-place for lovers. Perhaps some such thought crossed his mind as he paused once and looked back at the shadowy path that led by the meadows to the church. There was no one in sight when he reached the house. There was not a light in a single window, though the twilight was falling, and only two or three chimneys of the great stacks were smoking.

He waited a long time before anyone answered the door, waited on the doorstep, balancing himself first on one leg and then on the other, but he did not remember to scrape his feet. They really wanted scraping after that walk through the mud.

The old butler came at last, fumbling over the fastenings of the hall door, as if he had never opened it before in his life. His nerves were so shaken by Cecilia's flight that he did not know whether he was on his head or his heels. Nobody had ever eloped from Orchard Damerel before. Nobody was ever likely to elope again—not in his time. He was not at all sure whether her ladyship would see the young man—he had an earl's butler's contempt for schoolmasters—and he left him kicking up his heels in the dark hall while he went to inquire.

He came back presently with a message from the Countess. Her ladyship was very sorry, but she was so upset by the tragic incident of the day that she could not see anyone.

But the schoolmaster would not go away. He made the butler take another message to her ladyship, to the effect that his errand was pressing, that he could not go away without seeing her. He listened with his great ears outstretched—his ears had a way of pricking themselves up, perhaps with being always on the stretch, listening for answers that were slow in coming—and he heard the butler's feeble steps far, far away approaching.

He knew, by the sound of those steps, that her ladyship would see him, and he moistened his dry lips in an engaging way that he had, and wiped his forehead. It was dreadfully cold in that dark, draughty hall, where a fire had not been lighted for years and years; but the perspiration stood out in clammy drops on his forehead as he heard the butler's steps approaching.

He had guessed rightly. Her ladyship would see him. He followed the butler through the dark, shadowy rooms, and down a long passage, into a great dim, drab room, where, at the further end, by the fireplace, the Countess was sitting alone.

He came up to her shyly and awkwardly, with that undecided manner he had. He carried his hat in his hand, and his big cane; and his great boots, which he had forgotten to wipe, made dreadful marks on the carpet all the way.

The Countess looked up from her corner when he approached her. Traces of recent agitation were on her red face—it was red no longer, it was purple.

'What do you want to speak to me about? Why are you so anxious to see me?' she inquired sharply. 'It is not about the school, I hope; I have nothing more to do with the school. I have washed my hands of the school.'

'It is not about the school,' the young man said, moistening his dry lips.

'Sit down,' said the Countess impatiently. She could not bear to see him standing there twiddling his hat. 'You may as well sit down if you have anything to say.'

The schoolmaster sat down; he sat down at the very edge of the chair. If he had sat down a hair's-breadth nearer the edge, it would have toppled over with him.

'I came to speak to you about Miss Burrough——' he began awkwardly.

'I don't want to hear a word about Miss Burrough,' the Countess said, snapping him up. 'I don't want to hear her name ever mentioned again.'

'It is about Miss Burrough's situation,' the young man went on undaunted.

'Miss Burrough was my niece; Miss Burrough did not fill a situation!' the old woman said, losing her temper. 'What do you mean by talking about her situation, as if she were a housemaid?'

The young man ought to have been abashed, but he was only confused or puzzled; he was not the least ashamed.

'You will want someone to fill her place?' he went on doggedly.

'Of course I shall want someone to fill her place,' her ladyship said testily; 'but I don't see what that has to do with your visit.'

'I thought Mary—Miss Bailey——'

The Countess stopped him abruptly.

'Oh dear no!' she said stiffly, 'Mary Bailey wouldn't do at all. I've always been accustomed to have a lady.'

'But Ma—Miss Bailey is quite a lady. She has been well brought up. Her mother was a lady: she was the daughter of a solicitor. She married beneath her, but she brought Mary up in her own station.'

'I should have said a gentlewoman,' the Countess said, with some asperity. 'I have always been accustomed to have a gentlewoman about me. Mary Bailey would not do at all.'

She was nettled and offended at that allusion to Mary Bailey's mother being the daughter of a country attorney; it was putting her on the same level as herself.

'Mary is much better,' he went on desperately. He was not to be repressed. 'She is quite able to take a situation now. She would be very useful to your ladyship; she has taken a number of prizes for needlework; and she reads aloud beautifully.'

'Mary Bailey will not do at all. I could not have an invalid about me,' the old lady said sharply. 'I should have nothing to do but to nurse her; and when she got well, after a lot of feeding up and trouble, she would want to get married.'

'She would not want to get married for—for a long time—not until your ladyship could spare her; she would wait—we would both wait——'

'Fiddlesticks!' interrupted the Countess impatiently. 'What do you want to bring her down here for if you don't want to marry her? You'd better leave off thinking about Mary Bailey, Mr. Beckett, and stick to your work. I hear the school is in a disgraceful condition.'

And so she dismissed him.

The wheezy old butler took him back through the darkling rooms. They had seemed so grand to him when he had come in; they were all dim and drab and gray as he came back: they might have been covered with cobwebs for all the notice he took of them.

The wintry sun had sunk behind the moor, and the house stood sharply out against the pale gold of the

Over the hills hung a long dark line of clouds, and the gray mist of evening was stealing up from the valley, blotting and blurring the familiar landmarks—the great trees in the deer-park, the sloping sides of the coombe, with the dark water brawling below, the long green fields and the gray tower of the church.

The schoolmaster's back was towards the sunset, and his gray set face was towards the darkling sky and the creeping mist. His head had dropped upon his breast, and his attitude would have struck anyone meeting him there, in that lonely spot, as the attitude of a man who had given up hope—the attitude of despair.

It would have struck most men who had any sympathy with their fellow-creatures, but it did not strike Robert Lyon, who met him coming up to the house.

He was coming up to condole with her ladyship—it was his duty as the Rector of the parish to go to her in her trouble--and to tell her that his wife had sent for Phyllis. Phyllis would stay with her, at any rate for the present, until she could make up her mind who she would take to fill Cecilia's place.

Robert was absent and preoccupied as he came up the path towards the house in the winter sunset. He had had a good many things to worry him; he was not at all sure what the Countess would say to his marrying her niece in that clandestine way without consulting her first. It was his duty, he could do nothing else; but he was not at all sure that her ladyship would see it in that light. There were other things disturbing him, with which his errand to Lady Aylmerton had nothing to do. He had heard from Tattersall's that morning. Black Beauty had been put up for sale, and he had been knocked down for *one hundred pounds* less than the reserve price.

Of course he had been bought in. If Robert had not fixed a reserve, he would have been sold for twenty-five pounds. He had quite believed that story of Lady Alicia's brother's that he was 'worth two hundred of anybody's money,' and he had put what he thought a low reserve upon him.

He was dreadfully upset when that letter from Tattersall's reached him; he would not have told Joan anything about it for the world! The next thing to be considered was what to do with the horse. It was eating its head off in Tattersall's stables now instead of in his, and he would have to pay the cost of sending it back. This, and the commission, and the cost of its keep in London, would amount to a considerable sum, and it would be all loss. He was very much inclined to let it go for what it would fetch, and finish the business. He was revolving this in his mind, when he came across the schoolmaster walking moodily towards him, as if he had just left the house.

He could not at all think what had brought the man there on such a day as this above all others. He was sure that the Countess would not see him. What possible business could he have with her?

Could he have chosen this inauspicious time to go to her about the schools—the schools that were in such a disgraceful condition?

Robert was asking himself this question when he met the young man in the path. The moody fellow would have passed him with a sullen bow, but the Rector stopped him.

'Oh, I wanted to speak to you about the schools, Mr. Beckett,' he said, but he did not say it genially. 'The inspector is coming down a week earlier, and I'm afraid you will not be ready for him. I'll come over to-morrow morning and go through some of the subjects with the elder children. I hope I shall find them improved. Miss Bray has done wonders with the girls. The way she has worked them up in this short time is quite astonishing. She is an excellent teacher; she throws her heart into the work. There is nothing done without throwing one's heart into it.'

With this parting shot the Rector went on his way. He heard, or thought he heard, the moody, sullen fellow muttering to himself after he left him, and he paused at a turn in the road and looked after him, and saw him with his head still bent forward on his breast, and the gray mist closing around him.

CHAPTER XXVII.

ROBERT EXAMINES THE SCHOOL.

Robert Lyon returned home after that visit to Orchard Damerel rather damped in spirits. Everything had gone wrong. That wretched horse lay like a load upon his mind; the meeting with the schoolmaster had irritated him, though he could not explain why; and the interview with his patroness had not been a pleasant one.

The Countess had railed at him as it was not seemly for a member of his flock to rail at the parish priest; but her ladyship was not particular what she said, or how she said it, when she was very much moved. She was very much moved to-day, and she poured out the vials of her wrath upon the meek head of the clergyman who had tied the knot between the offending pair. She accused the Rector of aiding and abetting the elderly bridegroom, and being privy to the whole arrangement from the beginning. She would not listen to a single word of extenuation; and she turned up her nose—her poor vulgar red nose—at the mention of the word 'duty.'

There was only one duty he owed that was at all plain to her, the duty of refusing to perform the marriage ceremony without her knowledge and consent.

Robert came away angry and humiliated: he never came away from Orchard Damerel now without being angry and ashamed. The Countess never lost a chance of saying unpleasant things, and she was very fond of finding fault. If he could have got another presentation he would have thrown up the living—the beautiful house and grounds, the fruitful glebe, and the income of two hundred and eighty pounds a year! He would have thrown it all up.

It is possible to buy good things—not the best things—too dear, and this great gift, good as it was, he had bought dear. He had given much too high a price for it: he had forfeited his self respect, he told himself bitterly. 'He was not his own master; he was like a toad under a pair of harrows!'

In this frame of mind he came home after that inauspicious interview, and he was moody and silent all the evening. The next morning he had to face the question of the horse, the wonderful hunter that Lord George had given his honourable word was worth two hundred guineas. What is the worth of a lord if his word is not to be trusted?

It had been knocked down, bought in rather, for twenty-five pounds! Robert had put much too high a reserve upon it: if he had fixed a lower sum, so the clerk at Tattersall's informed him, the horse might have been sold. He had lain awake thinking about that horse all the night, when he ought to have been thinking about his Sunday sermon, and he had made up his mind he would take what he could get for it. It would never do to have it back.

He wrote off at once, directly after breakfast, and requested that Black Beauty might be put up again, this time fixing the reserve at the ridiculous sum of fifty pounds. When he had written this letter, he thought that he had washed his hands of the whole affair.

He could not think now where he should get the money to meet that wretched bill: he had quite depended upon selling Black Beauty for at least a hundred and fifty pounds, or he would not have signed it.

He got up from his writing-table moody and out of sorts. He was in a very sorry mood to examine those wretched children at the school, who had been expecting him for the last hour.

The children were tired of waiting, and were ill-tempered and sulky. The schoolmaster had been bullying them ever since nine o'clock, and had only succeeded in making them moody and defiant.

Robert spent two weary hours hammering away at the 'standards.' He had a try at them all, at least all that were taught in the boys' school, and he came to the conclusion, at the end of the two hours, that a worse-taught or a more ignorant set of boys he had never met with in his life. The school would disgrace the county, and there would be no grant.

'Well,' said the schoolmaster, when the examination

was over and Robert was frowning over his pencilled notes—' well,' he said, with his sickly smile, and moistening his pale lips as he spoke, ' they have not done so very badly, sir, have they?'

'They have done disgracefully,' Robert said severely. 'They could not have done worse. I thought, with this extension of time, you would have been able to do something with them. Miss Bray has done wonders with the girls. They were much more backward than the boys; through Miss Bailey's unfortunate illness they had been neglected all the summer; but Miss Bray has made up for the lost time, and the school is in excellent order. With all its advantages, the boys' school will compare very unfavourably with the girls' school in the examiner's report.'

Matilda Bray came into the schoolroom directly after the Rector had gone. She was a small, slight, prim young woman, and she wore spectacles. She was neatly dressed, with stiffly-starched white cuffs and collar, and a tightly-fitting dark gown. She had not a bow of ribbon about her, and she had not a hair awry, though she had been in school since nine o'clock in the morning and the girls had been obstinate and stupid enough to make her tear her hair out by handfuls. It was past one o'clock when the Rector went away, and she had not torn out—she had not disarranged—a single hair. She was exactly what a schoolmistress ought to be—a pattern of neatness.

'Oh, I beg your pardon, Mr. Beckett; I thought Mr. Lyon was here,' she said in a quick, chirping way, pausing on the threshold and looking round the schoolroom.

'He has just gone,' the schoolmaster said sullenly.

'What a long time he stayed! Has he been examining the school?'

She had a sharp, acid little voice, generally pitched in a high key—rather an unpleasant key—but she sweetened it and softened it wonderfully when she spoke to the schoolmaster, and a pink flush crept up under her freckled skin. She had heard all about Mary Bailey; she knew the story of the schoolmaster's disappointment; but she could not understand his ridiculous fidelity. No man in his senses would prefer a mawkish, sickly girl fifty miles away to a bright, active little next-door neighbour with a 'parchment' covered with the most beautiful testimonials.

At least Matilda Bray thought so as she stood in the doorway on that dull January morning with that unwonted rosy flush creeping up into her pale cheeks. They could not help being pale. She had been shut up in an ill-ventilated room for four hours with fifty children, big and little, and they had among them sucked all the red life-blood out of her cheeks. The stuffy schoolroom, and the long, long hours, and the fifty young vampires all draining her energies and consuming every particle of oxygen, would have finished off most girls—as they had finished off poor Mary Bailey—but Matilda was made of sterner stuff.

Three hours' work was all the School Board exacted, but Matilda Bray, in her zeal for the school—she was always thinking about that parchment of hers and the testimonials that the examiners endorsed upon it—kept the children an extra hour. She never spared herself when an examination was coming on, and she never spared the children. Sometimes the mothers used to complain, and sometimes—not always in time—the doctors interfered. But Matilda held on her way, and her parchment filled up beautifully.

'Yes,' the schoolmaster said, replying to her question moodily in his sulky way, 'he has wasted my time and his own, and he has driven everything I have been drilling into the children for the last month out of their heads.'

'Oh, I thought Mr. Lyon examined beautifully. He got on capitally with the girls; they weren't a bit afraid of him. You should have heard them answer!'

Matilda Bray tried to make her little sharp voice sympathetic, but she could not keep that ring of triumph out of it. She was so proud of her little success, of her cramming, of her discipline, and of her immaculate 'parchment.'

The schoolmaster detected that note of triumph in a moment, and he looked so fierce under his scowling eyebrows that the little creature on the doorstep quite trembled in her shoes.

'You've got the knack of making them answer, Miss Bray,' he said bitterly, 'and I haven't, and that makes all the difference.'

He turned his back upon her, and began putting away some books; but Matilda did not go away. He was a dreadfully ill-mannered young man. Manners are not in the School Board curriculum.

'Then, the examination was not satisfactory?' she said timidly.

'It was not at all satisfactory,' the schoolmaster answered quite crushingly.

He did not even turn round when he spoke to her. He was putting up some books on a shelf, and he had his back turned to her. She ought to have gone away then; if she had had any spirit she would have gone away, but she stood hesitating on the doorstep with the colour coming and going in her small, sharp face.

'I'm sorry to hear it,' she said, speaking with nervous haste in her anxiety to keep the quiver out of her voice; 'it will be such a loss to you to get a bad report. Do you think—I—I could help you?'

'You?' he said, and he turned half round and saw the insignificant little bit of a thing, with her freckled face and her spectacles, standing there—'you?'

'Yes,' she said humbly. 'I have a lot of time disengaged. I could take some of the backward boys in the evening. There is still a fortnight. I could do a great deal in a fortnight——'

He turned upon her fiercely with a wrathy, red light in his eyes and his face pale with passion.

'I—I am quite able to manage my own school,' he said ungraciously, his harsh voice quivering with ill-restrained anger as he spoke.

The pretty red colour dropped out of the girl's cheeks.

'I'm very sorry if I've offended you, Mr. Beckett,' she said meekly. 'I did not mean to offend you. If I could help you in any way I should be so glad. I have got plenty of time. Remember, if I can do anything to help you—don't think it's troubling me—I shall be very glad.'

She did not wait to hear what he said; she threw the shawl she carried on her arm over her head and ran back to her own rooms.

He stood looking after her with his heavy brows knitted together and his lips set. What did the young woman mean by offering to help him? Mary Bailey had never offered to help him.

CHAPTER XXVIII.

THE SCHOOLMASTER'S SECRET.

'PHYLLIS is coming down to-day,' Joan said at breakfast, when she had devoured her letters. She still devoured her letters. They were always pleasant letters; people did not worry Joan with their troubles. If they had got any, they kept them to themselves; they only told her pleasant things.

One does not devour letters when they are full of complaints, and other people's worries and misfortunes, and when they make large calls upon one's purse or one's sympathy.

'Coming down to-day?' Robert said, not very rapturously. 'I'm afraid Lady Aylmerton isn't expecting her. What will you do with her if she won't have her?'

'Do with her? Why, she will stay here, of course. I hope Lady Aylmerton won't have her, the grumpy old thing! She'll wear her to death, as she did poor Cecilia.'

'I think you will have to let Lady Aylmerton know, dear, that Phyllis is coming, that you are expecting her. She is touchy in little things; she would be offended if you didn't tell her when she is coming. Why don't you write a letter and send it over?'

'I think I'll go over, Rob. I could explain things better; and she's been expecting me to call for a long time.'

'I don't think you ought to drive the ponies, dear; they are sure to be fresh after having been shut up so long,' the Rector said doubtfully. 'Let Bennett drive you.'

'Why don't you drive me yourself, Robin?' Joan said, pouting. 'I hate Bennett's driving. You needn't go in. I don't think I would go in again, if I were you, until she apologizes.'

The Rector shrugged his shoulders. He would have to wait a long time for her ladyship to apologize. She might put a five-pound note in the plate at the next collection as a peace-offering, but she was not likely to apologize.

When the ponies were brought round after breakfast, Robert took his seat beside his wife in the carriage. He had just taken the reins in his hand, when Joan pointed out to him one of the school-children running with breathless haste across the lawn. It was an unpardonable liberty to take to run across the lawn in the soft winter weather. There was a big corner saved by crossing the grass, but everybody, even the Rector himself, went the long way round by the path.

'Oh, Robin, do you see that boy? Call to him to go back;' and Joan began to wave her little gloved hands to the rude boy to go back.

The boy did not take the least notice of her, and Robert did not raise his voice to send him back. Something in the boy's attitude struck him, and he waited with the reins in his hand for the boy to come up.

He came up breathless and panting.

'The sch—sch—schoolmaster——' he panted, and then he stopped for want of breath.

'What about the schoolmaster?' Robert asked, turning a little pale.

'Is—ill—very—ill. Mrs. Potter—thinks—he—is—dying——'

Mrs. Potter was the woman who cleaned the schools.

'Have they gone for a doctor?' the Rector asked hastily. He was not thinking very much about the schoolmaster, who had chosen such an inconvenient time to be sick; he was thinking about his wife, and hoping this news would not upset her.

'Yes—Miss Bray sent for a doctor—and—please, sir—she said—you—were—to come at once.'

'I'll look in as I pass. I'm going through the village;'

and then the Rector drove off; but he stopped before he reached the gate, and told the groom to get in.

They had to wait a few minutes for him while he fetched his hat and got into his driving-coat with the gilt buttons on it. Had it been a case of life or death, Joan would not have allowed him to get into the pony-carriage without that coat.

'I think you might as well drive over to the house first,' she said fretfully, 'and call at the school on the way back. I can't think why you let that man spoil our drive.'

'I'm afraid I must call on the way,' Robert said gravely. 'I don't think Miss Bray would have sent for me if it hadn't been something serious. I expect the poor fellow has worried himself into a fever.'

Then the groom came out in his new livery, and the carriage drove off. There was quite a crowd before the school-house door when Robert drew up. There had been no school that morning, and the boys were out in the playground, and there was a crowd of idlers round the door. Robert made his way through the crowd into the school-house—the rooms, rather, that the schoolmaster inhabited. There were two or three people in the lower room, and at the foot of the stairs was Matilda Bray.

Her face was quite white beneath the freckles, and she had taken off her glasses; he had never seen her before without her spectacles.

'Oh, I am so glad you have come!' she said eagerly, grasping his arm as she spoke, and drawing him up the stairs out of the way of the women who were gathered in the room beneath. 'He is very ill—he is dying! *He has taken something!*'

'Good heavens!' Robert exclaimed, turning as white as the girl beside him. 'You don't mean——'

'Hush, hush! Nobody knows—nobody suspects anything but myself. Oh, you must not let them know—you must keep the poor fellow's secret!'

'How do you know?' Robert asked hastily. 'Have you found anything?'

'No, not yet; I have been looking. There is nothing there;' and she pointed to the door of the room where the schoolmaster lay. They could hear him groaning as they stood outside on the landing.

Robert pushed the door open and went in.

The schoolmaster was sitting up in bed, supported by pillows, and two women, Mrs. Potter and another woman from the village, were bending over him. His face was drawn and discoloured, and his lips were white. He had been sick and groaning ever since the woman who tidied up his room found him an hour ago, and now he was lying on the pillow faint and almost insensible. Messengers had been despatched in various directions for the doctor, who had started on his round, but nothing had been done to help the poor groaning wretch on the bed.

Robert sent the women out of the room, and opened the window to let in the fresh morning air, and then he bent over the drawn face on the pillow.

'What have you taken?' he said sternly.

He was dreadfully angry with the poor writhing wretch who had not courage to face the hard problems of life that other men have to face; he could not help speaking sternly.

The man turned a shade more ghastly, and there was a faint quiver about his nostrils.

'I have taken nothing,' he moaned, and then he closed his eyes and writhed again in his agony.

Robert turned away impatiently to give some directions to the women.

He did not believe him. Nobody looking at his drawn, ghastly face and his clammy working hands, that were convulsively clutching the bed-clothes, could believe him.

The schoolmistress was on the stairs outside waiting when Robert came out.

'Well,' she said eagerly, 'have you found out—has he told you?'

'He has told me nothing,' the Rector said impatiently; and then he pushed by her and went down the stairs.

When he got to the bottom he remembered that Joan was waiting for him outside, and that the ponies were rather fresh.

'You had better drive on,' he said to Joan, 'the man is very ill; I cannot leave him at present. If you see

Joan made a little *moue*.

'I don't see why you should let that troublesome young man spoil our drive,' she said rather tartly. 'I believe you don't want to go with me, Robin, and you make this an excuse.'

The Rector smiled rather sadly. 'I could not leave just now,' he said gravely, 'not until the doctor comes.'

'I am sure you are making a horrid fuss for nothing. The man isn't worth it,' Joan murmured sulkily; and then she suffered herself to be driven away.

Perhaps Joan was right.

He was such a commonplace young man, and he had done such a silly, wicked thing; he was really not worth making a fuss about.

When Robert got back to the house the schoolmistress had turned the women out of the room, and she was there alone, searching in all the corners, searching for evidence. He helped her in her search, though he did not know what he was looking for.

It was a bare little room, with some trumpery pictures on the walls, and a few shabby books on a shelf in the corner, and some poor cheap photographs on the mantelpiece. There were three photographs on the mantelpiece, one in a velvet case that was open, and two in common frames, but they were all of one person, a slender, sickly-looking young woman with a melancholy smile.

The Rector paused before them, and looked at the poor, shabby things with a half-pitying smile. He could not see very much in Miss Bailey for a man to break his heart about.

The schoolmistress did not waste her time looking at them; she pushed them aside, and looked behind them to see if there was anything there—a scrap of paper, a packet, anything that would tell a tale.

The search was quite in vain; she poked and pottered about the room, prying into all the miserable man's little secrets, but she found nothing, and all the time he was groaning in the room above.

Someone had lighted a fire, but the ashes from overnight had not been swept up.

Robert had given up the search, and was going up the stairs, when the schoolmistress called him back. She was on her knees before the hearth, and she was raking out the ashes from beneath the grate.

'See,' she cried, 'see!'

She had a paper in her hand, a scrap of charred paper, but there was some writing upon it, and her hand shook as she held it up.

Robert snatched the paper from her and held it to the light, while she knelt there with her hands clasped, watching him with her eager eyes.

'There is certainly something here,' the Rector said, nervously adjusting his glasses. 'Good heavens! he has taken oxalic acid!'

The doctor came in while he was still examining the paper, and they read it together, and then Robert took him upstairs to see the poor misguided fellow who had done this wicked thing.

When they came down some time later, Matilda Bray was still kneeling before the hearth where they had left her, with her hands clasped, and her small white face sunk upon her bosom.

She got up mechanically when they came into the room, and walked rather shakily across to the window where they were talking together.

'He will not recover,' she said, in a sad, hopeless little voice; 'he will die. He has killed himself because of this girl, because I came here in her place. Oh, for her sake—think how he must have loved her!—keep his secret. No one knows—no one ever need know—people die suddenly every day. Oh, for the sake of Mary Bailey—poor Mary Bailey—keep his secret!'

The doctor looked at this strange young woman, pleading for another woman's lover, with something like astonishment. He thought he knew a great deal about women, but this was a new variety.

'I don't know that he is going to die, my dear,' he said kindly; 'he is in a bad case just now, but we won't talk about it if you don't wish. We don't want to raise a scandal.'

Matilda's voice faltered as she tried to thank him, and she hung her head to hide the tears which had come into her eyes.

Before Robert came away he left a woman in charge of the patient upstairs, and another woman below preparing the remedies ordered, hot jars, and mustard-poultices, and other like stimulating applications, and he promised to send brandy and port-wine and beef-tea over from the Rectory; but he took the scrap of paper the schoolmistress had fished from under the grate away in his pocket.

CHAPTER XXIX.

A HUMBLE HEROINE.

PHYLLIS came down the same night. Lady Aylmerton would not hear of her going to the Rectory, not for a single night. She appropriated her at once, and sent the lumbering old yellow chariot to the station to meet her, and whisk her off to Orchard Damerel without delay.

The schoolmaster was still living the next morning. Word had come up to the Rectory before breakfast that he had passed a quiet night, and that there was no change for the worse. Robert went over to the school-house after breakfast to see how matters were going on, and to arrange about the school. Something must be done with the boys: they could not have a holiday on the eve of the examination.

Robert had said nothing to Joan about the tragedy—the tragedy that might have been—at the school-house. It was no use upsetting her with these miserable details; besides, she would be sure to let the matter leak out, and it would be all over the village in no time.

On the way to the school he met the doctor, who had just paid a visit to his patient.

'The poor fellow is better,' he said, 'but he has had a narrow shave. It was the nearest thing I ever saw! He took enough of that stuff to kill two men. I can't think how he got over it.'

'Does he admit having taken it? Is he at all sorry?' the Rector asked anxiously.

'Sorry? Not he. I can't get a word out of him. He's a sulky, ill-conditioned fellow. I don't believe he's a bit grateful for what we've done for him. I shouldn't be surprised if he made another attempt.'

'God forbid!' Robert said with a shiver he could not repress. He felt himself to some extent responsible for this man's folly. He had been hard upon him, he told himself. He had not shown that sympathy for the poor commonplace fellow's weakness that he would—well, that he would have expected other people to show to him.

'He won't be about again for some time, and I don't think he'll be worth much then. He's not the sort of fellow you can be sure of. If I were in your place, Lyon, I should look out for another schoolmaster; depend upon it, he's a black sheep.'

Robert pondered the doctor's parting words as he walked in the direction of the school-house.

It was an easy solution to the difficulty to send him away, as he had sent Mary Bailey away. It is the best thing to be done with black sheep—the best thing, but not the only thing.

Suppose all the black sheep were to be sent away!

Matilda Bray was in the girls' school hammering away at her class. He could hear her sharp, high-pitched voice before he reached the gate; but she followed him closely into the school-house. Somebody must have been watching for his coming, for she was in the schoolmaster's room as soon as he was.

'Oh, Mr. Lyon!' she said breathlessly, with a little tremble in her voice, 'I wanted to speak to you before you went upstairs. I wanted to ask you—to—beg of you not to be hard upon him. You must not judge him by the same standard you judge other men by. Consider his case—it is quite an exceptional case. Oh, you don know what this disappointment has been to him—my being here, and the loss of all that he had set his heart upon! Put yourself in his place. Think, if everything had slipped away from you, as it has slipped away from him, how you could have borne it! You haven't seen, as I have seen, how crushed and beaten he has been since he came back; and this failure of the boys in the examination—he said they would not answer at all when you examined them—was the last straw. It broke him down; he could not stand up against it. How should you know, who are prosperous and happy, who have never known sorrow or disappointment, what it is to be hopeless and despairing? Think of this—oh, think of this—before you judge him!'

She poured out this torrent of words with an eagerness and entreaty that were pitiful, if they were not pathetic, with her trembling hands stretched out before her.

Robert was touched in spite of himself—touched and affected. He had not much compassion for weakness—other people's weakness—but this girl standing here, with her outstretched hands, and her immense compassion for a man who was nothing to her, who never could be anything to her, moved him with a sudden revulsion of sympathy and compassion.

'I shall not be hard upon him,' he said; 'God forbid that I should be hard upon him! How can I be sure that I should not have done the same if I had been in his place?'

And then he went upstairs and turned the women out of the sick-room, and had half an hour's talk with the patient.

The schoolmistress was not in the room when he came downstairs—she had gone back to her work; but she overtook him before he reached the gate.

'There is another thing I want to speak about,' she said in her eager way, with the pink colour coming and going in her cheeks. 'The school must not be neglected. It will be a long time before he is able to do anything, but we—you and I, if you will help me—can do a great deal. We can work the boys up for the examination. There is yet a fortnight; we can do a great deal in a fortnight. I can spare two hours a day, or more; if you can give two hours of a morning, we shall have them quite ready by the time. Think what it will be to him for the boys to pass well—to get a good report!'

Her eyes were shining, and there were two pink spots on her freckled cheeks, and her face was all aglow, as she stood bareheaded in the cold north wind on this bitter January morning.

It quite shamed Robert to see her standing there—such

a frail little thing—so eager to help; he could not refuse her if he would. He did not know what Joan would say to it, when he told her that he had promised to take the boys' school for two hours every morning till the schoolmaster got well. He could not picture Joan taking so much trouble for anyone; she was made on different lines—finer lines.

Robert was as good as his word. He devoted two hours every morning to the school, and before the week was over he had, as he expressed it, licked it into something like shape. The expression was not wholly metaphorical. He sent for a couple of strong canes on the first morning of his work, and he threw away the splinters before noon; but he had occasion to send for no more canes during his two weeks of Spartan rule.

There had not been any discipline to speak of in the school until he took it in hand.

'The boys haven't learned ob*ay*dience,' the trembling pupil-teacher explained on the first morning of the Rector's rule.

'They'll have to learn it now, then,' he answered, with his face set like a flint, and the new cane in his hand.

They learnt it before noon, and then there was smooth sailing for all parties.

The schoolmaster was not quite so well at the end of the week; he had a relapse just as he was getting about, and had to go to bed again. Robert was not quite sure that he had not been making another attempt, a feeble one this time; he could not get at anything very easily, shut up in the house and carefully watched.

He had not much confidence in him. He talked over the relapse of the schoolmaster with Miss Bray one day after school, and she gave him the key to the whole matter.

'I think the poor fellow is very anxious about the examination,' she said. 'If the report is bad there will be no grant. I think he has been counting upon the grant; if it were anything considerable he was going to take a house in the village and marry Mary Bailey.'

She could not keep her voice quite steady as she spoke; there was a little reedy thrill in it that Robert could not understand.

'I don't see how he could expect a grant,' Robert said impatiently, 'with the school in the condition it is.'

'It is not so bad as it was,' Matilda Bray interrupted eagerly. 'I took some of the elder boys last night; I have an evening class for girls, and the boys came in after, and I found they had improved so much lately. I'm sure if you go on taking the school until the examination they will not do at all badly, and there may be a small grant after all.'

This was some encouragement.

Robert plodded on at the school for another week. It was quite astonishing what progress the boys made during those last days. He could not understand their eagerness and anxiety; they were not like the same boys. Matilda Bray was quite right about the examination. They not only did not do at all badly, but they got quite a respectable grant, and the school was specially commended for discipline in the inspector's report.

Robert did not know until long after, and the schoolmaster, fuming and fretting in his chamber above, never knew, that Matilda Bray had had the backward boys in her own room every night during that last week working them up for the examination. Let us hope that her own 'parchment' did not suffer.

It was quite as well, perhaps, that Robert's hands were so full during this anxious time; the occupation, the teaching, and the caning kept his mind employed, and kept him from dwelling on his own personal troubles.

Black Beauty had come back.

It had not fetched the low reserve price that Robert had put upon it, and it had been sent back. It had been rather a costly experiment, the cost of sending him up to town and bringing him back, the double commission for putting him up for sale twice, and the cost of keeping him in the stable for a fortnight. It came to as much as he was worth—that is to say, if he had been sold for the sum that was bidden for him he would have just cleared his expenses.

But he was not sold; he had come back, like that most unwelcome coin, a bad penny, and Robert had to pay for the experiment.

Black Beauty had come back rather the worse for the journey; he had hurt his leg, sprained a muscle somewhere, and he limped painfully back to his old quarters in the Rectory stables; it was quite as much as he could do to limp those five miles. The veterinary, who was sent for the next day, recommended rest—a long rest; he did not give much hope of his being worth very much when he had taken the rest, but he was quite useless now. He had seen his best days, he said, when Lord George made that handsome exchange, and now he was worn out and good for nothing.

Robert did not tell his wife all this; he told her that Black Beauty had fallen lame and would not be fit for use for a long time, not until she was able to ride him again.

Lady Alicia came down to Wytchanger for a few weeks at Christmas, and Robert and his wife were invited to participate in all sorts of gaieties. There could be no question about Joan refusing, and Robert would not go without her. He had no heart to pay another visit to Wytchanger. The remembrance of that last visit was rather sore with him just now. He would not go near the place, he said; he had had to pay dearly enough for his fine friends on that last occasion.

The roads were shockingly bad at this season, so he had some excuse for not calling. He met Lord George and his brother-in-law coming back one day from hunting. His lordship was not riding the chestnut, he noticed; he was riding a very fine hunter, and he overtook Robert's slow cob easily.

'How d'ye do, Lyon?' he called out in his hearty way as he came up to him. 'Sorry to hear about your wife. By the bye, that chestnut I swopped with you turned out an awful screw. She fell dead lame within a week.'

'I'm very sorry,' Robert said, biting his lip to keep back an unbecoming note of irritation in his voice; he would not have let Lord George see that he was angry and indignant for the world. 'It was an unfortunate transaction.'

And then he suddenly remembered that he had a parochial visit to make at a farmhouse in an opposite direction, and he opened a gate and cantered the cob across a field.

He was not in the habit of riding across his parishioners' fields, but he could not trust himself with Lord George a minute longer. He did not believe a word about the chestnut. It had been warranted to him sound and sure-footed, and it was worth a dozen of Black Beauty. He quite understood why Lord George had gone out of his way to tell that fib. He knew quite well—everybody in the neighbourhood knew—about that journey of Black Beauty's to Tattersall's, and how he had come back like a bad penny. He was angry and humiliated to think that Lord George should have told him that fib. He was only beginning to find out that a horse is a dreadfully demoralizing animal, that he cannot be bought, or sold, or exchanged, without oh! such a lot of fibs being told about him.

CHAPTER XXX.

THE COUNTESS'S NEW COMPANION.

LADY AYLMERTON took to Phyllis at once. It is not much an old woman wants: only patience, consideration —and love. She is not likely to want them long; she cannot in the course of things want them very long, and it is hard to close the chapter without them.

Is there anything more pitiful in life than a loveless, solitary old age, a bare, bleak old age, stripped of affection and sympathy, and sinking beneath the accumulated snows of swift returning winters?

Lady Aylmerton had had her share of good things—the things that the world calls good, riches and honour—but she had not had much love. Perhaps she had never given any. And now in her old age, when the riches and honour were slipping away from her, she had nothing left. A hard, unloving, cantankerous, narrow-minded old woman, whose selfish fires burned low, buried beneath the white ashes of disappointment and regret. Cecilia's flight had shaken her; she could not bear things so well now as she once could.

She got on with Phyllis from the first: she could not help getting on with her. When Joan came to see her sister, a few days after her arrival, she found her as much at home at Orchard Damerel as if she had lived there all her life. She was not reading sermons like poor Cecilia, with her heart far away; she was sitting in the boudoir, where the Countess spent the greater part of her days now, beside the fireplace, beneath the little miniatures in the frame, and she was making Lady Damerel tell her all about them. Cecilia had sat beneath them for years, but she had never once asked a single question about them.

Joan's visit stopped the little family history that her ladyship was telling. She received the Rector's wife very graciously; she never bullied her as she bullied the Rector. The story of the schoolmaster's illness had reached her, the version known in the village, and she plied Joan with questions; she had forgotten all about Cecilia.

'Is it really true,' she asked, 'that the Rector is taking the school every morning, and frightening the boys out of their wits?'

Then Joan had to explain that Robert had really taken the schoolmaster's place, and that he had already broken two canes to splinters, and that the unruly boys that Beckett could do nothing with were as meek as mice.

'And about that horse,' her ladyship asked; 'is it really true that Mr. Lyon has sent a valuable hunter up to London to sell it, and that it has been returned dead lame; that he has lost his money, and has had the horse returned to him worthless?'

Joan acknowledged that it was quite true that the horse had come back, that no one would buy it, and that it had come back lame. It was her horse, she remarked rather tartly; Robert had bought it for her; and it would be quite well by the time she wanted to ride it.

Her ladyship sniffed in her unpleasant way, and made some ill-natured, impertinent remarks—at least, Joan said they were impertinent—about clergymen and their wives going a-hunting, and Joan got up in a tiff and went away. She had not come there simply to be bullied.

When she was gone, Phyllis went back to the miniatures—the three dear little faces in one frame that were looking down upon her from the mantelpiece.

'The boy in blue is Guy Damerel, and the little girls were his sisters. I wonder what they were called. Were they called after their mother, the beautiful countess?' she asked.

She was so eager and interested in the miniatures that her ladyship made an effort to remember their names.

'I never heard of one called Katherine,' she said thoughtfully. 'There was little Guy, who was grandfather to the Earl, and Theodora, who married Lord Lovelace; there is a picture of her hanging on the staircase, taken after her wedding. The other child, I think I have heard, died young.'

Phyllis stopped on her way downstairs to look at the portrait of Lady Lovelace. If the likeness were a true one, she had not inherited her mother's beauty, but only her grand air and her proud looks.

A cold, haughty, disdainful-looking woman with weary eyes, and thin, scornful lips. She had been looking down upon everybody in that proud way for more than a hundred years.

'Oh, you poor thing!' Phyllis said with a shiver as she ran down the stairs. 'I wouldn't have been you for the world.

She often looked, as she went through those great gilded rooms, for a grown-up likeness of Lady Lovelace's little sister; she was sure she should recognise it She could not mistake the sweet hazel eyes and the soft chestnut curls. She went through every portrait in the house, but she never met with any that had the faintest resemblance to the proud Lady Lovelace's baby sister. No doubt she had died young, and left nothing behind her but the little sweet face that had been smiling sadly down upon succeeding generations of Damerels for more than a century.

Phyllis took an interest in everything in this great, silent, mysterious house. She could not account to herself for the interest she took in it. Perhaps because of its strange history, and the stranger future that awaited it. When Lady Aylmerton died it would all be shut up like a tomb for nobody knew how many years.

The furniture would be covered up in brown holland, and the china locked away in cupboards, and the silver dishes would be consigned to a dark, dismal, burglar-proof den. Spiders would build in the corners of the big gilded rooms, and spread their dusky webs over everything. It would all grow gray and mouldy. The shutters would be closed, and no ray of sunlight would penetrate into the dim, ghostly house. It would be exactly like a tomb, only the marble statues would go on standing in their ridiculous attitudes, and the pictures on the walls would look down with their dull painted eyes on the gray desolation around.

Oh, how tired they would get!

Some day, when a hundred summers had flown, when everyone that was living now was dead and buried and forgotten, a fairy prince with joyful step would push his way through the laurels, and turn the key in the old rusted lock. With what a flutter at his heart he would mount the dusty stairs, with the old Damerels on the walls looking down upon him! How the long-pent-up stream of life would awake at his coming, and the silent halls, and the dim, voiceless corridors would resound again with the cheerful hubbub 'of feet that ran, and doors that clapt'!

Phyllis often occupied herself by thinking pensively of that far-off time, when the old Earl's debts should be all paid, and the estates freed and unencumbered, and the unborn fairy prince should come into his own.

Who would be there to welcome him? Who? The bones of those who strove in other days to pass that stony portal, if not exactly scattered blanching on the grass, would be mouldering beneath the stones of the Aylmerton chapel, or lying among the humble village folk in the green churchyard outside.

There would be no Damerel of his name to welcome him in this strange house so strangely his. The furniture beneath its holland coverings would have fallen to pieces, moth and mildew and decay would have done their silent work; only those old pictures of old Damerels on the walls—or what was left of them—would remain to tell of the former glories of the ancient house.

It was sad to think of this place, with all its treasures, being shut up year after year, everything decaying and falling to pieces. It made Phyllis quite angry to think of it. She had no patience with the unreasonable old Earl and his ridiculous will. She was quite sure, if she were Hugh Damerel, she would take possession of the place directly the Countess was dead, and would only be removed by violence.

Phyllis had plenty of time to indulge these absurd fancies. Lady Aylmerton gave her very little to do; she did not want so many sermons read to her now. Phyllis's energy and sweetness and good temper cheered the old woman wonderfully, and took off the edge of her appetite for sermons. She took a fancy to Phyllis the first day, and treated her from the first a great deal better than she had ever treated poor Cecilia.

After the first few days, when she had got accustomed to the great rooms, and the grandeur and the novelty of it had worn off, the silence and the monotony of her life would have been intolerable if it had not been for this affection of Lady Aylmerton's. The dull, wet February weather kept them prisoners in the great house for days together. It would have been a dreary time if there had not been some affection between them—if Phyllis had not had some pity and sympathy for the poor, lonely old woman who had outlived all her natural ties.

Joan paid very few visits to Orchard Damerel after that day when her ladyship snubbed her; she pleaded the state of her health and the cold weather; but Phyllis was allowed to come over once a week to the Rectory, and spend a whole afternoon with her sister—her 'day out,' as she used to call it. Perhaps the hardest part of her lot was that she had so little to do.

She had only to write letters for the Countess, and keep her accounts, and read to her, and talk. Cecilia had not been good at talking, though she could read sermons without going to sleep over them by the hour.

She had nothing to talk about but the servants, and the weather, and her ladyship's rheumatism.

Phyllis talked about the rheumatism now—one cannot live with an old woman who is racked with pain without very often talking about it—but she talked about other things too: about her mother and the boys, and what struggles she was making to keep them at school, of her poor sister Bertha and her unfortunate situation.

She interested the Countess in the joys and sorrows of other people; she took her attention off from her own ailments, and gave her something to think of. Her good spirits cheered the lonely old woman, and warmed and expanded her poor frozen old heart. By-and-by, when a baby came rather unexpectedly at the Rectory, her ladyship was in quite as much of a flutter as Phyllis. She despatched her at once to see it, and to bring her back a particular account of it, as if it differed materially from any other baby born into the world.

It was a puny, weakly little thing, if that constituted a difference. Phyllis was allowed to pay daily visits to the Rectory until Joan was about again; she usually came back so full of nursery news that it gave the Countess something to think about till the next visit. The wet, windy spring weather had brought on a sharp attack of rheumatism, and her ladyship was confined to the house, to her room sometimes, but she never kept Phyllis back on that account; when it was dry she went by the short-cut through the shrubbery and meadows on foot, and when it was wet she was driven over to the Rectory in the big yellow chariot.

One day, coming back through the shrubbery after one of these visits, she was frightened by hearing steps behind her. She had stayed later than usual, and the dusk was falling, and it was a lonely and retired spot. Nobody used that path except people going to the house, and it was late now for visitors.

Phyllis walked as fast as she could without breaking into a run, but the footsteps gained upon her.

They caught her up at last, and then, to her great surprise, she saw it was Mr. Hugh Damerel.

'Why did you run away from me?' he asked; 'did you think I was a burglar, a poacher poaching on my own preserves?'

'I did not know you were here,' she said in her quick, nervous way. 'I should not have been afraid if I had known it was you. I am always expecting to see you come walking up to the house.'

'Are you?' he said with the gloomy smile she remembered so well; 'I'm afraid they would not let me in if I came very often.'

'Oh yes, they would,' she said hotly; 'if no one else would let you in, I would.'

She blushed crimson after she had spoken: she was dreadfully ashamed of the warmth with which she had espoused this young man's cause.

'You?' he said in surprise.

'Yes,' she answered, detecting the note of surprise in his voice; 'but perhaps you do not know—you have not heard that I am living here. I am Lady Aylmerton's companion. I have taken Cecilia's place.'

The heir of Orchard Damerel did not exactly whistle, but he uttered an exclamation of surprise, and his face softened.

'I am very glad,' he said huskily, 'I am very glad you are here. It is another omen in my favour.'

There was a door that led into the house through the conservatory, that Phyllis often used, and that she had left unlatched. She opened the door for him to pass into his own house, and she closed it after him. He followed her through the darkling rooms to the big empty drawing-room, and she left him there while she went to tell Lady Aylmerton of his coming.

Her ladyship was not so well to-day; she was in a good deal of pain, and she was a little impatient at Phyllis having stayed away from her so long.

'Oh, you don't know what you have done, child,' she said peevishly. 'Mr. Damerel has no right to come into this house except by the front-door; he has no right to come in without knocking. You must never let him in that way again. What has he come down here for?'

'He has come down to see you,' Phyllis explained; 'he heard that you were ill.'

'Who told him I was ill? Does he think I am going to die? Has he come down to take possession?'

Phyllis soothed the old woman's anger; there was nothing for her to be angry about. Mr. Damerel was in the neighbourhood, and he had heard that her ladyship was ill, and he had come over to make inquiries.

What else could he do? It would have been very horrid of him, Phyllis said, if he had gone on his way without calling. She espoused his cause so warmly that the old woman was somewhat reconciled.

'He should have written,' she said peevishly; 'he knows what the trustees have settled—that he is not to come to the house without invitation or permission. He has come without either, and you have let him in, child—you have let him in without his first asking for admission. Oh dear, what will the trustees say!'

CHAPTER XXXI.

ON THE WINDOW-PANE.

Lady Aylmerton could not let Hugh Damerel go away without his dinner. She could not go down herself—she could not turn in bed without groaning—but she sent Phyllis down to take her place at the head of the table.

She was very particular on that point; Mr. Damerel was not to sit at the head of the table; he was to take the place of a guest, and Phyllis was to sit in her ladyship's place.

Phyllis had never dined with anyone but her ladyship before since she had been at Orchard Damerel, and she descended the big, ill-lit staircase in some trepidation. During Lady Aylmerton's illness she had not gone through the form of dressing for dinner, but she dressed to-day.

She had no old gown of the Countess's to put on, like Cecilia; she had only an old worn velvet frock, opening modestly at the throat, with some frillings of white lace falling on it and revealing her pretty white throat. She had only a single string of tiny yellow pearls to tie round it, which made it look whiter than ever. She caught sight of her face in the glass as she was tying the pearls round her throat, and saw two pink spots on her cheeks and a light in her gray eyes that she had never seen there before. She could not think what had come to her; she was sure Mr. Damerel would notice it—the ridiculous poppy colour flaring in her cheeks; she was quite ashamed to go down the stairs with those old, familiar portraits staring down upon her with their hard, watchful eyes.

If the staircase was dim, the drawing-room was unusually light. Peters had lighted the big chandelier over the table that was only lighted when guests were staying in the house, and he had put out the old, massive silver on the sideboard that was also only brought to light on state occasions. Phyllis had never seen so much silver on the table before, and the gardener had sent in some flowers.

She took it all in as she came into the room blushing dreadfully, with the pearls at her throat, and the soft folds of her velvet gown trailing on the carpet.

Hugh Damerel, standing on the hearth with his back to the fire, thought he had never seen any woman so winsome as this slight, girlish figure, with her blushing cheeks and her modest grace, coming into this stately room. The gilding and the rich hangings, the glitter of silver plate, the hot-house flowers, and the magnificent appointments of the grand old room, seemed a fitting surrounding for this shy, winsome creature.

He went forward and led her to her seat at the head of the table. The Countess need not have been so precise in her directions to Phyllis. The Earl of Aylmerton's heir made no attempt to claim it.

There was little conversation at table; the servants were in the room all the time, and Hugh Damerel never talked of his wrongs before the servants; he had no other subject to talk about. Though he had had a long journey, he had no appetite for his dinner. He could only lean back in his chair and look at the beautiful room, and the pictures of the old Damerels on the walls, the rich gilding and draperies, and the gold and silver plate on the sideboard. It was all his—all—and he was sitting here a guest on sufferance. He was only treated in this way, with this honour, to mark the distinction that he was there as a guest, and not the owner an· master of all.

Phyllis knew exactly what he felt; she was dreadfull sorry for him. She made a pretence of eating, but ther was a strange feeling in her throat that would hardly le her swallow a morsel. She could not think what was th matter with her throat. She was glad when the tim came that she could get up and go into the drawing-roon

This, too, had been lighted for company, and a big fir was blazing on the hearth. Phyllis sat down beside ı and began to think of that dreadful time she was alway picturing, when the house would be shut up like a tom and the moth and the spiders would have it all to them selves.

She was still thinking of it when Hugh Damerel cam in. He came in so softly, or she was so preoccupiec that she did not hear him cross the room until he wa standing by her side.

'I did not hear you come in,' she said, looking up witl that faint quiver in her eyelids he remembered so well.

He was standing beside the big marble mantelpiece with its carved statuary and its hideous red velve alcoves, and he looked down at her quivering eyelids, an· then he remarked that her eyes were full of tears.

'You were dreaming,' he said, with a voice that wa not quite steady. 'I—I wonder what you were dreamin about.'

'I was thinking how wicked it would be to shut thi place up,' she said, blushing a little beneath his eyes and trying to conceal her tears. She would not hav him see those foolish tears for the world. 'If you hav never been over it, you cannot understand what it is; i is full of lovely things.'

'Yes; it would be a pity.'

'It would be more than a pity—it would be wicked Oh, you don't know what treasures there are in thi house. I often go over it when I have nothing to do and peep into the rooms, and look at the beautiful ol(things, the embroideries, and the hangings, and th(splendid old furniture. If it's shut up for a hundre(years, the furniture will all have fallen to decay, and th(

moth will have eaten up the old needlework, and the lace, and the hangings. They have begun already. Oh, it is a cruel, cruel waste!'

'Yes,' he said, 'it is a cruel waste.'

She could not understand his taking it so quietly.

'It will be no benefit to anyone,' she went on, speaking rapidly; 'it will do no one any good shutting it up. It is a wicked, selfish thing to do. Think how wonderfully happy some people could be made living here, among all these beautiful things, using them carefully, and passing them on to those that came after! How much better it would be to have the place full of happy voices, and the pattering footsteps of children on the stairs, and their merry laughter echoing in the galleries, than shutting it up like a tomb!'

Hugh Damerel laughed, a dreary laugh that seemed to go travelling round the big, dusky room.

'No children of mine,' he said bitterly, 'are ever likely to wake the echoes in this house. There have been no children's footsteps on the stairs, no children's voices in those mouldy nurseries in the roof, for more than a century. The Earl was brought up at Aylmerton, and his father before him. He only came here to retrench when he could no longer live in his old style and splendour. It is long since any children's laughter was heard in this dismal place; you have well called it a tomb.'

'There are some dear little miniatures upstairs, in the Countess's boudoir, of some lovely children who lived here not so very long ago,' Phyllis said eagerly; 'they were her children.'

She nodded as she spoke in the direction of the famous picture by Gainsborough of the beautiful Countess Katherine.

Hugh Damerel glanced over his shoulder at the picture with faint interest; he had seen it dozens of times before.

'She was the Earl's great-grandmother,' he said; 'the miniatures, which I do not remember, must be of her son, Guy Damerel, the grandfather of the Earl. I did not know there were any other children; there was a blight upon the race; the children, if any were born to the

Damerels, died young. It had dwindled down generation after generation, until it died out, and not one of the old stock could be found to succeed to the title and inherit the mortgaged estates. If there had been one of the race left with the remotest claim, the curse would not have fallen upon me. Why was I ever called Hugh Damerel—why—why?'

The old unrest and impatience had come back to him, and he began to pace the room in his moody fretful way. He forgot all about Phyllis; he only remembered his wrongs, and how his life had been blighted by this lying mockery of an inheritance.

Phyllis had never seen him in his fierce mood before, and he frightened her with his mutterings and his execrations of the foolish old dotard who had bequeathed to him and his this great property, and these rich priceless heirlooms.

Phyllis suddenly remembered that the Countess would be missing her, and she got up from her seat by the fire and timidly wished him good-night.

He stopped in the middle of his walk, and took the little trembling hand she extended to him.

'I am a brute, Miss Penrose,' he said humbly. 'I am a selfish, inconsiderate brute. When I get on that miserable subject, I forget everything else—I forgot even you!'

He was penitent and ashamed, and well he might be. He had been behaving like a bear.

He was still penitent the next morning when he met Phyllis at breakfast. Lady Aylmerton had consented to his remaining in the house as a guest for the night. He was particularly cautioned by the housekeeper, whom her ladyship had charged with her message, that he was only invited to remain as a guest.

It was not the first time he had been reminded of his position in that house, but he accepted the invitation thankfully, almost humbly. He was glad to remain on any terms; he was in no hurry to go away. Lady Aylmerton was not likely to ask him to marry her new companion, as she had asked him to marry Cecilia; if she did, he would not be likely to give the same answer.

He remembered the little miniatures Phyllis had spoken

of as he was eating his breakfast the next morning, and he asked her to show him where they were to be found. Lady Aylmerton was in bed, and likely to be there for days, until the attack wore itself out; so that Phyllis took him up to the boudoir at once. There was no reason why he should not go up there. It was his own house; he was the owner of it, if only in name.

He had forgotten all about the miniatures over the mantelpiece that he had seen on his last visit, until Phyllis took him up into the lovely old room the Countess used as a boudoir, and showed him the case with the three little children's heads. He recollected them at once as he stood on the threshold in the sweet April sunshine. He remembered the occasion when he had last seen them, on that dull December morning when her ladyship had asked him to marry her niece. He quite shivered at the thought. He recollected the whole scene—the coarse, commonplace old woman in the shabby plaid shawl by the fireplace, the feathery flakes of snow on the window-ledge, the wintry landscape without, the fire crackling on the hearth, and the three little bright faces looking down upon the humiliating interview.

'And these were the children of the beautiful Countess Kate?' he said, examining them with some faint show of interest. 'I did not know that there were any girls. Do you happen to know who they were, and what became of them?'

'One of them, the eldest, married Lord Lovelace; there is a picture of her on the staircase. I always call her the proud Lady Lovelace. I believe she was very unhappy, and her children died before her.'

'And the other?' he asked.

'No one knows anything about the other little girl, not even her name. The Countess thinks that she died young. I have looked through all the rooms, and I cannot find any other likeness of her.'

'There is something written under the miniatures,' he said, taking the frame down from its place and carrying it over to the light. 'It looks like the names of the children; but I cannot make them out.'

There was something written in faded ink under each

of the little faces, but the characters were no longer traceable.

There was a letter *H*, a capital letter, under the third miniature, and the remains of a *t*—it was certainly a letter *t*; the crossing was faintly visible—in the middle of a name, and it was not a long name.

The writing would not tell him anything. He replaced the frame over the mantelpiece, and came back to the window where Phyllis was standing. A wide, fair prospect spread out before the window, green with the sweet fresh greenness of the year, and the blue April skies were above. The deer were sheltering beneath the great trees in the park, the oaken clumps and the spreading chestnuts, and a thrush—a dozen thrushes were singing in the branches, which were bare no longer, but bursting into leaf and flower.

Phyllis had looked from that window hundreds of times at the dreary, dreary landscape, but a change had come over the scene to-day, and it was dreary no longer.

The air was full of sunshine and song; the cloudy, windy, wintry days were all past, and spring had come—spring, with its eternal lesson of hope and promise.

Phyllis sighed as she turned away from the window; she did not know what she sighed for. Hugh Damerel had something to sigh for, but he set his lips hard and followed Phyllis silently out of the room.

She had the long morning all to herself, and she took him over the house—his own house, of the ways of which he was so strangely ignorant.

She led him through all the shut-up, silent chambers, that had not been used for years and years, that might never be used again for a century. They were getting mouldy already. They had been shut up all through the long winter without fire or ventilation, and they now struck damp and chilly, like a vault.

The furniture was covered up in holland cases, and the bedding was rolled up in bundles. It would not be worth much a hundred years hence. The beautiful down beds, and the prime goose-feather pillows and bolsters, would have grown musty and unfit for human use, and the old embroidered bed-hangings would be moth-eaten, and dry-rot would have got into the laths and woodwork of the huge carved bedsteads. It would be all useless lumber when the fairy prince came a hundred years hence, and peered curiously into these long-closed chambers. He would find very little here of worth. He would not be able to see his face in the mirrors, which were clouding already with damp and neglect; he would not be able to trust his weight on the decayed framework of the worm-eaten old chairs. There would be nothing left but the four walls, which already wanted painting dreadfully.

Yes, there would be something else, the heir remarked moodily. He had not much interest in these things that were falling year by year to decay and ruin; they were nothing to him—they were, indeed, never likely to be anything to him.

There would be the old carved ceilings of these gloomy state-rooms; they would not be likely to decay with the other things. Someone had whitewashed them over; they were so thick with whitewash that not a bit of the original oak was visible. This friendly vandalism would preserve them for another hundred years.

They did not leave a corner of the house unvisited. They left the dim, ghostly state-chambers of birth and death with something of a solemn feeling as they closed the doors upon them, like taking leave of the dead, and went silently up the staircase into the floor above, the garrets and sleeping-rooms of a vast army of retainers, befitting an earl's household, and the long-shut-up nurseries. No children's footsteps had pattered over the warped, uneven oak floors for more than a century. Mildew and dust lay thick upon the rickety old-fashioned furniture, on the cradle which the Earl's grandfather had been rocked in, on the high chair and the twisted-legged oak table where he had sat at meat. There was a child's crib in one corner—a clumsy contrivance with the sides missing—and a big oaken press, which had once been used as a receptacle for toys. There were no toys there now. The cupboard was quite empty, except for a colony of spiders which had taken up their abode there, and which scuttled away in a hurry when Phyllis opened the door and let the daylight in upon them.

Thick dust and shroud-like cobwebs covered up everything like a pall. The glass in the windows was blear and dim with age; it was old, old glass, and must have been put in those twisted leaden casements when the house was built. It could never have been bright and clear like spicspan modern glass; it was thick, and wavy, and uneven, and of a dull green colour, but it served its purpose, and let the daylight through. It had reflected the rosy sunsets through the flickering leaves, or the waving boughs of the giant elm-trees that stood sentinel over that western front, for over two hundred years.

There were some names faintly traced on the old blurred panes, and dates going back to the troubled days of the Stuarts. Phyllis had noticed the names scratched on the glass when she had paid a former visit to these deserted rooms, and she called Mr. Damerel's attention to them, two names side by side, 'Dorothy' and 'Hugh.'

He did not come over to look at them at once; he had found some other inscriptions, low down on another window, and he was trying his hardest to decipher them.

He came over presently, when he had made them out. The little childish scrawl had been scratched on the glass by the hand that had fought loyally for the King through all the Civil Wars, and was found lying cold and stiff in death, still clasping the unsheathed sword, on the plains of Marston Moor. His tomb, with a canopy over it and a recumbent figure in knightly armour, with the hound at his feet and the naked sword at his side, was in the Aylmerton chapel. Phyllis had seen it dozens of times, but the marble figure, with its pompous epitaph, did not bring back the brave Sir Hugh as the childish scrawl on the window-pane had done.

Hugh Damerel had found some inscriptions of a later date, three names scratched on the three lower panes of the adjoining window—'Guy' in a large, bold, sprawling hand, as if scratched with a sharp instrument, in the middle pane, and on either side a thin, indistinct inscription, that might have been scratched with a pin, 'Theodora' on one pane, and 'Hester' on the other.

The scratchings on the glass brought back the three dear little faces in the frame over the mantelpiece in the room below. Phyllis fancied she could hear their little feet pattering over the floor, and their merry childish laughter.

The tears came into her eyes as she closed the door of that mouldy old nursery, sacred to their innocent memories.

Hugh Damerel went away the same day. He had nothing to wait for. The Countess was ill, but not dying. She had no intention of dying just yet. There was nothing for him to do but get back to his pictures.

CHAPTER XXXII.

THAT LITTLE BILL.

A FEW days before the expiration of the three months when the bill Robert had signed fell due, he received a printed form apprising him of the fact, and offering to renew it if payment was just then inconvenient.

It was decidedly inconvenient.

It was absolutely impossible for Robert to meet it till his tithes came in, and he did not quite see how he should meet it then. If they were paid in full at that magnificent stipend of two hundred and eighty pounds a year, they could only amount to one hundred and forty pounds for the six months, allowing, as it was understood, six months' grace for the payment of the remainder.

If he paid the whole of his half-year's income when it came in, he would still be in debt the remaining forty pounds, and he would not have a penny to live upon during the next half-year.

Those Christmas bills, and the expenses of sending that wretched horse up and down to Tattersall's, and Joan's illness, had been a heavy pull upon this first quarter of the year. The hundred and fifty pounds was gone—quite gone; there was not a penny left of it. He was thinking of borrowing another hundred, the last transaction had seemed so easy and pleasant. It was only to invite a charming young gentleman down, and show him over the church, and give him some lunch, and the matter was arranged.

Robert wrote off at once, and said with perfect truthfulness that he was unable to meet the bill till such time as his tithes came in, and asked that it might be renewed, according to promise, for another three or six months.

The reply came prompt and to the point.

The philanthropist was quite willing to renew the bill to oblige Mr. Lyon on the payment of expenses incidental to the recovery of the bill, which was unfortunately out of his hands. Ten pounds might cover this transaction. On the payment of this sum, and the further sum of thirty pounds, the interest for the three months' extension applied for, the bill would be renewed.

Robert Lyon read this precious epistle with a gasp of astonishment. He could not believe his eyes. There must be a mistake somewhere. The young gentleman who had eaten his lunch and admired his church had assured him that the dating of the bill at three months instead of six was a mere matter of form. He had distinctly told him that it could be renewed at the expiration of that time without further cost. The twenty per cent. interest he had already paid covered all, everything.

Robert wrote off at once and demanded an explanation. He got it, as he had got his cheque, and that other reply to his letter, by return. The philanthropist added to his other virtues promptness and despatch. He did not keep a cheque dangling before a man's eyes for a week; he sent it to him by return.

Mr. William Wilberforce—he was called William—presented his compliments to Mr. Lyon, and sent him a copy of the rigmarole which he, Robert, had written out at the dictation of that bland young man, with his signature attached. 'He failed to see how Mr. Lyon, after reading that document (which must have escaped his memory), could ask if the bill was renewable without further charge.'

Robert owned with a groan that he had not understood a word of that document when he had written it, but he thought he saw the drift of it now. The game was up—it was no use kicking against the pricks, and there was nothing left to be done but to pay.

It is one thing to talk in a princely way about paying, and another thing to pay. Robert had not the least idea where he could raise the money; he could not even raise the forty pounds for the renewal of the bill. No one would give a pound a leg for Black Beauty, who was limping about the orchard a sorry spectacle of a hunter. There were Joan's ponies, and the carriage, and the cob which he drove in the dog-cart. It went to his heart to think of selling the ponies just as Joan was getting about again; and it was quite out of the question to sell the cob.

There would be nothing to bring things back from the station, or to go between the Rectory and Carlingford, if that were sold. They could not use the pony-carriage for a market-cart. Robert dropped his face into his hands and cursed his folly.

Many men have done the same thing, but it has not helped them very much. He could not understand how he could have been such a fool. He did not mince matters now; the time for mincing and romancing had gone, and he had to face facts.

He could not think, as he looked back on those happy thoughtless days, when he and Joan had taken possession of their new home, what could have possessed him!

He had scattered money—his little two thousand pounds—with the ease and prodigality of a man with an estate and a rent-roll.

He had spent his money as if it would never come to an end. He never thought it *could* come to an end. It was like his happiness; it was going to last for ever. He and Joan had been like two children; they had dreamed blissfully through their short, bright sunshiny day, and they had never thought of to-morrow.

They had been so happy! they had thought of nobody but themselves. The world was made for them; they had enjoyed it in their way, not denying themselves anything, filling the cup up to the brim—the very brim—and giving no thought to the morrow.

It is not much use being sorry when a thing is done. Robert could not bring himself to be very sorry—he had drunk deep of the cup of happiness; he would not have lost the memory, the full sweet flavour of that divine draught, for another two thousand pounds—for all the world. He could never live that six months over again.

No regrets or reproaches would have brought back the money that had been thrown away. It had been literally thrown away, a great deal of it; it had been thrown away upon things that were not needed, that could be done without, that would not have fetched a quarter the price if they had been sold again the next day.

Looking backward upon his folly, Robert Lyon could not understand how he could have been so utterly demented as to think that two thousand pounds would go on for ever.

He had fondly hoped that it would have gone on from year to year, coming in at intervals to fill up gaps, when the income he derived from his living was insufficient—and now it was all gone at the end of the first six months! There was nothing left for all the future but that poor little stipend that was anticipated, that was quite swallowed up, before it became due.

To make matters worse, Robert did not dare to tell his wife how matters stood; he had never breathed a word about that wretched bill to her, and he had not the courage to tell her now. She was not strong enough to bear it just yet, he told himself; it would be better to wait till she was stronger.

Joan had not made a very good getting up. She was looking thin and pale, the ghost of her bright self, and she was nervous and dispirited. She was not a bit like the old Joan of former days. The doctor said she wanted rousing, a change would do her good. There was nothing like a month's thorough change.

Robert sighed, and shook his head sadly, when the doctor suggested that expensive remedy. He did not see how he could get away, he said; he could not very well leave the parish at this season, not at any rate until after Easter. Joan did not catch the sigh, but she caught the tone in which those evasive words were spoken. She knew every tone in his voice: he could not hide that jarring note from her; and she saw those two upright lines come out in his forehead between his eyebrows. She did not remember to have seen two there till lately.

'I think I'd rather not go away yet, Robbie,' she said, when the doctor was gone—he had taken himself quite off now, with his bottles large and small, quite off until he was summoned again—'I'm sure it would do me more harm than good, and baby isn't at all strong. What *should* we do if she were ill while we were away?'

Joan's thin flushed face grew quite pale at the dreadful thought. She would not for worlds go away where the baby could not have all the care and attention and watching that she was accustomed to have.

'There is no place,' she said with great decision, 'for a little tiny wee baby like its own beautiful home. It does not want a change: why should it? It has had a good deal of change already.'

There was some truth in what Joan said, but Robert did not feel quite comfortable in ignoring altogether the doctor's prescription. The baby was a weak, puny little thing, and would not bear much buffeting about, and, as his wife had remarked, it had had a good deal of change already.

Easter would be here presently, with its beautiful services, and its sweet bright spring days full of hope and promise. Things would look better after Easter: the long gloomy winter would be gone, and the earth would blossom under their feet. Joan would get up her strength, and the baby would grow fat and rosy, and that dark cloud that hung over Robert like a pall would be dispelled, and everything would come right again.

The baby was to be christened at Easter, and Phyllis and Bertha were to be sponsors, and nothing would satisfy Joan now but that all the family—Bertha, and the boys, and her mother—should come down to the christening. She so wanted to show her mother her first-born.

The sight of their dear faces, she said, would do her more good than all the changes in the world.

Phyllis thought the idea 'splendid,' when she came over. It was exactly what she had been longing for ever since she came to Coombe Damerel. She knew how her mother and Bertha were hungering to see Joan's beautiful home. She had not told them half: they must see it for themselves to understand in what pleasant places the lines had fallen to Joan, and with what a goodly heritage a bountiful Providence had dowered her.

And, besides all this, there was the baby!

There were no school terms to stand in their way, for the boys were home for the holidays. There was nothing to prevent them from coming at once.

Joan wrote to her mother and Bertha that very night; she could not keep the great news a day longer. They were all to come down—all, every one. The country was looking lovely; everything was bursting into leaf and flower. The orchards were yellow with daffodils, the meadows with king-cups, and the wild cherry-blossom and the blackthorn in the hedges were in bloom. The cuckoo had already come, and there was a blackbird's nest in the elm-tree just outside her window. The boys could get as many birds' eggs as they liked. The lambs were bleating in the orchard, and there was a brood of downy young ducks on the pond—and baby was longing to see its grandmamma!

These, and a hundred other fond inducements, tripped off the end of Joan's joyful pen, as she wrote those pressing letters of invitation to the dear people at home. She filled four whole sheets, and if she had not been summoned to the nursery she would have filled four more.

There was no need for her to have held out all these delightful inducements to beguile those poor things from their dreary home in a back street to the beautiful green country. Mrs. Penrose could not read Joan's letter for the mist, the quite unaccountable mist, that swam before her eyes. It made all the words run together. Bertha told the boys the news long before her mother had finished reading the first page; her eyes were clear and bright, and were not troubled with dimness, except on very rare occasions.

The boys shouted like mad things. They had a wrestling-match in the back-garden on the strength of it, and paused in the middle to give three cheers for Joan. Chris, who was very keen upon birds' eggs, looked through his collection that afternoon, and threw away all the damaged specimens. There were some rare eggs among them, cuckoos', bitterns', hawks', plovers', and herons' eggs, but he threw them all away. He was going down into the finest birds'-nesting country in the world, and he would bring back with him something like specimens. So he threw those patched and mended old things away to begin with.

They came down two or three days before Easter. There were such a lot of them, and they brought such a heap of luggage—the boys' best clothes, and Mrs. Penrose's and Bertha's evening gowns. There was no saying for what great occasions they might be needed. Joan's great friends would be down at Easter, and they would meet the Earl and Lord George, of whom they had heard a great deal. Besides that, they would have to pay a visit to the Countess, and Phyllis would not like them to look dowdy. They filled their shabby old boxes up with the dinner-gowns and the evening things that had been packed away ever since Joan's wedding. Bertha worked from morning till night all those two last days before they went away, altering those evening gowns to the latest fashion.

Both the carriages from the Rectory were at the station to meet them—the pony-carriage for Mrs. Penrose and Bertha, and the dogcart for the boys and the luggage. It was like a royal procession. It was more than that: it was a procession of love, joy, happiness—happiness perfect and supreme!

CHAPTER XXXIII.

EASTERTIDE.

THAT long-anticipated visit of her own people did Joan a great deal more good than the most thorough change. The sight of their dear faces was better than the sight of the fairest prospect in the world. Her mother's face had grown older and thinner, she thought, since she had seen it last. It was lined and marred with a thousand sordid, petty cares, which left their marks behind quite as deep as nobler ones; but it grew youthful and tender, with that infinite tenderness of mother-love in it, when she folded Joan's tiny babe to her heart.

Seen through those tender eyes, Joan's little fragile Lent-lily was no longer puny and weak. It was a remarkably fine baby for its age; what could you expect of a babe of a month?

Everything was perfect and lovely, like the baby. There never was such a rectory-house, such lawns and gardens and stables, such a delightful country, such fishing, tubbing, riding, driving, and birds'-nesting. The days flew by like a dream; there was so much to crowd into them. The boys were out fishing or riding all the day; they had no time to search for birds' eggs. They scoured the country round on the back seat of Robert's dogcart, and nearly broke their necks a hundred times jumping in and jumping out in the most unexpected way on the least provocation. They rode poor old Black Beauty to death, and brought him home dead lame. He was not worth very much when they came, but he would not have fetched a pound a leg when they went away.

Robert, if the truth were told, was not sorry when they went away. They broke down his hedges, and trampled over his flower-garden, and ruined the lawn, and broke his fishing-tackle, and lamed his horses, and covered that back seat of his newly-varnished dogcart with scratches. They did exactly what boys have done from time immemorial. They would not be boys if they did not do these thoughtless things; they would be horrible priggish old men.

Bertha took her holiday more soberly, but she enjoyed it none the less. She enjoyed the sweet sights and sounds as only those who are shut up all the year in a shabby little house in a dingy street can enjoy beauty and freedom. The world was breaking into blossom under her feet, and the April skies were blue above, and everything was full of promise and hope.

She was not exactly envious of Joan as she wandered among the trim flower-beds, by the well-kept lawns, and through the orchards, where the branches were already white with blossom above her head, and the yellow daffodils were crowding up at her feet. She was not exactly envious of her more fortunate sister, but she felt that all this might have been hers, if it had not been for Joan and Phyllis—if they had not stood in her way.

The long, bright, sunshiny days were much too short to indulge in these foolish fancies. There was so much to be done. The church had to be decorated for Easter, and the Rector's wife could not help a bit. She could only look on for a few minutes, and then Robert came and called her away.

The Countess was well enough to spare Phyllis for a few hours, and while the sisters were kneeling together beside the font—the font in which Joan's baby was to be christened, and that took such a lot of decorating—Phyllis told her sister all about the disappointed heir.

She took her into the Aylmerton chapel and showed her the monuments of the Damerels, and the selfish old Earl, the painted arms in the windows, and the armorial bearings of the Aylmertons and Damerels, and the noble families they had married into, carven on roof and wall, and the gloomy hatchment over the screen. It had been put up seven years ago, when the Earl died, and it was there still.

'Will Mr. Damerel never come into the estate?' Bertha asked her sister, as they stood in the Aylmerton chapel among all these decaying memorials of the greatness and grandeur of the old house.

'Unless anything should happen, and the trustees should find out a way of paying the Earl's debts sooner than they expect, Mr. Damerel will never come into it in his lifetime,' Phyllis said, with a little sigh she could not keep back.

'Whom will it go to, then? Will it go to his children?'

'I don't think Mr. Damerel will ever marry,' Phyllis said, blushing scarlet. 'Unless anything quite unexpected should happen, it will never benefit him or his.'

'Happen!—what is likely to happen? and why will the foolish young man never marry? He ought to marry at once; he ought to lose no time in getting married. He has lost seven years already.'

'Nobody knows what may happen,' Phyllis said softly,

with that faint quiver of her drooping eyelids that her sister knew so well. 'Lady Aylmerton may do something for him at the last. I don't think he would ever marry for the sake of keeping this great unhappy fortune in the family. It has ruined his life; why should it ruin the lives of his children after him?'

'Oh, that's all nonsense,' Bertha said sharply. She had no patience with Phyllis and her dreamy notions. 'It is his duty to marry. It is quite preposterous to think of letting this great fortune, this wonderful inheritance, slip out of the family. It is simply robbing one's descendants.'

'If Mr. Damerel never has any children he cannot rob them,' Phyllis said softly; 'and—and I think he is better as he is.'

She was stooping over a spray of white cherry-blossom that would not stand upright in the window of the Aylmerton chapel, and Bertha did not see that her cheeks were crimson and her lips were trembling.

Perhaps it was the crimson streaming through the painted arms in the pane above; but that would not account for that tremulous quiver about her lips.

The sisters stayed in the church till the Easter decorations were all finished, till the last primrose was stuck in the moss that covered up the font, and the last bough of cherry-blossom was wreathed round the chancel rails. When it was all done, and the church looked like a garden, a lovely green garden, blazing with the first gold of the year, they came away and left an old woman to clear up the mess.

The churchyard was a scene of unwonted animation as they passed through it. The village children were trimming the graves, and some women were busy with brushes and buckets scrubbing the old moss-grown tombstones. They had forgotten, maybe, all the year those who lay beneath, and some they could never have known; but now, on this Easter Eve, according to the old West Country custom, they were garnishing their poor old tombstones, and trimming up their forgotten graves with the sweet emblems of 'the Resurrection and the Life.'

It brought the tears into Phyllis's eyes to see these busy, willing workers engaged in their tender offices. Bertha could not understand how people could find any pleasure in such an unpleasant, thankless task as scrubbing mouldy old tombstones, or clearing the weeds away from tangled, neglected graves. It could not possibly do any good to those who lay beneath. It was a bit of old-world folly and superstition.

While Bertha was walking round the little churchyard with her nose in the air, pitying these poor, ignorant rustics, Phyllis had crept back into the church. There were still some flowers left from the decorations; there was quite a heap in the porch that the old woman would clear away presently. Phyllis picked out a bunch of gold and green, rich yellow kingcups, and golden daffodils, and pale primroses, and carried them up beyond the screen into the Aylmerton chapel.

Nobody had remembered the old Earl, who had been so worshipped and feared in his life. No one had brought a scrubbing-brush and a pail and washed his old tombstone.

Phyllis selected all the golden flowers from her bunch and laid them reverently on the marble recumbent figure, with their sweet, solemn message of 'the Resurrection and the Life.'

She had still a few white, drooping blossoms in her hand, and she strewed them at the feet of the stately effigy of the beautiful Countess. She had trod upon flowers all her life, and—and surely she would tread upon flowers, unfading flowers, again.

The Countess came to church the next day in the old yellow chariot She had never been absent on an Easter day before, and she made an effort, in spite of her rheumatism, to come. Her ailments seldom lasted in the acute stage very long; she was in bed groaning one day and up the next. She had been in bed groaning only a few days ago, and she was at church to-day, to everybody's astonishment and Robert's dismay, sitting bolt upright in her high pew in the Aylmerton chapel.

Robert had not expected her ladyship; he thought she would be at home reading one of her edifying sermons, and he had not gone to that shabby bag in the Bluebeard cupboard and brought out a discoloured manuscript, and flattened it out, and put it into his sermon-case. He had written a short, simple discourse, addressed directly to the hearts of the simple folk who had been commemorating this Easter Day with that foolish, tender old superstitious observance of making ready for the joyful resurrection of those who lay sleeping in the yard outside. He had seen those spring-flowers on the old nameless graves as he had walked up the path, and the sight had touched him, and he had gone up into the pulpit and told his flock of a very different millennium from that far-off, uncertain event he was in the habit of preaching about.

He forgot all about her ladyship when he spoke of that quite certain joyful season the flowers on the graves outside foreshadowed—the flowers on the font, on the walls, on the altar symbolized—the new life of infinite joy and love and praise that lay beyond the narrow confines of time and sense.

It was like one of his old Stoke Lucy sermons.

The Countess was hobbling away after the congregation had filed out of the church, when she caught sight of the yellow flowers on her husband's tomb. She could not see very well; her eyes were failing as well as her legs; she could only see a sheen of gold and green on the white marble effigy of her lord.

Somebody had been thinking of *his* resurrection, and making ready for it. She could not think who had done it Cecilia had never put a single flower on his tomb in her life. She was very glad that someone had remembered him. It gave her something to think about for the rest of the day, and set her a-wondering whether any loving hands would lay the gold and the green on her cold stone when she lay beside him. Of all she had benefited in her long life, she could not think of any who would perform this tender office.

They christened the little weakly baby in the afternoon, and gave it its mother's old-fashioned name.

'It is an old family name,' Mrs. Penrose explained, when they had got back from church and were gathered round the fire in the library; 'it has been in the family for centuries. Joan was christened after my great-aunt; you have got her picture somewhere.'

Then somebody remembered that Aunt Joan's picture hung behind the library-door. They all went over to look at it, and while they looked at it they made a discovery, or, rather, they made two discoveries. They discovered that it was exactly like the baby—the family likeness had been faithfully carried on—and that it was not nearly so hideous as they had all voted it to be.

Aunt Joan had grown much better-looking, or they saw her with different eyes.

It depends so much upon the eyes you look at things with what you make them.

Phyllis had grown so accustomed to the old portraits on the walls of Orchard Damerel, the beautiful ancestors in their old-fashioned gowns, with the tender grace of a day long past still lingering about them, that she looked up at this despised picture of Aunt Joan with quite new eyes.

'I think it is a lovely picture,' she said presently; 'it is very like some at Orchard Damerel, some that they set a great value upon. I am very glad it was sent down here, that it was not sold with the rest.'

Joan smiled at Phyllis's earnestness; she did not see anything in the shabby old picture; but there certainly was a distinct resemblance to the baby.

They sat round the fire, making plans for the morrow, during that happy evening. Mrs. Penrose had not been over to Orchard Damerel yet, and Joan proposed to drive her over in the pony-carriage. It would be such a proud thing to drive her mother over in her own carriage, and show her all the beautiful things by the way. She had looked forward to that drive for months. What is the use of having beautiful things if those you love do not share them with you?

There were delightful plans made for the morrow. Bertha was to drive over in the dogcart, and the boys were to ride behind. They were to do a lot of birds'-nesting, while Bertha and her mother were in the house; there were some rare birds haunting the coombe, and the old nests in the great trees in the park had not been disturbed for years.

Easter had fallen late, as late as it *could* fall, this year; it was full spring, almost summer, and the air was balmy, and the flowers were crowding out in the hedges, and the orchards already white with blossom.

It was a quite perfect April morning; the boys had been out scouring the country since daybreak—they could not afford to lose an hour of this delightful holiday-time—and Bertha and her mother were loitering in the flower-garden. They had been loitering about the grounds since breakfast; about the orchards, and the paddock, and the home-farm, as they called the poultry-yard; they would loiter about these pleasant places until noon, when they would drive over in great state to Orchard Damerel to luncheon with the Countess, by her ladyship's special invitation.

Mrs. Penrose had never taken luncheon with a countess before, and she was rather disturbed in her mind about her toilette. She was not at all sure what she ought to wear on such an august occasion. She had brought down her best gown, a stiff silk that had seen a good deal of wear, and which had been discreetly covered with beads and lace, only its best points, its very best points, being visible. Bertha objected to her mother's 'beady gown,' as she somewhat irreverently termed this relic of bygone splendour, and suggested a more sober toilet; but Mrs. Penrose, for once in her life, was obdurate. She had brought down the beady gown, and she meant to wear it. If she did not wear it now she might not have another chance.

She was discussing that vital question with her first-born, who was the authority of the family on matters of etiquette, when a carriage with two men in it drove past them to the house.

Bertha observed them narrowly. She thought one of them might be Lord George; he might be coming to luncheon, and he had brought someone with him, perhaps Lady Alicia's husband, the member for the county.

On second thoughts she dismissed this idea from her mind. The second gentleman was of Jewish aspect; he was not the least like her ideal of a country squire. Perhaps he was a Rothschild staying in the house, a prince of financiers spending the Easter recess amid these sylvan scenes. She quite pictured in her mind what a relief it must be to the toil-worn great man to throw aside his greatness, and quit the pestilential money-making air of the City for these scenes of repose and peace. How his jaded body and mind must be invigorated by imbibing in copious draughts this pure, unbreathed air! He must feel quite a boy again as he angles for trout in that brawling stream beneath the falls. It was a pretty fancy.

Bertha was full of sympathy for that distinguished-looking stranger with the strongly marked Jewish cast of countenance.

The Rector was in his study when these visitors were announced, but he did not catch their names when the maidservant brought them in. He looked up from his table and saw these strangers of sinister aspect standing before him, and then, without a word being spoken, his heart sank into his boots.

He had no need to speak. The Israelite, who was an Israelite indeed, stepped forward and laid an open paper on his hands. He did not give it to him, he laid it on his hands, which were folded on the table before him. He had an impression, he was never quite sure that it was more than an impression, that the man laid his great, ugly, dirty hand on his shoulder.

'At the suit of Mr. William Wilberforce,' he heard someone say—someone a long way off—and for a few seconds he could not read what was written on that strip of blue paper on the table. The words all swam together, and he could not make any sense of them. He could only see the face of Joan; and the wee, wee face of the babe he had held in his arms at the font yesterday came between him and that paper.

He had a stifling feeling in his throat, as if he should choke for want of air, but he had no strength to rise from the table.

What did it all mean?

It meant that the philanthropist had put in an execution for the amount of his bill.

CHAPTER XXXIV.

THE FINANCIER.

Robert, in his ignorance, in his blind fatuity and belief in the philanthropic intentions of Mr. Wilberforce, had neglected to provide for the maturity of that wretched bill. He had not taken the commonest precautions to stave off the evil day. He had trusted that all would be well. Why should he not? He had taken the word of that bland young man, and had trusted that the matter would be arranged as he had stipulated.

A week ago a notice had reached him that the bill had not been met. He was quite aware that the bill had not been met without Mr. Wilberforce taking the trouble to send him that superfluous notice. Who should know better that it had not been met than he?

Robert had written off at once on the receipt of that ridiculous notice, and stated in the plainest terms the impossibility of his meeting the bill until his tithes came in. He had not sent the forty pounds asked for to cover the expense of renewing it, and the interest for the next three months. The affable young man had told him most distinctly that no further interest would be charged for the extension of time.

He had paid enough already, goodness knows, for this temporary loan. Thirty pounds for the loan of one hundred and fifty, and five pounds for expenses! Thirty-five pounds for three months—the idea was preposterous! If this were to go on it would amount to one hundred per cent. in the course of the year.

He could have borrowed the money at five per cent. of his bankers, if he had only gone to them in his trouble, and explained the matter to them.

Mr. Wilberforce had a large *clientèle* of clergy, the young man had informed Robert quite confidentially. Hundreds and hundreds of beneficed clergy applied to him yearly for temporary assistance to eke out their narrow incomes, or to enable them to meet some sudden and unexpected drain on their too slender resources. Hundreds and hundreds of unhappy men were being crushed daily beneath this awful load of *one hundred per cent.*

Mr. Wilberforce had vouchsafed no reply to Robert's indignant letter. He had put the law into force, and levied an execution upon all his goods and chattels.

When Robert recovered himself, and could see clearly enough to read the paper before him, and his voice came back so that he could speak without choking, and his legs were steady enough to carry him, he got up from the table, and, bidding the men wait his return, he left the room. He brushed by Mrs. Penrose and Bertha, who had just come in from the garden, in the hall, and went hurriedly up the stairs.

He could not have spoken to them if he had seen them; he could not have spoken to anyone. A dreadful, dreadful burden was upon him.

He had to tell Joan.

She was not in her own room—he was conscious of a feeling of relief when he opened the door, and saw she was not there. It gave him a little breathing space. He was so dazed, so bewildered, that he could not realize what had happened. He stumbled across the room and threw himself down on his knees beside the bed—beside the pillow that her innocent cheek had lately pressed—but no words would come to his lips. He could not utter a single prayer; he could only kneel there silent and mute in his bewilderment.

He had not far to look for Joan; he knew exactly where he should find her. She was only in the room beyond, the little dressing-room that she had turned into a nursery. The baby was sleeping in its cot, and Joan was standing beside it, looking down upon its peaceful, rosy slumber. She looked up and blushed when Robert entered the room; she flushed up like a poppy at being caught in this act of worship.

Robert closed the door behind him, and came over and stood beside the cot where his child was sleeping. Something in his step or in his manner made Joan look at him sharply. The poppy colour dropped out of her face as suddenly as it had come in.

'What is it, Robin?' she asked breathlessly, 'what?'

He had not spoken a word, but she had read that message of trouble in his face.

He put out his trembling hands and took hers, but he could not find any words to speak.

'Oh, Robin, what is this? what does it mean?'

'Darling!' was all he could say, 'darling!'

It was not very much, but it reassured her.

'Has anything happened,' she said eagerly, 'to mamma—to the boys?'

He shook his head.

'Nothing has happened to them,' he said.

'Then what——'

She did not finish the question; she stopped and gave a sigh of relief.

It could not be anything very bad. There was nothing the matter with the baby: it was sleeping like a top. There was nothing the matter with Robert—he was here by her side—there was nothing the matter with her mother or the girls. Whatever it was, it did not affect the safety of those she loved. Her heart gave a great bound of relief. Surely she could bear anything if these were safe.

Then Robert told her. He told her all. He told her with a quiver at his lips that he could not hide from her, and clammy drops of perspiration breaking out on his forehead.

She could not understand it at all. She could only just grasp the one dreadful fact, that the bright dazzling bubble of prosperity had burst.

She had her husband and her baby left; everything had not gone. It might have been worse—oh! so much worse.

'What will you do, Robert?' she said, speaking under her breath.

'There is nothing to be done but—but to let the men take the things. We shall never be able to hold up our heads again.'

'But it is not much, Robert. It is not quite two hundred pounds.' She had got the paper Robert had brought away with him in her hands, examining it. 'If—if we could get the money, the men would go away?'

'Yes, if we could get the money!' he said bitterly.

'We must try to get it: we must make an effort—we need not let anyone know. Oh, I wish mamma and the boys were not here!'

She was much cooler than Robert—cooler and braver; but that mention of her mother and the boys brought the colour into her face.

'And they are going to Orchard Damerel to luncheon. Do you think you could drive them over, Rob, and then I should have time to think?'

Robert shook his head.

'I don't think we should be allowed to take the horses out,' he said, hanging his head; 'there is a stipulation that nothing can be removed off the premises.'

'Then, I must write to Phyllis and tell her they are not coming, that something has happened to prevent them. Oh, if Phyllis were only here!'

Joan checked a little moan; she would not have uttered it for the world. Her cheeks were flushed, and her eyes were unusually bright, and she was nervously clasping and unclasping her little thin hands, but she gave no other sign of agitation. She had to strengthen her husband's heart; she had to keep him from breaking down.

She scribbled a little note to Phyllis, and she told Robert to send it up by a messenger to the house at once; and then she went downstairs and explained to her mother and Bertha that, these unexpected visitors coming in, Robert could not drive them over to Lady Aylmerton's to luncheon.

She ordered some wine and biscuits to be carried into the library to the men, and she sat down to table with her mother and the boys, and carved—or, rather, tried to carve—as if nothing had happened. It was a good thing their voracious young appetites kept her well employed, or she might have broken down. Bertha had put on quite a smart gown for the mid-day meal; she expected Lord George and the financier to be present. Joan had to explain that the visitors had come on business, and some refreshment had been served for them and Robert in the library. She did not say what business. There are all sorts of business that incumbents of country livings receive visitors upon—archidiaconal visitations, visits from rural deans, Ecclesiastical Commissioners, deputations from learned societies, county clubs, to say nothing of the unexpected presence of so august a person as the Bishop of the diocese himself.

The financier did not look the least like a bishop.

Bertha was still wondering who the distinguished visitors might be—she had quite settled in her mind that they were distinguished; if they had not been people of importance Robert would not have put off that visit to Orchard Damerel—when Phyllis arrived.

Joan caught sight of her crossing the lawn. Phyllis was quite sure from that hurried scribble of Joan's that something had happened; she had run all the way through the shrubbery and across the fields, taking the nearest cut, and when she reached the Rectory gate, instead of going round by the gravelled path, she ran across the lawn over the wet grass. Joan saw her sister coming, and, making some excuse, got up hastily from the table and went out into the hall to meet her.

Something seemed to be choking in her throat, and she could not speak a word to Phyllis when she came in at the open hall-door, bringing in the April sunshine with her. The sky had been overcast, and a shower had fallen; but the clouds had passed, and the sun had just shone out again, and it came shining into the open door with Phyllis.

Joan took her sister's hand silently and led her upstairs. She did not speak; she did not trust herself to look at her; she only drew her upstairs into her own room and closed the door after her—closed it and turned the key in the lock. Then, and not till then, she broke down. She broke down, with a little moan which she could not keep back, in Phyllis's arms.

'What is it?' Phyllis asked under her breath. She did not know why she whispered; she could not explain why she felt that this trouble which had fallen upon Joan was to be kept from the rest of the household. 'Is it the baby?—is it Robert?'

'No, no, no!' Joan sobbed almost passionately.

She had lost all command over herself; she could only sob and moan with her face on Phyllis's shoulder. She would not have had Robert see her weeping like that for the world.

Phyllis let her have her cry out. It was like the shower that had fallen—it was sharp and sudden and soon over, only, in Joan's case, when it was over the sun did not come out. Then, with her face still hidden on her shoulder, Joan told her sister all.

'It was not Robert's fault; you must not blame Robert. It is I who have been so silly and extravagant and led him into all sorts of foolish expenses. It is all my wicked, miserable pride,' she moaned.

Phyllis shook her head, and her eyelids quivered in that ridiculous way they had when she was much moved.

'I'm sure it was not your fault, darling, nor—nor Robert's. Poor Robert! You didn't either of you know the value of money; how should you? You have been living like two children in a fairy-tale; you thought the money would never come to an end. You've never had to pinch and scrape as we have had to do at home, or you would have known better. It was not your fault, you poor dear!'

This was all Phyllis could say to comfort her. It was not worth while to have got wet through in that shower if she could only say these trite, stupid things, and kiss Joan's damp cheeks, and fold her close in her loving arms.

'I wouldn't have mamma know for the world, or Bertha, or the boys. Mamma would break her heart; she is so proud of everything. Oh, you can't think, Phil, how proud and satisfied she is! She has brought down all her best things—that black silk with the flowers in it, that she used to set such store by, and her lace cap. She expected to meet all the best people in the county, and Bertha thought one of those men downstairs was Lord George.'

Joan could not help smiling in the midst of her tears, but Phyllis looked grave. Why should not she mistake him for Lord George? She had heard something about that most unfortunate transaction with Black Beauty, and she did not think very much of Lord George.

'What can you do to prevent them finding out? Can Robert keep the—the men out of sight?'

'No; they will go all over the house presently, into every room. They are going to take an inventory of the things—our things—our wedding presents—and the furniture—and—and the carriages and horses. They will not let Robert take one of them out of the yard.'

Here Joan broke down again, and it was a good thing that Phyllis's clinging arms were around her, and that her damp shoulder was handy for another flood of tears.

Phyllis was very near crying herself.

'Mamma and the boys must go home at once,' she said decidedly. 'They must go back to-day, and Robert must keep the men out of sight till they are gone.'

Joan was getting hysterical, and it was as much as Phyllis could do to soothe her.

'I'll manage that, dear. I'll manage it all if you'll let me; I won't hurt anybody's feelings, and—and I'll get them all out of the house in an hour.'

Phyllis was as good as her word; she locked Joan in with her baby—she was not at all in a fit state to be interviewed at present by anybody—and she went downstairs into the dining-room.

Mrs. Penrose and Bertha were still there, though they had long finished their meal, but the boys were out in the orchard, breaking down the fences and digging out a ferret which they had earthed in when they were summoned to luncheon.

'Joan's in dreadful trouble,' she explained, when she had greeted her mother and sister; 'she doesn't know what to do with those men. Robert didn't expect them until next week, when you were gone.'

Mrs. Penrose turned quite pale.

'You don't mean,' she said, 'that they have come to stay?'

'Oh yes, of course they have come to stay. They wouldn't come all this distance if they hadn't come to stay. It is so unfortunate you came now, mamma, instead of waiting till they had gone back; then you could have stayed as long as you liked.'

'I wonder Joan asked us to come down now, when she knew they were expected,' Bertha said sharply.

'She was so anxious to have the baby christened on Easter Day; she wrote without consulting Robert,' Phyllis said, meekly telling an unblushing fib. 'And they have come sooner than she had expected.'

'Surely in this great house Joan can find room for two people; it isn't like a dozen,' Bertha said crossly.

'My dear, it was my fault that Joan only furnished two extra rooms,' Mrs. Penrose said, with a sigh. 'I was so afraid they would begin on too large a scale, that I begged them to be careful. Joan was anxious to have three spare rooms, but I urged her only to furnish two to begin with. It is very awkward. I think we had better go back.'

'Do you think the boys would very much mind about going back?' Phyllis faltered.

She was dreadfully ashamed of herself for telling all these tarradiddles, and she was awfully sorry for the boys.

'I think they would be dreadfully disappointed. It is too bad of Joan to bring them down here, and to send them back in a hurry because some of Robert's friends choose to turn up quite unexpectedly.'

Bertha was hot and indignant; all her visions of being taken in to dinner by Lord George were dissipated. She had put on her smart frock for nothing, and she had a stinging, humiliating sense of being sent away in a hurry, turned out of the house to make room for strangers.

'I think we had better go, dear,' Mrs. Penrose said weakly.

'If you wouldn't mind, mother, I think it would be best,' Phyllis said, a trifle eagerly—she could not keep the eagerness out of her voice. 'It would be a great relief to Joan. She isn't strong yet, and things worry her so.'

'We will go at once. I wouldn't have Joan worried for the world. We can come down again——'

'*I* will never come down again!' Bertha said angrily; and she jumped up from the table and began to collect her work-things and the books she had been reading. 'It's shameful to have to go away in such a hurry; it's like being turned out of the house.'

'Can I help you pack?' Phyllis asked timidly, as her sister bounced out of the room.

'Oh no, thank you! We can do our own packing; we don't want any help in this house;' and Bertha banged the door after her in a way that—well, showed temper.

And then Phyllis had to go out into the orchard and find the boys, and explain matters to them. It was rather harder work reconciling the boys to going back, just as their long-looked-for holiday had begun, than it was reconciling Bertha. They could not be brought to see the necessity of going home at that short notice.

'If it's only the room that's wanted,' Chris said eagerly, 'there's no reason why we should go back. We can sleep anywhere. There are plenty of empty rooms, and we could sleep on the floor. We shouldn't at all mind sleeping on the floor.'

Then Phyllis had to explain that there were other reasons why they must go back. Robert had important visitors staying in the house, and it would be inconvenient to have boys about, and Joan was in weak health, and could not bear any worries.

The boys grumbled and gave in. Perhaps they saw from Phyllis's anxiety to get rid of them that there were other reasons. They went back to the house with heavy hearts, and packed up their fishing-rods, and their butterfly-nets, and their beetle-cases. They had not done half the things they were going to do. They had not got a single bird's egg. They had smashed all their old ones before they came away, and they had not found one to take back.

Considering all things, the boys behaved beautifully.

When Mrs. Penrose and Bertha came downstairs a couple of hours later with their travelling things on, Robert was in the hall to meet them. He was looking pale and worried, but he did not attempt to detain them.

'I am sorry you are going away in such a hurry,' he said. 'You must come down again soon, when the roses are in bloom. We have a fine show of roses.'

Joan had not the courage to see them off. She could only sit beside the cradle and weep.

'I think we had better tell mamma,' she sobbed, when Phyllis came to tell her that they were ready to start; 'who should be told if not mamma? I have never kept a trouble from her before in my life. What should I feel if baby were not to come to me when she was in trouble —*me*, above everybody else in the world? Oh, you don't know what a mother feels until you have a baby of your own, Phyllis!'

Joan was weak and overwrought; she had broken down completely.

'I would not have mamma know for the world!' Phyllis said indignantly. 'It would break her heart. Oh, you don't know how proud she is of you and your position! Poor mamma! it is all she has got to be proud of. She has lost everything but her pride in you. Let her keep this at any cost. Let her go away and feel that she is slighted, ill-used, anything, but let her keep this last little shred of pride.'

Joan could only sob and clasp her baby to her bosom, and implore it to never, never keep any secret from her.

While she was still weeping, Mrs. Penrose and Bertha came in to say good-bye; and then Phyllis had to explain that the worry of the men coming unexpectedly, and their having to go away in a hurry, had quite broken her down.

Whatever reproaches Bertha had been getting ready while she was packing the smart frocks and ribbons she had never had a chance of wearing, were silenced at the sight of Joan's drooping head, and the tears that were falling on the small pink face at her bosom; she had not a word to say. She could only kiss her wet cheeks, and murmur a little clinging, tender good-bye, and promise to come again soon—very soon.

CHAPTER XXXV.

MRS. PENROSE'S HUMILIATION.

Poor Mrs. Penrose's humiliation was not yet over. She had quite expected Joan's pony-carriage to be brought to the door for her, and the dogcart for the boys and the luggage—the same triumphal procession, minus the triumph, with which they had arrived at the Rectory.

There was no pony-carriage forthcoming; only the dogcart drove up to the door. They had brought a ridiculous quantity of luggage, and when that was packed in, and Mrs. Penrose had got up, there was only room for one more person behind. There was no room for the boys; there was only room for Bertha. It was rather undignified, sitting on the back seat of a dogcart, squeezed in among a lot of luggage.

Bertha flushed up hot and indignant; she did not know whether she could ride in that way. While she was still debating, the financier came out, with his great-coat over his arm, and his hat drawn down over his big Jewish nose, and jumped up on the back seat with the luggage, and the dogcart drove away.

Bertha and the boys were left standing in the porch.

'I'm afraid you will have to walk to the station,' Robert said, with a weak attempt at a smile. 'It is not very far by the fields—not more than three miles. You will get there almost as soon as the dogcart, but you will have to walk quickly.'

He did not attempt any apology or explanation of the financier taking that back seat. He only wished them 'good-bye' with his white smile, and recommended them to 'walk pretty quick.'

It was horribly humiliating having to go away in that hurried, undignified fashion. Phyllis was thankful that the dogcart had driven away down the road, and that her mother had not seen them scampering across the fields towards the railway-station.

She went with them as far as the gate that led into the highroad. A shower came on before they reached the gate—a pretty sharp April shower, and they stopped beneath a tree for shelter. If they had not stopped they would have got wet through, and they would have had to sit in their wet clothes for hours. They lost ten minutes by waiting for that shower, and if they meant to catch the train they would have to run all the rest of the way.

Phyllis started off to run with them, Phyllis and the boys, and Bertha, angry and indignant, lagged behind.

It was getting more and more undignified.

They had run half a mile over wet grass, and had arrived panting at the gate which led into the highroad, when a carriage drove by. It did not exactly drive by, it pulled up suddenly when they reached the gate, and then Phyllis saw it was Mr. Hugh Damerel. He had been watching them streaming across the fields for the last mile, running in that ridiculous fashion, and he could not make out who they could be. The last person he expected to see running races in a wet field was Lady Aylmerton's companion.

Phyllis could have cried for joy at the sight of that dogcart. Run as hard as they could for the rest of the way, they would hardly have reached Thetford before the train had left the station, and they would have had to come back to the Rectory, and would have caught that dreadful man left in charge cataloguing the things, and sticking nasty white labels on Joan's lovely new furniture.

Phyllis was not the least ashamed of being caught running in that ridiculous manner, with her skirts gathered up around her, and her hat flying off, hot and panting and breathless.

'Oh, Mr. Damerel!' she panted, 'I'm so glad—so glad——' And then she had to pause for breath.

Hugh Damerel looked from one to the other—the beautiful proud sister with her flushed face, and the hot, eager, panting boys. He took in the situation in a moment.

'You want to get to the station,' he said; 'can I be of any use?'

'Oh, if you would! If you could make room for my sister—this is my eldest sister, Bertha, Mr. Damerel—and the boys. This is Chris, and that is Clem. If you would drive them over to the station! Mamma is there waiting—and we stayed for the shower—and I'm sure they will be late.'

This was all the explanation Phyllis vouchsafed. In a moment Bertha was hauled up in front, and the boys had climbed up behind, and the horse's head was turned, and they were waving adieux and tearing away in the direction of the station. Phyllis watched them until they were out of sight, and then, for the first time, her eyes brimmed over. She was very glad Mr. Damerel was not there to see her; that she could have her little cry in silence.

When she got back to Orchard Damerel, she met Lady Aylmerton's maid in the hall, at the foot of the great staircase.

'Oh, I'm so glad you've come back, miss,' Wilkins said anxiously. 'Dear my lady is in such a state of mind about you! She's been asking for you all the afternoon. I think I'd go in and see her, if I were you, before you take your things off.'

Then Phyllis suddenly remembered that she had gone out without telling her ladyship that she was going. She had run off in a hurry on the receipt of Joan's letter, and she had not told anyone where she was going.

A presentiment of evil came over her as she went upstairs to the Countess's room. She was quite tired out with the running and the walking, and the anxiety and strain she had gone through; she had no spirit left in her. She was quite sure that Lady Aylmerton would send her away.

Her heart was in her boots when she went into the boudoir where her ladyship was sitting. The Countess looked up when Phyllis came in. She was looking pale and disturbed, with a drawn look about the eyes that Phyllis had never noticed before.

'I'm very sorry, Lady Aylmerton——' she began; and then she stopped; she could not understand that look in the Countess's face, as she sat muffled up in that old plaid shawl before the fire.

'What are you sorry about? Where have you been?' her ladyship asked in a rather thick voice.

Surely the voice was changed as well as the face?

'Oh, Lady Aylmerton, I'm sure you are ill! I'm sorry I stayed away so long.'

There was genuine concern in Phyllis's voice as she came over and stood before the muffled-up old figure in the great chair.

'There is nothing the matter—with me. I am—quite well,' her ladyship said crossly, with a strange hesitation in her speech.

Phyllis was really alarmed. She threw herself on her

knees before the old woman, and took her poor trembling hands in hers. She was astonished to feel how cold they were in that hot room, and how they trembled.

'Dear Lady Aylmerton,' she said anxiously, 'there is something the matter. You are not at all like yourself. I wish you would let me send for Mr. Wherry.'

Mr. Wherry was her ladyship's doctor.

'There is nothing to send for Wherry for,' her ladyship said fretfully. 'I am not ill, only tired, and stiff with the cold. I—I think I'll go to bed; I shall get warm there. I haven't been warm to-day.'

She made an effort to rise up from her chair as she spoke, but she fell back again. She could not get up without assistance.

'I've got stiff, I suppose, with waiting here for you so long,' she said peevishly, sinking back among her cushions.

'Oh, I'm so sorry!' Phyllis said; and then, to her ladyship's surprise, she burst out crying. 'I'm so sorry!'

She was kneeling on the ground before her, chafing her poor cold hands, and her tears were dropping upon them. So many things had happened to upset her nerves to-day, and now she had lost all command of herself, and was crying because an old woman's wrinkled hands were cold, and her speech was slow and thick.

Lady Aylmerton could not understand her. She had been groaning with rheumatism and spasms for years, but Cecilia had borne all her groaning unmoved. She had not shed a single tear.

They got the old woman to bed, and Phyllis sat beside her for the rest of the evening. She had no appetite for her dinner; it was not worth while to go downstairs into that empty dining-room, with all that hideous mockery of silver plate around her, if she could not swallow a mouthful. Her heart was sore and sick for Joan, and the trouble at the Rectory, and her conscience was pricking her dreadfully for the deception she had practised on her mother and Bertha.

She could not keep the tears out of her eyes as she sat beside the Countess's bed, and tried to read to her one of those old prophetic sermons. The poor old soul always flew to her sermons when her pains came upon her. She had nothing else to cling to but the hope of that speedy millennium when the wicked should be consumed and got out of the way, and her poor old body should be changed into something new and lovely, that would never decay or grow old, or be subject to any more groanings.

Phyllis did not put any heart into the dry, prosy sermon; her mind kept wandering away to the trouble at the Rectory, to Joan with her bowed head, and her tears dropping on the little baby face at her breast. She could not get that picture out of her mind; she kept losing her place and making mistakes, and finally she broke down, and her tears rained like Joan's, not on a little pink face, but on Dr. Cumming's sermons.

The old woman insisted on knowing what was the matter. She would not be put off. She got so angry and excited when Phyllis stammered and stumbled over some absurd explanation that she thought she was going off into a fit.

There was nothing to be done but to tell her. Phyllis was longing to tell somebody, and she was not at all unwilling to tell the Countess. Perhaps she would help them; who could tell?

'Bailiffs at the Rectory!' she muttered, in her thick strange voice. 'Bailiffs—at—the—Rectory! What could he expect—hunting and riding about the country—and neglecting the parish!'

'I'm sure Robert does not neglect the parish,' Phyllis said warmly; 'he must ride sometimes; he could not stay at home all day writing sermons.'

'What do you know about the parish?' the old woman said sharply; 'there are a lot of people in the place he has never visited since he has been here. None of the men go to church now, and he does not take the trouble to look after them. Does he forget that their souls will be required at his hands?'

'I'm sure Robert does a great deal of visiting,' Phyllis said stoutly, 'and he has to prepare two long sermons every Sunday.'

'Ay, ay, the sermons are well enough; *he gets 'em out of a book.*'

There was nothing more to be said, and Phyllis repented that she had told this cantankerous old woman about the trouble at the Rectory. She could not think what Robert would say; he would never forgive her. The Countess was silent after that last uncomfortable speech, and Phyllis thought she had fallen asleep. She was picturing Joan, upstairs as she had left her, weeping over the cradle, and the financier downstairs sticking those horrid little white labels on all the furniture, when a voice from the bed startled her.

'How much?'

The voice was thick and indistinct; it was not at all like the Countess's voice.

'How much?'

She had to ask the question twice before Phyllis understood her.

'How much?' she repeated. She could not at all think what her ladyship meant.

'How—much—money—does he owe?'

'Not very much; only two hundred pounds. He could pay it easily if the men could wait.'

The Countess made an impatient movement with her hand. Phyllis took the poor old wrinkled hand in hers and smoothed it; she thought her ladyship was exciting herself too much, and she did not like that strange thickness in her speech.

'Quick--give—me—that——'

She had snatched her hand away from Phyllis, and was pointing to a little desk that stood on a table near the window where she usually sat. The desk was open, and her writing things were lying ready at hand.

Phyllis brought the desk over and laid it on the bed beside the Countess; she could not think why she wanted to write a letter in such a hurry; and then she had to raise her up. It was much more difficult to get her up than usual; she had suddenly become quite helpless, and she would not have anyone called. Phyllis got her up into a sitting position with difficulty, and put the little open desk before her. She fumbled among the contents with nervous haste, but could not find what she wanted, and Phyllis had no idea what she was searching for.

'Cheque—book,' she said in her thick voice, that was more indistinct than ever.

It was more by the movement of her lips than the

sound that issued through them that Phyllis learned what she was seeking for.

'I am sure you are too ill to write, you poor dear!' Phyllis said. She was quite sure that it was not safe for Lady Aylmerton to excite herself. 'Can't it wait till to-morrow?'

The old woman shook her head.

'Too late,' she said; 'too late. Now——'

Phyllis saw it was useless to attempt to move her, and she found the cheque-book, and spread it open on the desk before her, and dipped a pen in the ink.

Her poor trembling fingers could scarcely grasp the pen, they had grown so feeble in these few minutes. She made more than one effort before she could fill up that cheque, and when it was written it looked as if a spider had trailed across it and left its mark behind. The signature at the foot was the plainest bit of writing upon it, the signature and the amount—two hundred pounds.

When her ladyship had written it, she gave it to Phyllis to blot; and then she saw—what she had not seen or dreamed of before—that it was made out to Robert.

'Oh, Lady Aylmerton!' she said, and she could not find a word more to say; she could only sink down on her knees and kiss the old wrinkled hand that had just written those magical words.

'Send—it—at once—at once; send a messenger.'

Phyllis did not want to be told twice. She rang the bell and despatched a servant with a hurried note to the Rectory, and told the man to bring back an answer.

He brought back an answer sooner than she expected. He had taken one of the well-fed carriage-horses, and had ridden it over to the Rectory, and was back again in no time. He brought back not only the answer, but the cheque. Robert had sent back the cheque.

The Countess watched Phyllis from the bed open the letter and take out the cheque, and she saw her face fall and heard the exclamation of disappointment she could not smother.

'What is it?' she asked.

'Oh, Lady Aylmerton, he has sent back the cheque!'

'Sent it back?'

'Yes. He sends his thanks, his grateful thanks, for your kindness, but he does not see how he can ever repay so large a sum. He writes in great trouble and distress; he has brought this disgrace on himself by his thoughtlessness—he calls it a harder name—by his folly and pride—and it is right that he only should suffer.'

'Quite right,' the old woman muttered from the bed—'quite right.'

She was silent for some time, and Phyllis thought she had fallen asleep; she dozed off so quickly now, awake one moment and asleep the next.

'Is—the—man—gone?' she asked presently.

The old difficulty seemed to have come back to her speech, the thickness and the indistinctness.

'He has come back, and he has brought the cheque with him,' Phyllis said, wringing her hands. 'Oh, what shall I do with the cheque?'

She was dreadfully afraid Lady Aylmerton would drop off to sleep and forget all about it, and Joan would have those horrible men in the house all the night.

'Do with it—do with it? Send it to him again—at once; tell him it is not a loan—it is a free gift.'

The last words were clear and distinct; there was no mistaking them, and again Phyllis knelt down and kissed the old woman's hand and thanked her in broken words.

Phyllis sent off the cheque that had been returned again, with Lady Aylmerton's message, and implored Robert to accept it and send the men away.

Joan opened the letter this time; she knew before she opened it that Phyllis had sent the cheque again, but she did not know that it was a gift—a free gift.

'Oh, thank God! thank God!' she cried, with the tears springing to her eyes, and that great, great load taken from her heart.

Robert did not remember to have heard Joan thank God for any special mercies before, not even when the baby came. It had always seemed to her that these great gifts, which had been showered down upon her so freely, were her due. She had never once remembered until now to thank God for them.

There was no question about sending the cheque back now. Robert wrote a hurried, incoherent letter of thanks, and sent it back by the messenger, and he promised to go up in the morning and thank her ladyship in person.

The first thing to be done was to get rid of the men. They were in the library when Robert went downstairs. They had taken an inventory of the furniture in the dining room and Joan's pretty drawing-room, and they had gone back to the library, and were looking at the backs of Robert's books—at least, they were looking at the backs of the books when he opened the library-door and came in. A moment or two before they were examining the old portrait of Joan's great-aunt behind the door.

'There's no doubt about it,' one of them had remarked.

'Not the least,' the financier had added, with an air of certainty; and then they had heard Robert's step in the passage outside, and had jumped down from the chairs, upon which they had been standing the better to examine the picture, with quite astonishing agility, and were busy reading the titles of the books on the shelves beneath when he came into the room.

Their faces fell quite a quarter of a yard when Robert laid the Countess's cheque before them, and insisted on their immediate withdrawal. Perhaps it was the unexpectedness of that quite unlooked-for event, the settlement of their claim in full; whatever it was, it took their breath away, and lengthened their unprepossessing countenances visibly. There was nothing to be done but to withdraw, there was nothing to wait for; but they withdrew with a very bad grace. They had hoped, they said, in a delightful insinuating way that had not been apparent until now, that the gentleman would have put them up for the night. There was no train out of Thetford till the morning, and the railway inn was five miles distant.

Robert remembered how his mother-in-law had been driven those five miles, with the financier occupying the back seat. That ignominious flight of Bertha and the boys streaming across the fields, with the April storm of wind and rain coming up behind them, was before his eyes, and he set his teeth hard, and desired the men to clear out. He gave them no quarter. They had given him no quarter; they would have nothing less than the pound of flesh, and they had got it. There was nothing for them to do but to go.

Before they went, they made Robert an offer. They tried to drive a bargain for that picture of Joan's great-aunt.

'Do you happen to value that picture of the old lady there behind the door?' the financier asked, blinking his black beady eyes. 'I know a man as wouldn't mind giving a twenty-pun note for her.'

Robert shook his head.

'The picture is not for sale,' he said.

'More's the pity,' said the financier, with a sigh; 'it's a-crackin' to pieces for want o' cleaning. The paint's all a-peelin' off; there'll be nothing left of it soon but the canvas. See, there's a crack right across the face, an' one of the heyes has begun to go already. Her'll only have one heye soon, an' the nose is a-goin'.'

There really was some truth in what he said. Joan's ancestress was in a shockingly bad condition. The paint, if not exactly peeling off, was cracking, or the varnish, with which it was unfeelingly daubed, was cracking dreadfully. The beautiful neck and arms were all over cracks, and the features, that bore such a remarkable resemblance to the baby's, were scarred by a wide seam that threatened destruction to that and all other likeness.

Robert had never noticed those cracks before; he had not seen them an hour ago; and a cloud of something like suspicion and anger came over his face, as he looked from one to the other of the wily countenances of his departing guests.

'It is a family portrait, and it is not for sale,' he said shortly.

'There won't be much portrait left of it soon,' the son of Israel said, as he tapped the picture knowingly with his knuckles. 'It's a-peelin' off as fast as it can. I know a picture like it, a family picture, of an ole gent wi' a bald 'ed, an' showin' a lot o' white front to his shirt, an' they wouldn't hear o' sellin' it for no price, 'cos he wor an ancestor. An' one fine morning the 'ousemaid—her thought the ancestor looked a little dusty—an' her flicked her broom over his bloomin' old face, an' it all came away—nose, and heyes, and double chin, and the 'aughty smile that he'd been a-smilin' a hundred years or more. There was nothin' left of him but the bald crown of his 'ed and his beautiful white shirt-front. He'd peeled right away.'

Still Robert shook his head.

'I don't think my friend would be particular for a tenner,' the financier continued; 'he wouldn't stick at thirty to save the picture. He's a great hand at restorin' old pictures; he'd make a new thing of it; you wouldn't know it again after he'd a-touched it up. Say thirty, sir, thirty pun down?'

'The picture is not for sale,' Robert said impatiently.

'Say fifty, sir, it's double what it's worth; but it's a cruel shame to see the picture a-peelin' away, an' not make an effort to safe it.'

Still Robert was unmoved.

That fifty pounds, he remembered, would have come in very handy just now; it cost him a good deal to refuse it.

'Well, sixty, then?' the financier pleaded.

Still Robert shook his head.

'Make it even money—say a hundred? More 'n double what it's worth.'

Robert changed colour, but he did not shake his head, and the Jew noted his irresolution.

'Shall we say a hundred pounds, then?' the financier said eagerly.

Robert paused before he answered the man. He was thinking how useful that hundred pounds would be: it would just tide him over that anxious time till his tithes came in. He was quite sure that Joan would not object to the picture of her great-aunt being parted with in this summary way; she would have jumped at that first offer of a twenty-pound note, and prided herself on the bargain.

'A hundred pounds!' the Jew repeated. Something in his voice struck upon Robert Lyon's ear as he stood undecided beneath the picture, with his hands thrust down deep into his empty pockets, rattling his keys.

It was not in his voice only there was a ring of elation, but his eyes were shining as they had certainly not shone while he was making that inventory of Joan's knick-knacks in the drawing-room. He could not keep that sparkle out of his eyes.

If he had worn a pair of blue glasses while he was making that munificent offer for the old family portrait, Robert would certainly have accepted it. It was that gleam in the fellow's eyes that made him hesitate.

'Guineas, then?' persisted the Jew eagerly. He was in such a hurry to conclude the bargain, the sweat broke out on his forehead while he was speaking.

'I have already told you I don't want to sell the picture,' Robert said, turning away.

The sight of the greasy little man filled him with intolerable loathing and disgust. He could not trust himself. He was dreadfully afraid that if he listened a moment longer he should take the fellow's money.

'A hundred and fifty?' pleaded the Jew. 'Don't say no to a hundred and fifty! You'll never have such another offer; the picture 'll have all peeled away in a year. Remember the ole gentleman's bald 'ed and his shirt-front.'

'The picture is not for sale,' Robert interrupted impatiently; and then he rang the bell for the servant to show the fellows out.

CHAPTER XXXVI.

LAST WORDS.

Robert had intended to go over to Orchard Damerel early the next morning, and thank the Countess in person for her timely help. He had fully intended to go over directly after breakfast; but long before that early meal, before he was dressed, indeed, a message came from Phyllis, begging him to come up to the house at once.

Something had happened.

Robert hurried up to the great house with all possible speed. He took the short-cut across the fields and through the shrubbery, in the April sunshine. It was such a sweet April morning it did not seem that there could be much amiss in the world. Everything was bursting into life; the new blood of the year was in every bough and branch and bud. The hills were melting with lovely colour, and glittering drops from a passing shower hung like precious stones on the trees; every blade of grass was glistening in the morning sunshine, and a blackbird was whistling in the trees overhead.

It did not seem that there could be very much the matter on such a morning as this.

Phyllis met Robert at the hall-door; she had just come out for a breath of air. She was looking tired and worn out, as if she had been up all night.

'Oh, Robert!' she said, when he came up to her, and she stretched out her hands towards him; and then the Rector noticed that her eyes were red with weeping, and that she was not quite herself.

'What is it?' he asked.

'Have you not heard? The Countess——'

'What has happened to the Countess?'

'She has had a—a seizure. She has not spoken since she sent that last message to you, "Tell him it is a free gift." Oh, I am so glad that they were such generous words—that her last act was such a kind, kind act!'

Phyllis broke quite down in a flood of tears, and Robert led her back to the house.

'Who is with Lady Aylmerton?' he said huskily.

He was moved, in spite of himself, at the suddenness of the news, and that unexpected act of generosity.

'The doctor has only just left her. He has been with her all night.'

'What does he say? Does he give any hope?' Robert asked eagerly.

'He does not give any hope; he says she may remain in this state for some days, and that she may regain consciousness for a little time towards the end.'

'The end!' It seemed dreadful to talk about *the end* in this calm way.

Phyllis led Robert upstairs into the darkened room, where the Countess of Aylmerton was lying in that death-like sleep which is the prelude to death itself. She had not moved since Phyllis had taken away the desk from before her, and the pen had fallen from her hand. It had comforted Phyllis, seeing her lying like this through all those anxious hours of the night, to remember that the last act those cold, stiff fingers had done—were ever likely to do—had been a kind act; that her last thoughts—the last thoughts of a selfish, sordid life—had been generous thoughts.

The face on the pillow, the poor old coarse face, was drawn and sharpened; it was not at all the face Robert had last seen in the Aylmerton pew at church. He took the cold hand that lay outside the coverlet in his. He was astonished, on that warm April morning, to find how cold it was; and he bent over the unconscious face on the pillow, and murmured a few broken words of gratitude. He was not sure that his words would fall on unheeding ears. If he had been sure, he would still have murmured his broken words of thanks. He could not go away without telling her what she had done for him.

Robert promised Phyllis he would come again in the afternoon, and he left instructions that he should be sent for at once if Lady Aylmerton showed any signs of returning consciousness. Before he went away, he asked Phyllis for Mr. Damerel's address, and then he learned for the first time that he was here in the neighbourhood, staying at the village inn, probably.

He called at the inn on his way back, and learned that Hugh Damerel had breakfasted early, and gone over to the Rectory. He was there when Robert got back, and he had told Joan all about that meeting in the lane, and how he had driven Bertha and the boys to the railway-station, and what a near shave they had to catch the train.

He had heard nothing about what had happened at Orchard Damerel until Robert came in. He could not understand the Rector's agitation, or Joan bursting into tears in that unexpected way, at the news of Lady Aylmerton's seizure. It did not particularly affect him. Her ladyship had never been very much to him. She had stood, or seemed to stand, between him and his, and she had extended her hospitality to him—the hospitality of his own house—in a way that had always filled him with an angry, impatient sense of injustice. He could not understand these people being genuinely sorry for her. She had never benefited him in her life, and that made all the difference.

'Oh, Robin, she will never know how thankful we are!' Joan sobbed.

'Yes, I think she will know some day,' Robert said thoughtfully. 'If the memory of the evil we have done, the opportunities we have missed here, follow us into that other life, I am sure the comfort of knowing that we have helped or benefited others will not be denied us.'

'I never heard of anyone the old woman ever helped or benefited,' Hugh Damerel said moodily; 'she nearly killed that niece of hers who had the pluck to run away, and—and I'm afraid she'll wear out that sister of yours, who is a thousand times too good for her.'

'Oh, you don't know!' Joan said between her sobs. It was such a new thing for Joan to weep for others; she generally laughed at other people's misfortunes, and now she was really crying in earnest. 'She was the best and kindest old woman in the world. Her last act was an act of generous, unlooked-for kindness. She must have had a good heart, a loving, generous, tender heart,' Joan sobbed.

It was really worth while to write that little cheque to leave such a memory behind. Only the stroke of a pen had won for the selfish, narrow-minded old woman the beatitude of those nobler virtues that no one had ever given her the credit of possessing. Oh, it is quite worth while to do one generous deed at the end of a selfish life, one work of mercy, charity, or love to walk the world after one has gone, and bless it!

Robert took Hugh Damerel into the library, and explained to him the reason of Joan's tearful gratitude. He told him all about his own folly and weakness, and the ruin that had overtaken him, and how Lady Aylmerton had generously come to the rescue. He told him all, he kept nothing back; his pride was quite dead within him; he had nothing to be ashamed of except his ignorance and ambition, and for being so foolish as to be taken in by the specious promises of the philanthropist.

Mr. Damerel admitted that the Countess had behaved 'like a brick.' He had a suspicion that Phyllis, whose part in the matter everyone seemed to have forgotten, had more to do with the sending of that cheque than the Countess. Perhaps he was prejudiced.

And then, while they were talking about the Philistines, and the job he had to get rid of them when their bill was paid, Robert remembered the ridiculous offer that the Jew broker had made for Joan's family picture.

'By Jove! it was a lucky thing you didn't take the fellow's offer,' Hugh Damerel said, when he had examined the picture. He did not have to jump on a chair to examine it. He could see it quite well from the floor, with the light shaded from his eyes in that dilettante way that artists affect when they begin to criticise other people's pictures.

'Lucky!' Robert said drearily; 'it was as much as I could do to keep myself from taking the fellow's offer, and I've regretted it ever since.'

Hugh Damerel looked at him curiously.

'Then you don't know the history of the picture?'

'No, I know nothing about it, except that it is the likeness of my wife's great-aunt—to be more accurate, her great-great-aunt.'

'And you would be willing to part with it? You attach no particular value to it?'

'No, I don't think anybody values it. It came to us quite by accident; it would have been carted away among a lot of rubbish but for the coincidence that the original bore my wife's name, or, rather, that my wife bears hers. Nobody living can remember the old lady; she died ages and ages ago. If her face begins to peel, as that Jew said it was peeling, and it comes away a feature at a time, she will be worse than a blot upon the wall. We shall have to send her upstairs to the lumber-room.'

'I don't think I'd send her upstairs just yet,' Mr. Damerel said dryly. 'I'd rather send her to be cleaned. By Jove! that fellow was right; she is peeling! There is not a moment to be lost. I would send her away to be cleaned. She will look very different when all that beastly varnish is taken off.'

'It will cost something to clean,' Robert said, staring at the cracked features of the portrait, with his hands in his empty pockets, rattling his keys in his idiotic manner. 'I have no money to throw away upon her.'

'The cost 'll be nothing, and it will save the picture. I know a man who would do it for a song. You leave it to me, Lyon, and I'll see you are not a penny out of pocket by it. Let me send it up to him and see what it'll cost. You don't mind trusting the picture with me?'

'Do what you like with it,' Robert said, with a smile.

'You've got some packing-cases about, for certain; you couldn't have got all these things down without packing-cases. Let's send it off at once. There isn't a minute to lose.'

Hugh Damerel was all eagerness to send the picture off. He got it down, with Robert's help, from its place behind the library door, and he hunted out a packing-case from the lumber in the barn, and he packed the picture and nailed down the case without anybody's assistance to speak of. He took off his coat, and turned up his shirt-sleeves, and worked away at that packing-case with an energy which Robert had never given him credit for, while he and Joan looked on.

When he had finished the packing, he nailed a card with an address in London upon the case, and sent Robert's man off with it to the railway-station. He sent it off before lunch, in time to catch the train that Bertha and the boys had caught by a shave the day before.

'I hope the hideous old frump will never come back again,' Joan said, as she watched the cart drive out of the yard.

Mr. Damerel laughed.

Joan had never heard him laugh before, and she looked at him with surprise. He did not look the least like the Earl of Aylmerton's gloomy heir, as he stood there in his shirt-sleeves, with the hammer in his hand that he had just used for nailing that address on, and the perspiration standing out in beads on his forehead.

He walked over with Robert after lunch to Orchard

Damerel to inquire after the Countess. Phyllis came to them in the bare, blank dining-room, where no preparations for any more meals were to be made for who should say how long? The house was so silent that they heard her light step on the oak stairs, and crossing the polished floor of the hall, before she opened the door.

Her face was pale and grave, as befitted the occasion, but she flushed up like a poppy when she saw who Robert's companion was; she could not keep the tell-tale colour out of her cheeks.

Lady Aylmerton was no better; there had been no change since the morning, and the doctor had given instructions that she was to be kept quiet, that no attempt was to be made to rouse her. Phyllis told Robert all this in a strange, breathless way; but she was looking at Mr. Damerel all the time. There seemed to be something on her mind she wanted to say to him, but she could not find the courage to say it. He did not attempt to make it easier for her to say; he walked up and down in his old restless manner, looking at the silver cups and dishes on the sideboard and the rich appointments of the stately room, while the old Damerels on the walls followed him with their dull, painted eyes. He stopped once before the window and looked out at the wide prospect. It was all the Damerel property as far as he could see. It was something to be the possessor of the beautiful hills, with the mist and the sunshine about them, but it did not seem to stir his pulses.

His face was pale and grave when he took Phyllis's hand before he left.

'I am going away,' he said. 'I came here to take a last look at the place before I went away, and to say good-bye. I am never likely to come back again; there is nothing to bring me back again.'

'Where are you going?' she said, with a soft thrill of eagerness in her voice and that flutter of her white eyelids that he remembered so well.

'I am going abroad,' he answered bitterly; 'there is nothing to keep me here. I am going out sheep-farming in Australia. I should only eat my heart out with impatience and disgust if I stayed in the old country. I shall never come back. I shall never hear the name of the accursed place again.'

'You will not go now?' Phyllis said.

Her eyes were shining, and there were two crimson spots burning on her cheeks.

'There is nothing to wait for,' he said, looking down at her with his melancholy eyes. 'Whether Lady Aylmerton lives or dies will make no difference to me.'

'Wait,' she said quickly—'wait. Oh, you don't know what a day may bring forth!'

He only smiled and shook his head.

'I have made all my arrangements,' he said; 'it is too late to draw back now. I sail to-morrow night.'

'Indeed, you must not go away now,' Phyllis pleaded, almost in tears. 'Oh, Robert, can you not prevail on Mr. Damerel to wait?'

Robert did not see that there was anything to detain the young man. No benefit could possibly accrue to him from the Countess's death; the disposition of the property would be unchanged. He would only wear his life away here brooding over his wrongs. The best thing that could happen to him would be to go away and forget that Orchard Damerel had ever existed.

He was so bent on going that he was not to be persuaded. Phyllis followed him into the hall, and said a reluctant good-bye to him in the porch. When he looked back she was still standing in the sunshine with her face hidden in her hands.

He came back white and trembling.

'It is so good of you to be sorry for me,' he said huskily, with a little break in his voice. 'God bless you, dear!'

He took her hands from before her face and kissed them, and then he saw that she was crying.

'What a brute I am to make you cry,' he said, 'I who would do anything in the world to make you happy!'

'Then stay another day,' Phyllis said earnestly. 'Oh, do not go away yet, Mr. Damerel!'

'I will stay until you tell me to go,' he answered, with a sudden passion in his voice and eyes.

Phyllis blushed and trembled.

'Will you come at once if I send for you?' she said softly, looking down. She could not meet the passion in his eyes.

'I will come at any moment of the day or night that you send for me,' he said. 'I have put myself in your hands.'

He spoke so humbly that she could not be hurt or offended with his words, but the sudden passion was still blazing in his eyes.

Phyllis looked at him steadily with that faint, curious flicker of her eyelids; her mouth quivered, and the colour died out of her cheeks.

CHAPTER XXXVII.

AN AUTO DA FÈ.

PHYLLIS sent for the Earl of Aylmerton's heir sooner than he expected. She sent for him in haste before daybreak the next morning.

There had been a change in the Countess during the night, and in the chill, dark hour before day broke, she showed signs of returning consciousness. Phyllis had despatched a messenger at once to summon Hugh Damerel, and she had also sent for Robert, as she had promised. Her ladyship would recover consciousness, the doctor had warned her, just before the end; she might recover it towards morning, and then the end would come rapidly.

Hugh Damerel arrived at the house before the Rector. He came up through the shrubbery in the gray dawning. He had no morbid terrors, and his nerves were not accustomed to shrink at the threatening of danger or the near presence of death; but a strange, unaccountable feeling possessed him as he came up to the house through the shadowy woods in the dim gray gloaming. An intangible presence seemed to follow him through that long silent walk across the fields, between the dim horizons, and beneath the wooded fringes of the park, into the gloom and silence of that great shut-up house. Was it Death, or Destiny, or his own hopeless future?

Phyllis came to him in the Countess's own room, the boudoir where she had made him that humiliating offer. He remembered that interview as he stood in the faded, old, gray room in that chill April dawning. He fancied he could see the old, shabby figure in the plaid shawl, huddled up in the great chair by the fireplace, as he waited for Phyllis. Everything was unchanged: the faded Turkey carpet, the quaint carved chairs, the spindle legged tables, the beautiful old china in the cabinets, the children's pictures over the mantelpiece, they were all as he had seen them on that unwilling morning

Phyllis came in as he was standing there on the Turkey rug, looking round at these familiar things, with the strange sense of that unreal presence that had followed him up to the house coming between him and them.

She came in, in a nervous, hasty way, and shut the door behind her.

'I am so glad you are come,' she said, speaking quickly, with a little break in her voice; 'the Countess has recovered consciousness, and made several efforts to speak. I am sure she would see you.'

'I don't think she would care to see me,' he answered bitterly; 'she can have no possible interest in me——'

He stopped suddenly; he saw the girl's eyes were full of tears.

'Oh, you don't know,' she said eagerly; 'when it comes to the end, one sees things so differently. It is so hard to go away, and not to have anyone to be sorry. It is so hard to die alone.'

'I will see her if you like, if you think it will be any comfort to her,' he said humbly.

'Come at once, then. Robert will be here presently, and she can only see one at a time.'

She drew him away with a light touch of her hand into the dark, gloomy passages, which seemed to echo to their muffled footsteps. The old house was haunted by echoes, dismal echoes of those who had come and gone down those dim corridors, whose faces were looking down at them from their gilded frames. At this gray hour of the new dawn, with the shadow of death hanging over the house, it seemed full of old ghosts and old sad memories of the past.

Phyllis opened a door at the end of the dark gallery, and beckoned Hugh Damerel to enter.

The Countess was talking to herself when they came in; that is, she was muttering a continuous stream of incoherent sounds, of which the watchers standing by could not understand a word, and she was gazing blankly before her at that awful veil which was very shortly to be withdrawn from before her fading eyes.

'Mr. Damerel has come to see you,' Phyllis said, bending over her.

He stepped forward into the light and took the hand that lay on the coverlet, and pressed the cold, stiffening fingers.

'I am very sorry,' he said; he could not find anything else to say.

He could not help remarking, as he looked down at the changed face on the pillow, how great was the change. It was like, but unlike, the coarse, commonplace face he remembered so well. It was coarse and commonplace no longer. It was as if an unseen hand had passed over the old worn face and ennobled it. The image of the earthly had been slipping off those still marble features during the hours of unconsciousness, and now, at the last, the bright image of the immortal was seen shining through the fading lineaments of weakness and decay.

Robert came in while Hugh Damerel was standing there looking down at the changed face.

'Dear Lady Aylmerton!' he said, taking the other hand in his.

It had been feebly groping the bed-clothes when he came in, but at the touch of Robert's warm, strong fingers it twined around them with the strange clinging tenacity of the dying.

He marked the change that had passed over the worn face on the pillow, but he could not understand what she was trying so hard to say. He could not catch a single word.

He could not but see that the end was not far off.

There were already the dews of death breaking out on the clammy forehead, and the shadows were creeping over the altered face, and the eyelids had drooped over the unseeing eyes.

Robert ought to have gone down on his knees at once, there was not a minute to lose; but he hesitated and looked down at his benefactress with a quivering lip, and a mist before his eyes.

'There is something I should like to say to Lady Aylmerton,' he said in a low voice to Phyllis; and he looked round at the attendants standing near.

Phyllis motioned them to leave the room; she would have gone away herself and taken Mr. Damerel with her, but Robert made a sign for them to stay.

'What I have to say I wish you both to hear,' he said huskily; and then he bent over the bed and addressed the dull, unheeding ears—at least, they seemed unheeding to those who stood by.

'I have done a wicked and foolish thing, Lady Aylmerton,' the Rector said. 'I ought to have told you before. Thank God, it is not too late to tell you now! I have deceived you from the beginning. I have taken this living from your hands under false pretences. The sermons I preached—that won for me your confidence—were not my own sermons; they did not even embody my own views. My convictions were opposed to them. I preached them Sunday after Sunday to deceive you. My father, who is now in heaven, wrote those sermons; he wrote them believing every word he wrote. They fell into my hands, and by accident, being driven for time, I preached the first of those sermons at Clifton; and you were present. You know the rest. When I found out what had led you to offer me this living, I had no other choice but to go on with the deception.'

It seemed quite a useless confession, tearing at his own heartstrings, and harrowing everyone's feelings with this sad, humiliating story of weakness and deceit. The old woman lying on the bed had done with the shams and mockeries of life; everything was slipping away from her—creeds, prejudices, doubts, fears, anxieties, all were slipping away. She could never be angry any more, and she would hear no more sermons. The Rector's confession did not move her a whit. He fancied, he might have been mistaken, that there was a faint flicker of her closed eyelids, and a feeble pressure of her clinging hand.

'I have come at this last moment to ask your forgiveness, Lady Aylmerton. God knows how sorry I am that I have not told you this before!'

Then, and not till then, he sank on his knees beside the bed, and offered up the prayers for the sick and dying; and when he got up, the feeble lips murmured an unintelligible 'Amen.'

They never spoke again. Whatever words they had tried so hard to say during the early part of the night were left unsaid.

Lady Aylmerton died at sunrise. When the April morning broke, gray and chill with early showers, she had passed beyond the mists and the shadows of the night.

Hugh Damerel stayed at Orchard Damerel—Phyllis would not hear of his going away; but Robert went home to bed—at least, he went back to the Rectory. Instead of going to bed, he went into his library, and ordered a fire to be lighted. He was cold and chilled, as everybody is at such times of mental depression, and he had a big blazing fire made in the ample grate, large enough to roast an ox. He had a great deal of roasting to do before he went to bed. He had to burn every one of those sermons in that Bluebeard cupboard. He burnt them one by one, and they took a good deal of burning. They burnt languidly, charring and shrivelling up on the outside, and remaining untouched in the middle. It seemed, indeed, as if the cold hand that penned them so long ago was holding them back from the flames.

It hurt Robert dreadfully, burning those unwilling sermons. It brought back to him the old time when they were written, the old parsonage house and the dear faces that had faded so long ago. He could see them all in the embers of those musty sermons—the long low building, with the hospitable open door, the Rectory garden, with the homely, old-fashioned flowers, and the paddock beyond, where the gray pony, who was always falling lame, was feeding. There was only that one small gray mare to carry the owner over that straggling, widespread moorland parish—one limping gray pony, and a low, ramshackle pony-carriage that was always overflowing with children.

Robert saw it again now, after all those long years, in those dying embers—the shabby carriage, the lame pony, the forgotten little faces, the well-remembered voices encouraging the lagging steed up the rectory hill.

'Well done, Cowslip! Good Cowslip! Dear old Cowslip! Well done, old girl!'

He knew the voices well. He recognised them every one, Jack's shrill treble above the rest—Jack, who had been sleeping beneath a small white stone outside the vestry-door these twenty years.

It cut Robert to the heart to burn those sermons, but he could not trust himself. He owed it to his tardy confession, his late repentance, to make this sacrifice, this *auto da fè*, and when he had made it, when the last reluctant ember had flickered up and died out, he went to bed.

CHAPTER XXXVIII.

YE COUNTESS KATE'S BOKE.

It was all over so soon. The next day was still dawning when Hugh Damerel went back to the gray old room. He waited there alone until Phyllis, treading softly over the oaken floor, should come to him with wet eyes, and a sad, solemn face, and tell him it was all over.

The silence of the great house was oppressive. He thought he heard Phyllis's light footstep a dozen times as he sat there listening, but it was only far-off creaks in the old wooden panelling on the oak staircase. Once or twice he opened the door to listen, and went out into the dark, gloomy passages. There was nobody coming or going, only the shadows of the heavy furniture on the floor, the stout oaken doors of the state-rooms, and the Damerels looking down from the walls.

He [illegible] the door softly and went back into th

and sat down in the window-seat, and looked out over the gray, misty country and the tree-tops and the clouds breaking on the horizon.

A dog was baying somewhere in the woods, and a single star was still shining in the pale daffodil sky; the wind was stirring the branches of the elm-trees, and the rooks were cawing sleepily in their nests. It was all gray and sweet and dim and fresh with the indescribable glow of the early morning, touched with the solemn calm of the night.

As he sat there, the new day in solemn pomp rose over all the sleeping world, and Phyllis, with her shining eyes and her wet cheeks, came into the room.

He rose up and took her hands and led her to a seat, the window-seat where he had been sitting, and opened the casement that the cool air from without should revive her. The fresh morning air was touched with the scent of the grass, and the blossom of the orchards, and the wild-flowers blooming in the woods. It seemed to give her new life after the exhausted air of that close room she had left.

'I am so glad you are here,' she said, when she could speak calmly, after the first flow of her grief was over; she had nothing to weep for, but Cecilia could not have been more moved. 'You must not go away; you must stay here till—till it is over. It is your right place. I have found out something; I don't know what it may mean, but I am sure you must not go away.'

'I have put myself in your hands,' he said, with a quiver of tenderness in his voice that she could not mistake; 'I will not leave here until you tell me to go.'

He did not ask her what she had found out.

'Then, you will never, never go away,' she said, under her breath, with a light shining in her eyes, and her breath coming quickly.

He could not understand her eagerness.

'See, see what I have found,' she said.

She put into his hands as she spoke a shabby old book, in a worn, dilapidated leather cover—an old manuscript-book full of writing in faded ink. He turned over the yellow, discoloured pages with a faint feeling of wonder.

He could not understand why she had put the book into his hands. It did not seem much of a find. There was nothing there that could concern him.

It was an old recipe-book, such as ladies used to delight in, in the old, simple days, when time was wont to hang heavy on their hands.

It was full of old-fashioned remedies for old-fashioned complaints, and mysterious compounds for evils that existed only in the superstitious imagination of our simple ancestors. There were instructions for concocting an endless variety of cosmetics and washes for the complexion, and recipes for every description of cake. There was really nothing in this absurd old book to interest a man.

'Why do you give me this?' Hugh Damerel asked, when he had turned over the pages.

He did not require a 'certain remedy for colic,' and he was indifferent to 'ye speedy removal of freckles.'

'Look! you have not seen all,' Phyllis said breathlessly; and she leaned over him, and turned back the yellow pages to the beginning.

There was a heading to the first page in a beautiful old-fashioned text-hand, ornamented with a great many flourishes, 'Ye Countess Kate's Recipe-Boke.' Still he could not understand.

'Look,' Phyllis said eagerly, 'look!'

And then he saw that two of the front pages of the 'boke' were pinned together. They were so closely pressed together, with the pages wrinkled and turned over in identical folds, that they looked exactly like one page—an old, yellow, wrinkled fly-leaf, with a pin in it.

He took the bent, rusty pin out, not knowing what he should find. He did not expect to find very much in that old cookery-book.

There were some entries yellow with age on the page that had been pinned over—entries of birth and death. The handwriting was the same as the writing in the other portion of the book. The same, with a difference that is apparent in most old family registers—the writing of youth, of maturity, of old age. There was more than half a century between the dates of the first entry and the last.

The first entry, which was fresher and less faded than the others, was written in a firm, clear, beautiful woman's hand. It was the entry of the birth of the Countess Kate's first-born.

'My sonne Guy was borne at a quarter to four of ye clocke, on Tuesday, January ye 16th, in ye yeare of our Lord 1730. He was crisenéd at ye churche of ye parishe, by the Reverend James Damerel, Rector of ye parishe, on Wednesday, February ye 23rd, ye 1st day of Lent.'

The next two entries related to her ladyship's daughters, the originals of the lovely miniatures over the fireplace in the Countess's room.

'My daughter Theodora was borne on ye 2nd day of May, in ye yeare of our Lord 1732, at five minutes past one of ye clocke. She was borne in ye night, and crisenéd at ye churche, by my lord's brother, ye Reverend James Damerel, Rector of ye parishe, on ye 24th day of June following.'

'My daughter Hester was borne on Sunday, ye 17th day of October, at twenty minutes past three of ye clocke, in ye yeare of our Lord 1735, and was crisenéd in ye parishe churche.'

'My daughter Theodora was married to Lord Lovelace on ye 2nd day of June, 1753, in ye parishe churche, by her uncle, ye Reverend James Damerel, assisted by ye Reverend Gilbert Legh, clerke in holy orders.'

'My daughter Lovelace gave birth to a sonne on ye 7th day of April, 1755, who was crisenéd Capel Molyneux, after his father.'

'She gave birth to a daughter on ye 20th day of June, 1756, at noon, which only survived its birth two days. Ye sweete infant was privately baptized.'

'My daughter Hester was married to Gilbert Legh, clerk in holy orders, from the house of her Aunt Priscilla in Westminster, at ye parishe churche, St. Margaret's, Westminster, to the great anger and mortification of my lord. She was married on ye 1st day of September, in ye yeare of our Lord 1760, without any of her own kinsfolk being present at ye sudden and secret wedding.'

'My daughter Legh died in child-bed on ye 2nd day of August, 1763, after having given birth to a daughter, who survived her. She was buried in ye chancel at Stoke Rawleigh, where her husband was ye curate-in-charge.'

'Ye infant daughter of my deare childe was cristenéd Judith on ye 3rd day of September, in her father's churche at Stoke Rawleigh.'

The next entry related to the other members of her ladyship's family.

'My sonne Guy married ye Lady Elizabeth Courtenay, fourth daughter of ye Earl of Devon, at her father's private chapelle at Powderham Castle in ye south of Devon, on ye 16th day of June, in ye yeare of our Lord 1763.'

'Ye Lady Elizabeth, wife of my son Guy, gave birth to a sonne on ye morning of July ye 3rd, at a quarter to three of ye clocke.'

'Ye childe was cristenéd Hugh Courtenay, in ye parishe churche, on ye 2nd day of August, 1765, by ye Reverend Bevis Damerel, rector of ye parishe.'

'Capel Molyneux, ye dearly loved sonne of my daughter Lovelace, died of a fever on ye 23rd day of December, 1771, to ye unspeakeable grief of his parents, after he had lived sixteen years in ye innocence of a childe, but with ye judgment and virtues of a man; he lies buried in ye vault at Bishop's Crawley, where all ye Lovelaces do lie.'

'My granddaughter Judith was married July ye 27th, 1789, in her father's parishe churche, to Hugh Damerel, a descendant of ye olde Sir Hugh, whose marble tomb, with a figure of himself in armour, and his wife and seven leetle children, is in ye chapelle at Orchard Damerel.'

The handwriting of this last entry was faint and shaky; it was the last entry in the handwriting of Countess Kate.

'What does it mean?' Phyllis said, when Hugh Damerel had come to the end, when he had finished reading the last entry. She was trembling all over, and her lips were quivering, and there was a tremulous flutter in her white eyelids that did not veil the eager, shining light in her eyes.

'It means,' he said, 'that the Earl of Aylmerton's ridiculous will is a bit of wastepaper.'

Phyllis turned quite white.

'Oh, you don't mean,' she gasped, 'that—that you are no longer the heir—that there is someone else? Oh, why did I ever take that pin out!'

Hugh Damerel took her trembling hands in his, and smiled in her white face.

'If you had not taken that pin out,' he said, in a voice he tried to keep steady, 'I should have gone away—I could not stay here; how could I?—and I should never have come back—but now——'

'But now?' Phyllis said breathlessly.

'How can I tell you?' he said, looking into her troubled face with a strange light in his eyes, and his face all aglow. 'Oh, my dear, how can I tell you what this discovery of yours is to me? Judith Legh was my grandmother. Her descendant, my father, was her only son—the legal heir to the Aylmerton title and estates.'

He could not keep the quiver of elation out of his voice.

'And the will?' Phyllis gasped; she could only gasp, she could not understand it yet.

'Your discovery has set the will aside. The Earl had no power to leave me what was mine already; he had nothing to bequeath but his debts.'

Mr. Greatorex and Cecilia came the next morning. They had arrived at Carlingford the previous night, and driven over to Orchard Damerel after breakfast.

Cecilia was much improved. She was not like the same person. She had grown stouter, fuller, perhaps, would be more exact, and she certainly looked taller in her fashionable gown, with the rich trailing skirt, as she came forward to greet Phyllis. She did not wear the Countess's old gowns now, and her sweet, soft, vapid face was languid and vacant no longer.

She shed a few small tears, not many, but she refused to go up into the room where the Countess lay, and see all that remained of her late kinswoman.

'I would rather remember her as I knew her,' Cecilia pleaded meekly. She had a morbid dread of seeing anything but pleasant sights. 'I should never be able to get her poor altered face out of my mind if I were to see her now.'

'Oh, but Lady Aylmerton is not changed for the worse; she has got the most beautiful face in the world! All the lines are smoothed out, and she looks quite young and lovely; she is like you——' 'Only nobler,' Phyllis was going to say, but she checked herself in time.

Cecilia would not be persuaded. She would not look once more on the dead face that had been part of her life so many years.

There were none of her own to mourn for the poor old Countess, to drop their warm tears upon her cold hands. They had not been generous hands or kind hands in life, but they had done a generous, kindly deed at the last, and, for the sake of the gracious deed, Phyllis kissed them and wept over them as she lay still and white in her lonely state.

There was plenty of room in that great house, with its many guest-chambers, for the late Earl's trustee and his wife, her ladyship's niece, without their being brought into unfeeling contact with the visible signs and outward trappings of woe; there was room enough for the living and the dead.

Mr. Greatorex no longer suggested to the Earl of Aylmerton's heir, after he had read those entries in 'Countess Kate's boke,' that he should knock at the hall door for admission before he ventured to enter Orchard Damerel, or that he should obtain permission from the trustees before he presumed to sleep beneath that roof. That old faded page had thrown a new light on his position. It had changed everything.

Hugh Damerel was no longer there as a beggar upon whom a ridiculous gift had been bestowed; he was there in his own right as the heir of the Damerels, the last living representative of the ancient race.

It was quite easy to verify those old entries of birth and marriage and death now that they had got the clue; it was only remarkable that they had not been discovered before.

No one could understand how the late Earl, in looking

about for one of his race and name to succeed to his heavily-weighted estates, had overlooked the descendants of his cousin Judith. There was an old rumour in the family that she had died in her infancy. All the old musty records in the muniment-room were silent about her. There was no mention made of the headstrong daughter of the race who had run away with her uncle's curate.

That page of her history had been turned down—pinned down, rather—more than a century ago; it would still have been pinned down if Phyllis had not come across it in her midnight vigil.

The trustees of the Earl of Aylmerton assembled in solemn state at the Countess's funeral. They buried her beside her lord in the Aylmerton chapel, and Robert read the burial-service over her.

He committed her poor, worn-out old body to that dark, damp receptacle, in sure and certain hope, without a quiver of doubt in his voice. He would not have felt so sure, though he would have repeated the same words, if it had not been for that last unlooked-for act of generosity. Nobody was any the loser by it. She had left her money, as she had always said she would leave it, to the Jews. She did not leave a single penny to any member of her own family.

She left her wardrobe to her maid; her old lace, her jewellery, and her fans were to be divided equally between her nieces; and her prophetic books, and Dr. Cumming's sermons, she left to Robert.

There were other matters connected with the estate that had brought the late Earl's trustees down to Orchard Damerel besides the Countess's funeral. They buried the old woman first, and read her last will and testament with the pompous solemnity befitting the occasion, and then they proceeded to enter into the real business that had called them together.

Mr. Greatorex had not been idle during the days that intervened between her ladyship's death and the meeting of the trustees. He had prepared and got together all the evidence that was wanted to prove Hugh Damerel's legal right to the great Aylmerton property. The position was quite altered; the discovery of those faded entries in the Countess Kate's shaky handwriting had set the late Earl's will aside, and consequently the occupation of the Aylmerton trustees was gone.

The Earl had nothing to leave but his debts. He was only a tenant for life, and his ridiculous will, that had given so much trouble to everybody, was not worth the paper it was written upon. He had certainly no right to saddle the estate with reckless mortgages paying outrageous interest. He was past being called to account now. He had behaved abominably, and the lawyer who had helped him to lay this heavy burden on the property was out of reach too. Those who had erred and those who had benefited were all beyond the reach of human censure.

It is no use being angry with the dead. Perhaps, if they are permitted to look back upon their sorry past, they are more angry and more grieved than the bitterest of their accusers.

Who would add to the poignancy of their remorse?

While the Earl of Aylmerton's trustees were discussing the altered situation, and saying hard things about the improvident Earl, whose mouldering old coffin they had just been looking down upon in the Aylmerton vault, Hugh Damerel went out into the April sunshine with Phyllis. He could not bear the close, stifling air of that musty muniment-room. There was a swimming in his head, and a mist before his eyes, and a lump in his throat; he could not breathe in that atmosphere. It was all so unreal, so unlooked-for; he was obliged to come out beneath the blue April skies, with the air of heaven about him, to be sure that he was in his right senses, that it was not a dream, and he asked Phyllis to come out with him.

Phyllis came with him, white and trembling; perhaps it was her black dress that made her look so white, and her eyes were red with weeping. No one could understand why she should weep for that cantankerous old woman.

Cecilia had shed a few becoming tears just before the funeral, when the mourners were gathered together in the big dining-room, where she had eaten so many dreary dinners opposite the old woman whose coffin was then being carried down the stairs and out of the hall-door. She had dried her tears as soon as the black procession was out of sight; she could not think what Phyllis was crying for. She could not care very much for the old woman, and she had not even mentioned her in her will.

Perhaps she was sorry to lose her situation. Hugh Damerel did not ask Phyllis what she was weeping for. It was rather a new thing for him to see women weep. He did not think red eyes at all unbecoming.

'Is it settled—have they decided anything?' Phyllis asked, when they had entered the shrubbery: she could not ask the question till she had passed out of sight of the great uncurtained windows of the house.

The blinds had all been drawn up after the funeral, and the many windows, like reproachful eyes, seemed watching her. It was so dreadful to ignore the dead so soon; she almost hesitated to ask the question.

'Nothing is settled,' he said, 'except that—that my fate is in your hands; that I go away never more to return or I remain here, whichever you bid me.'

'What do you mean?' Phyllis said, trembling, and putting out her hands to grasp some support.

She thought it was all settled by this time, and now he was talking of going away. Had they found anything more? Had they turned over another blurred and faded page?

Her neart stood quite still at the thought; she was trembling in every limb, she could hardly stand.

'I mean,' he said, 'that you alone can tell me to stay. There is a debt that I can never pay, a debt to which the poor old Earl's debts are but a feather-weight in the balance.'

'A debt?' she said, turning pale, and wringing her hands. 'How can I help you?'

He caught her two poor little outstretched hands in his, and looked down into her upturned face.

'Don't you see, dear,' he said, in a voice that was trembling like her own, 'that—that there are some debts that take a life-time to repay—that can never, never be fully paid?'

She looked up at him with her sweet anxious face; she could not at all understand what he meant. Something in his eyes told her what his lips had left unsaid. Her face flushed and paled; her eyes brightened and darkened.

'You—do—not—mean——' she said, with faltering accents, and the poppy colour rising scarlet in her cheeks, and a faint quiver of her white eyelids.

'But I do mean!' he said.

Cecilia, sitting at the window of the great gloomy drawing-room, where she had spent so many monotonous hours reading those dreary prophetic sermons, and playing those dreary old tunes on the grand piano in the corner, heard a step upon the gravel walk beneath. She turned round to see who was coming.

She was thinking of the old sad time, and wondering languidly how much of the Countess's old lace would fall to her share. Cecilia had a *penchant* for old lace, and there was a flounce of old *point de Medici* that she had set her heart upon. She was thinking of that old flounce when she heard the steps on the gravel beneath.

What enchantment had come over the scene? Hugh Damerel, with a girl by his side—a slim figure in a black robe with trailing skirts, a common black merino gown—was coming up the gravel-walk, not with a sad, mourning face to match her gown, but with peach-bloom cheeks, and a supreme look of happiness in her sweet eyes that poor Cecilia had never seen in any woman's eyes before. She had never seen it, alas! in her own eyes.

What was this? It was something she had missed in life.

Mr. Greatorex joined his wife at the window, as she stood with a strange feeling at her heart, looking down upon the happy lovers below. The hills were melting in the soft rosy glow of sunset; all the beautiful world beneath was shimmering and melting into greater loveliness. Through the purple mantle of cloud that had hung threatening all day on the horizon, a golden crown of sunlight had burst, and was streaming over the green glowing valley, and melting the mist on the hills.

'What does it mean?' Cecilia asked, in a whisper.

'It means, my dear, that Mr. Damerel—I beg his pardon, the Earl of Aylmerton—has made the first use of his succession to the Damerel property to discharge his greatest obligation. He would have been Mr. Damerel to the end of the chapter if that young lady had not made her wonderful discovery.'

CHAPTER XXXIX.

WINDFALLS.

THE Rector's wife had a good deal to think of in those dark days that intervened between the old Countess's death and her funeral. They were really dark days. Joan insisted on pulling down every blind in the house until Robert came back from the funeral. It was the only way she could show her respect for the old woman who had gone—who had gone so suddenly, without giving her a chance of thanking her.

Whether it was Lady Aylmerton's sudden death, or the trouble that had overtaken her own household—the trouble that had been so sharp while it lasted—one or the other, or perhaps both, had wrought a transformation in Joan.

The scales had fallen from her eyes.

How foolish, blind, infatuated she had been! Oh, how blind! She had thought about nothing but her own happiness and prosperity, her own happiness and Robert's. She had lived for it altogether; she had thought of nothing else. It had not answered. How could she expect it to answer? It had all come to an end abruptly. It was not too late—oh, thank Heaven! it was not too late—to begin afresh.

She began the next day, after lying awake all one night thinking—the night that Robert burned his sermons.

She began with the pony-carriage, which the groom drove into Carlingford the next morning, the carriage and the pair of ponies. She did not send them up to Tattersall's; she sent them back to the man of whom Robert had bought them.

'You will never be able to get on without them,' Robert said regretfully, while Joan was stroking their soft noses and giving them a parting lump of sugar before the groom drove them away.

'I shall be able to get on very well,' Joan said, laughing at his long face. She was obliged to laugh to hide her tears; she would not have had him see her crying for the world. 'I shall be too busy now to be driving about the country making calls. I have got something a thousand times better than a pony-carriage!'

She hugged the small atom in her arms and devoured it with kisses, and when she looked up from that sweet embrace there were no tears in her eyes to hide.

When the pony-carriage was gone, Joan suddenly discovered that there was not nearly enough work for a man to do in the stable, attending to that one horse—poor old Black Beauty was out at grass—and that the gardener, with a boy from the village to help him, could do the groom's work as well as his own.

It was not hard to persuade Robert about anything just now. He had been calling himself over the coals—rather hot coals—pretty freely lately; he had found out that he had made a great many mistakes.

'It shall be as you like, dear,' he said. 'I think we have made a mistake in thinking too much about appearances; a little too much of ourselves, perhaps, and not enough of other people, of our duties, our responsibilities.'

There was a little ache in Robert's voice as he spoke that Joan did not remember to have heard in it before, and the tears were smarting in his eyes.

'Darling!' Joan cried, in her old, impetuous way, with a sudden rush of tears, as she flung herself into his sheltering arms, 'darling! we will never, never think of appearances again. We will never, never care what people think about us! We have got each other—and the baby; what more can we want in the whole world?'

What indeed?

It was while Joan was in this mood that the schoolmaster came up to the Rectory and asked to see Robert.

The Rector had walked up to the house to make arrangements for the funeral, and Joan was alone in the darkened room, where the schoolmaster had held that first interview with her. She was not on the steps now. She was sitting in a low chair before the fire; the days were still chilly, and there was a small fire burning in the wide steel grate. Joan had already begun to economize in small things as well as in big, and the fire in the beautiful bright steel drawing-room grate was a mere handful to what it used to be in the old thoughtless days.

She was sitting quite close to the fire, and she had the baby in her arms, and she was crooning an old nursery lullaby to it when the schoolmaster came in.

'Mr. Lyon will be back presently, if you don't mind waiting,' she said, when he had explained that his errand was to the Rector.

'I would rather not wait,' he said nervously, 'I shall be too late if I wait. I have just had a telegram. Mary Bailey is ill—dying. If I want to see her alive, I must go at once. There is no time to lose; I must go by the next train.'

'Oh, I am so sorry!' Joan said, and then she looked at the young man with a new interest in her eyes.

How could she have thought him dull and stupid and commonplace, with that light of his faithful love shining in his eyes?

Joan never forgot that look. A poor, dull, stupid fellow standing there in the twilight, with the tears in his eyes, and his lips quivering, and that true, honest, faithful love in his tender heart.

'I am very sorry for Miss Bailey,' she said humbly 'I hope she is not quite so ill as you fear, but I am sure you ought to go to her at once. You need not wait to see Mr. Lyon; I am sure he will arrange about the school. You are late already to catch the mail; you have not a minute to lose. Stop—why shouldn't you drive over? The horse hasn't been out to-day; it will do it good to drive you to the station.'

She rang the bell as she spoke, and ordered the dog-cart to be brought round at once.

The man waited while it was brought round; he would not sit down; he stood, it seemed to Joan, on his old place in the carpet, and murmured his broken thanks.

'God reward you for your kindness,' he faltered in his broken voice, as he went away. 'If I am in time to see Mary Bailey alive, I shall bless you for it as long as I live.'

Joan, as she sat there crooning that low lullaby, heard the wheels of the dogcart scrunching over the gravel outside, but she did not see the stupid fellow take off his cap as he passed the darkened window of the room where she was sitting. There was no one there to see him, but the simple involuntary act looked like a benediction.

A strange thing happened the following day. Among the letters Robert took out of the post-bag was one from the picture-cleaner to whom Mr. Damerel had consigned that packing-case with the portrait of Joan's great-aunt.

It was dated from a West-End picture-gallery, and it bore the name of a well-known connoisseur. Robert had heard the name before—who has not?—though he knew nothing about the art-world. The picture-restorer said nothing about the cost of removing the network of cracks from the beautiful features of Joan's ancestress, but he asked some questions about the pedigree of the picture, the name of the lady whose portrait it was, and what relationship she bore to the present owner.

They were quite easy questions to answer. The lady was the youngest daughter of an old West-Country baronet, Sir Simon Worth. There were Worths still at Worth, but the title had long become extinct. Sir Simon was the last baronet. His daughter Joan's connection with the present owner was easy to trace. The picture had always descended as an heirloom to the female branch of the line, who bore the lady's old-world name. It had never been out of the family. Few pictures could have a better pedigree.

Robert had no idea why this information about his wife's picture was required. He gave all the particulars that he knew about it: the names, and the dates, and how it had come into his wife's possession; and then, for several days, he had so much else to think about that he forgot the picture. He forgot it as completely as if it had never existed. It went quite out of his mind.

There were sufficient reasons for his forgetting it. Things had happened so suddenly and unexpectedly lately, there was still such an air of unreality hanging over all, that Robert could not be quite sure whether he was awake or asleep.

The old Countess was dead and buried, sleeping beneath the marble pavement of the Aylmerton chapel. Hugh Damerel had come into his own. The old house would not be shut up for another hundred years, and its priceless heirlooms would not rot slowly away in the darkness and the dust. The light would be let into those darkened rooms, and the winds of heaven would sweep through them, and the dim, silent corridors would echo once more to merry voices and human laughter, and—perhaps—by-and-by the footsteps of children would patter over the oaken floor of those old nurseries and down the broad staircase, and the prattle of innocent voices would exorcise all the old ghosts and sad memories of the haunted house.

And Phyllis? Well, it was not possible to contemplate what the future had in store for Phyllis without wonder and awe. She was back at the Rectory now; there was nothing to keep her at Orchard Damerel after Cecilia had gone away, and taken that old *point de Medici* flounce away with her.

She had come back to stay with Joan. She had come back to the Rectory not quite the same Phyllis. She was graver, with a shy, tender light in her sweet eyes, as if she had drifted suddenly unawares into a peaceful calm. She was not going back to the old life; Joan would not hear of her going back; Bertha and her mother were to come to her here, and the boys were to come down again.

Phyllis shyly objected to this part of the programme. She had a little pet scheme of her own that she had set her heart upon. The boys were not to come down again just yet. They were to put off that long-looked-for visit until those shut-up chambers at Orchard Damerel should be swept and garnished, and she should be there to receive them. The birds'-nesting time would be over then, and the orchards would no longer be white with blossom; but there would be compensations—oh yes there would be compensations!

While the sisters were discussing these things, and the happy, happy days that were dawning for the boys and Bertha and their mother, who had gone through so much, Robert was working hard in his parish. Poor Mary Bailey was dead, and the schoolmaster had begged to stay for her funeral, and Robert had to spend all his mornings in the school. The boys were in better order now, and the work was not quite so hard; and that good little soul, Matilda Bray, was as ready as ever to help. She was such a capital disciplinarian that she could have managed both schools, the girls' and the boys', if Robert had let her.

The day the schoolmaster came back, an unexpected event happened. A windfall, a totally unexpected windfall, dropped down from the skies. It dropped straight into Joan's lap, where the baby happened to be lying.

The picture-restorer, who had asked so many questions about that picture of Joan's great-aunt, had asked another a few days previously. He had asked whether Robert would sell her.

'Sell her? Of course I would sell her,' Joan had answered when he had referred the question to her; 'the library looks ever so much better without her. I would sell her for a song, Robin, rather than have the hideous old frump sent back.'

The picture-restorer had taken Joan at her word. He had bought the portrait of her great-aunt for a song—rather a noble song. He had given four thousand pounds for her.

The portrait of the youngest daughter of Sir Simon Worth was painted by Sir Joshua Reynolds, and some particulars respecting the painting of this picture, which connoisseurs had sought in vain for, were recorded among the entries in the painter's pocket-book.

A princely buyer of the works of the great portrait-painter had offered this princely sum for the long-lost picture. The 'find' created quite a *furore* in the art-world among the lovers of the old English masters, but it created a greater *furore* in the quiet country Rectory at Coombe Damerel.

Robert gave the letter and the cheque to his wife, and she dropped it into her lap with a little cry.

'Oh, Robin!'

'Darling!' he said. He had not another word to say, and they looked at each other across the baby and the cheque. His heart was so full, and his eyes were so full, that he could not see them very plainly, not plainly enough to distinguish them one from the other; so he took them all in his arms, baby, and mother, and the wonderful windfall that had dropped down from the skies.

'What *does* it mean, Robin?' Joan asked, when her bewilderment allowed her to do anything but gasp, and clutch the baby to her bosom, lest it should melt away in the dream she was quite sure she was dreaming.

'It means, darling, that your great-aunt has brought us a fortune. We never treated her with the consideration she deserved while she was with us, and only now, after she has gone away from us for ever, have we discovered her worth.'

Joan could not believe it, Phyllis could not believe it, Robert could hardly believe it himself, though he rode over to his bankers at Carlingford the same day and deposited that wonderful cheque with them. He could not have slept with it in the house. Like Joan, he thought it was all a dream, and that he should awake presently and find that it had melted away.

No one could believe it but Hugh Damerel. He came over the morning the cheque arrived: he came over most mornings now; there was an attraction at the Rectory that was always drawing him away from that great gloomy house of Orchard Damerel.

It did not come upon him as a surprise; when he knocked the nails in that rude packing-case, and sent off Joan's ancestor to the prince of picture-dealers, he knew pretty well what would happen, and he was not the least surprised.

'Four thousand pounds, Robin!' Joan said, when she found the cheque crumpled up somewhere about the baby when she released herself from Robert's embrace; 'that will be two thousand pounds for mamma, and—and—two thousand pounds for us! We couldn't keep it all, Robin——'

'Of course we couldn't,' Robert said promptly.

'Poor dear mamma! what she will be able to do foi the boys!'

What more is there to tell?

When the late Earl's ridiculous old will was set aside, the trustees discovered that the property could be relieved from that heavy burden of debt without much difficulty. There was that great estate of Aylmerton which would fetch, if put into the market, more than was required to pay all the old Earl's debts, without touching a single heirloom, or an acre of the land belonging to Orchard Damerel.

It would leave enough, more than enough, to satisfy most men. The old family place, the china, the pictures, the ancient silver plate, the beautiful carved furniture, the tapestries, the books, and, above all, the old Bartolozzi prints, would remain intact. Not one of them would be touched.

They are there now, in their old places in the beautiful old house, which is presided over by a gracious mistress with a sweet shy face—a grave face, too, as if the burden of this greatness weighing upon her had added a new depth and earnestness to her nature. The old portraits of the Damerels are still looking down from their old places on the walls. They have seen so many changes in the old house since they hung there, that they have ceased to be surprised at anything. If their eyes were not dull and dim—not mere painted eyes—they would brighten as they looked down upon the ruddy freckled faces of two eager schoolboys, who never weary during the holidays they spend at Orchard Damerel of exploring the treasures of the old house with ever-increasing wonder and admiration.

There have been few changes at Coombe Damerel. A governess-cart, drawn by a quiet gray pony, who rejoices in the name of Cowslip, has taken the place of Joan's carriage and beautifully matching pair. She may be seen any day driving it through the village, and it stops much more often at cottage-doors than its magnificent predecessors. There is always a bright-looking nursemaid in the carriage with her, in charge of a beautiful brown baby, who has already established, during these many stoppages, a nodding acquaintance with every other baby in the parish.

Robert is doing his little best to elevate the humble folk among whom his lot has been cast. He had made a lot of mistakes at starting. There are a great many acts in every man's life that cannot be defended or explained.

That first year at Coombe Damerel had been a dismal record of failures, humiliating mistakes, and defeats. Perhaps it was not all loss. It is not always victory and triumph that make success, and blunders, mistakes, defeats, do not always make failure.

The village school is flourishing. The inspector's last report was the best, the very best, since the school was established, and the Government grant is to be considerably augmented.

Matilda Bray is still chirping about, as busy and active as ever, among her girls—she is still Matilda Bray. The schoolmaster, who is wearing a mourning band round his left arm for Mary Bailey, was training a rose-tree over her sitting-room window as Joan drove by the other day, and the silly fellow blushed furiously when he was caught in the act.

Perhaps the late Countess's intentions will be carried out after all, and the divided school-house will be made into one.

THE END.

BILLING AND SONS, PRINTERS, GUILDFORD.

MARIE ANTOINETTE ON THE EVE OF HER EXECUTION.

"All hope of Succour, but from Thee, is lost."

(SEE NEXT PAGE).

LIST OF BOOKS PUBLISHED BY

CHATTO & WINDUS

214 PICCADILLY, LONDON, W.

About (Edmond).—The Fellah: An Egyptian Novel. Translated by Sir RANDAL ROBERTS. Post 8vo, illustrated boards, 2*s.*

Adams (W. Davenport), Works by.
A Dictionary of the Drama: being a comprehensive Guide to the Plays, Playwrights, Players, and Playhouses of the United Kingdom and America, from the Earliest Times to the Present Day. Crown 8vo, half-bound, 12*s.* 6*d.* [*Preparing.*
Quips and Quiddities. Selected by W. DAVENPORT ADAMS. Post 8vo, cloth limp, 2*s.* 6*d.*

Agony Column (The) of 'The Times,' from 1800 to 1870. Edited, with an Introduction, by ALICE CLAY. Post 8vo, cloth limp, 2*s.* 6*d.*

Aidé (Hamilton), Novels by. Post 8vo, illustrated boards, 2*s.* each.
Carr of Carrlyon. | **Confidences.**

Albert (Mary).—Brooke Finchley's Daughter. Post 8vo, picture boards, 2*s.*; cloth limp, 2*s.* 6*d.*

Alden (W. L.).—A Lost Soul: Being the Confession and Defence of Charles Lindsay. Fcap. 8vo, cloth boards, 1*s.* 6*d.*

Alexander (Mrs.), Novels by. Post 8vo, illustrated boards, 2*s.* each.
Maid, Wife, or Widow? | **Valerie's Fate.**

Allen (F. M.).—Green as Grass. With a Frontispiece. Crown 8vo, cloth, 3*s.* 6*d.*

Allen (Grant), Works by.
The Evolutionist at Large. Crown 8vo, cloth extra, 6*s.*
Post-Prandial Philosophy. Crown 8vo, art linen, 3*s.* 6*d.*
Moorland Idylls. Crown 8vo, cloth decorated, 6*s.*

Crown 8vo, cloth extra, 3*s.* 6*d.* each; post 8vo, illustrated boards, 2*s.* each.

Philistia.	**In all Shades.**	**Dumaresq's Daughter.**
Babylon. 12 Illustrations.	**The Devil's Die.**	**The Duchess of Powysland**
Strange Stories. Frontis.	**This Mortal Coil.**	**Blood Royal.**
The Beckoning Hand.	**The Tents of Shem.** Frontis.	**Ivan Greet's Masterpiece.**
For Maimie's Sake.	**The Great Taboo.**	**The Scallywag.** 24 Illusts.

Crown 8vo, cloth extra, 3*s.* 6*d.* each.

At Market Value. | **Under Sealed Orders.**

Dr. Palliser's Patient. Fcap. 8vo, cloth boards, 1*s.* 6*d.*

Anderson (Mary).—Othello's Occupation: A Novel. Crown 8vo, cloth, 3*s.* 6*d.*

Arnold (Edwin Lester), Stories by.
The Wonderful Adventures of Phra the Phœnician. Crown 8vo, cloth extra, with 12 Illustrations by H. M. PAGET, 3*s.* 6*d.*; post 8vo, illustrated boards, 2*s.*
The Constable of St. Nicholas. With Frontispiece by S. L. WOOD. Crown 8vo, cloth, 3*s.* 6*d.*

Artemus Ward's Works. With Portrait and Facsimile. Crown 8vo, cloth extra, 7*s.* 6*d.*—Also a POPULAR EDITION, post 8vo, picture boards, 2*s.*
The Genial Sho[illegible]: The Life and Adventures of ARTEMUS WARD. By EDWARD P. HINGSTON. W[illegible] 3*s.* 6*d.*

Ashton (John), Works by. Crown 8vo, cloth extra, 7s. 6d. each.
History of the Chap-Books of the 18th Century. With 334 Illustrations.
Social Life in the Reign of Queen Anne. With 85 Illustrations.
Humour, Wit, and Satire of the Seventeenth Century. With 82 Illustrations.
English Caricature and Satire on Napoleon the First. With 115 Illustrations.
Modern Street Ballads. With 57 Illustrations.

Bacteria, Yeast Fungi, and Allied Species, A Synopsis of. By W. B. GROVE, B.A. With 87 Illustrations. Crown 8vo, cloth extra, 3s. 6d.

Bardsley (Rev. C. Wareing, M.A.), Works by.
English Surnames: Their Sources and Significations. Crown 8vo, cloth, 7s. 6d.
Curiosities of Puritan Nomenclature. Crown 8vo, cloth extra, 6s.

Baring Gould (Sabine, Author of 'John Herring,' &c.), Novels by.
Crown 8vo, cloth extra, 3s. 6d. each; post 8vo, illustrated boards, 2s. each.
Red Spider. | **Eve.**

Barr (Robert: Luke Sharp), Stories by. Cr. 8vo, cl., 3s. 6d. each.
In a Steamer Chair. With Frontispiece and Vignette by DEMAIN HAMMOND.
From Whose Bourne, &c. With 47 Illustrations by HAL HURST and others.

A Woman Intervenes. With 8 Illustrations by HAL HURST. Crown 8vo, cloth extra, 6s.
Revenge! With numerous Illustrations. Crown 8vo, cloth extra, 6s. [*Shortly.*

Barrett (Frank), Novels by.
Post 8vo, illustrated boards, 2s. each; cloth, 2s. 6d. each.
Fettered for Life.
The Sin of Olga Zassoulich.
Between Life and Death.
Folly Morrison. | **Honest Davie.**
Little Lady Linton.
A Prodigal's Progress.
John Ford; and **His Helpmate.**
A Recoiling Vengeance.
Lieut. Barnabas. | **Found Guilty.**
For Love and Honour.
The Woman of the Iron Bracelets. Cr. 8vo, cloth, 3s. 6d.; post 8vo, boards, 2s.; cl. limp, 2s. 6d.
The Harding Scandal. 2 vols., 10s. net.

Barrett (Joan).—Monte Carlo Stories. Fcap. 8vo, cloth, 1s. 6d.

Beaconsfield, Lord. By T. P. O'CONNOR, M.P. Cr. 8vo, cloth, 5s.

Beauchamp (Shelsley).—Grantley Grange. Post 8vo, boards, 2s.

Beautiful Pictures by British Artists: A Gathering of Favourites from the Picture Galleries, engraved on Steel. Imperial 4to, cloth extra, gilt edges, 21s.

Besant (Sir Walter) and James Rice, Novels by.
Crown 8vo, cloth extra, 3s. 6d. each; post 8vo, illustrated boards, 2s. each; cloth limp, 2s. 6d. each.
Ready-Money Mortiboy.
My Little Girl.
With Harp and Crown.
This Son of Vulcan.
The Golden Butterfly.
The Monks of Thelema.
By Celia's Arbour.
The Chaplain of the Fleet.
The Seamy Side.
The Case of Mr. Lucraft, &c.
'Twas in Trafalgar's Bay, &c.
The Ten Years' Tenant, &c.
*** There is also a LIBRARY EDITION of the above Twelve Volumes, handsomely set in new type on a large crown 8vo page, and bound in cloth extra, 6s. each; and a POPULAR EDITION of **The Golden Butterfly,** medium 8vo, 6d.; cloth, 1s.—NEW EDITIONS, printed in large type on crown 8vo laid paper, bound in figured cloth, 3s. 6d. each, are also in course of publication.

Besant (Sir Walter), Novels by.
Crown 8vo, cloth extra, 3s. 6d. each; post 8vo, illustrated boards, 2s. each; cloth limp, 2s. 6d. each.
All Sorts and Conditions of Men. With 12 Illustrations by FRED. BARNARD.
The Captains' Room, &c. With Frontispiece by E. J. WHEELER.
All in a Garden Fair. With 6 Illustrations by HARRY FURNISS.
Dorothy Forster. With Frontispiece by CHARLES GREEN.
Uncle Jack, and other Stories. | **Children of Gibeon.**
The World Went Very Well Then. With 12 Illustrations by A. FORESTIER.
Herr Paulus: His Rise, his Greatness, and his Fall. | **The Bell of St. Paul's.**
For Faith and Freedom. With Illustrations by A. FORESTIER and F. WADDY.
To Call Her Mine, &c. With 9 Illustrations by A. FORESTIER.
The Holy Rose, &c. With Frontispiece by F. BARNARD.
Armorel of Lyonesse: A Romance of To-day. With 12 Illustrations by F. BARNARD.
St. Katherine's by the Tower. With 12 Illustrations by C. GREEN.
Verbena Camellia Stephanotis, &c. With a Frontispiece by GORDON BROWNE.
The Ivory Gate. | **The Rebel Queen.**

Beyond the Dreams of Avarice. With 12 Illusts. by W. H. HYDE. Crown 8vo, cloth extra, 3s. 6d.
In Deacon's Orders, &c. With Frontispiece by A. FORESTIER. Crown 8vo, cloth, 6s.
The Master Craftsman. 2 vols., crown 8vo, 10s. net. [*May*

Fifty Years Ago. With 144 Plates and Woodcuts. Crown 8vo, cloth extra, 5s.
The Eulogy of Richard Jefferies. With Portrait. Crown 8vo, cloth extra, 6s.
London. With 125 Illustrations. Demy 8vo, cloth extra, 7s. 6d.
Westminster. With Etched Frontispiece by F. S. WALKER, R.P.E., and 130 Illustrations by WILLIAM PATTEN and others. Demy 8vo, cloth, 18s.
Sir Richard Whittington. With Frontispiece. Crown 8vo, art linen, 3s. 6d.
Gaspard de Coligny. With a Portrait. Crown 8vo, art linen, 3s. 6d.
As we Are: As we May Be: Social Essays. Crown 8vo, linen, 6s. [*Shortly.*

Bechstein (Ludwig).—As Pretty as Seven, and other German Stories. With Additional Tales by the Brothers GRIMM, and 98 Illustrations by RICHTER. Square 8vo, cloth extra, 6s. 6d.; gilt edges, 7s. 6d.

Beerbohm (Julius).—Wanderings in Patagonia; or, Life among the Ostrich-Hunters. With Illustrations. Crown 8vo, cloth extra, 3s. 6d.

Bellew (Frank).—The Art of Amusing: A Collection of Graceful Arts, Games, Tricks, Puzzles, and Charades. With 300 Illustrations. Crown 8vo, cloth extra, 4s. 6d.

Bennett (W. C., LL.D.).—Songs for Sailors. Post 8vo, cl. limp, 2s.

Bewick (Thomas) and his Pupils. By AUSTIN DOBSON. With 95 Illustrations. Square 8vo, cloth extra, 6s.

Bierce (Ambrose).—In the Midst of Life: Tales of Soldiers and Civilians. Crown 8vo, cloth extra, 6s.; post 8vo, illustrated boards, 2s.

Bill Nye's History of the United States. With 146 Illustrations by F. OPPER. Crown 8vo, cloth extra, 3s. 6d.

Bire (Edmond).—Diary of a Citizen of Paris during 'The Terror.' Translated and Edited by JOHN DE VILLIERS. With 2 Photogravures. Two Vols., 8vo, cloth, 21s. [*Shortly.*

Blackburn's (Henry) Art Handbooks.

Academy Notes, 1875, 1877-86, 1889, 1890, 1892-1895, Illustrated, each 1s.
Academy Notes, 1896. 1s. [*May.*
Academy Notes, 1875-79. Complete in One Vol., with 600 Illustrations. Cloth, 6s.
Academy Notes, 1880-84. Complete in One Vol., with 700 Illustrations. Cloth, 6s.
Academy Notes, 1890-94. Complete in One Vol., with 800 Illustrations. Cloth, 7s. 6d.
Grosvenor Notes, 1877. 6d.
Grosvenor Notes, separate years from **1878-1890,** each 1s.
Grosvenor Notes, Vol. I., **1877-82.** With 300 Illustrations. Demy 8vo, cloth, 6s.
Grosvenor Notes, Vol. II., **1883-87.** With 300 Illustrations. Demy 8vo, cloth, 6s.
Grosvenor Notes, Vol. III., **1888-90.** With 230 Illustrations. Demy 8vo cloth, 3s. 6d.
The New Gallery, 1888-1895. With numerous Illustrations, each 1s.
The New Gallery, Vol. I., **1888-1892.** With 250 Illustrations. Demy 8vo, cloth, 6s.
English Pictures at the National Gallery. With 114 Illustrations. 1s.
Old Masters at the National Gallery. With 128 Illustrations. 1s. 6d.
Illustrated Catalogue to the National Gallery. With 242 Illusts. Demy 8vo, cloth, 3s.
The Paris Salon, 1895. With 300 Facsimile Sketches. 3s.

Blind (Mathilde), Poems by.

The Ascent of Man. Crown 8vo, cloth, 5s.
Dramas in Miniature. With a Frontispiece by F. MADOX BROWN. Crown 8vo, cloth, 5s.
Songs and Sonnets. Fcap. 8vo, vellum and gold, 5s.
Birds of Passage: Songs of the Orient and Occident. Second Edition. Crown 8vo, linen, 6s. net.

Bourget (Paul).—A Living Lie. Translated by JOHN DE VILLIERS. With special Preface for the English Edition. Crown 8vo, cloth, 3s. 6d.

Bourne (H. R. Fox), Books by.

English Merchants: Memoirs in Illustration of the Progress of British Commerce. With numerous Illustrations. Crown 8vo, cloth extra, 7s. 6d.
English Newspapers: Chapters in the History of Journalism. Two Vols., demy 8vo, cloth, 25s.
The Other Side of the Emin Pasha Relief Expedition. Crown 8vo, cloth, 6s.

Bowers (George).—Leaves from a Hunting Journal. Coloured Plates. Oblong folio, half-bound, 21s.

Boyle (Frederick), Works by. Post 8vo, illustrated bds., 2s. each.

Chronicles of No-Man's Land. | **Camp Notes.** | **Savage Life.**

Brand (John).—Observations on Popular Antiquities; chiefly illustrating the Origin of our Vulgar Customs, Ceremonies, and Superstitions. With the Additions of Sir HENRY ELLIS, and numerous Illustrations. Crown 8vo, cloth extra, 7s. 6d.

Brewer (Rev. Dr.), Works by.

The Reader's Handbook of Allusions, References, Plots, and Stories. Seventeenth Thousand. Crown 8vo, cloth extra, 7s. 6d.
Authors and their Works, with the Dates: Being the Appendices to 'The Reader's Handbook,' separately printed. Crown 8vo, cloth limp, 2s.
A Dictionary of Miracles. Crown 8vo, cloth extra, 7s. 6d.

Brewster (Sir David), Works by. Post 8vo, cloth, 4s 6d. each.

More Worlds than One: Creed of the Philosopher and Hope of the Christian. With Plates.
The Martyrs of Science: GALILEO, TYCHO BRAHE, and KEPLER. With Portraits.
Letters on Natural Magic. With numerous Illustrations.

Brillat-Savarin.—Gastronomy as a Fine Art. Translated by R. E. ANDERSON, M.A. Post 8vo, half-bound, 2s.

Brydges (Harold).—Uncle Sam at Home. With 91 Illustrations. Post 8vo, illustrated boards, 2s.; cloth limp, 2s. 6d.

Buchanan (Robert), Novels, &c., by.

Crown 8vo, cloth extra, 3s. 6d. each; post 8vo, illustrated boards, 2s. each.

The Shadow of the Sword.
A Child of Nature. With Frontispiece.
God and the Man. With 11 Illustrations by FRED. BARNARD.
The Martyrdom of Madeline. With Frontispiece by A. W. COOPER.
Love Me for Ever. With Frontispiece.
Annan Water. | **Foxglove Manor.**
The New Abelard.
Matt: A Story of a Caravan. With Frontispiece.
The Master of the Mine. With Frontispiece.
The Heir of Linne. | **Woman and the Man.**

Crown 8vo, cloth extra, 3s. 6d. each.

Red and White Heather. | **Rachel Dene.**

Lady Kilpatrick. Crown 8vo, cloth extra, 6s.
The Wandering Jew: a Christmas Carol. Crown 8vo, cloth, 6s.

The Charlatan. By ROBERT BUCHANAN and HENRY MURRAY. With a Frontispiece by T. H. ROBINSON. Crown 8vo, cloth, 3s. 6d.

Burton (Richard F.).—The Book of the Sword. With over 400 Illustrations. Demy 4to, cloth extra, 32s.

Burton (Robert).—The Anatomy of Melancholy. With Translations of the Quotations. Demy 8vo, cloth extra, 7s. 6d.
Melancholy Anatomised: An Abridgment of BURTON'S ANATOMY. Post 8vo, half-bd., 2s. 6d.

Caine (T. Hall), Novels by. Crown 8vo, cloth extra, 3s. 6d. each.; post 8vo, illustrated boards, 2s. each; cloth limp, 2s. 6d. each.

The Shadow of a Crime. | **A Son of Hagar.** | **The Deemster.**

A LIBRARY EDITION of **The Deemster** is now ready; and one of **The Shadow of a Crime** is in preparation, set in new type, crown 8vo, cloth decorated, 6s. each.

Cameron (Commander V. Lovett).—The Cruise of the 'Black Prince' Privateer. Post 8vo, picture boards, 2s.

Cameron (Mrs. H. Lovett), Novels by. Post 8vo, illust. bds. 2s. ea.
Juliet's Guardian. | **Deceivers Ever.**

Carlyle (Jane Welsh), Life of. By Mrs. ALEXANDER IRELAND. With Portrait and Facsimile Letter. Small demy 8vo, cloth extra, 7s. 6d.

Carlyle (Thomas).—On the Choice of Books. Post 8vo, cl., 1s. 6d.
Correspondence of Thomas Carlyle and R. W. Emerson, 1834-1872. Edited by C. E. NORTON. With Portraits. Two Vols., crown 8vo, cloth, 24s.

Carruth (Hayden).—The Adventures of Jones. With 17 Illustrations. Fcap. 8vo, cloth, 2s.

Chambers (Robert W.), Stories of Paris Life by. Long fcap. 8vo, cloth, 2s. 6d. each.
The King in Yellow. | **In the Quarter.**

Chapman's (George), Works. Vol. I., Plays Complete, including the Doubtful Ones.—Vol. II., Poems and Minor Translations, with Essay by A. C. SWINBURNE.—Vol. III., Translations of the Iliad and Odyssey. Three Vols., crown 8vo, cloth, 6s. each.

Chapple (J. Mitchell).—The Minor Chord: The Story of a Prima Donna. Crown 8vo, cloth, 3s. 6d.

Chatto (W. A.) and J. Jackson.—A Treatise on Wood Engraving, Historical and Practical. With Chapter by H. G. BOHN, and 450 fine Illusts. Large 4to, half-leather, 28s.

Chaucer for Children: A Golden Key. By Mrs. H. R. HAWEIS. With 8 Coloured Plates and 30 Woodcuts. Crown 4to, cloth extra, 3s. 6d.
Chaucer for Schools. By Mrs. H. R. HAWEIS. Demy 8vo, cloth limp, 2s. 6d.

Chess, The Laws and Practice of. With an Analysis of the Openings. By HOWARD STAUNTON. Edited by R. B. WORMALD. Crown 8vo, cloth, 5s.
The Minor Tactics of Chess: A Treatise on the Deployment of the Forces in obedience to Strategic Principle. By F. K. YOUNG and E. C. HOWELL. Long fcap. 8vo, cloth, 2s. 6d.
The Hastings Chess Tournament Book (Aug.-Sept., 1895). Containing the Official Report of the 231 Games played in the Tournament, with Notes by the Players, and Diagrams of Interesting Positions; Portraits and Biographical Sketches of the Chess Masters; and an Account of the Congress and its surroundings. Crown 8vo, cloth extra, 7s. 6d. net. [*Shortly.*

Clare (Austin).—For the Love of a Lass. Post 8vo. 2s.; cl., 2s. 6d.

Clive (Mrs. Archer), Novels by. Post 8vo, illust. boards, 2s. each.
Paul Ferroll. | **Why Paul Ferroll Killed his Wife.**

Clodd (Edward, F.R.A.S.).—Myths and Dreams. Cr. 8vo, 3s. 6d.

Cobban (J. Maclaren), Novels by.

The Cure of Souls. Post 8vo, illustrated boards, 2s.
The Red Sultan. Crown 8vo, cloth extra, 3s. 6d.; post 8vo, illustrated boards, 2s.
The Burden of Isabel. Crown 8vo, cloth extra, 3s. 6d.

Coleman (John).—Players and Playwrights I have Known. Two Vols., demy 8vo, cloth, 24s.

Coleridge (M. E.).—The Seven Sleepers of Ephesus. Cloth, 1s. 6d.

Collins (C. Allston).—The Bar Sinister. Post 8vo, boards, 2s.

Collins (John Churton, M.A.), Books by.

Illustrations of Tennyson. Crown 8vo, cloth extra, 6s.
Jonathan Swift: A Biographical and Critical Study. Crown 8vo, cloth extra, 8s.

Collins (Mortimer and Frances), Novels by.

Crown 8vo, cloth extra, 3s. 6d. each; post 8vo, illustrated boards, 2s. each.

From Midnight to Midnight. | **Blacksmith and Scholar.**
Transmigration. | **You Play me False.** | **A Village Comedy.**

Post 8vo, illustrated boards, 2s. each.

Sweet Anne Page. | **A Fight with Fortune.** | **Sweet and Twenty.** | **Frances.**

Collins (Wilkie), Novels by.

Crown 8vo, cloth extra, 3s. 6d. each; post 8vo, illustrated boards, 2s. each; cloth limp, 2s. 6d. each.

Antonina. With a Frontispiece by Sir JOHN GILBERT, R.A.
Basil. Illustrated by Sir JOHN GILBERT, R.A., and J. MAHONEY.
Hide and Seek. Illustrated by Sir JOHN GILBERT, R.A., and J. MAHONEY.
After Dark. With Illustrations by A. B. HOUGHTON. | **The Two Destinies.**
The Dead Secret. With a Frontispiece by Sir JOHN GILBERT, R.A.
Queen of Hearts. With a Frontispiece by Sir JOHN GILBERT, R.A.
The Woman in White. With Illustrations by Sir JOHN GILBERT, R.A., and F. A. FRASER.
No Name. With Illustrations by Sir J. E. MILLAIS, R.A., and A. W. COOPER.
My Miscellanies. With a Steel-plate Portrait of WILKIE COLLINS.
Armadale. With Illustrations by G. H. THOMAS.
The Moonstone. With Illustrations by G. DU MAURIER and F. A. FRASER.
Man and Wife. With Illustrations by WILLIAM SMALL.
Poor Miss Finch. Illustrated by G. DU MAURIER and EDWARD HUGHES.
Miss or Mrs.? With Illustrations by S. L. FILDES, R.A., and HENRY WOODS, A.R.A.
The New Magdalen. Illustrated by G. DU MAURIER and C. S. REINHARDT.
The Frozen Deep. Illustrated by G. DU MAURIER and J. MAHONEY.
The Law and the Lady. With Illustrations by S. L. FILDES, R.A., and SYDNEY HALL.
The Haunted Hotel. With Illustrations by ARTHUR HOPKINS.
The Fallen Leaves. | **Heart and Science.** | **The Evil Genius.**
Jezebel's Daughter. | **'I Say No.'** | **Little Novels.** Frontis.
The Black Robe. | **A Rogue's Life.** | **The Legacy of Cain.**
Blind Love. With a Preface by Sir WALTER BESANT, and Illustrations by A. FORESTIER.

POPULAR EDITIONS. Medium 8vo, 6d. each; cloth, 1s. each.

The Woman in White. | **The Moonstone.**

The Woman in White and **The Moonstone** in One Volume, medium 8vo, cloth, 2s.

Colman's (George) Humorous Works: 'Broad Grins,' 'My Nightgown and Slippers,' &c. With Life and Frontispiece. Crown 8vo, cloth extra, 7s. 6d.

Colquhoun (M. J.).—Every Inch a Soldier. Post 8vo, boards, 2s.

Colt-breaking, Hints on. By W. M. HUTCHISON. Cr. 8vo, cl., 3s. 6d.

Convalescent Cookery. By CATHERINE RYAN. Cr. 8vo, 1s.; cl., 1s. 6d.

Conway (Moncure D.), Works by.

Demonology and Devil-Lore. With 65 Illustrations. Two Vols., demy 8vo, cloth, 28s.
George Washington's Rules of Civility. Fcap. 8vo, Japanese vellum, 2s. 6d.

Cook (Dutton), Novels by.

Paul Foster's Daughter. Crown 8vo, cloth extra, 3s. 6d.; post 8vo, illustrated boards, 2s.
Leo. Post 8vo, illustrated boards, 2s.

Cooper (Edward H.).—Geoffory Hamilton. Cr. 8vo, cloth, 3s. 6d.

Cornwall.—Popular Romances of the West of England; or, The Drolls, Traditions, and Superstitions of Old Cornwall. Collected by ROBERT HUNT, F.R.S. With two Steel Plates by GEORGE CRUIKSHANK. Crown 8vo, cloth, 7s. 6d.

Cotes (V. Cecil).—Two Girls on a Barge. With 44 Illustrations by F. H. TOWNSEND. Post 8vo, cloth, 2s. 6d.

Craddock (C. Egbert), Stories by.
The Prophet of the Great Smoky Mountains. Post 8vo, illustrated boards, 2s.
His Vanished Star. Crown 8vo, cloth extra, 3s. 6d.

Cram (Ralph Adams).—Black Spirits and White. Fcap. 8vo, cloth 1s. 6d.

Crellin (H. N.) Books by.
Romances of the Old Seraglio. With 28 Illustrations by S. L. WOOD. Crown 8vo, cloth, 3s. 6d.
Tales of the Caliph. Crown 8vo, cloth, 2s.
The Nazarenes: A Drama. Crown 8vo, 1s.

Crim (Matt.).—Adventures of a Fair Rebel. Crown 8vo, cloth extra, with a Frontispiece by DAN. BEARD, 3s. 6d.; post 8vo, illustrated boards, 2s.

Crockett (S. R.) and others.—Tales of Our Coast. By S. R. CROCKETT, GILBERT PARKER, HAROLD FREDERIC, 'Q.,' and W. CLARK RUSSELL. With 12 Illustrations by FRANK BRANGWYN. Crown 8vo, cloth, 3s. 6d. [*Shortly.*

Croker (Mrs. B. M.), Novels by. Crown 8vo, cloth extra, 3s. 6d. each; post 8vo, illustrated boards 2s. each; cloth limp, 2s. 6d. each.
Pretty Miss Neville. | **Diana Barrington.** | **A Family Likeness.**
A Bird of Passage. | **Proper Pride.** | **'To Let.'**
Village Tales and Jungle Tragedies.

Crown 8vo, cloth extra, 3s. 6d. each.
Mr. Jervis. | **The Real Lady Hilda.**
Married or Single? Three Vols., crown 8vo, 15s. net.

Cruikshank's Comic Almanack. Complete in Two SERIES: The FIRST, from 1835 to 1843; the SECOND, from 1844 to 1853. A Gathering of the Best Humour of THACKERAY, HOOD, MAYHEW, ALBERT SMITH, A'BECKETT, ROBERT BROUGH, &c. With numerous Steel Engravings and Woodcuts by GEORGE CRUIKSHANK, HINE, LANDELLS, &c. Two Vols., crown 8vo, cloth gilt, 7s. 6d. each.
The Life of George Cruikshank. By BLANCHARD JERROLD. With 84 Illustrations and a Bibliography. Crown 8vo, cloth extra, 6s.

Cumming (C. F. Gordon), Works by. Demy 8vo, cl. ex., 8s. 6d. ea.
In the Hebrides. With an Autotype Frontispiece and 23 Illustrations.
In the Himalayas and on the Indian Plains. With 42 Illustrations.
Two Happy Years in Ceylon. With 28 Illustrations.
Via Cornwall to Egypt. With a Photogravure Frontispiece. Demy 8vo, cloth, 7s. 6d.

Cussans (John E.).—A Handbook of Heraldry; with Instructions for Tracing Pedigrees and Deciphering Ancient MSS., &c. Fourth Edition, revised, with 408 Woodcuts and 2 Coloured Plates. Crown 8vo, cloth extra, 6s.

Cyples (W.).—Hearts of Gold. Cr. 8vo, cl., 3s. 6d.; post 8vo, bds., 2s.

Daniel (George).—Merrie England in the Olden Time. With Illustrations by ROBERT CRUIKSHANK. Crown 8vo, cloth extra, 3s. 6d.

Daudet (Alphonse).—The Evangelist; or, Port Salvation. Crown 8vo, cloth extra, 3s. 6d.; post 8vo, illustrated boards, 2s.

Davenant (Francis, M.A.).—Hints for Parents on the Choice of a Profession for their Sons when **Starting in Life.** Crown 8vo, 1s.; cloth, 1s. 6d.

Davidson (Hugh Coleman).—Mr. Sadler's Daughters. With a Frontispiece by STANLEY WOOD. Crown 8vo, cloth extra, 3s. 6d.

Davies (Dr. N. E. Yorke-), Works by. Cr. 8vo, 1s. ea.; cl., 1s. 6d. ea.
One Thousand Medical Maxims and Surgical Hints.
Nursery Hints: A Mother's Guide in Health and Disease.
Foods for the Fat: A Treatise on Corpulency, and a Dietary for its Cure.
Aids to Long Life. Crown 8vo, 2s.; cloth limp, 2s. 6d.

Davies' (Sir John) Complete Poetical Works. Collected and Edited, with Introduction and Notes, by Rev. A. B. GROSART, D.D. Two Vols., crown 8vo, cloth, 12s.

Dawson (Erasmus, M.B.).—The Fountain of Youth. Crown 8vo, cloth extra, with Two Illustrations by HUME NISBET, 3s. 6d.; post 8vo, illustrated boards, 2s.

De Guerin (Maurice), The Journal of. Edited by G. S. TREBUTIEN. With a Memoir by SAINTE-BEUVE. Translated from the 20th French Edition by JESSIE P. FROTHINGHAM. Fcap. 8vo, half-bound, 2s. 6d.

De Maistre (Xavier).—A Journey Round my Room. Translated by Sir HENRY ATTWELL. Post 8vo, cloth limp, 2s. 6d.

De Mille (James).—A Castle in Spain. Crown 8vo, cloth extra, with a Frontispiece, 3s. 6d.; post 8vo, illustrated boards, 2s.

Derby (The): The Blue Ribbon of the Turf. With Brief Accounts of THE OAKS. By LOUIS HENRY CURZON. Crown 8vo, cloth limp, 2s. 6d.

Derwent (Leith), Novels by. Cr. 8vo, cl., 3s. 6d. ea.; post 8vo, 2s. ea.
Our Lady of Tears. | **Circe's Lovers.**

Dewar (T. R.).—A Ramble Round the Globe. With 220 Illustrations. Crown 8vo, cloth extra, 7s. 6d.

Dickens (Charles), Novels by. Post 8vo, illustrated boards, 2s. each.
Sketches by Boz. | **Nicholas Nickleby.** | **Oliver Twist.**

About England with Dickens. By ALFRED RIMMER. With 57 Illustrations by C. A. VANDERHOOF, ALFRED RIMMER, and others. Square 8vo, cloth extra, 7s. 6d.

Dictionaries.

A Dictionary of Miracles: Imitative, Realistic, and Dogmatic. By the Rev. E. C. BREWER, LL.D. Crown 8vo, cloth extra, 7s. 6d.
The Reader's Handbook of Allusions, References, Plots, and Stories. By the Rev. E. C. BREWER, LL.D. With an ENGLISH BIBLIOGRAPHY. Crown 8vo, cloth extra, 7s. 6d.
Authors and their Works, with the Dates. Crown 8vo, cloth limp, 2s.
Familiar Short Sayings of Great Men. With Historical and Explanatory Notes by SAMUEL A. BENT, A.M. Crown 8vo, cloth extra, 7s. 6d.
The Slang Dictionary: Etymological, Historical, and Anecdotal. Crown 8vo, cloth, 6s. 6d.
Words, Facts, and Phrases: A Dictionary of Curious, Quaint, and Out-of-the-Way Matters. By ELIEZER EDWARDS. Crown 8vo, cloth extra, 7s. 6d.

Diderot.—The Paradox of Acting. Translated, with Notes, by WALTER HERRIES POLLOCK. With Preface by Sir HENRY IRVING. Crown 8vo, parchment, 4s. 6d.

Dobson (Austin), Works by.
Thomas Bewick and his Pupils. With 95 Illustrations. Square 8vo, cloth, 6s.
Four Frenchwomen. With Four Portraits. Crown 8vo, buckram, gilt top, 6s.
Eighteenth Century Vignettes. TWO SERIES. Crown 8vo, buckram, 6s. each.—A THIRD SERIES is in preparation.

Dobson (W. T.).—Poetical Ingenuities and Eccentricities. Post 8vo, cloth limp, 2s. 6d.

Donovan (Dick), Detective Stories by.

Post 8vo, illustrated boards, 2s. each; cloth limp, 2s. 6d. each.

The Man-Hunter. | **Wanted.**
Caught at Last.
Tracked and Taken.
Who Poisoned Hetty Duncan?
Suspicion Aroused.
A Detective's Triumphs.
In the Grip of the Law.
From Information Received.
Link by Link. | **Dark Deeds.**
Riddles Read.

Crown 8vo, cloth extra, 3s. 6d. each; post 8vo, illustrated boards, 2s. each; cloth, 2s. 6d. each.
The Man from Manchester. With 23 Illustrations.
Tracked to Doom. With Six full-page Illustrations by GORDON BROWNE.

The Mystery of Jamaica Terrace. Crown 8vo, cloth, 3s. 6d.

Doyle (A. Conan).—The Firm of Girdlestone. Cr. 8vo, cl., 3s. 6d.

Dramatists, The Old. Crown 8vo, cl. ex., with Portraits, 6s. per Vol.
Ben Jonson's Works. With Notes, Critical and Explanatory, and a Biographical Memoir by WILLIAM GIFFORD. Edited by Colonel CUNNINGHAM. Three Vols.
Chapman's Works. Three Vols. Vol. I. contains the Plays complete; Vol. II., Poems and Minor Translations, with an Essay by A. C. SWINBURNE; Vol. III., Translations of the Iliad and Odyssey.
Marlowe's Works. Edited, with Notes, by Colonel CUNNINGHAM. One Vol.
Massinger's Plays. From GIFFORD'S Text. Edited by Colonel CUNNINGHAM. One Vol.

Duncan (Sara Jeannette: MRS. EVERARD COTES), Works by.

Crown 8vo, cloth extra, 7s. 6d. each.

A Social Departure. With 111 Illustrations by F. H. TOWNSEND.
An American Girl in London. With 80 Illustrations by F. H. TOWNSEND.
The Simple Adventures of a Memsahib. With 37 Illustrations by F. H. TOWNSEND.

Crown 8vo, cloth extra, 3s. 6d. each.

A Daughter of To-Day. | **Vernon's Aunt.** With 47 Illustrations by HAL HURST.

Dyer (T. F. Thiselton).—The Folk-Lore of Plants. Cr. 8vo, cl., 6s.

Early English Poets. Edited, with Introductions and Annotations, by Rev. A. B. GROSART, D.D. Crown 8vo, cloth boards, 6s. per Volume.
Fletcher's (Giles) Complete Poems. One Vol.
Davies' (Sir John) Complete Poetical Works. Two Vols.
Herrick's (Robert) Complete Collected Poems. Three Vols.
Sidney's (Sir Philip) Complete Poetical Works. Three Vols.

Edgcumbe (Sir E. R. Pearce).—Zephyrus: A Holiday in Brazil and on the River Plate. With 41 Illustrations. Crown 8vo, cloth extra, 5s.

Edison, The Life and Inventions of Thomas A. By W. K. L. and ANTONIA D[illegible] [illegible]TCALT, &c. Demy 4to, cloth gilt, 18s.

Edwardes (Mrs. Annie), Novels by.
Post 8vo, illustrated boards, 2s. each.
Archie Lovell. | **A Point of Honour.**

Edwards (Eliezer).—Words, Facts, and Phrases: A Dictionary of Curious, Quaint, and Out-of-the-Way Matters. Crown 8vo, cloth, 7s. 6d.

Edwards (M. Betham-), Novels by.
Kitty. Post 8vo, boards, 2s.; cloth, 2s. 6d. | **Felicia.** Post 8vo, illustrated boards, 2s.

Egerton (Rev. J. C., M.A.). — Sussex Folk and Sussex Ways. With Introduction by Rev. Dr. H. WACE, and Four Illustrations. Crown 8vo, cloth extra, 5s.

Eggleston (Edward).—Roxy: A Novel. Post 8vo, illust. boards, 2s.

Englishman's House, The: A Practical Guide for Selecting or Building a House. By C. J. RICHARDSON. Coloured Frontispiece and 534 Illusts. Cr. 8vo, cloth, 7s. 6d.

Ewald (Alex. Charles, F.S.A.), Works by.
The Life and Times of Prince Charles Stuart, Count of Albany (THE YOUNG PRETENDER). With a Portrait. Crown 8vo, cloth extra, 7s. 6d.
Stories from the State Papers. With Autotype Frontispiece. Crown 8vo, cloth, 6s.

Eyes, Our: How to Preserve Them. By JOHN BROWNING. Cr. 8vo, 1s.

Familiar Short Sayings of Great Men. By SAMUEL ARTHUR BENT, A.M. Fifth Edition, Revised and Enlarged. Crown 8vo, cloth extra, 7s. 6d.

Faraday (Michael), Works by. Post 8vo, cloth extra, 4s. 6d. each.
The Chemical History of a Candle: Lectures delivered before a Juvenile Audience. Edited by WILLIAM CROOKES, F.C.S. With numerous Illustrations.
On the Various Forces of Nature, and their Relations to each other. Edited by WILLIAM CROOKES, F.C.S. With Illustrations.

Farrer (J. Anson), Works by.
Military Manners and Customs. Crown 8vo, cloth extra, 6s.
War: Three Essays, reprinted from 'Military Manners and Customs.' Crown 8vo, 1s.; cloth, 1s. 6d.

Fenn (G. Manville), Novels by.
Crown 8vo, cloth extra, 3s. 6d. each; post 8vo, illustrated boards, 2s. each.
The New Mistress. | **Witness to the Deed.**
The Tiger Lily: A Tale of Two Passions.

The White Virgin. Crown 8vo, cloth extra, 3s. 6d.

Fin-Bec.—The Cupboard Papers: Observations on the Art of Living and Dining. Post 8vo, cloth limp, 2s. 6d.

Fireworks, The Complete Art of Making; or, The Pyrotechnist's Treasury. By THOMAS KENTISH. With 267 Illustrations. Crown 8vo, cloth, 5s.

First Book, My. By WALTER BESANT, JAMES PAYN, W. CLARK RUSSELL, GRANT ALLEN, HALL CAINE, GEORGE R. SIMS, RUDYARD KIPLING, A. CONAN DOYLE, M. E. BRADDON, F. W. ROBINSON, H. RIDER HAGGARD, R. M. BALLANTYNE, I. ZANGWILL, MORLEY ROBERTS, D. CHRISTIE MURRAY, MARY CORELLI, J. K. JEROME, JOHN STRANGE WINTER, BRET HARTE, 'Q.,' ROBERT BUCHANAN, and R. L. STEVENSON. With a Prefatory Story by JEROME K. JEROME, and 185 Illustrations. Small demy 8vo, cloth extra, 7s. 6d.

Fitzgerald (Percy), Works by.
The World Behind the Scenes. Crown 8vo, cloth extra, 3s. 6d.
Little Essays: Passages from the Letters of CHARLES LAMB. Post 8vo, cloth, 2s. 6d.
A Day's Tour: A Journey through France and Belgium. With Sketches. Crown 4to, 1s.
Fatal Zero. Crown 8vo, cloth extra, 3s. 6d.; post 8vo, illustrated boards, 2s.

Post 8vo, illustrated boards, 2s. each.

Bella Donna.	**The Lady of Brantome.**	**The Second Mrs. Tillotson.**
Polly.	**Never Forgotten.**	**Seventy-five Brooke Street.**

The Life of James Boswell (of Auchinleck). With Illusts. Two Vols., demy 8vo, cloth, 24s.
The Savoy Opera. With 60 Illustrations and Portraits. Crown 8vo, cloth, 3s. 6d.
Sir Henry Irving: Twenty Years at the Lyceum. With Portrait. Crown 8vo, 1s.; cloth, 1s. 6d.

Flammarion (Camille), Works by.
Popular Astronomy: A General Description of the Heavens. Translated by J. ELLARD GORE, F.R.A.S. With Three Plates and 288 Illustrations. Medium 8vo, cloth, 16s.
Urania: A Romance. With 87 Illustrations. Crown 8vo, cloth extra, 5s.

Fletcher's (Giles, B.D.) Complete Poems: Christ's Victorie in Heaven, Christ's Victorie on Earth, Christ's Triumph over Death, and Minor Poems. With Notes by Rev. A. B. GROSART, D.D. Crown 8vo, cloth boards, 6s.

Fonblanque (Albany).—Filthy Lucre. Post 8vo, illust. boards, 2s.

Francillon (R. E.), Novels by.

Crown 8vo, cloth extra, 3s. 6d. each; post 8vo, illustrated boards, 2s. each.

One by One. | **A Real Queen.** | **A Dog and his Shadow.**
Ropes of Sand. Illustrated.

Post 8vo, illustrated boards, 2s. each.

Queen Cophetua. | **Olympia.** | **Romances of the Law.** | **King or Knave?**

Jack Doyle's Daughter. Crown 8vo, cloth, 3s. 6d.
Esther's Glove. Fcap. 8vo, picture cover, 1s.

Frederic (Harold), Novels by. Post 8vo, illust. boards, 2s. each.
Seth's Brother's Wife. | **The Lawton Girl.**

French Literature, A History of. By HENRY VAN LAUN. Three Vols., demy 8vo, cloth boards, 7s. 6d. each.

Friswell (Hain).—One of Two: A Novel. Post 8vo, illust. bds., 2s.

Frost (Thomas), Works by. Crown 8vo, cloth extra, 3s. 6d. each.
Circus Life and Circus Celebrities. | **Lives of the Conjurers.**
The Old Showmen and the Old London Fairs.

Fry's (Herbert) Royal Guide to the London Charities. Edited by JOHN LANE. Published Annually. Crown 8vo, cloth, 1s. 6d.

Gardening Books. Post 8vo, 1s. each; cloth limp, 1s. 6d. each.
A Year's Work in Garden and Greenhouse. By GEORGE GLENNY.
Household Horticulture. By TOM and JANE JERROLD. Illustrated.
The Garden that Paid the Rent. By TOM JERROLD.

My Garden Wild. By FRANCIS G. HEATH. Crown 8vo, cloth extra, 6s.

Gardner (Mrs. Alan).—Rifle and Spear with the Rajpoots: Being the Narrative of a Winter's Travel and Sport in Northern India. With numerous Illustrations by the Author and F. H. TOWNSEND. Demy 4to, half-bound, 21s.

Garrett (Edward).—The Capel Girls: A Novel. Crown 8vo, cloth extra, with two Illustrations, 3s. 6d.; post 8vo, illustrated boards, 2s.

Gaulot (Paul).—The Red Shirts: A Story of the Revolution. Translated by JOHN DE VILLIERS. With a Frontispiece by STANLEY WOOD. Crown 8vo, cloth, 3s. 6d.

Gentleman's Magazine, The. 1s. Monthly. Contains Stories, Articles upon Literature, Science, Biography, and Art, and **'Table Talk'** by SYLVANUS URBAN.
*** *Bound Volumes for recent years kept in stock, 8s. 6d. each. Cases for binding, 2s.*

Gentleman's Annual, The. Published Annually in November. 1s.

German Popular Stories. Collected by the Brothers GRIMM and Translated by EDGAR TAYLOR. With Introduction by JOHN RUSKIN, and 22 Steel Plates after GEORGE CRUIKSHANK. Square 8vo, cloth, 6s. 6d.; gilt edges, 7s. 6d.

Gibbon (Charles), Novels by.

Crown 8vo, cloth extra, 3s. 6d. each; post 8vo, illustrated boards, 2s. each.

Robin Gray. Frontispiece. | **The Golden Shaft.** Frontispiece. | **Loving a Dream.**

Post 8vo, illustrated boards, 2s. each.

The Flower of the Forest.
The Dead Heart.
For Lack of Gold.
What Will the World Say?
For the King. | **A Hard Knot.**
Queen of the Meadow.
In Pastures Green.
In Love and War.
A Heart's Problem.
By Mead and Stream.
The Braes of Yarrow.
Fancy Free. | **Of High Degree.**
In Honour Bound.
Heart's Delight. | **Blood-Money.**

Gibney (Somerville).—Sentenced! Crown 8vo, 1s.; cloth, 1s. 6d.

Gilbert (W. S.), Original Plays by. In Three Series, 2s. 6d. each.
The FIRST SERIES contains: The Wicked World—Pygmalion and Galatea—Charity—The Princess—The Palace of Truth—Trial by Jury.
The SECOND SERIES: Broken Hearts—Engaged—Sweethearts—Gretchen—Dan'l Druce—Tom Cobb—H.M.S. 'Pinafore'—The Sorcerer—The Pirates of Penzance.
The THIRD SERIES: Comedy and Tragedy—Foggerty's Fairy—Rosencrantz and Guildenstern—Patience—Princess Ida—The Mikado—Ruddigore—The Yeomen of the Guard—The Gondoliers—The Mountebanks—Utopia.

Eight Original Comic Operas written by W. S. GILBERT. Containing: The Sorcerer—H.M.S. 'Pinafore'—The Pirates of Penzance—Iolanthe—Patience—Princess Ida—The Mikado—Trial by Jury. Demy 8vo, cloth limp, 2s. 6d.

The Gilbert and Sullivan Birthday Book: Quotations for Every Day in the Year, selected from Plays by W. S. GILBERT set to Music by Sir A. SULLIVAN. Compiled by ALEX. WATSON. Royal [illegible]

illbert (William), Novels by. Post 8vo, illustrated bds., 2s. each.
Dr. Austin's Guests. | **James Duke, Costermonger.**
The Wizard of the Mountain.

lanville (Ernest), Novels by.
Crown 8vo, cloth extra, 3s. 6d. each; post 8vo, illustrated boards, 2s. each.
The Lost Heiress: A Tale of Love, Battle, and Adventure. With Two Illustrations by H. NISBET.
The Fossicker: A Romance of Mashonaland. With Two Illustrations by HUME NISBET.
A Fair Colonist. With a Frontispiece by STANLEY WOOD.

The Golden Rock. With a Frontispiece by STANLEY WOOD. Crown 8vo, cloth extra, 3s. 6d.
Kloof Yarns. Crown 8vo, picture cover, 1s.; cloth, 1s. 6d.

lenny (George).—A Year's Work in Garden and Greenhouse: Practical Advice as to the Management of the Flower, Fruit, and Frame Garden. Post 8vo, 1s.; cloth, 1s. 6d.

odwin (William).—Lives of the Necromancers. Post 8vo, cl., 2s.

Golden Treasury of Thought, The: An Encyclopædia of QUOTATIONS. Edited by THEODORE TAYLOR. Crown 8vo, cloth gilt, 7s. 6d.

Gontaut, Memoirs of the Duchesse de (Gouvernante to the Children of France), 1773-1836. With Two Photogravures. Two Vols., demy 8vo, cloth extra, 21s.

oodman (E. J.).—The Fate of Herbert Wayne. Cr. 8vo, 3s. 6d.

raham (Leonard).—The Professor's Wife: A Story. Fcp. 8vo, 1s.

reeks and Romans, The Life of the, described from Antique Monuments. By ERNST GUHL and W. KONER. Edited by Dr. F. HUEFFER. With 545 Illustrations. Large crown 8vo, cloth extra, 7s. 6d.

reenwood (James), Works by. Crown 8vo, cloth extra, 3s. 6d. each.
The Wilds of London. | **Low-Life Deeps.**

reville (Henry), Novels by.
Nikanor. Translated by ELIZA E. CHASE. Post 8vo, illustrated boards, 2s.
A Noble Woman. Crown 8vo, cloth extra, 5s.; post 8vo, illustrated boards, 2s.

Griffith (Cecil).—Corinthia Marazion: A Novel. Crown 8vo, cloth extra, 3s. 6d.; post 8vo, illustrated boards, 2s.

Grundy (Sydney).—The Days of his Vanity: A Passage in the Life of a Young Man. Crown 8vo, cloth extra, 3s. 6d.: post 8vo, illustrated boards, 2s.

Habberton (John, Author of 'Helen's Babies'), **Novels by.**
Post 8vo, illustrated boards, 2s. each; cloth limp, 2s. 6d. each.
Brueton's Bayou. | **Country Luck.**

Hair, The: Its Treatment in Health, Weakness, and Disease. Translated from the German of Dr. J. PINCUS. Crown 8vo, 1s.; cloth, 1s. 6d.

Hake (Dr. Thomas Gordon), Poems by. Cr. 8vo, cl. ex., 6s. each.
New Symbols. | **Legends of the Morrow.** | **The Serpent Play.**

Maiden Ecstasy. Small 4to, cloth extra, 8s.

Hall (Owen).—The Track of a Storm. Crown 8vo, cloth, 6s.

Hall (Mrs. S. C.).—Sketches of Irish Character. With numerous Illustrations on Steel and Wood by MACLISE, GILBERT, HARVEY, and GEORGE CRUIKSHANK. Small demy 8vo, cloth extra, 7s. 6d.

Halliday (Andrew).—Every-day Papers. Post 8vo, boards, 2s.

Handwriting, The Philosophy of. With over 100 Facsimiles and Explanatory Text. By DON FELIX DE SALAMANCA. Post 8vo, cloth limp, 2s. 6d.

Hanky-Panky: Easy and Difficult Tricks, White Magic, Sleight of Hand, &c. Edited by W. H. CREMER. With 200 Illustrations. Crown 8vo, cloth extra, 4s. 6d.

Hardy (Lady Duffus).—Paul Wynter's Sacrifice. Post 8vo, bds., 2s.

Hardy (Thomas).—Under the Greenwood Tree. Crown 8vo, cloth extra, with Portrait and 15 Illustrations, 3s. 6d.; post 8vo, illustrated boards, 2s. cloth limp, 2s. 6d.

Harper (Charles G.), Works by. Demy 8vo, cloth extra, 16s. each.
The Brighton Road. With Photogravure Frontispiece and 90 Illustrations.
From Paddington to Penzance: The Record of a Summer Tramp. With 105 Illustrations.

Harwood (J. Berwick).—The Tenth Earl. Post 8vo, boards, 2s.

Harte's (Bret) Collected Works. Revised by the Author. LIBRARY EDITION, in Eight Volumes, crown 8vo, cloth extra, 6s. each.

Vol. I. COMPLETE POETICAL AND DRAMATIC WORKS. With Steel-plate Portrait.
,, II. THE LUCK OF ROARING CAMP—BOHEMIAN PAPERS—AMERICAN LEGENDS
,, III. TALES OF THE ARGONAUTS—EASTERN SKETCHES.
,, IV. GABRIEL CONROY. | Vol. V. STORIES—CONDENSED NOVELS, &c.
,, VI. TALES OF THE PACIFIC SLOPE.
,, VII. TALES OF THE PACIFIC SLOPE—II. With Portrait by JOHN PETTIE, R.A.
,, VIII. TALES OF THE PINE AND THE CYPRESS.

The Select Works of Bret Harte, in Prose and Poetry. With Introductory Essay by J. M. BELLEW, Portrait of the Author, and 50 Illustrations. Crown 8vo, cloth extra, 7s. 6d.
Bret Harte's Poetical Works. Printed on hand-made paper. Crown 8vo, buckram, 4s. 6d.
The Queen of the Pirate Isle. With 28 Original Drawings by KATE GREENAWAY, reproduced in Colours by EDMUND EVANS. Small 4to, cloth, 5s.

Crown 8vo, cloth extra, 3s. 6d. each; post 8vo, picture boards, 2s. each.
A Waif of the Plains. With 60 Illustrations by STANLEY L. WOOD.
A Ward of the Golden Gate. With 59 Illustrations by STANLEY L. WOOD.

Crown 8vo, cloth extra, 3s. 6d. each.
A Sappho of Green Springs, &c. With Two Illustrations by HUME NISBET.
Colonel Starbottle's Client, and Some Other People. With a Frontispiece.
Susy: A Novel. With Frontispiece and Vignette by J. A. CHRISTIE.
Sally Dows, &c. With 47 Illustrations by W. D. ALMOND and others.
A Protegee of Jack Hamlin's. With 26 Illustrations by W. SMALL and others.
The Bell-Ringer of Angel's, &c. With 39 Illustrations by DUDLEY HARDY and others
Clarence: A Story of the American War. With Eight Illustrations by A. JULE GOODMAN.

Post 8vo, illustrated boards, 2s. each.
Gabriel Conroy. | **The Luck of Roaring Camp, &c.**
An Heiress of Red Dog, &c. | **Californian Stories.**

Post 8vo, illustrated boards, 2s. each; cloth, 2s. 6d. each.
Flip. | **Maruja.** | **A Phyllis of the Sierras.**

Fcap. 8vo, picture cover, 1s. each.
Snow-Bound at Eagle's. | **Jeff Briggs's Love Story.**

Haweis (Mrs. H. R.), Books by.
The Art of Beauty. With Coloured Frontispiece and 91 Illustrations. Square 8vo, cloth bds., 6s.
The Art of Decoration. With Coloured Frontispiece and 74 Illustrations. Sq. 8vo, cloth bds., 6s.
The Art of Dress. With 32 Illustrations. Post 8vo, 1s.; cloth, 1s. 6d.
Chaucer for Schools. Demy 8vo, cloth limp, 2s. 6d.
Chaucer for Children. With 38 Illustrations (8 Coloured). Crown 4to, cloth extra, 3s. 6d.

Haweis (Rev. H. R., M.A.), Books by.
American Humorists: WASHINGTON IRVING, OLIVER WENDELL HOLMES, JAMES RUSSELL LOWELL, ARTEMUS WARD, MARK TWAIN, and BRET HARTE. Third Edition. Crown 8vo, cloth extra, 6s.
Travel and Talk, 1885, 1893, 1895: America—New Zealand—Tasmania—Ceylon. With Photogravure Frontispieces. Two Vols., crown 8vo, cloth, 21s.

Hawthorne (Julian), Novels by.
Crown 8vo, cloth extra, 3s. 6d. each; post 8vo, illustrated boards, 2s. each.
Garth. | **Ellice Quentin.** | **Beatrix Randolph.** With Four Illusts.
Sebastian Strome. | **David Poindexter's Disappearance.**
Fortune's Fool. | **Dust.** Four Illusts. | **The Spectre of the Camera.**

Post 8vo, illustrated boards, 2s. each.
Miss Cadogna. | **Love—or a Name.**
Mrs. Gainsborough's Diamonds. Fcap. 8vo, illustrated cover, 1s.

Hawthorne (Nathaniel).—Our Old Home. Annotated with Passages from the Author's Note-books, and Illustrated with 31 Photogravures. Two Vols., cr. 8vo, 15s.

Heath (Francis George).—My Garden Wild, and What I Grew There. Crown 8vo, cloth extra, gilt edges, 6s.

Helps (Sir Arthur), Works by. Post 8vo, cloth limp, 2s. 6d. each.
Animals and their Masters. | **Social Pressure.**
Ivan de Biron: A Novel. Crown 8vo, cloth extra, 3s. 6d.; post 8vo, illustrated boards, 2s.

Henderson (Isaac).—Agatha Page: A Novel. Cr. 8vo, cl., 3s. 6d.

Henty (G. A.), Novels by.
Rujub the Juggler. With Eight Illustrations by STANLEY L. WOOD. Crown 8vo, cloth, 3s. 6d.; post 8vo, illustrated boards, 2s.
Dorothy's Double. Crown 8vo, cloth, 3s. 6d.

Herman (Henry).—A Leading Lady. Post 8vo, bds., 2s.; cl., 2s. 6d.

Herrick's (Robert) Hesperides, Noble Numbers, and Complete Collected Poems. With Memorial-Introduction and Notes by the Rev. A. B. GROSART, D.D., Steel Portrait ... 18s.

Hertzka (Dr. Theodor).—Freeland: A Social Anticipation. Translated by ARTHUR RANSOM. Crown 8vo, cloth extra, 6s.

Hesse-Wartegg (Chevalier Ernst von).—Tunis: The Land and the People. With 22 Illustrations. Crown 8vo, cloth extra, 3s. 6d.

Hill (Headon).—Zambra the Detective. Post 8vo, bds., 2s.; cl., 2s. 6d.

Hill (John), Works by.
Treason-Felony. Post 8vo, boards, 2s. | **The Common Ancestor.** Cr. 8vo, cloth, 3s. 6d.

Hindley (Charles), Works by.
Tavern Anecdotes and Sayings: Including Reminiscences connected with Coffee Houses, Clubs, &c. With Illustrations. Crown 8vo, cloth extra, 3s. 6d.
The Life and Adventures of a Cheap Jack. Crown 8vo, cloth extra, 3s. 6d.

Hodges (Sydney).—When Leaves were Green. 3 vols., 15s. net.

Hoey (Mrs. Cashel).—The Lover's Creed. Post 8vo, boards, 2s.

Hollingshead (John).—Niagara Spray. Crown 8vo, 1s.

Holmes (Gordon, M.D.)—The Science of Voice Production and Voice Preservation. Crown 8vo, 1s.; cloth, 1s. 6d.

Holmes (Oliver Wendell), Works by.
The Autocrat of the Breakfast-Table. Illustrated by J. GORDON THOMSON. Post 8vo, cloth limp, 2s. 6d.—Another Edition, post 8vo, cloth, 2s.
The Autocrat of the Breakfast-Table and **The Professor at the Breakfast-Table.** In One Vol. Post 8vo, half-bound, 2s.

Hood's (Thomas) Choice Works in Prose and Verse. With Life of the Author, Portrait, and 200 Illustrations. Crown 8vo, cloth extra, 7s. 6d.
Hood's Whims and Oddities. With 85 Illustrations. Post 8vo, half-bound, 2s.

Hood (Tom).—From Nowhere to the North Pole: A Noah's Arkæological Narrative. With 25 Illustrations by W. BRUNTON and E. C. BARNES. Cr. 8vo, cloth, 6s.

Hook's (Theodore) Choice Humorous Works; including his Ludicrous Adventures, Bons Mots, Puns, and Hoaxes. With Life of the Author, Portraits, Facsimiles, and Illustrations. Crown 8vo, cloth extra, 7s. 6d.

Hooper (Mrs. Geo.).—The House of Raby. Post 8vo, boards, 2s.

Hopkins (Tighe).—''Twixt Love and Duty.' Post 8vo, boards, 2s.

Horne (R. Hengist).—Orion: An Epic Poem. With Photograph Portrait by SUMMERS. Tenth Edition. Crown 8vo, cloth extra, 7s.

Hungerford (Mrs., Author of 'Molly Bawn'), **Novels by.**
Post 8vo, illustrated boards, 2s. each; cloth limp, 2s. 6d. each.
A Maiden All Forlorn. | **In Durance Vile.** | **A Mental Struggle.**
Marvel. | **A Modern Circe.**

Crown 8vo, cloth extra, 3s. 6d. each; post 8vo, illustrated boards, 2s. each; cloth limp, 2s. 6d. each.
Lady Verner's Flight. | **The Red-House Mystery.**

The Three Graces. With 6 Illustrations. Crown 8vo, cloth extra, 3s. 6d.
The Professor's Experiment. Three Vols., crown 8vo, 15s. net.
A Point of Conscience. Three Vols., crown 8vo, 15s. net.

Hunt's (Leigh) Essays: A Tale for a Chimney Corner, &c. Edited by EDMUND OLLIER. Post 8vo, half-bound, 2s.

Hunt (Mrs. Alfred), Novels by.
Crown 8vo, cloth extra, 3s. 6d. each; post 8vo, illustrated boards, 2s. each.
The Leaden Casket. | **Self-Condemned.** | **That Other Person.**

Thornicroft's Model. Post 8vo, boards, 2s. | **Mrs. Juliet.** Crown 8vo, cloth extra, 3s. 6d.

Hutchison (W. M.).—Hints on Colt-breaking. With 25 Illustrations. Crown 8vo, cloth extra, 3s. 6d.

Hydrophobia: An Account of M. PASTEUR'S System; The Technique of his Method, and Statistics. By RENAUD SUZOR, M.B. Crown 8vo, cloth extra, 6s.

Hyne (C. J. Cutcliffe).—Honour of Thieves. Cr. 8vo, cloth, 3s. 6d.

Idler (The): An Illustrated Magazine. Edited by J. K. JEROME. 1s. Monthly. The First EIGHT VOLS. are [illegible] ng, 1s. 6d. each.

Impressions (The) of Aureole. Crown 8vo, printed on blush-rose paper and handsomely bound, 6s.

Indoor Paupers. By ONE OF THEM. Crown 8vo, 1s. ; cloth, 1s. 6d.

Ingelow (Jean).—Fated to be Free. Post 8vo, illustrated bds., 2s.

Innkeeper's Handbook (The) and Licensed Victualler's Manual. By J. TREVOR-DAVIES. Crown 8vo, 1s. ; cloth, 1s. 6d.

Irish Wit and Humour, Songs of. Collected and Edited by A. PERCEVAL GRAVES. Post 8vo, cloth limp, 2s. 6d.

Irving (Sir Henry) : A Record of over Twenty Years at the Lyceum. By PERCY FITZGERALD. With Portrait. Crown 8vo, 1s. ; cloth, 1s. 6d.

James (C. T. C.). — A Romance of the Queen's Hounds. Post 8vo, picture cover, 1s. ; cloth limp, 1s. 6d.

Jameson (William).—My Dead Self. Post 8vo, bds., 2s. ; cl., 2s. 6d.

Japp (Alex. H., LL.D.).—Dramatic Pictures, &c. Cr. 8vo, cloth, 5s.

Jay (Harriett), Novels by. Post 8vo, illustrated boards, 2s. each.
The Dark Colleen. | **The Queen of Connaught.**

Jefferies (Richard), Works by. Post 8vo, cloth limp, 2s. 6d. each.
Nature near London. | **The Life of the Fields.** | **The Open Air.**
*** Also the HAND-MADE PAPER EDITION, crown 8vo, buckram, gilt top, 6s. each.

The Eulogy of Richard Jefferies. By Sir WALTER BESANT. With a Photograph Portrait. Crown 8vo, cloth extra, 6s.

Jennings (Henry J.), Works by.
Curiosities of Criticism. Post 8vo, cloth limp, 2s. 6d.
Lord Tennyson : A Biographical Sketch. With Portrait. Post 8vo, 1s. ; cloth, 1s. 6d.

Jerome (Jerome K.), Books by.
Stageland. With 64 Illustrations by J. BERNARD PARTRIDGE. Fcap. 4to, picture cover, 1s.
John Ingerfield, &c. With 9 Illusts. by A. S. BOYD and JOHN GULICH. Fcap. 8vo, pic. cov. 1s. 6d.
The Prude's Progress : A Comedy by J. K. JEROME and EDEN PHILLPOTTS. Cr. 8vo, 1s. 6d.

Jerrold (Douglas).—The Barber's Chair ; and The Hedgehog Letters. Post 8vo, printed on laid paper and half-bound, 2s.

Jerrold (Tom), Works by. Post 8vo, 1s. ea. ; cloth limp, 1s. 6d. each.
The Garden that Paid the Rent.
Household Horticulture : A Gossip about Flowers. Illustrated.

Jesse (Edward).—Scenes and Occupations of a Country Life. Post 8vo, cloth limp, 2s.

Jones (William, F.S.A.), Works by. Cr. 8vo, cl. extra, 7s. 6d. each.
Finger-Ring Lore : Historical, Legendary, and Anecdotal. With nearly 300 Illustrations. Second Edition, Revised and Enlarged.
Credulities, Past and Present. Including the Sea and Seamen, Miners, Talismans, Word and Letter Divination, Exorcising and Blessing of Animals, Birds, Eggs, Luck, &c. With Frontispiece.
Crowns and Coronations : A History of Regalia. With 100 Illustrations.

Jonson's (Ben) Works. With Notes Critical and Explanatory, and a Biographical Memoir by WILLIAM GIFFORD. Edited by Colonel CUNNINGHAM. Three Vols. crown 8vo, cloth extra, 6s. each.

Josephus, The Complete Works of. Translated by WHISTON. Containing 'The Antiquities of the Jews' and 'The Wars of the Jews.' With 52 Illustrations and Maps. Two Vols., demy 8vo, half-bound, 12s. 6d.

Kempt (Robert).—Pencil and Palette : Chapters on Art and Artists. Post 8vo, cloth limp, 2s. 6d.

Kershaw (Mark). — Colonial Facts and Fictions : Humorous Sketches. Post 8vo, illustrated boards, 2s. ; cloth, 2s. 6d.

Keyser (Arthur).—Cut by the Mess. Crown 8vo, 1s. ; cloth, 1s. 6d.

King (R. Ashe), Novels by. Cr. 8vo, cl., 3s. 6d. ea.; post 8vo, bds., 2s. ea.
A Drawn Game. | **'The Wearing of the Green.'**

...oards, 2s. each.
Passio **Bell Barry.**

Knight (William, M.R.C.S., and Edward, L.R.C.P.). — The Patient's Vade Mecum: How to Get Most Benefit from Medical Advice. Cr. 8vo, 1s.; cl. 1s. 6d.

Knights (The) of the Lion: A Romance of the Thirteenth Century. Edited, with an Introduction, by the MARQUESS OF LORNE, K.T. Crown 8vo, cloth extra, 6s.

Lamb's (Charles) Complete Works in Prose and Verse, including 'Poetry for Children' and 'Prince Dorus.' Edited, with Notes and Introduction, by R. H. SHEPHERD. With Two Portraits and Facsimile of the 'Essay on Roast Pig.' Crown 8vo, half-bd., 7s. 6d.
The Essays of Elia. Post 8vo, printed on laid paper and half-bound, 2s.
Little Essays: Sketches and Characters by CHARLES LAMB, selected from his Letters by PERCY FITZGERALD. Post 8vo, cloth limp, 2s. 6d.
The Dramatic Essays of Charles Lamb. With Introduction and Notes by BRANDER MATTHEWS, and Steel-plate Portrait. Fcap. 8vo, half-bound, 2s. 6d.

Landor (Walter Savage).—Citation and Examination of William Shakspeare, &c., before Sir Thomas Lucy, touching Deer-stealing, 19th September, 1582. To which is added, **A Conference of Master Edmund Spenser** with the Earl of Essex, touching the State of Ireland, 1595. Fcap. 8vo, half-Roxburghe, 2s. 6d.

Lane (Edward William).—The Thousand and One Nights, commonly called in England **The Arabian Nights' Entertainments.** Translated from the Arabic, with Notes. Illustrated with many hundred Engravings from Designs by HARVEY. Edited by EDWARD STANLEY POOLE. With Preface by STANLEY LANE-POOLE. Three Vols., demy 8vo, cloth, 7s. 6d. ea.

Larwood (Jacob), Works by.
The Story of the London Parks. With Illustrations. Crown 8vo, cloth extra, 3s. 6d.
Anecdotes of the Clergy. Post 8vo, laid paper, half-bound, 2s.

Post 8vo, cloth limp, 2s. 6d. each.
Forensic Anecdotes. | **Theatrical Anecdotes.**

Lehmann (R. C.), Works by. Post 8vo, 1s. each; cloth, 1s. 6d. each.
Harry Fludyer at Cambridge.
Conversational Hints for Young Shooters: A Guide to Polite Talk.

Leigh (Henry S.), Works by.
Carols of Cockayne. Printed on hand-made paper, bound in buckram, 5s.
Jeux d'Esprit. Edited by HENRY S. LEIGH. Post 8vo, cloth limp, 2s. 6d.

Leland (C. Godfrey). — A Manual of Mending and Repairing. With Diagrams. Crown 8vo, cloth, 5s. [*Shortly.*

Lepelletier (Edmond). — Madame Sans-Gène. Translated from the French by JOHN DE VILLIERS. Crown 8vo, cloth extra, 3s. 6d.

Leys (John).—The Lindsays: A Romance. Post 8vo, illust. bds., 2s.

Lindsay (Harry).—Rhoda Roberts: A Welsh Mining Story. Crown 8vo, cloth, 3s. 6d.

Linton (E. Lynn), Works by.

Crown 8vo, cloth extra, 3s. 6d. each; post 8vo, illustrated boards, 2s. each.
Patricia Kemball. | **Ione.**
The Atonement of Leam Dundas.
The World Well Lost. With 12 Illusts.
Under which Lord? With 12 Illustrations.
'My Love!' | **Sowing the Wind.**
Paston Carew, Millionaire and Miser.
The One Too Many.

Post 8vo, illustrated boards, 2s. each.
The Rebel of the Family. | **With a Silken Thread.**

Post 8vo, cloth limp, 2s. 6d. each.
Witch Stories. | **Ourselves:** Essays on Women.
Freeshooting: Extracts from the Works of Mrs. LYNN LINTON.

Lucy (Henry W.).—Gideon Fleyce: A Novel. Crown 8vo, cloth extra, 3s. 6d.; post 8vo, illustrated boards, 2s.

Macalpine (Avery), Novels by.
Teresa Itasca. Crown 8vo, cloth extra, 1s.
Broken Wings. With Six Illustrations by W. J. HENNESSY. Crown 8vo, cloth extra, 6s.

MacColl (Hugh), Novels by.
Mr. Stranger's Sealed Packet. Post 8vo, illustrated boards, 2s.
Ednor Whitlock. Crown 8vo, cloth extra, 6s.

Macdonell (Agnes).—Quaker Cousins. Post 8vo, boards, 2s.

MacGregor (Robert).—Pastimes and Players: Notes on Popular Games. Post 8vo, cloth limp, 2s. 6d.

Mackay (Charles, LL.D.). — Interludes and Undertones; or, Music at Twilight. Crown 8vo, cloth extra, 6s.

McCarthy (Justin, M.P.), Works by.

A History of Our Own Times, from the Accession of Queen Victoria to the General Election of 1880. Four Vols., demy 8vo, cloth extra, 12s. each.—Also a POPULAR EDITION, in Four Vols., crown 8vo, cloth extra, 6s. each.—And the JUBILEE EDITION, with an Appendix of Events to the end of 1886, in Two Vols., large crown 8vo, cloth extra, 7s. 6d. each.
A Short History of Our Own Times. One Vol., crown 8vo, cloth extra, 6s.—Also a CHEAP POPULAR EDITION, post 8vo, cloth limp, 2s. 6d.
A History of the Four Georges. Four Vols., demy 8vo, cl. ex., 12s. each. [Vols. I. & II. *ready*

Crown 8vo, cloth extra, 3s. 6d. each; post 8vo, illustrated boards, 2s. each; cloth limp, 2s. 6d. each.

The Waterdale Neighbours.
My Enemy's Daughter.
A Fair Saxon.
Linley Rochford.
Dear Lady Disdain.
Miss Misanthrope. With 12 Illustrations.
Donna Quixote. With 12 Illustrations.
The Comet of a Season.
Maid of Athens. With 12 Illustrations.
Camiola: A Girl with a Fortune.
The Dictator.
Red Diamonds.

'The Right Honourable.' By JUSTIN MCCARTHY, M.P., and Mrs. CAMPBELL PRAED. Crown 8vo, cloth extra, 6s.

McCarthy (Justin Huntly), Works by.

The French Revolution. (Constituent Assembly, 1789-91). Four Vols., demy 8vo, cloth extra, 12s. each. Vols. I. & II. *ready;* Vols. III. & IV. *in the press*
An Outline of the History of Ireland. Crown 8vo, 1s.; cloth, 1s. 6d.
Ireland Since the Union: Sketches of Irish History, 1798-1886. Crown 8vo, cloth, 6s.

Hafiz in London: Poems. Small 8vo, gold cloth, 3s. 6d.

Our Sensation Novel. Crown 8vo, picture cover, 1s.; cloth limp, 1s. 6d.
Doom: An Atlantic Episode. Crown 8vo, picture cover, 1s.
Dolly: A Sketch. Crown 8vo, picture cover, 1s.; cloth limp, 1s. 6d.
Lily Lass: A Romance. Crown 8vo, picture cover, 1s.; cloth limp, 1s. 6d.
The Thousand and One Days. With Two Photogravures. Two Vols., crown 8vo, half-bd., 12s.
A London Legend. Crown 8vo, cloth, 3s. 6d.

MacDonald (George, LL.D.), Books by.

Works of Fancy and Imagination. Ten Vols., 16mo, cloth, gilt edges, in cloth case, 21s.; or the Volumes may be had separately, in Grolier cloth, at 2s. 6d. each.
Vol. I. WITHIN AND WITHOUT.—THE HIDDEN LIFE.
„ II. THE DISCIPLE.—THE GOSPEL WOMEN.—BOOK OF SONNETS.—ORGAN SONGS.
„ III. VIOLIN SONGS.—SONGS OF THE DAYS AND NIGHTS.—A BOOK OF DREAMS.—ROADSIDE POEMS.—POEMS FOR CHILDREN.
„ IV. PARABLES.—BALLADS.—SCOTCH SONGS.
„ V. & VI. PHANTASTES: A Faerie Romance.
Vol. VII. THE PORTENT.
„ VIII. THE LIGHT PRINCESS.—THE GIANT'S HEART.—SHADOWS.
„ IX. CROSS PURPOSES.—THE GOLDEN KEY.—THE CARASOYN.—LITTLE DAYLIGHT.
„ X. THE CRUEL PAINTER.—THE WOW O' RIVVEN.—THE CASTLE.—THE BROKEN SWORDS.—THE GRAY WOLF.—UNCLE CORNELIUS.

Poetical Works of George MacDonald. Collected and Arranged by the Author. Two Vols. crown 8vo, buckram, 12s.
A Threefold Cord. Edited by GEORGE MACDONALD. Post 8vo, cloth, 5s.

Phantastes: A Faerie Romance. With 25 Illustrations by J. BELL. Crown 8vo, cloth extra, 3s. 6d.
Heather and Snow: A Novel. Crown 8vo, cloth extra, 3s. 6d.; post 8vo, illustrated boards, 2s.
Lilith: A Romance. SECOND EDITION. Crown 8vo, cloth extra, 6s.

Maclise Portrait Gallery (The) of Illustrious Literary Characters: 85 Portraits

by DANIEL MACLISE: with Memoirs—Biographical, Critical, Bibliographical, and Anecdotal—illustrative of the Literature of the former half of the Present Century, by WILLIAM BATES, B.A. Crown 8vo, cloth extra, 7s. 6d.

Macquoid (Mrs.), Works by. Square 8vo, cloth extra, 6s. each.

In the Ardennes. With 50 Illustrations by THOMAS R. MACQUOID.
Pictures and Legends from Normandy and Brittany. 34 Illusts. by T. R. MACQUOID.
Through Normandy. With 92 Illustrations by T. R. MACQUOID, and a Map.
Through Brittany. With 35 Illustrations by T. R. MACQUOID, and a Map.
About Yorkshire. With 67 Illustrations by T. R. MACQUOID.

Post 8vo, illustrated boards, 2s. each.

The Evil Eye, and other Stories.
Lost Rose, and other Stories.

Magician's Own Book, The: Performances with Eggs, Hats, &c.

Edited by W. H. CREMER. With 200 Illustrations. Crown 8vo, cloth extra, 4s. 6d.

Magic Lantern, The, and its Management: Including full Practical Directions.

By T. C. HEPWORTH. With 10 Illustrations. Crown 8vo, 1s.; cloth, 1s. 6d.

Magna Charta: An Exact Facsimile of the Original in the British Museum,

3 feet by 2 feet, with Arms and Seals emblazoned in Gold and Colours, 5s.

Mallory (Sir Thomas). — Mort d'Arthur: The Stories of King Arthur and of the Knights of the Round Table.

(A Selection.) Edited by B. MONTGOMERIE RANKING. Post 8vo, cloth limp, 2s.

Mallock (W. H.), Works by.
The New Republic. Post 8vo, picture cover, 2s.; cloth limp, 2s. 6d.
The New Paul & Virginia: Positivism on an Island. Post 8vo, cloth, 2s. 6d.
A Romance of the Nineteenth Century. Crown 8vo, cloth 6s.; post 8vo, illust. boards, 2s.

Poems. Small 4to, parchment, 8s.
Is Life Worth Living? Crown 8vo, cloth extra, 6s.

Mark Twain, Books by. Crown 8vo, cloth extra, 7s. 6d. each.
The Choice Works of Mark Twain. Revised and Corrected throughout by the Author. With Life, Portrait, and numerous Illustrations.
Roughing It; and The Innocents at Home. With 200 Illustrations by F. A. FRASER.
Mark Twain's Library of Humour. With 197 Illustrations.

Crown 8vo, cloth extra (illustrated), 7s. 6d. each; post 8vo, illustrated boards, 2s. each.
The Innocents Abroad; or, The New Pilgrim's Progress. With 234 Illustrations. (The Two Shilling Edition is entitled **Mark Twain's Pleasure Trip.**)
The Gilded Age. By MARK TWAIN and C. D. WARNER. With 212 Illustrations.
The Adventures of Tom Sawyer. With 111 Illustrations.
A Tramp Abroad. With 314 Illustrations.
The Prince and the Pauper. With 190 Illustrations.
Life on the Mississippi. With 300 Illustrations.
The Adventures of Huckleberry Finn. With 174 Illustrations by E. W. KEMBLE.
A Yankee at the Court of King Arthur. With 220 Illustrations by DAN BEARD.

Crown 8vo, cloth extra, 3s. 6d. each.
The American Claimant. With 81 Illustrations by HAL HURST and others.
Tom Sawyer Abroad. With 26 Illustrations by DAN. BEARD.
Pudd'nhead Wilson. With Portrait and Six Illustrations by LOUIS LOEB.
Tom Sawyer, Detective, &c. With numerous Illustrations. [*Shortly.*

The £1,000,000 Bank-Note. Crown 8vo, cloth, 3s. 6d.; post 8vo, picture boards 2s.

Post 8vo, illustrated boards, 2s. each.
The Stolen White Elephant. | **Mark Twain's Sketches.**

Marks (H. S., R.A.), Pen and Pencil Sketches by. With Four Photogravures and 126 Illustrations. Two Vols. demy 8vo, cloth, 32s.

Marlowe's Works. Including his Translations. Edited, with Notes and Introductions, by Colonel CUNNINGHAM. Crown 8vo, cloth extra, 6s.

Marryat (Florence), Novels by. Post 8vo, illust. boards, 2s. each.
A Harvest of Wild Oats. | **Fighting the Air.**
Open! Sesame! | **Written in Fire.**

Massinger's Plays. From the Text of WILLIAM GIFFORD. Edited by Col. CUNNINGHAM. Crown 8vo, cloth extra, 6s.

Masterman (J.).—Half-a-Dozen Daughters. Post 8vo, boards, 2s.

Matthews (Brander).—A Secret of the Sea, &c. Post 8vo, illustrated boards, 2s.; cloth limp, 2s. 6d.

Mayhew (Henry).—London Characters, and the Humorous Side of London Life. With numerous Illustrations. Crown 8vo, cloth, 3s. 6d.

Meade (L. T.), Novels by.
A Soldier of Fortune. Crown 8vo, cloth, 3s. 6d.; post 8vo, illustrated boards, 2s.
In an Iron Grip. Crown 8vo, cloth, 3s. 6d.
The Voice of the Charmer. Three Vols., 15s. net.

Merrick (Leonard).—The Man who was Good. Post 8vo, illustrated boards, 2s.

Mexican Mustang (On a), through Texas to the Rio Grande. By A. E. SWEET and J. ARMOY KNOX. With 265 Illustrations. Crown 8vo, cloth extra, 7s. 6d.

Middlemass (Jean), Novels by. Post 8vo, illust. boards, 2s. each.
Touch and Go. | **Mr. Dorillion.**

Miller (Mrs. F. Fenwick).—Physiology for the Young; or, The House of Life. With numerous Illustrations. Post 8vo, cloth limp, 2s. 6d.

Milton (J. L.), Works by. Post 8vo, 1s. each; cloth, 1s. 6d. each.
The Hygiene of the Skin. With Directions for Diet, Soaps, Baths, Wines, &c.
The Bath in Diseases of the Skin.
The Laws of Life, and their Relation to Diseases of the Skin.

Minto (Wm.).—Was She Good or Bad? Cr. 8vo, 1s.; cloth, 1s. 6d.

Mitford (Bertram), Novels by. Crown 8vo, cloth extra, 3s. 6d. each.
The Gun-Runner: A Romance of Zululand. With a Frontispiece by STANLEY L. WOOD.
The Luck of Gerard Ridgeley. With a Frontispiece by STANLEY L. WOOD.
The King's Assegai. With Six full-page Illustrations by STANLEY L. WOOD.
Renshaw Fanning's Quest. With a Frontispiece by STANLEY L. WOOD.

Molesworth (Mrs.), Novels by.
Hathercourt Rectory. Post 8vo, illustrated boards, 2s.
That Girl in Black. Crown 8vo, cloth, 1s. 6d.

Moncrieff (W. D. Scott-).—The Abdication: An Historical Drama. With Seven Etchings by JOHN PETTIE, W. Q. ORCHARDSON, J. MACWHIRTER, COLIN HUNTER, R. MACBETH and TOM GRAHAM. Imperial 4to, buckram, 21s.

Moore (Thomas), Works by.
The Epicurean; and **Alciphron.** Post 8vo, half-bound, 2s.
Prose and Verse; including Suppressed Passages from the MEMOIRS OF LORD BYRON. Edited by R. H. SHEPHERD. With Portrait. Crown 8vo, cloth extra, 7s. 6d.

Muddock (J. E.) Stories by.
Stories Weird and Wonderful. Post 8vo, illustrated boards, 2s.; cloth, 2s. 6d.
The Dead Man's Secret. With Frontispiece by F. BARNARD. Post 8vo, picture boards, 2s.
From the Bosom of the Deep. Post 8vo, illustrated boards, 2s.
Maid Marian and Robin Hood. With 12 Illusts. by STANLEY WOOD. Cr. 8vo, cloth extra, 3s. 6d.
Basile the Jester. With Frontispiece by STANLEY WOOD. Crown 8vo, cloth, 3s. 6d.

Murray (D. Christie), Novels by.
Crown 8vo, cloth extra, 3s. 6d. each; post 8vo, illustrated boards, 2s. each.

A Life's Atonement.
Joseph's Coat. 12 Illusts.
Coals of Fire. 3 Illusts.
Val Strange.
Hearts.
The Way of the World.
A Model Father.
Old Blazer's Hero.
Cynic Fortune. Frontisp.
By the Gate of the Sea.
A Bit of Human Nature.
First Person Singular.
Bob Martin's Little Girl.
Time's Revenges.
A Wasted Crime.
In Direst Peril.

Mount Despair, &c. With Frontispiece by GRENVILLE MANTON. Crown 8vo, cloth, 3s. 6d.
The Making of a Novelist: An Experiment in Autobiography. With a Collotype Portrait and Vignette. Crown 8vo, art linen, 6s.

Murray (D. Christie) and Henry Herman, Novels by.
Crown 8vo, cloth extra, 3s. 6d. each; post 8vo, illustrated boards, 2s. each.
One Traveller Returns. | **The Bishops' Bible.**
Paul Jones's Alias, &c. With Illustrations by A. FORESTIER and G. NICOLET.

Murray (Henry), Novels by.
Post 8vo, illustrated boards, 2s. each; cloth, 2s. 6d. each.
A Game of Bluff. | **A Song of Sixpence.**

Newbolt (Henry).—Taken from the Enemy. Fcp. 8vo, cloth, 1s. 6d.

Nisbet (Hume), Books by.
'Bail Up.' Crown 8vo, cloth extra, 3s. 6d.; post 8vo, illustrated boards, 2s.
Dr. Bernard St. Vincent. Post 8vo, illustrated boards, 2s.

Lessons in Art. With 21 Illustrations. Crown 8vo, cloth extra, 2s. 6d.
Where Art Begins. With 27 Illustrations. Square 8vo, cloth extra, 7s. 6d.

Norris (W. E.), Novels by. Crown 8vo, cloth, 3s. 6d. each.
Saint Ann's. | **Billy Bellew.** With Frontispiece. [*Shortly.*

O'Hanlon (Alice), Novels by. Post 8vo, illustrated boards, 2s. each.
The Unforeseen. | **Chance? or Fate?**

Ouida, Novels by. Cr. 8vo, cl., 3s. 6d. ea.; post 8vo, illust. bds., 2s. ea.

Held in Bondage.
Tricotrin.
Strathmore.
Chandos.
Cecil Castlemaine's Gage
Under Two Flags.
Puck. | **Idalia.**
Folle-Farine.
A Dog of Flanders.
Pascarel. | **Signa.**
Two Wooden Shoes.
In a Winter City.
Ariadne. | **Friendship.**
A Village Commune.
Moths. | **Pipistrello.**
In Maremma. | **Wanda.**
Bimbi. | **Syrlin.**
Frescoes. | **Othmar.**
Princess Napraxine.
Guilderoy. | **Ruffino.**
Two Offenders.

Square 8vo, cloth extra, 5s. each.
Bimbi. With Nine Illustrations by EDMUND H. GARRETT.
A Dog of Flanders, &c. With Six Illustrations by EDMUND H. GARRETT.

Santa Barbara, &c. Square 8vo, cloth, 6s.; crown 8vo, cloth, 3s. 6d.; post 8vo, illustrated boards, 2s.
Under Two Flags. POPULAR EDITION. Medium 8vo, 6d.; cloth, 1s.

Wisdom, Wit, and Pathos, selected from the Works of OUIDA by F. SYDNEY MORRIS. Post 8vo, cloth extra, 5s.—CHEAP EDITION, illustrated boards, 2s.

Pope's Poetical Works. Post 8vo, cloth limp, 2s.

Praed (Mrs. Campbell), Novels by. Post 8vo, illust. bds., 2s. each.
The Romance of a Station. | **The Soul of Countess Adrian.**

Crown 8vo, cloth, 3s. 6d. each; post 8vo, boards, 2s. each.
Outlaw and Lawmaker. | **Christina Chard.** With Frontispiece by W. PAGET.
Mrs. Tregaskiss. Three Vols., crown 8vo, 15s. net.

Price (E. C.), Novels by.

Crown 8vo, cloth extra, 3s. 6d. each; post 8vo, illustrated boards, 2s. each.
Valentina. | **The Foreigners.** | **Mrs. Lancaster's Rival.**
Gerald. Post 8vo, illustrated boards, 2s.

Princess Olga.—Radna: A Novel. Crown 8vo, cloth extra, 6s.

Proctor (Richard A., B.A.), Works by.
Flowers of the Sky. With 55 Illustrations. Small crown 8vo, cloth extra, 3s. 6d.
Easy Star Lessons. With Star Maps for every Night in the Year. Crown 8vo, cloth, 6s.
Familiar Science Studies. Crown 8vo, cloth extra, 6s.
Saturn and its System. With 13 Steel Plates. Demy 8vo, cloth extra, 10s. 6d.
Mysteries of Time and Space. With numerous Illustrations. Crown 8vo, cloth extra, 6s.
The Universe of Suns, &c. With numerous Illustrations. Crown 8vo, cloth extra, 6s.
Wages and Wants of Science Workers. Crown 8vo, 1s. 6d.

Pryce (Richard).—Miss Maxwell's Affections. Crown 8vo, cloth, with Frontispiece by HAL LUDLOW, 3s. 6d.; post 8vo, illustrated boards, 2s.

Rambosson (J.).—Popular Astronomy. Translated by C. B. PITMAN. With Coloured Frontispiece and numerous Illustrations. Crown 8vo, cloth extra, 7s. 6d.

Randolph (Lieut.-Col. George, U.S.A.).—Aunt Abigail Dykes: A Novel. Crown 8vo, cloth extra, 7s. 6d.

Reade's (Charles) Novels.

Crown 8vo, cloth extra, mostly illustrated, 3s. 6d. each; post 8vo, illustrated boards, 2s. each.
Peg Woffington. | **Christie Johnstone.**
'It is Never Too Late to Mend.'
The Course of True Love Never Did Run Smooth.
The Autobiography of a Thief; Jack of all Trades; and **James Lambert.**
Love Me Little, Love Me Long.
The Double Marriage.
The Cloister and the Hearth.
Hard Cash. | **Griffith Gaunt.**
Foul Play. | **Put Yourself in His Place.**
A Terrible Temptation.
A Simpleton. | **The Wandering Heir.**
A Woman-Hater.
Singleheart and Doubleface.
Good Stories of Men and other Animals.
The Jilt, and other Stories.
A Perilous Secret. | **Readiana.**

A New Collected LIBRARY EDITION, complete in Seventeen Volumes, set in new long primer type, printed on laid paper, and elegantly bound in cloth, price 3s. 6d. each, is now in course of publication. The volumes will appear in the following order:—

1. **Peg Woffington;** and **Christie Johnstone.**
2. **Hard Cash.**
3. **The Cloister and the Hearth.** With a Preface by Sir WALTER BESANT.
4. **'It is Never too Late to Mend.'**
5. **The Course of True Love Never Did Run Smooth;** and **Singleheart and Doubleface.**
6. **The Autobiography of a Thief; Jack of all Trades; A Hero and a Martyr;** and **The Wandering Heir.**
7. **Love Me Little, Love me Long.**
8. **The Double Marriage.** [April.
9. **Griffith Gaunt.** [May.
10. **Foul Play.** [June.
11. **Put Yourself in His Place.** [July.
12. **A Terrible Temptation.** [August.
13. **A Simpleton.** [Sept.
14. **A Woman-Hater.** [Oct.
15. **The Jilt,** and other Stories; and **Good Stories of Men & other Animals.** [Nov.
16. **A Perilous Secret.** [Dec.
17. **Readiana; & Bible Characters.** [Jan. '97

POPULAR EDITIONS, medium 8vo, 6d. each; cloth, 1s. each.
'It is Never Too Late to Mend.' | **The Cloister and the Hearth.**
Peg Woffington; and **Christie Johnstone.**

'It is Never Too Late to Mend' and **The Cloister and the Hearth** in One Volume, medium 8vo, cloth, 2s.

Christie Johnstone. With Frontispiece. Choicely printed in Elzevir style. Fcap. 8vo, half-Roxb. 2s. 6d.
Peg Woffington. Choicely printed in Elzevir style. Fcap. 8vo, half-Roxburghe, 2s. 6d.
The Cloister and the Hearth. In Four Vols., post 8vo, with an Introduction by Sir WALTER BESANT, and a Frontispiece to each Vol., 14s. the set; and the ILLUSTRATED LIBRARY EDITION, with Illustrations on every page, Two Vols., crown 8vo, cloth gilt, 42s. net.
Bible Characters. Fcap. 8vo, leatherette, 1s.

Selections from the Works of Charles Reade. With an Introduction by Mrs. ALEX. IRELAND. Crown 8vo, buckram, with Portrait, 6s.; CHEAP EDITION, post 8vo, cloth limp, 2s. 6d.

Riddell (Mrs. J. H.), Novels by.
Weird Stories. Crown 8vo, cloth extra, 3s. 6d.; post 8vo, illustrated boards, 2s.

Post 8vo, illustrated boards, 2s. each.
The Uninhabited House. | **Fairy Water.**
The Prince of Wales's Garden Party. | **Her Mother's Darling.**
The Mystery [illegible] | **The Nun's Curse.** | **Idle Tales.**

Rimmer (Alfred), Works by. Square 8vo, cloth gilt, 7s. 6d. each.
Our Old Country Towns. With 55 Illustrations by the Author.
Rambles Round Eton and Harrow. With 50 Illustrations by the Author.
About England with Dickens. With 58 Illustrations by C. A. VANDERHOOF and A. RIMMER.

Rives (Amelie).—Barbara Dering. Crown 8vo, cloth extra, 3s. 6d.; post 8vo, illustrated boards, 2s.

Robinson Crusoe. By DANIEL DEFOE. With 37 Illustrations by GEORGE CRUIKSHANK. Post 8vo, half-cloth, 2s.; cloth extra, gilt edges, 2s. 6d.

Robinson (F. W.), Novels by.
Women are Strange. Post 8vo, illustrated boards, 2s.
The Hands of Justice. Crown 8vo, cloth extra, 3s. 6d.; post 8vo, illustrated boards, 2s.

The Woman in the Dark. Two Vols., 10s. net.

Robinson (Phil), Works by. Crown 8vo, cloth extra, 6s. each.
The Poets' Birds. | **The Poets' Beasts.**
The Poets and Nature: Reptiles, Fishes, and Insects.

Rochefoucauld's Maxims and Moral Reflections. With Notes and an Introductory Essay by SAINTE-BEUVE. Post 8vo, cloth limp, 2s.

Roll of Battle Abbey, The: A List of the Principal Warriors who came from Normandy with William the Conqueror, 1066. Printed in Gold and Colours, 5s.

Rosengarten (A.).—A Handbook of Architectural Styles. Translated by W. COLLETT-SANDARS. With 630 Illustrations. Crown 8vo, cloth extra, 7s. 6d.

Rowley (Hon. Hugh), Works by. Post 8vo, cloth, 2s. 6d. each.
Puniana: Riddles and Jokes. With numerous Illustrations.
More Puniana. Profusely Illustrated.

Runciman (James), Stories by. Post 8vo, bds., 2s. ea.; cl., 2s. 6d. ea.
Skippers and Shellbacks. | **Grace Balmaign's Sweetheart.**
Schools and Scholars.

Russell (Dora), Novels by. Crown 8vo, cloth, 3s. 6d. each.
A Country Sweetheart. | **The Drift of Fate.**

Russell (W. Clark), Books and Novels by.

Crown 8vo, cloth extra, 6s. each; post 8vo, illustrated boards, 2s. each; cloth limp, 2s. 6d. each.

Round the Galley-Fire. | **A Book for the Hammock.**
In the Middle Watch. | **The Mystery of the 'Ocean Star.'**
A Voyage to the Cape. | **The Romance of Jenny Harlowe.**

Crown 8vo, cloth extra, 3s. 6d. each; post 8vo, illustrated boards, 2s. each; cloth limp, 2s. 6d. each.

An Ocean Tragedy. | **My Shipmate Louise.** | **Alone on a Wide Wide Sea.**

Crown 8vo, cloth, 3s. 6d. each.

Is He the Man? | **The Phantom Death, &c.** With Frontispiece.
The Good Ship 'Mohock.' | **The Convict Ship.** [*Shortly.*

On the Fo'k'sle Head. Post 8vo, illustrated boards, 2s.; cloth limp, 2s. 6d.
Heart of Oak. Three Vols., crown 8vo, 15s. net.
The Tale of the Ten. Three Vols., crown 8vo, 15s. net.

Saint Aubyn (Alan), Novels by.

Crown 8vo, cloth extra, 3s. 6d. each; post 8vo, illustrated boards, 2s. each.

A Fellow of Trinity. With a Note by OLIVER WENDELL HOLMES and a Frontispiece.
The Junior Dean. | **The Master of St. Benedict's.** | **To His Own Master.**
Orchard Damerel.

Fcap. 8vo, cloth boards, 1s. 6d. each.

The Old Maid's Sweetheart. | **Modest Little Sara.**

Crown 8vo, cloth extra, 3s. 6d. each.

In the Face of the World. | **The Tremlett Diamonds.**

Sala (George A.).—Gaslight and Daylight. Post 8vo, boards, 2s.

Sanson.—Seven Generations of Executioners: Memoirs of the Sanson Family (1688 to 1847). Crown 8vo, cloth extra, 3s. 6d.

Saunders (John), Novels by.

Crown 8vo, cloth extra, 3s. 6d. each; post 8vo, illustrated boards, 2s. each.

Guy Waterman. | **The Lion in the Path.** | **The Two Dreamers.**

Bound to the Wheel. Crown 8

Saunders (Katharine), Novels by.
Crown 8vo, cloth extra, 3s. 6d. each; post 8vo, illustrated boards, 2s. each.

Margaret and Elizabeth. | **Heart Salvage.**
The High Mills. | **Sebastian.**

Joan Merryweather. Post 8vo, illustrated boards, 2s.
Gideon's Rock. Crown 8vo, cloth extra, 3s. 6d.

Scotland Yard, Past and Present: Experiences of Thirty-seven Years. By Ex-Chief-Inspector CAVANAGH. Post 8vo, illustrated boards, 2s.; cloth, 2s. 6d.

Secret Out, The: One Thousand Tricks with Cards; with Entertaining Experiments in Drawing-room or 'White' Magic. By W. H. CREMER. With 300 Illustrations. Crown 8vo, cloth extra, 4s. 6d.

Seguin (L. G.), Works by.
The Country of the Passion Play (Oberammergau) and the Highlands of Bavaria. With Map and 37 Illustrations. Crown 8vo, cloth extra, 3s. 6d.
Walks in Algiers. With Two Maps and 16 Illustrations. Crown 8vo, cloth extra, 6s.

Senior (Wm.).—By Stream and Sea. Post 8vo, cloth, 2s. 6d.

Sergeant (Adeline).—Dr. Endicott's Experiment. Crown 8vo, buckram, 3s. 6d.

Shakespeare for Children: Lamb's Tales from Shakespeare. With Illustrations, coloured and plain, by J. MOYR SMITH. Crown 4to, cloth gilt, 3s. 6d.

Sharp (William).—Children of To-morrow. Crown 8vo, cloth, 6s.

Shelley's (Percy Bysshe) Complete Works in Verse and Prose. Edited, Prefaced, and Annotated by R. HERNE SHEPHERD. Five Vols., crown 8vo, cloth, 3s. 6d. each.
Poetical Works, in Three Vols.:
Vol. I. Introduction by the Editor; Posthumous Fragments of Margaret Nicholson; Shelley's Correspondence with Stockdale; The Wandering Jew; Queen Mab, with the Notes; Alastor, and other Poems; Rosalind and Helen; Prometheus Unbound; Adonais, &c.
,, II. Laon and Cythna; The Cenci; Julian and Maddalo; Swellfoot the Tyrant; The Witch of Atlas; Epipsychidion; Hellas.
,, III. Posthumous Poems; The Masque of Anarchy; and other Pieces.
Prose Works, in Two Vols.:
Vol. I. The Two Romances of Zastrozzi and St. Irvyne; the Dublin and Marlow Pamphlets; A Refutation of Deism; Letters to Leigh Hunt, and some Minor Writings and Fragments.
,, II. The Essays; Letters from Abroad; Translations and Fragments, edited by Mrs. SHELLEY. With a Biography of Shelley, and an Index of the Prose Works.
*** Also a few copies of a LARGE-PAPER EDITION, 5 vols., cloth, £2 12s. 6d.

Sherard (R. H.).—Rogues: A Novel. Crown 8vo, 1s.; cloth, 1s. 6d.

Sheridan (General P. H.), Personal Memoirs of. With Portraits, Maps, and Facsimiles. Two Vols., demy 8vo, cloth, 24s.

Sheridan's (Richard Brinsley) Complete Works, with Life and Anecdotes. Including his Dramatic Writings, his Works in Prose and Poetry, Translations, Speeches, and Jokes. With 10 Illustrations. Crown 8vo, half-bound, 7s. 6d.
The Rivals, The School for Scandal, and other Plays. Post 8vo, half-bound, 2s.
Sheridan's Comedies: The Rivals and **The School for Scandal.** Edited, with an Introduction and Notes to each Play, and a Biographical Sketch, by BRANDER MATTHEWS. With Illustrations. Demy 8vo, half-parchment, 12s. 6d.

Sidney's (Sir Philip) Complete Poetical Works, including all those in 'Arcadia.' With Portrait, Memorial-Introduction, Notes, &c., by the Rev. A. B. GROSART, D.D. Three Vols., crown 8vo, cloth boards, 18s.

Sims (George R.), Works by.
Post 8vo, illustrated boards, 2s. each; cloth limp, 2s. 6d. each.

Rogues and Vagabonds.
The Ring o' Bells.
Mary Jane's Memoirs.
Mary Jane Married.
Tinkletop's Crime.
Zeph: A Circus Story, &c.
Tales of To-day.
Dramas of Life. With 60 Illustrations.
Memoirs of a Landlady.
My Two Wives.
Scenes from the Show.
The Ten Commandments: Stories.

Crown 8vo, picture cover, 1s. each; cloth, 1s. 6d. each.
How the Poor Live; and **Horrible London.**
The Dagonet Reciter and Reader: Being Readings and Recitations in Prose and Verse, selected from his own Works by GEORGE R. SIMS.
The Case of George Candlemas. | **Dagonet Ditties.** (From *The Referee.*)

Dagonet A

Signboards: Their History, including Anecdotes of Famous Taverns and Remarkable Characters. By JACOB LARWOOD and JOHN CAMDEN HOTTEN. With Coloured Frontispiece and 94 Illustrations. Crown 8vo, cloth extra, 7s. 6d.

Sister Dora: A Biography. By MARGARET LONSDALE. With Four Illustrations. Demy 8vo, picture cover, 4d.; cloth, 6d.

Sketchley (Arthur).—A Match in the Dark. Post 8vo, boards, 2s.

Slang Dictionary (The): Etymological, Historical, and Anecdotal. Crown 8vo, cloth extra, 6s. 6d.

Smart (Hawley).—Without Love or Licence: A Novel. Crown 8vo, cloth extra, 3s. 6d.; post 8vo, illustrated boards, 2s.

Smith (J. Moyr), Works by.
The Prince of Argolis. With 130 Illustrations. Post 8vo, cloth extra, 3s. 6d.
The Wooing of the Water Witch. With numerous Illustrations. Post 8vo, cloth, 6s.

Society in London. Crown 8vo, 1s.; cloth, 1s. 6d.

Society in Paris: The Upper Ten Thousand. A Series of Letters from Count PAUL VASILI to a Young French Diplomat. Crown 8vo, cloth, 6s.

Somerset (Lord Henry).—Songs of Adieu. Small 4to, Jap. vel., 6s.

Spalding (T. A., LL.B.).—Elizabethan Demonology: An Essay on the Belief in the Existence of Devils. Crown 8vo, cloth extra, 5s.

Speight (T. W.), Novels by.

Post 8vo, illustrated boards, 2s. each.

The Mysteries of Heron Dyke. | **Back to Life.**
By Devious Ways, &c. | **The Loudwater Tragedy.**
Hoodwinked; & Sandycroft Mystery. | **Burgo's Romance.**
The Golden Hoop. | **Quittance in Full.**

Post 8vo, cloth limp, 1s. 6d. each.

A Barren Title. | **Wife or No Wife?**

Crown 8vo, cloth extra, 3s. 6d. each.

A Secret of the Sea. | **The Grey Monk.**

The Sandycroft Mystery. Crown 8vo, picture cover, 1s.
The Master of Trenance. Three Vols., crown 8vo, 15s. net.
A Husband from the Sea. Post 8vo, illustrated boards, 2s.

Spenser for Children. By M. H. TOWRY. With Coloured Illustrations by WALTER J. MORGAN. Crown 4to, cloth extra, 3s. 6d.

Stafford (John).—Doris and I, &c. Crown 8vo, cloth, 3s. 6d.

Starry Heavens (The): A POETICAL BIRTHDAY BOOK. Royal 16mo, cloth extra, 2s. 6d.

Stedman (E. C.), Works by. Crown 8vo, cloth extra, 9s. each.
Victorian Poets. | **The Poets of America.**

Stephens (Riccardo, M.B.).—The Cruciform Mark: The Strange Story of RICHARD TREGENNA, Bachelor of Medicine (Univ. Edinb.) Crown 8vo, cloth, 6s.

Sterndale (R. Armitage).—The Afghan Knife: A Novel. Crown 8vo, cloth extra, 3s. 6d.; post 8vo, illustrated boards, 2s.

Stevenson (R. Louis), Works by. Post 8vo, cloth limp, 2s. 6d. ea.
Travels with a Donkey. With a Frontispiece by WALTER CRANE.
An Inland Voyage. With a Frontispiece by WALTER CRANE.

Crown 8vo, buckram, gilt top, 6s. each.

Familiar Studies of Men and Books.
The Silverado Squatters. With Frontispiece by J. D. STRONG.
The Merry Men. | **Underwoods:** Poems.
Memories and Portraits.
Virginibus Puerisque, and other Papers. | **Ballads.** | **Prince Otto.**
Across the Plains, with other Memories and Essays.

New Arabian Nights. Crown 8vo, buckram, gilt top, 6s.; post 8vo, illustrated boards, 2s.
The Suicide Club; and **The Rajah's Diamond.** (From NEW ARABIAN NIGHTS.) With Eight Illustrations by W. J. HENNESSY. Crown 8vo, cloth, 5s.
The Edinburgh Edition of the Works of Robert Louis Stevenson. Twenty-seven Vols., demy 8vo. This Edition (which is limited to 1,000 copies) is sold only in Sets, the price of which may be learned from the Booksellers. The First Volume was published Nov., 1894.

Songs of Travel. Crown 8vo, buckram, 5s. [Shortly.
Weir of Hermiston. (R. L. STEVENSON'S LAST WORK.) Large crown 8vo, 6s. [May.

Stoddard (C. Warren).—Summer Cruising in the South Seas. Illustrated by WALLIS MACKAY. Crown 8vo, cloth extra, 3s. 6d.

Stories from Foreign Novelists. With Notices by HELEN and ALICE ZIMMERN. Crown 8vo, cloth extra, 3s. 6d.; post 8vo, illustrated boards, 2s.

Strange Manuscript (A) Found in a Copper Cylinder. Crown 8vo, cloth extra, with 19 Illustrations by GILBERT GAUL, 5s.; post 8vo, illustrated boards, 2s.

Strange Secrets. Told by PERCY FITZGERALD, CONAN DOYLE, FLORENCE MARRYAT, &c. Post 8vo, illustrated boards, 2s.

Strutt (Joseph). — The Sports and Pastimes of the People of England; including the Rural and Domestic Recreations, May Games, Mummeries, Shows, &c., from the Earliest Period to the Present Time. Edited by WILLIAM HONE. With 140 Illustrations. Crown 8vo, cloth extra, 7s. 6d.

Swift's (Dean) Choice Works, in Prose and Verse. With Memoir, Portrait, and Facsimiles of the Maps in 'Gulliver's Travels.' Crown 8vo, cloth, 7s. 6d.
Gulliver's Travels, and **A Tale of a Tub.** Post 8vo, half-bound, 2s.
Jonathan Swift: A Study. By J. CHURTON COLLINS. Crown 8vo, cloth extra, 8s.

Swinburne (Algernon C.), Works by.

Selections from the Poetical Works of A. C. Swinburne. Fcap. 8vo, 6s.
Atalanta in Calydon. Crown 8vo, 6s.
Chastelard: A Tragedy. Crown 8vo, 7s.
Poems and Ballads. FIRST SERIES. Crown 8vo, or fcap. 8vo, 9s.
Poems and Ballads. SECOND SERIES. Crown 8vo, 9s.
Poems & Ballads. THIRD SERIES. Cr. 8vo, 7s.
Songs before Sunrise. Crown 8vo, 10s. 6d.
Bothwell: A Tragedy. Crown 8vo, 12s. 6d.
Songs of Two Nations. Crown 8vo, 6s.
George Chapman. (*See* Vol. II. of G. CHAPMAN'S Works.) Crown 8vo, 6s.
Essays and Studies. Crown 8vo, 12s.
Erechtheus: A Tragedy. Crown 8vo, 6s.
A Note on Charlotte Bronte. Cr. 8vo, 6s.
A Study of Shakespeare. Crown 8vo, 8s.
Songs of the Springtides. Crown 8vo, 6s.
Studies in Song. Crown 8vo, 7s.
Mary Stuart: A Tragedy. Crown 8vo, 8s.
Tristram of Lyonesse. Crown 8vo, 9s.
A Century of Roundels. Small 4to, 8s.
A Midsummer Holiday. Crown 8vo, 7s.
Marino Faliero: A Tragedy. Crown 8vo, 6s.
A Study of Victor Hugo. Crown 8vo, 6s.
Miscellanies. Crown 8vo, 12s.
Locrine: A Tragedy. Crown 8vo, 6s.
A Study of Ben Jonson. Crown 8vo, 7s.
The Sisters: A Tragedy. Crown 8vo, 6s.
Astrophel, &c. Crown 8vo, 7s.
Studies in Prose and Poetry. Cr. 8vo, 9s.

Syntax's (Dr.) Three Tours: In Search of the Picturesque, in Search of Consolation, and in Search of a Wife. With ROWLANDSON'S Coloured Illustrations, and Life of the Author by J. C. HOTTEN. Crown 8vo, cloth extra, 7s. 6d.

Taine's History of English Literature. Translated by HENRY VAN LAUN. Four Vols., small demy 8vo, cloth boards, 30s.—POPULAR EDITION, Two Vols., large crown 8vo, cloth extra, 15s.

Taylor (Bayard). — Diversions of the Echo Club: Burlesques of Modern Writers. Post 8vo, cloth limp, 2s.

Taylor (Dr. J. E., F.L.S.), Works by. Crown 8vo, cloth, 5s. each.
The Sagacity and Morality of Plants: A Sketch of the Life and Conduct of the Vegetable Kingdom. With a Coloured Frontispiece and 100 Illustrations.
Our Common British Fossils, and Where to Find Them. With 331 Illustrations.
The Playtime Naturalist. With 366 Illustrations.

Taylor (Tom). — Historical Dramas. Containing 'Clancarty,' 'Jeanne Darc,' 'Twixt Axe and Crown,' 'The Fool's Revenge,' 'Arkwright's Wife,' 'Anne Boleyn,' 'Plot and Passion.' Crown 8vo, cloth extra, 7s. 6d.

⁎ The Plays may also be had separately, at 1s. each.

Tennyson (Lord): A Biographical Sketch. By H. J. JENNINGS. Post 8vo, portrait cover, 1s.; cloth, 1s. 6d.

Thackerayana: Notes and Anecdotes. With Coloured Frontispiece and Hundreds of Sketches by WILLIAM MAKEPEACE THACKERAY. Crown 8vo, cloth extra, 7s. 6d.

Thames, A New Pictorial History of the. By A. S. KRAUSSE. With 340 Illustrations. Post 8vo, 1s.; cloth, 1s. 6d.

Thiers (Adolphe). — History of the Consulate and Empire of France under Napoleon. Translated by D. FORBES CAMPBELL and JOHN STEBBING. With 36 Steel Plates. 12 Vols., demy 8vo, cloth extra, 12s. each.

Thomas (Bertha), Novels by. Cr. 8vo, cl., 3s. 6d. ea.; post 8vo, 2s. ea.
The Violin-Player. | **Proud Maisie.**

Cressida. Post 8vo, illustrated boards, 2s.

Thomson's Seasons, and The Castle of Indolence. With Introduction by ALLAN CUNNINGHAM, and 48 Illustrations. Post 8vo, half-bound, 2s.

Thornbury (Walter), Books by.
The Life and Correspondence of J. M. W. Turner. With Illustrations in Colours. Crown 8vo, cloth extra, 7s. 6d.

Post 8vo, illustrated boards, 2s. each.
Old Stories Re-told. | **Tales for the Marines.**

Timbs (John), Works by. Crown 8vo, cloth extra, 7s. 6d. each.
The History of Clubs and Club Life in London: Anecdotes of its Famous Coffee-houses, Hostelries, and Taverns. With 42 Illustrations.
English Eccentrics and Eccentricities: Stories of Delusions, Impostures, Sporting Scenes, Eccentric Artists, Theatrical Folk, &c. With 48 Illustrations.

Transvaal (The). By JOHN DE VILLIERS. With Map. Crown 8vo, 1s.

Trollope (Anthony), Novels by.
Crown 8vo, cloth extra, 3s. 6d. each; post 8vo, illustrated boards, 2s. each.
The Way We Live Now. | **Mr. Scarborough's Family.**
Frau Frohmann. | **The Land-Leaguers.**

Post 8vo, illustrated boards, 2s. each.
Kept in the Dark. | **The American Senator.**
The Golden Lion of Granpere. | **John Caldigate.** | **Marion Fay.**

Trollope (Frances E.), Novels by.
Crown 8vo, cloth extra, 3s. 6d. each; post 8vo, illustrated boards, 2s. each.
Like Ships Upon the Sea. | **Mabel's Progress.** | **Anne Furness.**

Trollope (T. A.).—Diamond Cut Diamond. Post 8vo, illust. bds., 2s.

Trowbridge (J. T.).—Farnell's Folly. Post 8vo, illust. boards, 2s.

Tytler (C. C. Fraser-).—Mistress Judith: A Novel. Crown 8vo, cloth extra, 3s. 6d.; post 8vo, illustrated boards, 2s.

Tytler (Sarah), Novels by.
Crown 8vo, cloth extra, 3s. 6d. each; post 8vo, illustrated boards, 2s. each.
Lady Bell. | **Buried Diamonds.** | **The Blackhall Ghosts.**

Post 8vo, illustrated boards, 2s. each.
What She Came Through. | **The Huguenot Family.**
Citoyenne Jacqueline. | **Noblesse Oblige.**
The Bride's Pass. | **Beauty and the Beast.**
Saint Mungo's City. | **Disappeared.**

The Macdonald Lass. With Frontispiece. Crown 8vo, cloth, 3s. 6d.

Upward (Allen), Novels by.
The Queen Against Owen. Crown 8vo, cloth, with Frontispiece, 3s. 6d.; post 8vo, boards, 2s.
The Prince of Balkistan. Crown 8vo, cloth extra, 3s. 6d.
A Crown of Straw. Crown 8vo, cloth, 6s.

Vashti and Esther. By the Writer of 'Belle's' Letters in *The World*. Crown 8vo, cloth extra, 3s. 6d.

Villari (Linda).—A Double Bond: A Story. Fcap. 8vo, 1s.

Vizetelly (Ernest A.).—The Scorpion: A Romance of Spain. With a Frontispiece. Crown 8vo, cloth extra, 3s. 6d.

Walton and Cotton's Complete Angler; or, The Contemplative Man's Recreation, by IZAAK WALTON; and Instructions How to Angle, for a Trout or Grayling in a clear Stream, by CHARLES COTTON. With Memoirs and Notes by Sir HARRIS NICOLAS, and 61 Illustrations. Crown 8vo, cloth antique, 7s. 6d.

Walt Whitman, Poems by. Edited, with Introduction, by WILLIAM M. ROSSETTI. With Portrait. Crown 8vo, hand-made paper and buckram, 6s.

Ward (Herbert), Books by.
Five Years with the Congo Cannibals. With 92 Illustrations. Royal 8vo, cloth, 14s.
My Life with Stanley's Rear Guard. With Map. Post 8vo, 1s.; cloth, 1s. 6d.

Walford (Edward, M.A.), Works by.

Walford's County Families of the United Kingdom (1896). Containing the Descent, Birth, Marriage, Education, &c., of 12,000 Heads of Families, their Heirs, Offices, Addresses, Clubs, &c. Royal 8vo, cloth gilt, 50*s*.
Walford's Shilling Peerage (1896). Containing a List of the House of Lords, Scotch and Irish Peers, &c. 32mo, cloth, 1*s*.
Walford's Shilling Baronetage (1896). Containing a List of the Baronets of the United Kingdom, Biographical Notices, Addresses, &c. 32mo, cloth, 1*s*.
Walford's Shilling Knightage (1896). Containing a List of the Knights of the United Kingdom, Biographical Notices, Addresses, &c. 32mo, cloth, 1*s*.
Walford's Shilling House of Commons (1896). Containing a List of all the Members of the New Parliament, their Addresses, Clubs, &c. 32mo, cloth, 1*s*.
Walford's Complete Peerage, Baronetage, Knightage, and House of Commons (1896). Royal 32mo, cloth, gilt edges, 5*s*.

Tales of our Great Families. Crown 8vo, cloth extra, 3*s*. 6*d*.

Warner (Charles Dudley).—A Roundabout Journey. Crown 8vo, cloth extra, 6*s*.

Warrant to Execute Charles I. A Facsimile, with the 59 Signatures and Seals. Printed on paper 22 in. by 14 in. 2*s*.

Warrant to Execute Mary Queen of Scots. A Facsimile, including Queen Elizabeth's Signature and the Great Seal. 2*s*.

Washington's (George) Rules of Civility Traced to their Sources and Restored by MONCURE D. CONWAY. Fcap. 8vo, Japanese vellum, 2*s*. 6*d*.

Wassermann (Lillias), Novels by.

The Daffodils. Crown 8vo, 1*s*.; cloth, 1*s*. 6*d*.

The Marquis of Carabas. By AARON WATSON and LILLIAS WASSERMANN. Post 8vo, illustrated boards, 2*s*.

Weather, How to Foretell the, with the Pocket Spectroscope. By F. W. CORY. With Ten Illustrations. Crown 8vo, 1*s*.; cloth, 1*s*. 6*d*.

Webber (Byron).—Fun, Frolic, and Fancy. With 43 Illustrations by PHIL MAY and CHARLES MAY. Fcap. 4to, cloth, 5*s*.

Westall (William), Novels by.

Trust-Money. Post 8vo, illustrated boards, 2*s*.; cloth, 2*s*. 6*d*.
Sons of Belial. Two Vols., crown 8vo, 10*s*. net.

Westbury (Atha).—The Shadow of Hilton Fernbrook: A Romance of Maoriland. Crown 8vo, cloth, 3*s*. 6*d*. [*Shortly*.

Whist, How to Play Solo. By ABRAHAM S. WILKS and CHARLES F. PARDON. Post 8vo, cloth limp, 2*s*.

White (Gilbert).—The Natural History of Selborne. Post 8vo, printed on laid paper and half-bound, 2*s*.

Williams (W. Mattieu, F.R.A.S.), Works by.

Science in Short Chapters. Crown 8vo, cloth extra, 7*s*. 6*d*.
A Simple Treatise on Heat. With Illustrations. Crown 8vo, cloth, 2*s*. 6*d*.
The Chemistry of Cookery. Crown 8vo, cloth extra, 6*s*.
The Chemistry of Iron and Steel Making. Crown 8vo, cloth extra, 9*s*.
A Vindication of Phrenology. With Portrait and 43 Illusts. Demy 8vo, cloth extra, 12*s*. 6*d*.

Williamson (Mrs. F. H.).—A Child Widow. Post 8vo, bds., 2*s*.

Wills (W. H., M.D.).—An Easy-going Fellow. Crown 8vo, cloth, 6*s*. [*Shortly*.

Wilson (Dr. Andrew, F.R.S.E.), Works by.

Chapters on Evolution. With 259 Illustrations. Crown 8vo, cloth extra, 7*s*. 6*d*.
Leaves from a Naturalist's Note-Book. Post 8vo, cloth limp, 2*s*. 6*d*.
Leisure-Time Studies. With Illustrations. Crown 8vo, cloth extra, 6*s*.
Studies in Life and Sense. With numerous Illustrations. Crown 8vo, cloth extra, 6*s*.
Common Accidents: How to Treat Them. With Illustrations. Crown 8vo, 1*s*.; cloth, 1*s*. 6*d*.
Glimpses of Nature. With 35 Illustrations. Crown 8vo, cloth extra, 3*s*. 6*d*.

Winter (J. S.), Stories by. Post 8vo, illustrated boards, 2*s*. each; cloth limp, 2*s*. 6*d*. each.

Cavalry Life. | **Regimental Legends.**

A Soldier's Children. With 34 Illustrations by E. G. THOMSON and E. STUART HARDY. Crown 8vo, cloth extra, 3*s*. 6*d*.

Wissmann (Hermann von). — My Second Journey through Equatorial [illegible], cloth, 16*s*.

Wood (H. F.), Detective Stories by. Post 8vo, boards, 2s. each.
The Passenger from Scotland Yard. | **The Englishman of the Rue Cain.**

Wood (Lady).—Sabina: A Novel. Post 8vo, illustrated boards, 2s.

Woolley (Celia Parker).—Rachel Armstrong; or, Love and Theology. Post 8vo, illustrated boards, 2s.; cloth, 2s. 6d.

Wright (Thomas), Works by. Crown 8vo, cloth extra, 7s. 6d. each.
The Caricature History of the Georges. With 400 Caricatures, Squibs, &c.
History of Caricature and of the Grotesque in Art, Literature, Sculpture, and Painting. Illustrated by F. W. FAIRHOLT, F.S.A.

Wynman (Margaret).—My Flirtations. With 13 Illustrations by J. BERNARD PARTRIDGE. Post 8vo, cloth, 3s. 6d.

Yates (Edmund), Novels by. Post 8vo, illustrated boards, 2s. each.
Land at Last. | **The Forlorn Hope.** | **Castaway.**

Zangwill (I.).—Ghetto Tragedies. With Three Illustrations by A. S. BOYD. Fcap. 8vo, picture cover, 1s. net.

Zola (Emile), Novels by. Crown 8vo, cloth extra, 3s. 6d. each.
The Fat and the Thin. Translated by ERNEST A. VIZETELLY.
Money. Translated by ERNEST A. VIZETELLY.
The Downfall. Translated by E. A. VIZETELLY.
The Dream. Translated by ELIZA CHASE. With Eight Illustrations by JEANNIOT.
Doctor Pascal. Translated by E. A. VIZETELLY. With Portrait of the Author.
Lourdes. Translated by ERNEST A. VIZETELLY.
Rome. Translated by ERNEST A. VIZETELLY. [*Shortly.*

SOME BOOKS CLASSIFIED IN SERIES.

**** For fuller cataloguing, see alphabetical arrangement, pp. 1–26.*

The Mayfair Library. Post 8vo, cloth limp, 2s. 6d. per Volume.

A Journey Round My Room. By X. DE MAISTRE. Translated by Sir HENRY ATTWELL.
Quips and Quiddities. By W. D. ADAMS.
The Agony Column of 'The Times.'
Melancholy Anatomised: Abridgment of BURTON.
Poetical Ingenuities. By W. T. DOBSON.
The Cupboard Papers. By FIN-BEC.
W. S. Gilbert's Plays. Three Series.
Songs of Irish Wit and Humour.
Animals and their Masters. By Sir A. HELPS.
Social Pressure. By Sir A. HELPS.
Curiosities of Criticism. By H. J. JENNINGS.
The Autocrat of the Breakfast-Table. By OLIVER WENDELL HOLMES.
Pencil and Palette. By R. KEMPT.
Little Essays: from LAMB'S LETTERS.
Forensic Anecdotes. By JACOB LARWOOD.
Theatrical Anecdotes. By JACOB LARWOOD.
Jeux d'Esprit. Edited by HENRY S. LEIGH.
Witch Stories. By E. LYNN LINTON.
Ourselves. By E. LYNN LINTON.
Pastimes and Players. By R. MACGREGOR.
New Paul and Virginia. By W. H. MALLOCK.
The New Republic. By W. H. MALLOCK.
Puck on Pegasus. By H. C. PENNELL.
Pegasus Re-saddled. By H. C. PENNELL.
Muses of Mayfair. Edited by H. C. PENNELL.
Thoreau: His Life and Aims. By H. A. PAGE.
Puniana. By Hon. HUGH ROWLEY.
More Puniana. By Hon. HUGH ROWLEY.
The Philosophy of Handwriting.
By Stream and Sea. By WILLIAM SENIOR.
Leaves from a Naturalist's Note-Book. By Dr. ANDREW WILSON.

The Golden Library. Post 8vo, cloth limp, 2s. per Volume.

Diversions of the Echo Club. BAYARD TAYLOR.
Songs for Sailors. By W. C. BENNETT.
Lives of the Necromancers. By W. GODWIN.
The Poetical Works of Alexander Pope.
Scenes of Country Life. By EDWARD JESSE.
Tale for a Chimney Corner. By LEIGH HUNT.
The Autocrat of the Breakfast Table. By OLIVER WENDELL HOLMES.
La Mort d'Arthur: Selections from MALLORY.
Provincial Letters of Blaise Pascal.
Maxims and Reflections of Rochefoucauld.

The Wanderer's Library. Crown 8vo, cloth extra, 3s. 6d. each.

Wanderings in Patagonia. By JULIUS BEERBOHM. Illustrated.
Merrie England in the Olden Time. By C. DANIEL. Illustrated by ROBERT CRUIKSHANK.
Circus Life. By THOMAS FROST.
Lives of the Conjurers. By THOMAS FROST.
The Old Showmen and the Old London Fairs. By THOMAS FROST.
Low-Life Deeps. By JAMES GREENWOOD.
The Wilds of London. By JAMES GREENWOOD.
Tunis. By Chev. HESSE-WARTEGG. 22 Illusts.
Life and Adventures of a Cheap Jack.
World Behind the Scenes. By P. FITZGERALD.
Tavern Anecdotes and Sayings.
The Genial Showman. By E. P. HINGSTON.
Story of London Parks. By JACOB LARWOOD.
London Characters. By HENRY MAYHEW.
Seven Generations of Executioners.
Summer Cruising in the South Seas. By C. WARREN STODDARD. Illustrated.

BOOKS IN SERIES—*continued.*

Handy Novels. Fcap. 8vo, cloth boards, 1s. 6d. each.

The Old Maid's Sweetheart. By A. ST. AUBYN.
Modest Little Sara. By ALAN ST. AUBYN.
Seven Sleepers of Ephesus. M. E. COLERIDGE.
Taken from the Enemy. By H. NEWBOLT.
A Lost Soul. By W. L. ALDEN.
Dr. Palliser's Patient. By GRANT ALLEN.
Monte Carlo Stories. By JOAN BARRETT.
Black Spirits and White. By R. A. CRAM.

My Library. Printed on laid paper, post 8vo, half-Roxburghe, 2s. 6d. each.

Citation and Examination of William Shakspeare. By W. S. LANDOR.
The Journal of Maurice de Guerin.
Christie Johnstone. By CHARLES READE.
Peg Woffington. By CHARLES READE.
The Dramatic Essays of Charles Lamb.

The Pocket Library. Post 8vo, printed on laid paper and hf.-bd., 2s. each.

The Essays of Elia. By CHARLES LAMB.
Robinson Crusoe. Illustrated by G. CRUIKSHANK.
Whims and Oddities. By THOMAS HOOD.
The Barber's Chair. By DOUGLAS JERROLD.
Gastronomy. By BRILLAT-SAVARIN.
The Epicurean, &c. By THOMAS MOORE.
Leigh Hunt's Essays. Edited by E. OLLIER.
White's Natural History of Selborne.
Gulliver's Travels, &c. By Dean SWIFT.
Plays by RICHARD BRINSLEY SHERIDAN.
Anecdotes of the Clergy. By JACOB LARWOOD.
Thomson's Seasons. Illustrated.
Autocrat of the Breakfast-Table and The Professor at the Breakfast-Table. By O. W. HOLMES.

THE PICCADILLY NOVELS.

LIBRARY EDITIONS OF NOVELS, many Illustrated, crown 8vo, cloth extra, 3s. 6d. each.

By F. M. ALLEN.

Green as Grass.

By GRANT ALLEN.

Philistia.
Strange Stories.
Babylon.
For Maimie's Sake.
In all Shades.
The Beckoning Hand.
The Devil's Die.
This Mortal Coil.
The Tents of Shem.
The Great Taboo.
Dumaresq's Daughter.
Duchess of Powysland.
Blood Royal.
Ivan Greet's Masterpiece.
The Scallywag.
At Market Value.
Under Sealed Orders.

By MARY ANDERSON.

Othello's Occupation.

By EDWIN L. ARNOLD.

Phra the Phoenician. | Constable of St. Nicholas.

By ROBERT BARR.

In a Steamer Chair. | From Whose Bourne.

By FRANK BARRETT.

The Woman of the Iron Bracelets.

By 'BELLE.'

Vashti and Esther.

By Sir W. BESANT and J. RICE.

Ready-Money Mortiboy.
My Little Girl.
With Harp and Crown.
This Son of Vulcan.
The Golden Butterfly.
The Monks of Thelema.
By Celia's Arbour.
Chaplain of the Fleet.
The Seamy Side.
The Case of Mr. Lucraft.
In Trafalgar's Bay.
The Ten Years' Tenant.

By Sir WALTER BESANT.

All Sorts and Conditions of Men.
The Captains' Room.
All in a Garden Fair.
Dorothy Forster.
Uncle Jack.
The World Went Very Well Then.
Children of Gibeon.
Herr Paulus.
For Faith and Freedom.
To Call Her Mine.
The Bell of St. Paul's.
The Holy Rose.
Armorel of Lyonesse.
S. Katherine's by Tower
Verbena Camellia Stephanotis.
The Ivory Gate.
The Rebel Queen.
Beyond the Dreams of Avarice.

By PAUL BOURGET.

A Living Lie.

By ROBERT BUCHANAN.

Shadow of the Sword.
A Child of Nature.
God and the Man.
Martyrdom of Madeline
Love Me for Ever.
Annan Water.
Foxglove Manor.
The New Abelard
Matt. | Rachel Dene.
Master of the Mine.
The Heir of Linne.
Woman and the Man.
Red and White Heather.

ROB. BUCHANAN & HY. MURRAY.

The Charlatan.

By J. MITCHELL CHAPPLE.

The Minor Chord.

By HALL CAINE.

The Shadow of a Crime. | The Deemster.
A Son of Hagar.

By MACLAREN COBBAN.

The Red Sultan. | The Burden of Isabel.

By MORT. & FRANCES COLLINS.

Transmigration.
Blacksmith & Scholar.
The Village Comedy.
From Midnight to Midnight.
You Play me False.

By WILKIE COLLINS.

Armadale. | AfterDark.
No Name.
Antonina.
Basil.
Hide and Seek.
The Dead Secret.
Queen of Hearts.
My Miscellanies.
The Woman in White.
The Moonstone.
Man and Wife.
Poor Miss Finch.
Miss or Mrs. ?
The New Magdalen.
The Frozen Deep.
The Two Destinies
The Law and the Lady.
The Haunted Hotel.
The Fallen Leaves.
Jezebel's Daughter.
The Black Robe.
Heart and Science.
'I Say No.'
Little Novels.
The Evil Genius.
The Legacy of Cain.
A Rogue's Life.
Blind Love.

By DUTTON COOK.

Paul Foster's Daughter.

By E. H. COOPER.

Geoffory Hamilton.

By V. CECIL COTES.

Two Girls on a Barge.

By C. EGBERT CRADDOCK.

His Vanished Star.

By H. N. CRELLIN.

Romances of the Old Seraglio.

By MATT CRIM.

The Adventures of a Fair Rebel.

By S. R. CROCKETT and others.

Tales of Our Coast.

By B. M. CROKER.

Diana Barrington.
Proper Pride.
A Family Likeness.
Pretty Miss Neville.
A Bird of Passage.
'To Let.'
Mr. Jervis
Village Tales & Jungle Tragedies.
The Real Lady Hilda.

By WILLIAM CYPLES.

Hearts of Gold.

By ALPHONSE DAUDET.

The Evangelist; or, Port Salvation.

By H. COLEMAN DAVIDSON.

Mr. Sadler's Daughters.

By ERASMUS DAWSON.

The Fountain of Youth.

By JAMES DE MILLE.

A Castle in Spain.

THE PICCADILLY (3/6) NOVELS—*continued.*

By J. LEITH DERWENT.
Our Lady of Tears. | Circe's Lovers.

By DICK DONOVAN.
Tracked to Doom.
Man from Manchester.
The Mystery of Jamaica Terrace.

By A. CONAN DOYLE.
The Firm of Girdlestone.

By S. JEANNETTE DUNCAN.
A Daughter of To-day. | Vernon's Aunt.

By G. MANVILLE FENN.
The New Mistress.
Witness to the Deed.
The Tiger Lily.
The White Virgin.

By PERCY FITZGERALD.
Fatal Zero.

By R. E. FRANCILLON.
One by One.
A Dog and his Shadow.
A Real Queen.
Ropes of Sand.
Jack Doyle's Daughter.

Prefaced by Sir BARTLE FRERE.
Pandurang Hari.

BY EDWARD GARRETT.
The Capel Girls.

By PAUL GAULOT.
The Red Shirts.

By CHARLES GIBBON.
Robin Gray.
Loving a Dream.
The Golden Shaft.

By E. GLANVILLE.
The Lost Heiress.
A Fair Colonist.
The Fossicker.
The Golden Rock.

By E. J. GOODMAN.
The Fate of Herbert Wayne.

By Rev. S. BARING GOULD.
Red Spider. | Eve.

By CECIL GRIFFITH.
Corinthia Marazion.

By SYDNEY GRUNDY.
The Days of his Vanity.

By THOMAS HARDY.
Under the Greenwood Tree.

By BRET HARTE.
A Waif of the Plains.
A Ward of the Golden Gate.
A Sappho of Green Springs.
Col. Starbottle's Client.
Susy.
Sally Dows.
A Protégée of Jack Hamlin's.
Bell-Ringer of Angel's.
Clarence.

By JULIAN HAWTHORNE.
Garth.
Ellice Quentin.
Sebastian Strome.
Dust.
Fortune's Fool.
Beatrix Randolph.
David Poindexter's Disappearance.
The Spectre of the Camera.

By Sir A. HELPS.
Ivan de Biron.

By I. HENDERSON.
Agatha Page.

By G. A. HENTY.
Rujub the Juggler. | Dorothy's Double.

By JOHN HILL.
The Common Ancestor.

By Mrs. HUNGERFORD.
Lady Verner's Flight.
The Red-House Mystery.
The Three Graces.

By Mrs. ALFRED HUNT.
The Leaden Casket.
That Other Person.
Self Condemned.
Mrs. Juliet.

By C. J. CUTCLIFFE HYNE.
Honour of Thieves.

By R. ASHE KING.
A Drawn Game.
'The Wearing of the Green.'

By EDMOND LEPELLETIER.
Madame Sans-Gêne.

By HARRY LINDSAY.
Rhoda Roberts.

By E. LYNN LINTON.
Patricia Kemball.
Under which Lord?
'My Love!'
Ione.
Paston Carew.
Sowing the Wind.
The Atonement of Leam Dundas.
The World Well Lost.
The One Too Many.

By HENRY W. LUCY.
Gideon Fleyce.

By JUSTIN McCARTHY.
A Fair Saxon.
Linley Rochford.
Dear Lady Disdain.
Camiola.
Waterdale Neighbours.
My Enemy's Daughter.
Miss Misanthrope.
Donna Quixote.
Red Diamonds.
Maid of Athens.
The Dictator.
The Comet of a Season.

By JUSTIN H. McCARTHY.
A London Legend.

By GEORGE MACDONALD.
Heather and Snow. | Phantastes.

By L. T. MEADE.
A Soldier of Fortune. | In an Iron Grip.

By BERTRAM MITFORD.
The Gun-Runner.
The Luck of Gerard Ridgeley.
The King's Assegai.
Renshaw Fanning's Quest.

By J. E. MUDDOCK.
Maid Marian and Robin Hood.
Basile the Jester.

By D. CHRISTIE MURRAY.
A Life's Atonement.
Joseph's Coat.
Coals of Fire.
Old Blazer's Hero.
Val Strange. | Hearts.
A Model Father.
By the Gate of the Sea.
A Bit of Human Nature.
First Person Singular.
Cynic Fortune.
The Way of the World.
Bob Martin's Little Girl.
Time's Revenges.
A Wasted Crime.
In Direst Peril.
Mount Despair.

By MURRAY and HERMAN.
The Bishops' Bible.
One Traveller Returns.
Paul Jones's Alias.

By HUME NISBET.
'Bail Up!'

By W. E. NORRIS.
Saint Ann's. | Billy Bellew.

By G. OHNET.
A Weird Gift.

By OUIDA.
Held in Bondage.
Strathmore.
Chandos.
Under Two Flags.
Idalia.
Cecil Castlemaine's Gage.
Tricotrin.
Puck.
Folle Farine.
A Dog of Flanders.
Pascarel.
Signa.
Princess Napraxine.
Ariadne.
Two Little Wooden Shoes.
In a Winter City.
Friendship.
Moths.
Ruffino.
Pipistrello.
A Village Commune.
Bimbi.
Wanda.
Frescoes. | Othmar.
In Maremma.
Syrlin. | Guilderoy.
Santa Barbara.
Two Offenders.

By MARGARET A. PAUL.
Gentle and Simple.

By JAMES PAYN.
Lost Sir Massingberd.
Less Black than We're Painted.
A Confidential Agent.
A Grape from a Thorn.
In Peril and Privation.
The Mystery of Mirbridge.
By Proxy.
The Canon's Ward.
Walter's Word.
High Spirits.
Under One Roof.
Glow-worm Tales.
The Talk of the Town.
Holiday Tasks.
For Cash Only.
The Burnt Million.
The Word and the Will.
Sunny Stories.
A Trying Patient.

THE PICCADILLY (3/6) NOVELS—*continued.*

By Mrs. CAMPBELL PRAED.
Outlaw and Lawmaker. | Christina Chard.

By E. C. PRICE.
Valentina. | Mrs. Lancaster's Rival.
The Foreigners.

By RICHARD PRYCE.
Miss Maxwell's Affections.

By CHARLES READE.
It is Never Too Late to Mend.
The Double Marriage.
Love Me Little, Love Me Long.
The Cloister and the Hearth.
The Course of True Love.
The Autobiography of a Thief.
Put Yourself in His Place.
A Terrible Temptation.
The Jilt.
Singleheart and Doubleface.
Good Stories of Men and other Animals.
Hard Cash.
Peg Woffington.
Christie Johnstone.
Griffith Gaunt.
Foul Play.
The Wandering Heir.
A Woman-Hater.
A Simpleton.
A Perilous Secret.
Readiana.

By Mrs. J. H. RIDDELL.
Weird Stories.

By AMELIE RIVES.
Barbara Dering.

By F. W. ROBINSON.
The Hands of Justice.

By DORA RUSSELL.
A Country Sweetheart. | The Drift of Fate.

By W. CLARK RUSSELL.
Ocean Tragedy.
My Shipmate Louise.
Alone on Wide Wide Sea
The Phantom Death.
Is He the Man?
The Good Ship 'Mohock.'
The Convict Ship.

By JOHN SAUNDERS.
Guy Waterman.
Bound to the Wheel.
The Two Dreamers.
The Lion in the Path.

By KATHARINE SAUNDERS.
Margaret and Elizabeth
Gideon's Rock.
The High Mills.
Heart Salvage.
Sebastian.

By ADELINE SERGEANT.
Dr. Endicott's Experiment.

By HAWLEY SMART.
Without Love or Licence.

By T. W. SPEIGHT.
A Secret of the Sea. | The Grey Monk.

By ALAN ST. AUBYN.
A Fellow of Trinity.
The Junior Dean.
Master of St. Benedict's.
To his Own Master.
In Face of the World.
Orchard Damerel.
The Tremlett Diamonds

By JOHN STAFFORD.
Doris and I.

By R. A. STERNDALE.
The Afghan Knife.

By BERTHA THOMAS.
Proud Maisie. | The Violin-Player.

By ANTHONY TROLLOPE.
The Way we Live Now.
Frau Frohmann.
Scarborough's Family.
The Land-Leaguers.

By FRANCES E. TROLLOPE.
Like Ships upon the Sea.
Anne Furness.
Mabel's Progress.

By IVAN TURGENIEFF, &c.
Stories from Foreign Novelists.

By MARK TWAIN.
The American Claimant.
The £1,000,000 Bank-note.
Tom Sawyer Abroad.
Pudd'nhead Wilson.
Tom Sawyer, Detective.

By C. C. FRASER-TYTLER.
Mistress Judith.

By SARAH TYTLER.
Lady Bell.
Buried Diamonds.
The Blackhall Ghosts.
The Macdonald Lass.

By ALLEN UPWARD.
The Queen against Owen.
The Prince of Balkistan.

By E. A. VIZETELLY.
The Scorpion: A Romance of Spain.

By ATHA WESTBURY.
The Shadow of Hilton Fernbrook.

By JOHN STRANGE WINTER.
A Soldier's Children.

By MARGARET WYNMAN.
My Flirtations.

By E. ZOLA.
The Downfall.
The Dream.
Dr. Pascal.
Money. | Lourdes.
The Fat and the Thin.
Rome.

CHEAP EDITIONS OF POPULAR NOVELS.

Post 8vo, illustrated boards, 2s. each.

By ARTEMUS WARD.
Artemus Ward Complete.

By EDMOND ABOUT.
The Fellah.

By HAMILTON AÏDÉ.
Carr of Carrlyon. | Confidences.

By MARY ALBERT.
Brooke Finchley's Daughter.

By Mrs. ALEXANDER.
Maid, Wife or Widow? | Valerie's Fate.

By GRANT ALLEN.
Philistia.
Strange Stories.
Babylon
For Maimie's Sake.
In all Shades.
The Beckoning Hand.
The Devil's Die.
The Tents of Shem.
The Great Taboo.
Dumaresq's Daughter.
Duchess of Powysland.
Blood Royal.
Ivan Greet's Masterpiece.
The Scallywag.
This Mortal Coil.

By E. LESTER ARNOLD.
Phra the Phœnician.

By SHELSLEY BEAUCHAMP.
Grantley Grange.

BY FRANK BARRETT.
Fettered for Life.
Little Lady Linton.
Between Life & Death.
The Sin of Olga Zassoulich.
Folly Morrison.
Lieut. Barnabas.
Honest Davie.
A Prodigal's Progress.
Found Guilty.
A Recoiling Vengeance.
For Love and Honour.
John Ford; and His Helpmate.
The Woman of the Iron Bracelets.

By Sir W. BESANT and J. RICE.
Ready-Money Mortiboy
My Little Girl.
With Harp and Crown.
This Son of Vulcan.
The Golden Butterfly.
The Monks of Thelema.
By Celia's Arbour.
Chaplain of the Fleet.
The Seamy Side.
The Case of Mr. Lucraft.
In Trafalgar's Bay.
The Ten Years' Tenant.

By Sir WALTER BESANT.
All Sorts and Conditions of Men.
The Captains' Room.
All in a Garden Fair.
Dorothy Forster.
Uncle Jack.
The World Went Very Well Then.
Children of Gibeon.
Herr Paulus.
For Faith and Freedom.
To Call Her Mine.
The Bell of St. Paul's.
The Holy Rose.
Armorel of Lyonesse.
S. Katherine's by Tower.
Verbena Camellia Stephanotis
The Ivory Gate.
The Rebel Queen.

By AMBROSE BIERCE.
In the Midst of Life.

TWO-SHILLING NOVELS—*continued.*

By FREDERICK BOYLE.

Camp Notes. | Chronicles of No-man's Land.
Savage Life.

BY BRET HARTE.

Californian Stories. | Flip. | Maruja.
Gabriel Conroy. | A Phyllis of the Sierras.
The Luck of Roaring Camp. | A Waif of the Plains.
An Heiress of Red Dog. | A Ward of the Golden Gate.

By HAROLD BRYDGES.

Uncle Sam at Home.

By ROBERT BUCHANAN.

Shadow of the Sword. | The Martyrdom of Madeline.
A Child of Nature. | The New Abelard.
God and the Man. | Matt.
Love Me for Ever. | The Heir of Linne.
Foxglove Manor. | Woman and the Man.
The Master of the Mine.
Annan Water.

By HALL CAINE.

The Shadow of a Crime. | The Deemster.
A Son of Hagar.

By Commander CAMERON.

The Cruise of the 'Black Prince.'

By Mrs. LOVETT CAMERON.

Deceivers Ever. | Juliet's Guardian.

By HAYDEN CARRUTH.

The Adventures of Jones.

By AUSTIN CLARE.

For the Love of a Lass.

By Mrs. ARCHER CLIVE.

Paul Ferroll.
Why Paul Ferroll Killed his Wife.

By MACLAREN COBBAN.

The Cure of Souls. | The Red Sultan.

By C. ALLSTON COLLINS.

The Bar Sinister.

By MORT. & FRANCES COLLINS.

Sweet Anne Page. | Sweet and Twenty.
Transmigration. | The Village Comedy.
From Midnight to Midnight. | You Play me False.
A Fight with Fortune. | Blacksmith and Scholar
Frances.

By WILKIE COLLINS.

Armadale. | AfterDark. | My Miscellanies.
No Name. | The Woman in White.
Antonina. | The Moonstone.
Basil. | Man and Wife.
Hide and Seek. | Poor Miss Finch.
The Dead Secret. | The Fallen Leaves.
Queen of Hearts. | Jezebel's Daughter.
Miss or Mrs.? | The Black Robe.
The New Magdalen. | Heart and Science.
The Frozen Deep. | 'I Say No!'
The Law and the Lady | The Evil Genius.
The Two Destinies. | Little Novels.
The Haunted Hotel. | Legacy of Cain.
A Rogue's Life. | Blind Love.

By M. J. COLQUHOUN.

Every Inch a Soldier.

By DUTTON COOK.

Leo. | Paul Foster's Daughter.

By C. EGBERT CRADDOCK.

The Prophet of the Great Smoky Mountains.

By MATT CRIM.

The Adventures of a Fair Rebel.

By B. M. CROKER.

Pretty Miss Neville. | Proper Pride.
Diana Barrington. | A Family Likeness.
'To Let.' | Village Tales and Jungle Tragedies.
A Bird of Passage.

By W. CYPLES.

Hearts of Gold.

By ALPHONSE DAUDET.

The Evangelist; or, Port Salvation.

By ERASMUS DAWSON.

The Fountain of Youth.

By JAMES DE MILLE.

A Castle in Spain.

By J. LEITH DERWENT.

Our Lady of Tears. | Circe's Lovers.

By CHARLES DICKENS.

Sketches by Boz. | Nicholas Nickleby.
Oliver Twist.

By DICK DONOVAN.

The Man-Hunter. | In the Grip of the Law.
Tracked and Taken. | From Information Received.
Caught at Last! | Tracked to Doom.
Wanted! | Link by Link
Who Poisoned Hetty Duncan? | Suspicion Aroused.
Man from Manchester. | Dark Deeds.
A Detective's Triumphs | Riddles Read.

By Mrs. ANNIE EDWARDES.

A Point of Honour. | Archie Lovell.

By M. BETHAM-EDWARDS.

Felicia. | Kitty.

By EDWARD EGGLESTON.

Roxy.

By G. MANVILLE FENN.

The New Mistress. | The Tiger Lily.
Witness to the Deed.

By PERCY FITZGERALD.

Bella Donna. | Second Mrs. Tillotson.
Never Forgotten. | Seventy-five Brooke Street.
Polly.
Fatal Zero. | The Lady of Brantome.

By P. FITZGERALD and others.

Strange Secrets.

By ALBANY DE FONBLANQUE.

Filthy Lucre.

By R. E. FRANCILLON.

Olympia. | King or Knave?
One by One. | Romances of the Law.
A Real Queen. | Ropes of Sand.
Queen Cophetua. | A Dog and his Shadow.

By HAROLD FREDERIC.

Seth's Brother's Wife. | The Lawton Girl.

Prefaced by Sir BARTLE FRERE.

Pandurang Hari.

By HAIN FRISWELL.

One of Two.

By EDWARD GARRETT.

The Capel Girls.

By GILBERT GAUL.

A Strange Manuscript.

By CHARLES GIBBON.

Robin Gray. | In Honour Bound.
Fancy Free. | Flower of the Forest.
For Lack of Gold. | The Braes of Yarrow.
What will World Say? | The Golden Shaft.
In Love and War. | Of High Degree.
For the King. | By Mead and Stream.
In Pastures Green. | Loving a Dream.
Queen of the Meadow. | A Hard Knot.
A Heart's Problem. | Heart's Delight.
The Dead Heart. | Blood-Money.

By WILLIAM GILBERT.

Dr. Austin's Guests. | The Wizard of the Mountain.
James Duke.

By ERNEST GLANVILLE.

The Lost Heiress. | The Fossicker.
A Fair Colonist.

By Rev. S. BARING GOULD.

Red Spider. | Eve.

By HENRY GREVILLE.

A Noble Woman. | Nikanor.

By CECIL GRIFFITH.

Corinthia Marazion.

By SYDNEY GRUNDY.

The Days of his Vanity.

By JOHN HABBERTON.

Brueton's Bayou. | Country Luck.

By ANDREW HALLIDAY.

Every-day Papers.

By Lady DUFFUS HARDY.

Paul Wynter's Sacrifice.

TWO-SHILLING NOVELS—*continued.*

By THOMAS HARDY.
Under the Greenwood Tree.

By J. BERWICK HARWOOD.
The Tenth Earl.

By JULIAN HAWTHORNE.
Garth.
Ellice Quentin.
Fortune's Fool.
Miss Cadogna.
Sebastian Strome.
Dust.
Beatrix Randolph.
Love—or a Name.
David Poindexter's Disappearance.
The Spectre of the Camera.

By Sir ARTHUR HELPS.
Ivan de Biron.

By G. A. HENTY.
Rujub the Juggler.

By HENRY HERMAN.
A Leading Lady.

By HEADON HILL.
Zambra the Detective.

By JOHN HILL.
Treason Felony.

By Mrs. CASHEL HOEY.
The Lover's Creed.

By Mrs. GEORGE HOOPER.
The House of Raby.

By TIGHE HOPKINS.
Twixt Love and Duty.

By Mrs. HUNGERFORD.
A Maiden all Forlorn.
In Durance Vile.
Marvel.
A Mental Struggle.
A Modern Circe.
Lady Verner's Flight.
The Red House Mystery

By Mrs. ALFRED HUNT.
Thornicroft's Model.
That Other Person.
Self-Condemned.
The Leaden Casket.

By JEAN INGELOW.
Fated to be Free.

By WM. JAMESON.
My Dead Self.

By HARRIETT JAY.
The Dark Colleen.
Queen of Connaught.

By MARK KERSHAW.
Colonial Facts and Fictions.

By R. ASHE KING.
A Drawn Game.
'The Wearing of the Green.'
Passion's Slave.
Bell Barry.

By JOHN LEYS.
The Lindsays.

By E. LYNN LINTON.
Patricia Kemball.
The World Well Lost.
Under which Lord?
Paston Carew.
'My Love!'
Ione.
The Atonement of Leam Dundas.
With a Silken Thread.
Rebel of the Family.
Sowing the Wind.
The One Too Many.

By HENRY W. LUCY.
Gideon Fleyce.

By JUSTIN McCARTHY.
Dear Lady Disdain.
Waterdale Neighbours.
My Enemy's Daughter.
A Fair Saxon.
Linley Rochford.
Miss Misanthrope.
Camiola.
Donna Quixote.
Maid of Athens.
The Comet of a Season.
The Dictator.
Red Diamonds.

By HUGH MACCOLL.
Mr. Stranger's Sealed Packet.

By GEORGE MACDONALD.
Heather and Snow.

By AGNES MACDONELL.
Quaker Cousins.

By KATHARINE S. MACQUOID.
The Evil Eye.
Lost Rose.

By W. H. MALLOCK.
A Romance of the Nineteenth Century.
The New Republic.

By FLORENCE MARRYAT.
Open! Sesame!
Fighting the Air.
A Harvest of Wild Oats.
Written in Fire.

By J. MASTERMAN.
Half-a-dozen Daughters.

By BRANDER MATTHEWS.
A Secret of the Sea.

By L. T. MEADE.
A Soldier of Fortune.

By LEONARD MERRICK.
The Man who was Good.

By JEAN MIDDLEMASS.
Touch and Go.
Mr. Dorillion.

By Mrs. MOLESWORTH.
Hathercourt Rectory.

By J. E. MUDDOCK.
Stories Weird and Wonderful.
The Dead Man's Secret.
From the Bosom of the Deep.

By D. CHRISTIE MURRAY.
A Model Father.
Joseph's Coat.
Coals of Fire.
Val Strange.
Old Blazer's Hero.
Hearts.
The Way of the World.
Cynic Fortune.
A Life's Atonement.
By the Gate of the Sea.
A Bit of Human Nature.
First Person Singular.
Bob Martin's Little Girl
Time's Revenges.
A Wasted Crime.
In Direst Peril.

By MURRAY and HERMAN.
One Traveller Returns.
Paul Jones's Alias.
The Bishops' Bible.

By HENRY MURRAY.
A Game of Bluff.
A Song of Sixpence.

By HUME NISBET.
'Bail Up!'
Dr. Bernard St. Vincent.

By ALICE O'HANLON.
The Unforeseen.
Chance? or Fate?

By GEORGES OHNET.
Dr. Rameau.
A Last Love.
A Weird Gift.

By Mrs. OLIPHANT.
Whiteladies.
The Primrose Path.
The Greatest Heiress in England.

By Mrs. ROBERT O'REILLY.
Phœbe's Fortunes.

By OUIDA.
Held in Bondage.
Strathmore.
Chandos.
Idalia.
Under Two Flags.
Cecil Castlemaine's Gage
Tricotrin.
Puck.
Folle Farine.
A Dog of Flanders.
Pascarel.
Signa.
Princess Napraxine.
In a Winter City.
Ariadne.
Friendship.
Two Lit. Wooden Shoes.
Moths.
Bimbi.
Pipistrello.
A Village Commune.
Wanda.
Othmar.
Frescoes.
In Maremma.
Guilderoy.
Ruffino.
Syrlin.
Santa Barbara.
Two Offenders.
Ouida's Wisdom, Wit, and Pathos.

By MARGARET AGNES PAUL.
Gentle and Simple.

By C. L. PIRKIS.
Lady Lovelace.

By EDGAR A. POE.
The Mystery of Marie Roget.

By Mrs. CAMPBELL PRAED.
The Romance of a Station.
The Soul of Countess Adrian.
Outlaw and Lawmaker.
Christina Chard.

By E. C. PRICE.
Valentina.
The Foreigners.
Mrs. Lancaster's Rival.
Gerald.

By RICHARD PRYCE.
Miss Maxwell's Affections.

TWO-SHILLING NOVELS—*continued.*

By JAMES PAYN.

Bentinck's Tutor.
Murphy's Master.
A County Family.
At Her Mercy.
Cecil's Tryst.
The Clyffards of Clyffe.
The Foster Brothers.
Found Dead.
The Best of Husbands.
Walter's Word.
Halves.
Fallen Fortunes.
Humorous Stories.
£200 Reward.
A Marine Residence.
Mirk Abbey.
By Proxy.
Under One Roof.
High Spirits.
Carlyon's Year.
From Exile.
For Cash Only.
Kit.
The Canon's Ward.
The Talk of the Town.
Holiday Tasks.
A Perfect Treasure.
What He Cost Her.
A Confidential Agent.
Glow-worm Tales.
The Burnt Million.
Sunny Stories.
Lost Sir Massingberd.
A Woman's Vengeance.
The Family Scapegrace.
Gwendoline's Harvest.
Like Father, Like Son.
Married Beneath Him.
Not Wooed, but Won.
Less Black than We're Painted.
Some Private Views.
A Grape from a Thorn.
The Mystery of Mirbridge.
The Word and the Will.
A Prince of the Blood.
A Trying Patient.

By CHARLES READE.

It is Never Too Late to Mend.
Christie Johnstone.
The Double Marriage.
Put Yourself in His Place
Love Me Little, Love Me Long.
The Cloister and the Hearth.
The Course of True Love.
The Jilt.
The Autobiography of a Thief.
A Terrible Temptation.
Foul Play.
The Wandering Heir.
Hard Cash.
Singleheart and Doubleface.
Good Stories of Men and other Animals.
Peg Woffington.
Griffith Gaunt.
A Perilous Secret.
A Simpleton.
Readiana.
A Woman-Hater.

By Mrs. J. H. RIDDELL.

Weird Stories.
Fairy Water.
Her Mother's Darling.
The Prince of Wales's Garden Party.
The Uninhabited House.
The Mystery in Palace Gardens.
The Nun's Curse.
Idle Tales.

By AMELIE RIVES.

Barbara Dering.

By F. W. ROBINSON.

Women are Strange. | The Hands of Justice.

By JAMES RUNCIMAN.

Skippers and Shellbacks. | Schools and Scholars.
Grace Balmaign's Sweetheart.

By W. CLARK RUSSELL.

Round the Galley Fire.
On the Fo'k'sle Head.
In the Middle Watch.
A Voyage to the Cape.
A Book for the Hammock.
The Mystery of the 'Ocean Star.'
The Romance of Jenny Harlowe.
An Ocean Tragedy.
My Shipmate Louise.
Alone on a Wide Wide Sea.

By GEORGE AUGUSTUS SALA.

Gaslight and Daylight.

By JOHN SAUNDERS.

Guy Waterman.
The Two Dreamers.
The Lion in the Path.

By KATHARINE SAUNDERS.

Joan Merryweather.
The High Mills.
Heart Salvage.
Sebastian.
Margaret and Elizabeth.

By GEORGE R. SIMS.

Rogues and Vagabonds.
The Ring o' Bells.
Mary Jane's Memoirs.
Mary Jane Married.
Tales of To-day.
Dramas of Life.
Tinkletop's Crime.
Zeph.
My Two Wives.
Memoirs of a Landlady.
Scenes from the Show.
The 10 Commandments.

By ARTHUR SKETCHLEY.

Match in the Dark.

By HAWLEY SMART.

Without Love or Licence.

By T. W. SPEIGHT.

The Mysteries of Heron Dyke.
The Golden Hoop.
Hoodwinked.
By Devious Ways.
Back to Life.
The Loudwater Tragedy.
Burgo's Romance.
Quittance in Full.
A Husband from the Sea

By ALAN ST. AUBYN.

A Fellow of Trinity.
The Junior Dean.
Master of St. Benedict's
To His Own Master.
Orchard Damerel.

By R. A. STERNDALE.

The Afghan Knife.

By R. LOUIS STEVENSON.

New Arabian Nights. | Prince Otto.

By BERTHA THOMAS.

Cressida.
Proud Maisie.
The Violin-Player.

By WALTER THORNBURY.

Tales for the Marines. | Old Stories Retold.

By T. ADOLPHUS TROLLOPE.

Diamond Cut Diamond.

By F. ELEANOR TROLLOPE

Like Ships upon the Sea.
Anne Furness.
Mabel's Progress.

By ANTHONY TROLLOPE.

Frau Frohmann.
Marion Fay.
Kept in the Dark.
John Caldigate.
The Way We Live Now.
The Land-Leaguers.
The American Senator.
Mr. Scarborough's Family.
GoldenLion of Granpere

By J. T. TROWBRIDGE.

Farnell's Folly.

By IVAN TURGENIEFF, &c.

Stories from Foreign Novelists.

By MARK TWAIN.

A Pleasure Trip on the Continent.
The Gilded Age.
Huckleberry Finn.
MarkTwain's Sketches.
Tom Sawyer.
A Tramp Abroad.
Stolen White Elephant.
Life on the Mississippi.
The Prince and the Pauper.
A Yankee at the Court of King Arthur.
The £1,000,000 Bank-Note.

By C. C. FRASER-TYTLER.

Mistress Judith.

By SARAH TYTLER.

The Bride's Pass.
Buried Diamonds.
St. Mungo's City.
Lady Bell.
Noblesse Oblige.
Disappeared.
The Huguenot Family.
The Blackhall Ghosts.
What SheCameThrough
Beauty and the Beast.
Citoyenne Jaqueline.

By ALLEN UPWARD.

The Queen against Owen.

By AARON WATSON and LILLIAS WASSERMANN.

The Marquis of Carabas.

By WILLIAM WESTALL.

Trust-Money.

By Mrs. F. H. WILLIAMSON.

A Child Widow.

By J. S. WINTER.

Cavalry Life. | Regimental Legends.

By H. F. WOOD.

The Passenger from Scotland Yard.
The Englishman of the Rue Cain.

By Lady WOOD.

Sabina.

By CELIA PARKER WOOLLEY.

Rachel Armstrong; or, Love and Theology.

By EDMUND YATES.

The Forlorn Hope.
Land at Last.
Castaway.

OGDEN, SMALE AND CO. L... ...LL, E.C.

Pears' Soap

The delicate skin of Infants and Children is particularly liable to injury from coarse and unrefined Toilet Soap, which is commonly adulterated with the most pernicious ingredients; hence, frequently, *its irritability, redness, and blotchy appearance of the Skin from which many Children suffer.*

The purity of PEARS' SOAP is guaranteed by the special recommendation of the late

SIR ERASMUS WILSON,

F.R.S.

President of the Royal Colleg of Surgeons of England.

Edmund Evans, Racquet Ct., Fleet St., London, E.C.

www.ingramcontent.com/pod-product-compliance
Lightning Source LLC
Chambersburg PA
CBHW020937030726
47496CB00005B/1228
* 9 7 8 3 3 3 7 0 4 4 3 7 4 *